PRAISE
THE TAME MAN

"Dana Burnell's dazzling debut is anything but tame, a tale of intrigue that turns corners at breakneck speed, catapulting the reader into a world where the past haunts as dauntingly as the present threatens."

SCOTT ALEXANDER HESS,

author of *Skyscraper* and *The Butcher's Sons*

(named a *Kirkus Reviews* Best Book)

"Reminiscent of scenes from the darker writings of James Thurber. . . themes explore how commitment is portrayed and betrayed. Those in search of a multi-layered tale need look no further than this one!"

U.S. REVIEW OF BOOKS

"Burnell's witty, pitch-perfect prose subtly interweaves dark comedy with a murder mystery, creating a reading experience reminiscent of Martin Amis's London Fields. The Tame Man is a vertiginous, hilarious reanimation of Blair-Era suburban London."

STACY JOHN HAIGNY,

author of *Red Front Connection*

"Vivid and realistic characters . . . A brilliant story that pulls you in from the start and doesn't let you go until the jaw-dropping ending."

INTERNATIONAL REVIEW OF BOOKS,

Gold Badge Winner

THE TAME MAN

DANA BURNELL

AIA PUBLISHING

THE TAME MAN
Dana Burnell

Copyright © 2023
Published by AIA Publishing, Australia

ABN: 32736122056

http://www.aiapublishing.com

ISBN: 978-1-922329-49-3

*Thanks to my parents
and to the Black Cat Café for
the man in the floral shirt.*

Fame is a bee.
It has a song—
It has a sting—
Ah, too, it has a wing.

- EMILY DICKINSON

I. HOW THEY MET   1

II. THE MARRIAGE   59

III. THE DEATH   197

I

HOW THEY MET

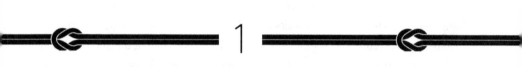

RUBICON BAINES STOOD BENEATH THE four-sided clock at Waterloo Station, waiting for her childhood friend. Jenn was twelve minutes late and every minute gave Rubicon hopes she wouldn't show at all.

Rubicon had caught the 2:28 train in from Richmond, keeping one eye on the trollied Irishman who slumped next to her exuding cider fumes and sandalwood. He'd slurred something in her ear as she slid into the beige vinyl seat, something about giving her a proper seeing-to. "Promises!" Rubicon had said to the Hyacinth Bucket type seated opposite, as the Irishman passed out on her shoulder, "Always full of *promises*, aren't they?" The older lady tightened her lips into a thin ribbon of disapproval, and Rubicon winked at her. Ah England, she thought. I love it so. Rubicon watched the low brick buildings sliding slowly by the dirty, rain-splashed train window. Roofs of red clay and small round chimneys.

Low-ceilinged, cozy, angry, verbal, cynical, moreish England.

The train slid on. Low damp roofs of South London contrasting with the modern architecture that was springing up near the city; the Gherkin gleaming like a dirty missile in the distance, construction cranes swinging slowly to their purpose. In 2004 the UK was adapting to the blinging and terrorized twenty-first century— rising again, shaking Thatcher's dust from its feet. The Iraq War was in its second year; photos had recently been leaked from Abu Ghraib.

THIS WAS IN NOVEMBER OF that year; the women hadn't seen each other in over two decades. Rubicon was not looking forward to seeing her old friend, who'd somehow tracked her down via the Internet. She knew they would not talk politics: instead, she anticipated an afternoon of platitudinal boredom, being forced to look at photos of their 80s' childhood hometown. (And after seeing the photos, Rubicon decided, in Pinekill it still *was* the '80s; everybody was older and some enrobed in fat, but still gamely sporting mullets and stonewash.)

Although Rubicon nowadays rarely ate more than a few scant snacks each day, she went into W.H. Smith, bought a packet of Wotsits, and tore the packet open. An obscene cloud of orange dust puffed out, and she picked at the chemical cheese straws. So that's lunch then, thought Rubicon. The last thing London needs is another fat Yank.

At the height of her prom-queen popularity, Jenn had airily taken to calling everybody "Sweetie." She'd better not "Sweetie" me, Rubicon thought, as she bit down hard on a Wotsit. Forty-one is a bit old to stomach patronizing diminutives. Slouching beneath the Waterloo clock in her charity shop Helmut Lang jeans and the poncho made of random scraps of suede, Rubicon kept waiting.

Jenn was now eighteen minutes late.

The Midwest. Rubicon crumpled the Wotsits wrapper in her hand, tossed it into a bin and rubbed some orange dust off her fingers. The broad vowels and unearned friendliness, the flat-landed farms and the stone-set certainties that seem comforting, then laughable, then vaguely threatening. Pinekill.

Twenty-five minutes late. At thirty minutes, Rubicon would stop waiting. She'd take the Piccadilly line to Pandora's, her favorite consignment shop in Knightsbridge, and buy herself a designer dress for tonight; something so simple it was daunting. And later she would see Mark.

Mark was the only thing on earth she loved as much as she'd loved fame. Rubicon was (or rather, had briefly been) famous. And like fame, she'd lost him— but there was hope. Now there was hope.

Then she saw Jennifer.

ൟ

How can someone ride an escalator like an American? Jennifer managed it. Despite her small stature, she sailed up that thing looking like a figure on the prow of the SS Ronald Reagan. Still determinedly yellow of hair and full of body, petite with round pink arms and strong shoulders over an hourglass figure. Jennifer's cheeks had remained full and as red as Indiana apples, but her eyebrows now pointed down in a sharp V toward her button nose. Sometime in the past she'd tweezed them badly and too thin; they would never fully grow back. With thick horse-like hair restrained by a scrunchie, Jenn emerged from the bowels of Waterloo. Big blue eyes looking around: searching, searching for Rubicon—who suddenly wanted to hide behind the W.H. Smith sign. The blue eyes widened as Jenn recognized her old friend skulking near the bookstore.

"Rubi! Is that *you!?* Oh my GOD!"

It sounded like "GAAD." The Midwestern accent.

Rubicon's frozen smile registered Jenn's T-shirt, pleated, high-waisted, narrow-ankled denims ("Mummy jeans" in the UK), and her feet swaddled in shapeless white gym shoes. It was the outfit of an overgrown toddler. She wore a fanny pack and a large fleece coat cinched around her waist. Jenn tripped pulling her roller-bag off the escalator, and collided with a sneer of raven-haired hipsters in bone-tight skinny jeans.

"Watch yerself, Septic."

"Yeh—wouldn't want to fall on that fat arse of yours."

"Lovely tits, though . . ."

Rubicon stepped forward. She adjusted her poncho and strode toward her old friend, waving long arms to shoo the hipsters away. "Piss off, you lot. Are you okay, Jenn?"

Jenn pretended she hadn't heard what the kids said to her, and leaped forward to grip Rubicon in a fervent embrace. "Rubi! You're so pretty now!"

They hugged, and to Rubicon it seemed Jenn's rounded arms contained hoops of steel. "Oh Rubi, it's *so great* to see you. Paris was just the worst place ever— so *rude*. That's why I wore this T-shirt. Ha!" She stood back for a moment and pointed to the flag emblazoned across her chest; a coiled rattlesnake representing the thirteen colonies with warning words, "Don't Tread on Me" written beneath.

Somehow this brought a rush of embarrassed affection for Jenn which Rubicon hadn't expected. Jenn was just so *wrong* over here, so clearly *wrong* that it made Rubicon feel clever and knowing, svelte and self-sufficient, and rather protective of her old friend.

"Oh lord, Jenn. You can't wear that—propaganda. We'll have to take you shopping."

"Ooh—I'm dying to go to Harrods!" Jenn hugged Rubicon again and rocked her from side to side.

Rubicon kept an eye on Jenn's suitcase, but also let herself glance at the two of them in the W.H. Smith window reflection. Jenn's head fit just beneath Rubicon's chin. Look at us, she thought. It's funny when past connections lose their power, when what was once major becomes minor.

Why was I so *stressed* about seeing her? When they'd been kids, Jenn had seemed to take up all the oxygen in the room, had never left Rubicon room to shout, to expand. But now Rubicon was surprised by a burst of affection. After all, Jenn couldn't inhale all of London; she couldn't grab all that Rubicon had done and become. Even if the last few years had been hard . . . Plus, in a few hours she'll be on her way to Edinburgh.

As for Jenn, she was so happy to see Rubicon that she'd already decided to miss the Edinburgh train. But she didn't mention it.

.ഏ.

TWENTY MINUTES LATER THEY WERE coming up from Charing Cross tube station. The tube was crowded, so they'd become separated and couldn't talk. Jennifer looked at her tall friend and thought how funny it was that she'd recognized her right off, even after twenty plus years. Rubicon stood across the car, gazing down at her own feet. Jenn thought, she's still got that look she took on just before high school—like a bird perching briefly, just itching to take off. But kind of scared too. Rubi would stand on one leg sometimes, the other foot propped against the side of her calf, put her hands on her hips, and lean forward slightly with those dark eyes of hers looking up, that messy hair trembling. She'd just stand there like that, back then, in the sloppy joe line at lunch or at the back of the volleyball court during girls' P.E.

Jenn remembered that some of the football team started calling Rubi the Gargoyle, until she stopped them. "Enough," she told Mike Bellwether, the tight end who was her beau. "Or you'll be parking alone from now on." Rubi had dated Mike briefly in the eighth grade. He'd said it was like feeling up his little brother. "You know what that feels like?" asked Jenn pertly.

The two women were silent as they climbed the stairs from the tube station. Jennifer thought the steps were steep and filthy, but suddenly as they rounded the last corner of the staircase, she saw a patch of cold blue light which expanded as they kept climbing. There was a thrilling sense of movement outside, from birds and people and buses; the pale light grew, and a fizzle of excitement burst in Jenn's stomach. The light of London spread over her, and she could smell a funny combination of things, wet cardboard and burned leaves and charcoal (with a back note of urine). Jenn was so glad to be out of France, which stank of sulfur and tobacco. She felt she'd always known that she and Rubi would be together again.

And at the top of the steps . . . there it was! London! Right in front of her. It reminded her of those paintings they'd seen on those field trips to the Art Institute of Chicago. She and Rubi weren't friends by high school, but Jenn remembered the long bus rides, the thick naugahyde on the seats and the ribbed rubber floor of the bus. The floor she and the other kids would stamp their feet on while singing, "We Wanna Go To Burger King! Burger Burger KING KING KING." Rubi had sat in the back of the bus as they drove upstate, staring resentfully out at the expanse of grain fields waving alongside them. Rubi had become a vegetarian by then, and no longer ate Quarter Pounders. The minute she'd learned Rubi was now a vegetarian, Jenn had assumed that her ex-and-forever friend would end up moving to Chicago someday, where there were all sorts of people like that. But, being Rubi, she got fancy. London.

Rubicon had left Illinois plump with ambition and a scholarship to St. Martin's College of Arts. London!

And Jenn could see why. Those pictures in the Art Institute? The ones some beer millionaire's wife had bought a hundred years ago and hauled over from the old country? They reminded her of London, or vice versa. Coming up out of the tube, Jenn saw a world with a low, fast-moving sky, where it seemed like the buildings had swallowed light and the clouds had eaten darkness, and somehow this quietly mixed every color of the rainbow within all the browns and grays of the stone buildings.

Jenn grabbed Rubicon's arm in a tight grip. "Boy!" she said, "is this place ever better than Paris!"

Rubicon laughed.

Trafalgar Square heaved around them, all roads pointing directly to where the two friends stood. Buskers and human statues surrounded by clutches of tourists, the smell of burned nuts and fried food; they all lifted Jenn's spirits. Pigeons swooping around all fluttery like they'd just had their feelings hurt. A high and storming fountain surrounded by four great lions, each around twenty feet off the ground. Rubicon grabbed Jenn's muscular arm and pulled her friend across the street, narrowly avoiding a black taxi that barreled toward them.

When they'd reached safety, Jenn's eye was caught by the first tabloid headline she'd ever seen: *Good Time Pen and the PM's Big Ben*. There was a picture of a pneumatic blond, bristling with hair extensions and sucking her thumb. A smaller image, grainier and clearly not a studio photograph, was of a gray-haired man in a suit, walking out of a doorway holding his briefcase over his face.

It would have seemed ridiculous if someone had told Jenn that *their* faces—hers and Rubicon's— would appear on the cover of the same tabloid paper in less than a year, that rhymes would be made with *their* names. That the tabloids would minutely detail Rubicon and Jenn's friendship: the childhood days spent swearing allegiance to the flag—which snapped brightly in the wind beneath the vast, inescapable Illinois sky—and to each other. Slumber parties in aluminum-sided ranch houses, onion dip with Lay's chips as midnight snacks. Followed by the usual, painful adolescent faltering of friendship as Rubicon turned away from Jenn's blithe, forceful optimism and toward the lure of new punk stoner friends. The types who slumped against the cinderblock school walls, smirking a passive rebellion.

ON THIS NOVEMBER DAY, HOWEVER, Jenn just laughed at the headline and allowed Rubi to lead her across another, narrower street and toward a large building with a big flat triangle on the top.

Jennifer noticed lots of men milling around London, compared to back home. Men everywhere. Men, small and skinny, with big loose sort of teeth, pink faces and funny haircuts, some wearing fitted wool suits with stripes and bright colored shirts. Tall men with high beer bellies and veined noses. Lots of students too. Jenn didn't trust students, because shouldn't they have jobs? What's the point of just hanging out for four years of your life? (Jenn never had—unlike Rubicon, she never got the chance.)

Then there were the women who rushed by looking like Rubicon— no hips at all, pale faces, and unkempt but somehow expensive-looking hair. No lipstick,

8

and narrow mouths. Jenn noticed the way Londoners looked at the tourists only glancingly, like pillars of flesh to be avoided; they didn't even register them as *people*. She wanted to buy them all a hairbrush. I mean, is there anything wrong with a little hair-brushing now and again? She asked Rubicon, who smiled patronizingly. "Well, the weather in London is a challenge, and people here like to look a little casual, a bit cheeky." Rubicon pushed open a double door into a building marked National Portrait Gallery and gestured Jenn inside.

Jenn had no idea what "cheeky" meant. She assumed, rightly, that it wasn't a look she would ever go for.

The two women walked up the marble stairs of the National Portrait Gallery as Rubicon pointed out pictures of those who were famous, infamous, or merely ugly. The truth was, Jennifer was mostly taking in Rubicon.

She used to have the same accent as me, Jenn thought. Your basic Illinois one, with a little howdy of a Southern twang. It's a friendly accent, one that lets you know we don't think we're above ourselves or fancy or anything. Now she talks different. Instead of saying her double t's like we do back home, where "pudding" and "putting" sound the same, now she carefully hits those "t's" like they're something fancy on a platter she's presenting to you. It's wrong to lose your accent. It's like—like—Jennifer couldn't finish that sentence, but she felt there was pretentiousness to it.

An elevator took them the final few flights up to the Gallery Restaurant.

As they rose slowly in the tight glass enclosure, Jenn described to Rubicon how the World War II exhibit in Paris barely even mentioned the good old US of A. "Like we didn't have a little something to do with *that!* And—well—the men."

"What about them?"

"The stuff they'd say to me. Well, I don't know exactly what it was—but I knew what they wanted. It made me feel a little weird. Honestly, I was scared." Jenn hadn't been scared. A few men in the metro whispered to Jenn; she'd stood as still as she could when their bodies brushed against hers, the tobacco smell on their breath making her feel faint, her pelvis yearning forward, though she tried to stop it.

"Hmm," Rubicon mused. "You should've taken one of them back to your hotel and let them give you a proper seeing-to." The small elevator lurched to a stop.

"Yuck!" Jenn squeezed out the small door. "You're so bad!" Rubicon seemed to know what Jenn meant, which was kind of nice. Rubi never used to know about guys. Not even basic junior high stuff, like how to make sure they noticed you ignoring them.

She slapped Rubicon on the arm like when they were kids, and was rewarded by a sudden flashing smile. "I would never—I mean—I'm a *widow*." They stepped into an airy marble-and-steel bar with a long window that ran along the side of the entire room. A waiter sprang forward, both sullen and subservient. Rubicon raised two long fingers from within that suede poncho of hers.

As they sat down on low chairs that looked like they were made of knit silver, Jenn leaned forward. "Rubi, have *you* ever—"

The table was small and rectangular, with a white tablecloth and little salt-and-pepper ceramic boxes on it, like Jenn had seen in Crate & Barrel catalogs.

"Have I ever what?"

She said "whot," Jenn noticed; Rubicon's accent switched on and off like a neon sign. "Have I ever shagged a random bloke—a guy—in France? Absolutely."

Jenn gawped at how casual she was about it, and how Rubicon milked the word "absolutely" in a way that sounded dirty and almost smelled of unmade hotel beds and musky maleness. Jenn suddenly felt warm, and removed her fanny pack.

"You're trying to shock me, aren't you? Well, I might not've made it out of Pinekill, but I know you'd never have done that. What with diseases and everything. Right?"

Rubicon said nothing, just wore a Mona Lisa smile and fanned herself with the menu card.

Jenn gasped. "Did you?"

Rubicon raised one eyebrow and shrugged.

"*Ohh . . .*" Jenn was impressed.

A coffee machine hissed nearby, and the clinking sound of bottles of wine being lined up to sweat on the bar. Large glass jars filled with cookies that looked more elegant than tasty. Pistachio and Elderflower. Organic Muesli and Orange Essence. The restaurant seemed to overlook all of London: the lions in Trafalgar Square, the Houses of Parliament resembling castles of drizzled sand, and Big Ben, listing so slightly to one side. People below scurrying in odd dashes or standing still in softly spilling rainfall. Inside the restaurant there seemed to be only couples—during the workday!—only couples murmuring to each other, and Jenn noticed the women wore dark drapey clothes like she'd seen in Paris, but here the effect was random, messier. In London it seemed to be the men who were neater, in their high-patterned suits. Tidy men sitting across from frank-eyed women with uncombed hair, men who looked down into their whiskey glasses and then up again as they laughed softly, like they had all day for these women.

Jennifer wondered for the first time if maybe people like big cities because they can get away with being bad. The possibilities were endless; bringing men back to hotels or even in that tight elevator—and no one knows, ever, what you did and said and asked for. Jenn flushed. No one except God, she reminded herself. God trusts you to do the right thing. God is like a small-town neighbor who is always watching you from his living-room window.

"I wish the waiter would come back," she said. "I sure am hungry."

"He'll be along." Rubicon removed her gloves, and Jenn saw her friend's fingers were raw and bitten-looking; they looked dirty and that surprised her. Nearby, two middle-aged women (probably sisters, for both had auburn hair and aquiline noses) turned to look, briefly, at Rubicon and then exchanged glances. They'd recognized the short dark licks of hair standing flamelike around her head, her seeming cool chic . . . it still happened, occasionally, that people remembered Rubicon.

RUBICON, AS MENTIONED EARLIER, WAS famous. Or had been. In the early 90s, for a brief and shining moment of the Waif Era, Rubicon had hosted an ITV show called *It's Pants!* The show made snarky fun of music videos' many egregious excesses, so it was an inexpensive, high-concept format. Rubicon had been discovered by a TV producer in a Chelsea nightclub with her nose dusted with mooched cocaine, cawing with laughter and loudly taking the piss out of nearby Sloane Rangers and their shoulder pads and court shoes. She'd been whisked in to audition in torn yet fiercely individualistic clothing of her own making, and used a voice she'd created for the occasion: the nasal vowels of Illinois triangulating between the clipped arrogance of Chelsea and the pushing "Innit?" of the East End street kids.

It's Pants! became a massive hit, and Rubicon had been one of the ladettes of the era. She was papped on the piss with one hand down her pants and the other holding an ever-draining pint glass. Newspaper columns predicted her cirrhotic decline, but the only addiction Rubicon really had was to fame.

However, after a year or so, the *It's Pants* ratings began to drop as the '80s' music video footage repeated itself, and the paucity of the format became clear. A cooler irony came into style for television presenters, and Rubicon's mocking and squawking began to seem tiresome.

The show was canceled and she was gone; she was done.

The funny thing was, that when fame abandoned her (and Rubicon had loved fame more than anything—except maybe that man, once), she had thought of Jennifer. One day, about three months after the show had been canceled, Rubicon had been walking by a shop and caught a glimpse of her face in the mirrored window. Her shadowy, hawklike eyes were fixed forward, darkened by confusion—and her mouth. It was the mouth that most particularly reminded her of Jenn. Lipsticked and stretched in a mirthless smile, a smile of confusion and pain, a smile of loss.

It was the way Jenn used to gaze at her in the Pinekill High School lunchroom, after Rubicon had ended their friendship.

.୨ୣ.

Now the two old Pinekill friends gazed, in a moment of awkward silence, out of the National Gallery Café's window. The Thames could just be seen. To Jenn it looked like a creek but wider, green and algaeic, with the rain falling into it like a soft question the river rushed to overwhelm. Above the buildings the sky was streaked and low, smaller than skies are in America.

Make an effort, thought Jenn.

When's her train? wondered Rubicon.

They ordered. A coffee and cookie for Jenn. Rubicon (rather shockingly to Jenn) asked for a glass of wine. The slope-shouldered waiter had dishwater hair and pale, chewed lips. He began to place water glasses, creamer, sugar, and spoons on the small table. Jennifer's bag was in the way.

"Would you mind moving your bum bag, miss?"

"What?"

The waiter pointed disdainfully at the offending object, a black sack with canvas straps at either end that Jenn had placed on the table. It looked like a vinyl snake that'd swallowed a squirrel.

"Your bum bag. Would you move it, please?"

"Ohhh! You mean my fanny pack? Oh! Lemme just—" Jenn placed the bag firmly in her lap and patted it.

The waiter's eyes brightened for half a moment before returning to a subservient grudge, though not before Rubicon caught his glance and smiled, her sharp incisors flashing just for a moment.

"What's so funny?" said Jenn, after the waiter wandered bonelessly off again.

"Well, 'fanny' means your vagina, over here. Your suzy."

"What?"

"To them, 'fanny' means vagina. They call it 'bum bag.' Because it hangs over your bottom."

Again, Jenn noticed Rubicon getting the utmost mileage, a world of naughtiness, from a word. "Bottom"—the o slightly inhaled, the t's pronounced distinctly. "Oh jeez," she said, looking over her shoulder to where the waiter was morosely pouring red wine into a large glass, his shoulders hunched in resentment of his job and of his flagrant superiority over his customers.

"So I just told him I'd grab my . . . vagina bag?"

"Yeah, kind of."

"Hmm." Jenn looked over at the waiter again. He was gloomily wiping a Beaujolais Nouveau stain from his trouser leg. "Do you think that means I should ask *him* to move his ball sac?"

Rubicon choked on her glass of water. "Jenn!"

The two laughed in unison, like it was 1977 and they were at an Andy Gibb concert, with their hair curled into gravity-defying wings, and matching and covertly applied blue eyeshadow gleaming under the lights of Rockford Armory Stadium. When the waiter returned with their drinks, Jenn immediately quieted, but Rubicon found she couldn't stifle her laughter. She bit her lips and looked down, somehow ended up staring directly at the waiter's crotch, and then caught Jenn's eye.

The waiter glanced suspiciously at Rubicon's red face, and left the table with a stiff, disapproving walk.

"I thought you were one of those Christian God-botherers, Jenn."

"Oh, I'm a Christian. There's God in Christ, no doubt about that. But God gave us eyes and thoughts, so why not enjoy 'em harmlessly—that's what I say."

"Amen to that, I guess." Rubicon took a relieved sip of her wine, and thought this wasn't going to be such a bad couple of hours. Jenn was kind of funny, in her small-town way, and the shadows out over Trafalgar Square were already growing longer.

As shadows lengthened, the wind kicked up.

.୨୧.

"I'M SORRY ABOUT MIKE. I should've written." Rubicon's glass was nearly empty, her apology long overdue. "I didn't know he'd fina—that he'd died until a few months after. I always felt bad about what I said at graduation. About your engagement."

Jenn didn't look at Rubicon but brightly examined her plate as if another quinoa cardamom cookie might suddenly appear there. "Oh, Rubi. That's okay. I know you never liked him."

Rubicon ran her fingers through her cropped hair. "Well, no, I didn't. But why the hell I thought it was my place to say so—"

"Maybe you were just trying to save me from making a mistake."

Rubicon slowly tilted her head back and forth, as if Jenn's was one way of looking at it, but not the right one. Then she began to look around for a clock, but Jenn's hand slid across the table and grasped Rubicon's arm.

"You want to know why you were right about Mike? And why I married him?"

"You don't have to tell me anyth—"

"No. I want to. I never got to . . . Lemme have a sip of your wine, okay?"

As Jenn took a solid gulp, Rubicon watched her and thought, Poor Old Jenn. She would look okay if she just got rid of that ridiculous waterfall ponytail and about half of her makeup, maybe bought some decent clothing.

Jenn held the bowl of the big glass while drinking and thought the wine tasted like cherries, black cherries and velvet. What was she going to tell Rubicon about Mike? She wondered. She would need to make it good, let her know that she missed something, that she'd missed Jen . . . She wanted to tell her what happened that night. It had sat in her so long.

Jenn was in Europe. And she finally had Rubi to talk to, after all these years. God knows she couldn't have talked to Mike. Or anyone in Pinekill, and ruin their opinion of her as the saint who'd taken care of the paralyzed ex-tight end. Funny, she thought she'd been lonely in Pinekill, particularly toward the end there just a few months ago when Mike refused even to eat, just decided to die . . . but nothing, nothing had made her as lonely as France had.

One thing no one had mentioned about travel to Jenn, and she couldn't figure out why, was that it was lonely making. (Of course, at that point she didn't have prison to compare it to.)

Jenn noticed Rubicon's eye begin to wander toward the clock again. "Okay. Let's each get a glass of that wine, and I'll tell you about the night of the accident."

Rubicon raised hawklike brows and an assertive hand in the waiter's direction. As she ordered, Jenn gazed at her. Rubi! Her old friend who listened to Jenn talk about boys, all those years when she couldn't get any herself. Jenn remembered those outfits they wore trick or treating, herself dressed like Wonder Woman and Rubi as a package of Marlboros. In junior high she'd entertain Rubi by telling her about the boys who'd called, night after night, and they'd talked together about what the Mikes and Bobs and Toms had said to her that day.

Jenn had never understood why their friendship had ended.

One gulp of wine went to her head, and Jenn's heart just melted when she noticed how Rubi's front teeth still crossed sweetly over each other just like when they grew in when she was eight. Those teeth had always made Jenn think of a kitten's folded paws, for some reason. The rest of her friend might have been "Rubicon" nowadays, but that smile was pure Rubi.

The sweet smile of the anxious little girl who'd worn her Garanimals shorts and Fresca T-shirt every day, day in and day out for two summers. She bet Rubi was all alone now too. She had that look about her, under all the fancy clothes. She should put on some nice peach blush.

Jenn saw her reflection in the darkening window and remembered all the people drinking in the daytime in Paris—the faces they made when you asked for a nice glass of milk there! Rubi's face was pale as milk, actually, but her nostrils were veined and flushed. Anyway, Rubi's dark eyes were also the same, big and somehow kind of smudged beneath those unplucked brows so big and dark and lord so serious, one raised just a little bit higher than the other.

"So," Jenn began, putting the wine glass down. "Last time we spoke, ever, was at graduation. You marched right up to me and said I was dumb to marry Mike and he was a waste of protoplasm. I had to look it up."

"Oh Jesus."

Jenn's thick fingers hovered over the bowl of nibbles, nuts, chocolate and dried fruit that the waiter had brought over with the drinks. She flicked nuts aside and pulled out the dark chocolate chips. Rubi did look awfully ashamed of herself, and you could suddenly see all these crepey lines around her eyes. This made Jenn feel better. After all, she'd been the married one—*she* grew up and faced her responsibilities, didn't run away but managed the family bakery all those years, while Rubi disappeared. Jenn wanted to let Rubi know how fast she'd had to grow up, how much she'd lost . . . and also that Rubi had been kind of right. Really right, actually.

"You also said he was a selfish bonehead."

"Christ. You were right to be pissed off—I'd barely spoken to either of you for years. For all I know he was working for Greenpeace on the weekends. Or fighting to free Mandela."

Jenn laughed a sharp short "Ha!", flicked another nut aside, and grabbed a chocolate chip. "Oh, Mike was always trying to free something all right. His johnson from his pants."

Rubicon had wondered what that set got up to, with their brightly shouting confidence and Members Only jackets. "Seriously? But you guys were into all that Christian music and those Jesus Loves Life dances and that sh—stuff."

"Oh, we were bombed at those things. It was the '80s, you know? Since my family had the bakery, I could steal whippet dispensers easy. Plus Mike's family always had some Red White & Blue beer in their basement fridge. But . . ." Jenn took a dreamy sip of Beaujolais. This was the first time she'd had a drink in years. "Oh, I loved Amy Grant. Wonder what happened to her. No. With Mike it was always trying to get something for nothing. Morning, noon and night, blow jobs!" Aggrieved Illinois vowel tones bounced off the windows.

A blond man in a camel-hair coat at the next table scraped his eyes away from his elegant companion, who was drawling complacently about a mini-break in the Cotswolds, to regard Jenn thoughtfully.

"Indoor voice, Jenn." Rubicon smiled and pushed the bowl of nibbles closer to Jenn's side of the table.

Jenn gazed out over Trafalgar Square, at the streetlights beginning to turn on in a soft gold glow, and thought she could do anything she wanted here, just like Rubi.

So she gazed speculatively back at the man in the camel coat. Unlike him, who looked like he'd been born with a full set of silver spoons in his mouth, she'd been working all her life. *She* deserved a goshdarn mini-break. The man broke the gaze, cowed by the frank hostility and appraisal he saw in Jenn's aqua-shadowed eyes. She turned back to Rubi.

"I mean, they're called jobs for a *reason.*"

Rubicon nodded thoughtfully at this piece of non-originality, as Jenn took another sip of wine, her coral fingernails resembling Barbie flesh against the blood-red fluid in the glass. "So. I finally did it with Mike. It was the beginning of baseball season, and he said he loved me, and I was sick of finding a hair at the back of my throat. Pretty icky. Next thing I know—"

"No no, wait a minute. Where did this great event occur? Somehow I don't

see Laverne giving you guys a spliff and telling you the sofa bed was available."
Laverne had been Jenn's mother, who'd told the girls that virginity was like
precious Lenox china; once broken you're never really valuable again. Laverne
had sublimated a lifetime of lust into fixations on Robert Goulet, craft projects, and
fried cheese balls rolled in dark brown sugar.

"No, we did it at his Aunt Margaret's house while she was in Valparaiso for
the Frigidaire convention. Mike didn't even make me dinner—just bought us a
couple of Big Macs, cracked a few Red White & Blues." Jenn looked a little dreamy.
"Remember when they served Big Macs in those yellow Styrofoam containers?"

"Yep." Rubicon sounded like a Pinekill girl again, her vowel tones broader. "I
ate one of those in two bites on a ten dollar bet. Shat black slime for a week. That's
what turned me vegetarian."

Jenn laughed and Big Ben chimed, and suddenly a pigeon flew up and stood
outside the windowsill, and the sky outside grew more and more like those Art
Institute pictures, with every color in the world inside it, and she thanked Jesus
again for the good price she got for selling the bakery, and for bringing Rubicon
back to listen to her stories.

God always clears a way, Jenn thought. Or almost always. She hiccuped,
sharply, just once.

"Take it easy now, Jenn," said Rubicon. "They don't allow drinkers in
Scotland, you know. Very strict about that."

Forget Scotland, Jenn thought. She pushed her wine to the other side of the
table. "Anyway. Mike said he was going to pull out, but then he forgot—like a
bonehead. And it kind of hurt, so after, I just curled up on the couch with an ice
pack, while he watched the Cubs game and ate his Big Mac. When I said I wanted
a ride home, he goes, "But Sandberg's coming up to bat!"

"Holy crap—Sandberg. I had a thing for him. Sorry. I'm impressed Mike left
one of the Big Macs for you. That's chivalry, baby."

"I was just so pee-ed off and bummed by the sex thing that I told him I was
leaving and that he was totally dumped. I threw the ice pack at his head, got out of
there and walked home along side streets so he couldn't find me. He kept calling me
over the next few weeks, but I told him—DUMPED."

"So he proposed in order to get you back?"

"Gosh no." There was no more chocolate in the bowl of nibbles, so Jenn
fished out a pistachio.

Rubicon watched her place the nut between her small sharp teeth, and crack down hard. They were unnerving, those teeth. Tiny, white and oddly plentiful.

"It was like this. One morning two weeks later I woke up really sudden—because I'd felt something move. Fluttering inside. Like an excited drum roll or something, just trembling with love inside me."

"Oh." Rubicon shrugged. "I see. Love. You loved Mike despite his flaws. And you listened to your heart." Rubicon licked salt from her fingertips. "Sweet."

"Nothing sweet about it, Rubi. That fathead. The fluttering wasn't *love*. I knew love wasn't couch sex and a Big Mac. What I felt was The Quickening. I knew it right away. You remember that, right? What Mrs. Turbov taught us from that D.H. Lawrence story we had to read in Senior English?"

"The quicken? No, I don't remember that. I hated Lawrence, the bully."

"It's the quicken*ing*. When life begins."

"C'mon. Two weeks? No way you could know that early."

"I knew. I was pregnant. I knew. The quickening, that's the moment it turns from just cells into a person, a baby. I felt it. So I had to marry Mike."

Rubicon hadn't known Jenn had a kid. She thought her mother (who'd died in '92) would've mentioned if Jenn and Mike had had a child. Casually thrown it into conversation as another thing Jenn did that Rubicon hadn't. Like take care of her parents plus Mike for all those years, like stay in Pinekill and let life suck the marrow out of her soul via hourly wages and stonewashed denim. Rubicon had actually been a little impressed by Jenn not becoming a mother, because if anyone seemed destined for the complacencies of Pinekill mommydom, it was Jenn.

"You guys had a kid? I'm sorry, I never knew."

"No." Jenn looked down, and her over-plucked eyebrows trembled.

Rubicon felt uncomfortable. The restaurant was emptying now in preparation for the switch from tea to evening service, and she spared a passing thought for Jenn's train to Edinburgh. "Jenn. Maybe we should—" She began waving for the waiter, who was on the other side of the room, staring blankly out of the window.

Jenn just kept talking. "We didn't have a kid. Because Mike killed it the night of the accident. So you were right, Rubi." As Jenn's face lost its painted luminosity and gathered darkness into it, she said bitterly, "The guy was a total waste of protoplasm."

Rubicon's hand fell.

2

JENN LEANED BACK IN HER chair and spoke quietly. "When I told Mike we would be blessed with a baby, he was at school warming up before a baseball game. It was like in the movies—him on one side of the chain link fence, me on the other. I said, I don't want to marry you—but that's what we're gonna do for a while. He froze. Like a chipmunk at an ammo convention."

"I bet." Rubicon nodded, remembering that chain link fence and how it separated the athletes from the smokers.

"So he pitched an awful game, got pulled after the third inning, and when he went back to his car I was sitting in it, waiting."

"The Bruiser. That was his car's name, right?"

"Yep. Told him we were going home and telling his folks what was up. Mrs. Bellwether cried some, and his dad just got real quiet for a while, but then he said we could live in their house. Told Mike he'd have to sell the Bruiser and get something a little more practical. That's when Mike started screaming."

"That fucking car. Everyone hated that loud bastard of a car, with all those Jesus fish stickers."

"Yeah . . . well. He'd taken the muffler off. So anyway, Mike's screaming

'Everything's gonna change! I don't want everything to change!' And his dad says, 'Do you think Jenn did?' And I started crying, which his dad didn't like. Sooo . . ." Jenn pushed her wineglass away and scratched her head.

Jenn's words tumbled over each other in their catharsis—details of a life and a world that seemed to Rubicon like frames from an old sixteen millimeter movie, or some half-remembered but torturously vivid dream come to life. The details made Rubicon feel defensive at first. Jenn had trapped *herself*, Rubicon thought, trapped herself in that cheerleading nonsense and that Christian music bullshit—willingly ensnared herself in the blaring self-satisfaction of American culture.

But somehow, Jenn was also bringing Rubicon back to a vision of Pinekill that she hadn't experienced since she was a small child. Remembering a certain mythic stoicism to the place, beneath the sanitary complacencies of commerce. The brutality of Illinois winters, the grim leaping urgency of deer in hunting season. The scent of autumn, its clean air perfumed with burning wood and the sweet rot of apples. Smothering summers, like a hot wet cloth pressed over your nose and mouth so you panted like a felled animal. And sunsets—oh those sunsets, weaving lavendered glory over the banality of what man had done to the land. Sunsets that were a mockery of progress, like Pinekill itself, but also humbling, silencing visions of unconquerable beauty.

As Jenn spoke, Rubicon began looking at her in a different way. Not from the height of an expat's condescension toward a compatriot reeling from decades of America's drip-tap of fear and trans fats—but on the level. Straight on. As Jenn kept talking about that late summer night in 1981, Rubicon's hand, long-fingered but also always dingy from newsprint, reached halfway across the table and was still.

"Did you never consider an abortion?"

Jenn's eyebrows lowered.

"Rubi. The baby had *quickened*. It was *alive*. I'd already messed up doing all that sex stuff—though God knows it wasn't much fun. What if Mary aborted Jesus?"

"I don't think she was given the option. In much of anything."

"Yeah, Mike tried to talk me into going to Chicago. I was like, you wouldn't take me up there to go shopping, and now you want to spend money on *that?* No way, mister. But I decided I'd shut him up with a lot of sex since I was stuck with him. So I'd got Mike quieted down. Then I put the word out about the wedding, and it all looked okay. Maybe not to you, but I figured it was God's plan that I have my baby and take it from there. I knew I'd always have a job at the bakery."

"Jesus, Jenn. But . . . all I heard about was the accident. And that you took care of Mike from then on."

Jenn brushed muesli crumbs from the American flag on her chest. "It was after you left. I was nearly four months gone by that time. So one night I got a call from Junelle Seaver."

"Jeez." Rubicon had fallen straight back into the Pinekill lexicon, dragged there by this little glimpse of the Peyton Place she'd shaken off from her Doc Marten boots. "Junelle. I bought calculus homework off her."

"Yeah, she's good at math. She was our accountant. Her harelip scar's kind of sunk into her face by now, so she's not so bitchy as she used to be. Anyway, she calls me, and thank God my parents were watching Magnum P.I. so they didn't answer, because she says Mike's at Mississippi Taco getting super-drunk and talking about how he's gonna leave town. And leave me."

"And good goddamn riddance."

For the first time Jenn became annoyed with Rubicon. Her sharply tweezed eyebrows drew down into a deeper V, and her teeth bared in a hostile smile.

Rubicon realized what all those little teeth reminded her of—a piranha. So many teeth, so tiny and strong. Piranha Barbie. She suddenly remembered why it had been hard to dump Jenn as a friend all those years ago—she could be fierce when she was called on to defend her view of the world (of herself). The bright certainty of her empty blue eyes was unsettling.

"Rubi. I know you've decided to forget about Pinekill, but I was *not* going to be the town joke; the knocked-up abandoned cheerleader. That didn't happen back then. And it sure as sugar didn't happen to *me*." Icy eyes glared at chic Rubicon, who found herself wanting to shrink away.

"Sorry. It was tough."

The blue eyes calmed, and those teeth disappeared behind the gleaming coral lips. Jenn's banality locked back in place again—but Rubicon remembered that moment. How it had made her respect Jenn a little more (or at least hesitate before expressing casual contempt for her philosophies). How it had made her think again that poor Jenn wouldn't look bad if someone just cleaned her up a bit. But she just said, "It was a tough one for you."

Jenn nodded blandly, her coral lips closed. "Obviously I wasn't letting him leave. I climbed out onto that tar deck outside my window—you remember that?"

Rubicon nodded. She glanced over at the Houses of Parliament, but didn't see them. Her nose was filled with the scent of hot tar and of teenage skin coated in baby oil; her tongue tasted the fetid fizziness of a stolen and shared Schlitz beer, warm from Illinois sun and mixing with the sweetness of Bonnie Bell Root Beer Lip Smackers. Summer in Pinekill.

Jenn watched the minute hand on Big Ben twitch forward. "So," she added hurriedly, "I shimmied down the muckleberry tree and pushed my Nova out of the driveway so my folks wouldn't hear, and started it up while it was rolling. Drove down to Mississippi Taco like a bat out of you-know-where. Leave *me?* Nope. No."

Rubicon nodded.

"Mike was standing in the parking lot when I pulled up. He was doing a beer bong with J.T. Marcus and didn't notice me. But J.T. did. J.T.—who by the way lost a hand in the first Gulf War so he's an American hero but is still a jerk—nearly fell over laughing. He started shouting to Mike, saying he should run before I hog-tied him. 'What about me?' I said. 'I'm already hog-tied, from the inside. And Mike did it, so shut your mouth, J.T.!' Mike picked up something and began running to the back of the parking lot, and I realized it was a duffel bag. He really was gonna leave! He jumped into the Bruiser and I was like 'No Way.' I was back in the Nova before he fishtailed out of the parking lot, and you can bet I nearly ran J.T. over as I left."

"Damn, Jenn. It's like that Coppola film from the '80s."

"I don't know about that, but I went after Mike heck for leather. I figured normally there was no chance of me catching him, since the Bruiser had a police engine—but it also had a drunk bonehead at the wheel. He was skidding all over the road and stripping the gears. I remembered that Marksman Rd. would corner him by the ravines, so I threw the car off 68 and hit the back roads." The big blue eyes filled with wonder. "And Rubi, I swear that baby was inside me, she was fluttering in my stomach, just *egging* me on. 'Come on, Mommy, come on—catch Daddy for me, catch my daddy.' I said, 'Right, baby. I'm gonna get our man.' And I hit the gas. It'd rained a lot so the road was wet and covered in dragged pebbles, but I swear to God that baby made it so I could see the spine in every leaf on the road. Every bug that hit the windshield, I could see its butt pass through its brain. Excuse the language."

"No problem." Rubicon was so absorbed that she didn't notice that the waiter now stood nearby, polishing glasses in the vacantly thorough way waiters take on when they're eavesdropping.

"So I get to the ravines ahead of him and just pull the car sideways in the middle of that fork where the split oak grew—you remember that? There were always accidents there?"

"Yeah—idiots TP'd that tree every Halloween."

"Mike and I did that junior year. It was fun." Jennifer took a final sip of her glass of wine. "So I hit the brakes, blocking the road so he *has* to stop, and I hear the Bruiser roaring closer to me—Mike can't see me yet, but of course I can hear that engine. And he's coming closer, and I'm thinking, kind of crazy-like, 'Maybe Mike and I can leave town together? Maybe I can just get in the Bruiser and we'll *go* and see what's out there?' But then Mike rounds the corner going super-fast, the car's skidding on leaves and I remembered the baby—a baby needs a home—and suddenly the Bruiser's just flying at me, I could see Mike's eyes as big as ping pong balls . . ."

"Holy shit, Jenn. Did you jump out of the car?"

Jenn's eyebrows again lowered at the center of the V. "Heck no, Rubi. I figured he'd brake. He loved the Bruiser too much not to brake, I figured."

"Jesus."

"But he just kept coming. And it was dark in the ravines, with all those low branches, so you'd think I couldn't see, but I saw he had that crazy drunk look in his eyes, and I guess mine were just daring him. *Daring* him to mess with me and my baby." Again the teeth appeared, again the unnerving combination of ferocity and emptiness within Jenn's eyes.

The portrait gallery café had nearly emptied by now. If Rubicon thought at all about trains to Edinburgh, she thought, vaguely, that there'd be a later one.

Rubicon made quite a few mistakes that afternoon. First, she decided to treat Jenn as a joke, based on appearances. Then she was disconcerted by Jenn's force of character and allowed herself to forget how dangerous a narrow certainty can be. And finally, she thought it wouldn't be such a bad thing if Jenn caught a later train to Scotland.

Stupid, stupid Rubicon. Stupider than when she'd been eighteen and had ruthlessly left that small town, knowing that if she didn't leave, Pinekill would define her.

That's the thing about the past. It's not enough to escape it once. You've got to keep doing it. You need to escape it again and again. You've got to be ruthless in the repetition.

The waiter cleaned a glass and looked outside.

It was dark in London now.

.ᴏᴇ.

"I DON'T KNOW HOW FREAKIN' fast he was going. It—he—" Jenn felt her face turn red; the wine had made her skin feel thick and itchy. "That SOB." Jenn's lips tightened over the words.

Rubicon remembered that part of the female socialization of Pinekill was that girls don't swear (or actually that only rich girls can swear, because they didn't need to worry about what people thought of them).

"He said later that he tried to swerve—but I didn't see it. Everything just suddenly went into like a slideshow, and the whites of his eyes turned into the brights of his car coming right at me. He hit exactly at the front passenger side opposite where I was sitting and waiting for him. Where *we* were sitting—the baby and me."

"Holy shit." Rubicon could see it all—the ravines, the only low and twisted road in Pinekill, the wet leaves on the ground and black branches overhead. Mike's face, his thick gleaming floppy hair and his stupid letter jacket, only eighteen but his face already florid from beer bongs and hormone-riddled meat, small foxlike eyes inflamed from the intestinal challenge of Mississippi Taco's jalapeño salsa.

"When the Bruiser hit us, it kind of went all silent, but my head slammed sideways hard and cracked the driver's side window. I had my seatbelt on and there was a lurch in my gut. I saw Mike smash through his windshield and suddenly his body's stuck there, sort of over me, half in and half out of the windshield with his face all shredded up. I saw he'd got one eye hanging out of the socket, and it looked kind of blue and filmy under the blood. Then I realize I'm covered in blood too—it felt cold, which I thought was weird. Cold blood."

The waiter had gone back to straightening cutlery on nearby tables, and Rubicon felt proud of providing entertainment for him. She assumed Jenn's story was an improvement on the usual parade of mother/daughter tea parties awash in Ylang-Ylang and cross-generational tension.

"Suddenly I'm screaming and screaming, which was stupid, because no one was around—"

"Jesus, Jenn, your boyfriend was hanging over you like a flesh piñata. Of course you were screaming."

Jenn's eyes brightened in amusement. "Oh, Rubi. I wasn't screaming for *Mike*. He'd made all this happen, that fathead. It was the baby. She'd got . . . suddenly blood wasn't just coming from my head, but it was all over the seat and my pajama bottoms. And my stomach felt like it was twisting." Jenn's voice quieted, and the waiter strained to hear. "I'd figured I'd name her Lovina. Isn't that pretty?" Her broad Midwestern vowels took on an almost unspeakable tenderness, like petals unfolding. "Lovina."

Rubicon said nothing, just leaned forward, for once not aware of the elegant drape of her poncho or the severe chicness of her boots. Or not much aware. Again she was back in southern Illinois, under the damp branches of that oak tree in the middle of the Pinekill ravines. Covered in cold blood and surrounded by twisted metal, while crickets creak an early autumn's song from an indifferent distance and a mangled boy moans overhead.

"And no cell phones then," Rubicon said.

"Nope."

"What'd you do?"

Jenn shrugged. "Well, I tried to crawl out the passenger side, but I passed out. When I came to, the ambulance was there and I was being strapped to some long plank. I put my hand over my crotch, to try to keep Lovina safe, but she was dead. I knew she was dead. I looked over to where the Bruiser was, but I couldn't see Mike. They'd put a hefty bag over him—I thought he was dead too, but it turned out that's how they kept him warm. Next day they took Lovina out of me, and told me I couldn't ever have another. I later read that she would've been super-small still, like the size of a—OH RATS! Look!"

Jenn's coral fingertips flew to her matching bow-shaped lips, and the blue mascaraed eyes opened to perfect roundness. She was staring out the window at Trafalgar Square, where the sky was now darkest periwinkle blue and the streets illuminated by golden street lights and the tight bright boxes of black cabs. Big Ben loomed benevolently, and dimly through the windows, they could hear the click of stiletto heels and the more solid clack of male shoes swarming toward the pubs.

"Oh, Rubi—I missed that train!"

"It's okay, Jenn, there'll be another in an hour or so." Rubicon stared, almost dazed, out the window at her adopted city, at its wealth and civilization, its soothing urban grime—the ravines still seemed more real to her just then, with that poor dumb bastard writhing beneath a hefty bag.

But Jenn leaped up and waved her arms at the nearby waiter like she was semaphoring from a faraway hilltop. "No—there's not another train until 11:50 tonight! I checked it. And my B&B—" she grabbed her fanny pack, and started tossing euros and pound coins and dollars on the table. "They don't let you in after midnight. And I don't want to be a bother . . ."

Rubicon looked at her old childhood friend and suddenly felt what an oddly good thing—an integrating thing—it had been to see her. It had awakened her to the astonishing power of the past, how she had allowed petty childhood insecurities to force her into shallow comparisons. Pinekill or London, life is hard for women— and options don't exactly crack open as time passes. Rubicon believed she had put behind her the childhood sense that she was never pretty and perky and positive and proactive enough. God, America had been demanding. Right now, however, all of it was in the past. And none of it, she said to herself, had really been Jenn's fault.

Poor Jenn. Poor Jenn lost that damn kid and ended up spoon-feeding crippled Mike Bellwether for twenty-odd years out of some misbegotten sense of . . . guilt? Responsibility?

"C'mon, Rubi—we've got to go! Where'd that waiter head to, anyways?" Jenn looked around with manicured hands on her heavy hips, and Rubicon gazed at her with affection. Why not give the ex-cheerleader a good evening in London, and then put her on that late train?

Why not indeed?

Jenn fumbled down the front of her shirt for her passport wallet. A glimpse of pink flesh overflowed a faded eggshell-colored bra. "Let's get moving, Rubi!" She said again.

"No." Rubicon remained seated, pulled out her cell phone, and snapped it open. "We're changing plans. I'll call your B&B and tell 'em you're arriving tomorrow morning. And then you know what?"

Jenn froze, but a slow smile spread across her face. Lips wide and coral and those tiny teeth, all those tiny teeth gleaming.

"What?"

"We're going to a party."

"Oh wow! Really? But—but I don't think I look fancy enough for a London party."

Rubicon's dark, mocking eyes were gentler than usual.

"Well then, we'll go shopping. Did you budget for shopping?"

"I sure did—Harrods! Whose party?"

"Not Harrods. And, oh, no one much—just the guy I kind of have a thing about."

"Rubi!"

Sophisticated Rubicon blushed, and thought how she'd never had an American friend to properly gush over guys with.

"I'll tell you about it at the shop. It's complicated. His wife died last year."

Jenn almost skipped in excitement at it all, the glass of wine and Rubi here, right here with her, London and the buildings and the now blue-black light of Trafalgar Square.

"Does he love you? Why not Harrods? I'd really like to go to H——"

"No. Harrods is a rip-off this time of year. We're going to Pandora's, the designer resale Mecca of Knightsbridge. Valentino, darling. And Versace, and Moschino. Though——" She looked at Jenn's body musingly. "You might be a little more DVF. Hmm."

"My *waist* isn't as big as it looks, really. It's just" —Jenn clutched two £20 notes in her hand as she looked resignedly down at her body— "everything else is."

Rubicon felt pity for her old friend that she wouldn't have been able to imagine a few hours before. "Jenn, put your money away. Of course this is my treat." With her long elegant fingers clad in a sheen of impossibly soft leather (the gloves had been a gift from her wealthy friend Arabella years ago), Rubicon slapped down an HSBC card, and silently prayed that her overdraft had not deactivated the card.

As the waiter silently took the card and left to run it through the machine, Rubicon's eyes followed him in silent prayer. She didn't notice the gleam of triumph pass over Jenn's face. Rubicon was too busy praying that her credit would work.

It did.

As they walked out of the National Portrait Gallery, Rubicon wondered how the hell you dress a figure that's short but somehow *all* curves (something she'd never dealt with before).

JENN'S EYES DANCED AS SHE kept drinking in Trafalgar Square, black taxi cabs glowing from within, shopping, parties, and—the thing that they're all for and about, really, she thought—men.

If Rubi could find one, so could she, right? And did this guy have a thing for Rubi too? Well, Rubi was so self-sufficient she was almost like a guy herself. Just look at her stride along! But Jenn was different. She had spent her life lying next to Mike Bellwether as he breathed laboriously, paralyzed from the waist down, his male smell combining with his medications into a scent that made her think of ether and rotting wood. Even so, sometimes, when Mike was in a narcotic daze, she would go to her knees next to his bed and breathe in his scent. That was the only time he would let her near him.

The two women kept walking down the stairs, and passed gilt-framed portraits of famous rogues and courtesans.

"Should we bring wine to the party, Rubi? Or food—food's more fun, right?"

"Crap," said Rubicon (two hours ago she would've said "Bugger"). "I told Mark I'd bring something to eat. Pain in the ass—we'll pick up something."

"I can throw something together. I love to cook."

"Really?" Rubicon's patronizing expression was back, her face reflecting that, to her, cooking was a useless but amusing skill, akin to being able to play the banjo with one's feet. "Okay, we'll hit the Waitrose on the way to the party."

Rubicon pulled open the door marked "Way Out," and she and Jenn left the National Portrait Gallery.

They walked toward the tube and their lives as tabloid fodder.

.୨ଓ.

JENN SUCCESSFULLY MISSED HER TRAIN. If you'd asked her (which she'd have found rude), she'd have sworn up and down that she never meant to miss it; would have opened glassy blue eyes wide and said, "I was honestly so *bummed*!" Jenn was one of those people who when they lie always use the word 'honestly' in order to convince themselves they're telling the truth.

However, from the minute she'd seen Rubicon at Waterloo, Jenn had felt an odd certainty that their lives were going to become entwined again. That by sheer force of will she could make it happen. Rubicon—so distant and so familiar, so chic and so unkempt, so confident in this big, wonderful dirty city and with her new clipped accent—had something Jenn wanted.

She didn't know quite exactly what it was, or how the heck she was going to get it. She just knew she would, and she was right.

Thanks to Jenn missing her train, the two erstwhile friends from Illinois shopped and went to a party and fought over a guy and presided over a murder that sold thousands of newspaper columns. So, despite the fact that both were over forty in the dawning age of Botox and liposuction and collagen implants, instead of buying, Rubicon and Jenn ended up selling (newspapers). Which goes to show that even nowadays it can still be age before beauty, if you have a juicy enough story for the media. Cast your pearls before those swine and the gutter scribes scramble to retrieve opalescent rounds from the dust and string them along the usual lines: Who's the good woman? Who's the bad?

Of course, there was much debate in the press. Many said that Jennifer, at worst, was a good girl gone wrong. Which means she gets to be bad, but with approval. Yes, the papers admit, she killed. She's also a little dim, a God-botherer and a Yank; but she's a mom doing her all for her family. Plus blond and full-figured, which helps. And Rubicon? Well, no approval for poor lonely Rubicon. She had an affair with a married man and turned her friend in for murder. Also American, but loud, and once was famous for her on-air obnoxiousness. And . . . she doesn't like kids (collective gasp of disapproval for that one). Yes. There is mileage in presenting Rubicon as the bad one.

HOWEVER, ON THIS NOVEMBER NIGHT, the two women stood outside the Charing Cross tube as the sky darkened, as Rubicon's black poncho was whipped into mad batlike constructs, as they were buffeted on all sides by cold rain and damp tourists. Jenn stood patiently waiting, just looking around. Students in willfully tattered tights scuffed by unseeingly, businessmen arrowed toward pubs as they fingered pre-pint snacks of salt and vinegar crisps, old men in shabby tweeds had bits of pigeon-colored damp newspaper sticking to their rubber-soled shoes, and there was a nearby telephone kiosk filled with postcard pictures of a topless girl whose breasts were depressingly stretch-marked beneath the words, "Naughty Nicky's Got the Hump—call 0208."

Rubicon wondered if she could get Jenn to spring for a taxi. Part of her still wished she was alone on the tube back to Richmond, but some long-dormant section of her mind was also ignited with images of Pinekill. Its wide expanses, the straight narrow roads' endless progression through the grain belt. The memories of nights outside Mississippi Taco, with a Diet Rite in her left hand and a Beef Buster Taco leaking its searing salsa down her ambitious throat as she sat on the hood of her car and imagined . . . imagined being anywhere than under those endless false-hope skies.

Jenn had never got out.

She looked down at Jenn, petite and stolid, whose hair was like molded plastic which remained curiously unmoving in the wind, and who stood with her legs akimbo as if no buffeting would budge her— that goddamn fanny pack, those bright unfocused eyes, that patriotic T-shirt warped over a dovelike figure that'd give Naughty Nicky a run for her money. Just then a splash of rain hit Jenn in the eye, and Rubicon raised an imperious hand. She was going to hail a cab. Damn the expense.

She'd just pretend to fumble for her wallet, and let Jenn pay.

A bit later, as the cab pulled up in Knightsbridge and Jenn saw how the thousands of round lights wrapped around Harrods gleamed with the energizing intensity of capitalistic desire, and that everywhere here, too, men spilled out of pubs, smoking on the sidewalk with a casual grip on their pint glasses, hitching their trousers up as women walked by. Jenn inhaled slowly. Then she applied more lipstick and smacked her full lips together.

London!

Dodging raindrops and litter, Rubicon grabbed Jenn's hand as they ran across the street and up the steep curb opposite. Leading Jenn away from Harrods' hypnotic lights was like trying to pull a collie off a pile of rotten leaves, Rubicon thought. She was beginning to regret her decision, but nothing like she would later on.

History repeats the same defeats. Rubicon had sung this into a hairbrush many times when young, so she should've known better.

They moved along the narrow darkness of Cheval Place, toward a store with a low, crooked wooden awning. Bare bulbs hung from thick black cords, and focused women moved along the racks of clothes with sharp elbows pointed toward their neighbors. Rich women's castoffs!

Rubi pushed Jenn toward the area where new (and expensive) girdles, bras and shapewear were sold. First thing, she thought, is to get Jenn a decent foundation garment.

Strap those things *down*.

Later, as Rubi piled dress after dress into Jenn's arms, stiff silk ones in jewel tones and clinging jersey wraps that slithered softly toward the floor, Jenn reminded her that she was going to spill about her "boyfriend." They stood in the dressing room, their faces reflected within the images of opposing mirrors, a hundred Rubicons towering over a hundred Jenns with her shirt off.

"He's not my boyfriend. I just kind of, for a long time I've—I just think he's great. But he's a widower. A lovely bloke. I mean, a sweet guy. I've known him so long . . . like I say, we're just friends now—Also, he's got a son, though that kid creeps me out. Jenn—you have to try on a shaping garment beneath that dress. It looks like a couple of hams are wrestling down there."

Why didn't Rubicon say she loved Mark wholeheartedly? That the sad depth of his dark brown eyes was both intoxicating and calming to her, that the sound of his hesitant voice on the telephone plumbed a tenderness in Rubicon she possessed only for him? Why didn't she say she'd been watching over the years of his deteriorating marriage, sometimes from afar and sometimes from up close, too close, an ache in her throat, as his broad back began to shrink down upon itself and shoulder blades to jut as if apologizing for taking up too much room? Why didn't she say all of that?

Because if Jenn had realized how much—and more to the point, how long—Rubicon had loved Mark, she would've come off as the plain, pathetic friend again. But, if Rubicon glossed over the years of longing, this night at Mark's would all come off as a fresh and glamorous status quo, not a period of awkward transition as Rubicon waited for Mark to recover from his (ghastly) wife's death. Jenn would see how accepted Rubi was in Mark's life and his house, almost the casual co-hostess of his party, the honest assessor of his child and staunch ally in his post-Arabella life. In a few months, Rubicon could maybe drop Jenn a line, tell her about how Mark and she were now together. Going to car-boot sales and farmers' markets. Their toes meeting beneath the table at pub lunches. Rubicon sighed, remembering long ago. How his hand had once stroked her hair as they sat together on the sofa, watching *Only Fools and Horses* on the telly. Just before she'd idiotically introduced him to posh, grabby, freckled and seemingly charming Arabella.

As it was, Jenn just thought that Rubicon had a crush. And that Rubi hadn't changed; she couldn't be bothered with the essentials. Like loving the man's son, no matter what. Children are as sensitive to criticism as a butterfly's wings are to human fingerprints. A rough hand can be eternally damaging. Rubi—thought Jenn as she fishtailed her arms through the tight foundation garment—never really got her priorities right. She supposed that was why it was so easy for her to leave home and never come back.

"Ugh! Oh, okay." The thick elastic jammed on Jenn's head. Her arms stuck up straight, her shoulders trapped, but then she wriggled a bit and the girdle somehow shifted over and down a bit. Jenn's voice was muffled by the Lycra, but she spoke solemnly. "You should never say kids are a drag, Rubi. They are our mirrors, our gift and our gold." Jenn kept wriggling, but the foundation garment somehow tightened around her upper arms. She gasped. "Giving kids chance after chance will always pay off in the end. How'd this guy's wife die? What's his name? Ugh—I can't get this ..."

"Here." Rubicon grabbed the bottom edge of the garment and tugged and twisted at it. She grunted, and Jenn bit her lips so as not to cry out as the elastic caught her flesh. The exuberance of Jenn's body was undimmed by time and loneliness. She has, Rubicon thought, the kind of figure that makes half the population not take you seriously, and the other (male) half take you very seriously indeed. Christ—thought Rubicon, as she tugged the girdle over Jenn's chest—what a drag to lug those cassavas around.

But of course she didn't say that. "Mark. He's a doctor. A widower, too. His wife was murdered last year. So naturally he's been pretty devastated."

With a fierce effort, Jenn pulled hard, and the spandex trap grudgingly slid down. Her hairdo had come out of its ponytail and was flattened over her head, and the rain had caused her heavy mascara to smear in panda formations—but her eyes flashed with avid interest.

"What?" Jenn said. "Say that again?"

"That his wife was killed. He came home from surgery one night last year and found her dead. Well, his son found her first. She was stabbed. Cops don't know who did it—an addict, maybe. Looking for drug money." Rubicon's eyes met Jenn's in the mirror.

"That's awful! But—" Jenn's eyes caught Rubicon's in the mirror. "A *surgeon*, huh? Whoa!"

"No—surgery's what they call a doctor's office here. He's just a regular doctor. A GP."

"Well, still!" Jenn whistled. "Pretty fancy, Rubes!"

The two women simultaneously fell silent. They tilted their heads and looked at Jenn's reflection in the long rectangular mirror. Rubicon nodded. It was a good beginning.

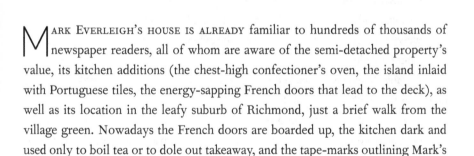

3

M ARK EVERLEIGH'S HOUSE IS ALREADY familiar to hundreds of thousands of newspaper readers, all of whom are aware of the semi-detached property's value, its kitchen additions (the chest-high confectioner's oven, the island inlaid with Portuguese tiles, the energy-sapping French doors that lead to the deck), as well as its location in the leafy suburb of Richmond, just a brief walk from the village green. Nowadays the French doors are boarded up, the kitchen dark and used only to boil tea or to dole out takeaway, and the tape-marks outlining Mark's body long gone.

And as for that island? Well, Portuguese tiles chip easily and become very shabby after a while, and it's a bitch to clean out their grouting. Only someone profoundly impractical would select them for their kitchen. That would be Arabella, Mark's first wife, Rubicon's old friend, nearly a year dead on the damp November night of this party. The island is pivotal, though. At the time, all the DIY and rehab shows on TV focused on the island—how handy it is to have a chunk of cabinetry smack in the middle of your kitchen. How professional, how necessary for a modern cook—one simply *must* spend money to change the kitchen (no, one's life!) with an island. And both of their bodies ended up near there, Arabella's and Mark's, on the bamboo floor (an elegant sand color) clutching the island for support as their lives' blood ran out. Their deaths occurred eighteen months apart, but on that same spot. One might think this is meaningful, but it's simple logic. The kitchen's where people hang out.

.·ഗ·.

HOWEVER, ON THIS COLD NOVEMBER night Mark Everleigh was (obviously) still alive and trying to put the past behind him, or the parts of it he could. This was his first party since his wife's death. Mark had been on the Marylebone high street that afternoon to see a psychologist about his recurring dream that he, with joyous intention, was running the family Volvo wagon over his wife and son. He'd then reverse the car and crush them both again. In the dream Mark would open the Volvo's door to inspect the damage beneath the wheels. There he'd find the bloodied gristle and bone-shattered remains of Arabella and Simon intermingled, united in death as they'd never been in life.

The psychologist's appointment hadn't worked out too well. The doctor had a rather nasty pale mustache and chewed her pencil noisily as Mark shifted on a low Swedish chair and recounted his dream. At the detail about him inspecting the bodies, the psychologist flinched, and Mark knew she believed that he had killed his wife.

Many people did.

So now Mark, as he walked on the subtly varnished hardwood floors of his lovely semi-detached house in Southwest London, putting out bowls of gourmet crisps and pretzels, was feeling disgusted with himself. Disgusted at his weakness in having paid a dodgy half-trained doctor—one who was apparently incapable of using tweezers (Arabella, he knew, had plucked her shapely brows and incipient chin hairs every morning)—and who'd glance at the door any time Mark made a sudden movement. He'd left the appointment early, deciding to drop by Harrods to buy some chocolate biscuits for his party tonight.

At least that would be money usefully spent.

He'd known all along he couldn't tell the psychologist the truth, anyway. So why go? Mark had hoped that half-truths, simply talking, would help.

He should've known better. Sharing half-truths does nothing for the psyche or the soul—unless, of course, you are fortunate or foolish enough to believe they are the whole truth. Mark was neither.

OVER THE LAST YEAR MARK had become used to watching as people heard his name and then paused while trying to remember why it seemed familiar, waiting for the moment the penny would drop and they'd remember it had been in the newspapers. The tabloids. How Arabella had been found dead in that kitchen (a bottle of Tilex nearby. Had she been surprised while trying vainly to clean those Portuguese tiles? Atypical). It had happened one evening when Mark was late at surgery and Simon had gone to the cinema with friends. How the police had been bad enough, with their expressions moving from professional respect to open suspicion as they'd torn through the house but failed to find the knife. A similar search of Mark's surgery revealed nothing—but he felt their conviction that the husband always did it. It's never the passing tramp, the hired man, the freak accident (with a knife? To her throat?).

Perhaps everyone, Mark included, had simply seen too many women slaughtered on TV. Perhaps everyone was right to think in these TV movie clichés. Mark had not killed his wife but he'd yearned for her death, or at least her *silence*.

And he knew his son had done the same.

SO ARABELLA'S DEATH HAD BEEN bad enough, but then the press got involved. Rubicon was seen at the funeral, and her stale celebrity bumped the murder coverage up to page four in the tabloids. Next, the tabs learned about Mark and Arabella's "open" marriage. How spicy—how evolved! Eventually the more intriguing, humiliating truth had emerged—that the marriage was only open on her side. Mark had sadly waited for Arabella to come home at night with her eyes unfocussed by drink and sex, her freckled skin rough from another man's beard. By now everyone knew that Mark had been asked to "help the police with their investigations" and that the police had requested a warrant to prolong his questioning.

What the neighbors said about him to the press certainly hadn't helped. About the worst things that could be said, in fact. Mark's shoulders slumped as he thought about it: A gentle bloke, they'd stated. Wouldn't hurt a fly. Can you imagine? Every murderous, murderer's cliché.

Wouldn't hurt a fly.

Mark sighed, thinking (not for the first time) of how unfair it was that in relationships there was always that unbalance of power, always the one person who did the loving and the other who was loved. He had (once) loved Arabella. Arabella had loved . . . indiscriminately. Mark had then been astonished by how much he loved his son. It was a tremulous and fierce love that seemed to be deepened—almost enriched—by his evolving mistrust of the boy and Simon's wary contempt for him.

Mark looked into the gold-framed mirror over the gas fireplace in Arabella's elegant kitchen/lounge extension. His face—did he *look* like a murderer? He couldn't see it, though he knew some did. The sandy hair, still brush-like and full in the center, but wandering back over the temples. The mild brown eyes. His eyebrows, well—he couldn't do much about them; they'd always had a certain troglodytic heaviness. Thick black brows were the only thing that made him seem authoritative, and he'd learned early on to lower his chin and stare out from under them. Those brows would make Dennis Thatcher look imperious, he'd been told. Not that it'd fooled Arabella. Simon had his father's face, but with green eyes and a misleadingly cheerful-looking up-tilted nose.

Mark sighed, and wished he'd bought more hors d'oeuvres. Rubicon said she'd bring some, but she was as ghastly a cook as he, and probably would also buy crisps and maybe some Marks and Spencer's quiches. Anyway, it was always nice to see her.

Wouldn't hurt a fly. And the other damning phrase: *He keeps to himself a lot.* Which one would, of course, with a wife who not only shagged for Southwest London but also liked to shout it to the world, along with your own sexual inadequacies and peccadilloes.

The Brayson's dinner that last summer: Arabella and Simon were next door for a casual weekday barbeque. When the surgery had closed and Mark joined his family, he could tell something was off right away. Vanessa sat with a tight false smile on her face, talking (or rather listening) to Arabella as Jack grilled sausages and peppers on his new, ridiculously large, outdoor hybrid grill. Arabella was delicately holding a frozen margarita, with her fingers oily from spanakopita canapés. Tequila—added to the bourgeois nature of a summer barbeque—made her discontent, reckless. Mark noticed how the tiki torches near Arabella's seat gave her eyes a dangerous flickering brightness. Upon seeing her husband, Arabella wiped her mouth with the heel of her hand (how had it been so elegant? How had she been able to do such coarse things and manage elegance?), and loudly inquired if Jack Brayson thought the next generation of English men would be so fixated on the same dull sexual peccadilloes.

"Because there he is. Our Lord of Tits and Sodomy." Arabella laughed and gestured toward her husband. "*Such* a bore, Mark is. You'd think the clitoris was that red button American Presidents press to start nuclear war. Terrified of it! Are *you*, Jack?" Vanessa Brayson's pale face had looked at Mark wearily, with absolutely no expectation that he'd stop this nonsense, before she sharply informed her husband that the gourmet sausages were burning on the grill. "One must be *so* careful . . ." she'd added as Jack seized the tongs.

"One can be too bloody careful," muttered Arabella darkly, her small freckled face florid from tequila. Her left hand suddenly reached out talon-like to grasp Mark's thigh as he wearily sat down next to her. "For example, Mark washes his willy before sex." She tittered gaily, her slender throat (the one that was later so efficiently sliced) exposed. Mark had loathed her then, loathed her even more when she'd cawed across the lawn to her son, "Simon, always remember that your willy *should* be dirty—it should be *rich* with oils, rank as patchouli."

The fourteen-year-old boy had glanced up from his handheld video game and looked at his mother with opaque, weary eyes. Mark's throat tightened.

The meal was served and began in silence. Everybody felt a little awkward as they ate their Sainsbury's Best chicken and fennel sausages. Pity, because they were perfectly seared.

A SOUND DREW MARK BACK to the present, and he realized Rubicon was standing on the back deck just outside the French doors. She was bespattered with rain and waving at him with her usual wary, ill-hidden devotion. Awkward, that. Now she stood there in the dark with plastic bags from Waitrose dangling from her fingers, resembling an elegant bird perched on the stained teak deck. He gestured her in, and her dark, shadowed face split into a grin. As she opened the doors, Mark noticed a shapeless, bedraggled figure behind her.

"Mark! How's it going?" Rubicon kissed him on the corner of his mouth. He fought the urge to wipe the cold rainwater from his face.

"Hallo, Rubicon. Well . . . fans of Nigella will be disappointed." He looked unhappily down at the bowl he was holding, which contained 'gourmet' crisps made with quartered black pepper and stick-like shards of rosemary.

"No worries. I've brought the cavalry—or rather, someone who actually likes to cook." Rubicon stepped aside and referred Mark to the damp blond figure standing stolidly behind her. Muscular, but clearly a small woman, with mascara running down her face in clownish grotesquerie and hair sticking to her forehead like damp ferns.

"Hey there!" The figure chirruped like they were old friends.

How tired Mark was of meeting people. Terrible thought for a host to have, but nonetheless true. Flawed, sick, frightened, foolish, indecisive people, just like himself. Or simply endlessly predictably *boring*, again like himself. This specimen was clearly American, rather short and stout, with the hairstyle of an adolescent girl and the face of a cross matron. A horrible shapeless fleece jacket and the usual childish trainers on her feet. Her brows pointed down over a button nose, and she clutched the handle of a roller suitcase.

This solid American stepped in out of the dark rainy night, dropped the handle of her suitcase with a bang, placed her hands on her hips, and looked around. "Cute place you got here! Fancy. Rubi says you don't cook, so I bought the fixings for a really good app or two. She said you'd have butter—do you? I use a lot of butter."

Jenn was already pushing past him toward the island, and Mark caught Rubicon's eye. She tilted her head to the side with a shy, funny look he'd never seen before and shrugged one shoulder.

"Mark, meet a denizen of Pinekill, Illinois."

The stocky figure leaned over the island counter and stuck her hand out. Her eyes were blue, round, and bright with bossiness. "Yeah, Rubi and I go way back. Best friends from the year dot! My name's Jenn."

"I'm Mark Everleigh. Lovely to meet you. Butter we have. And any friend of . . . Rubi's."

Their hands met. He noticed how small and cold her hands were, and how powerful their grip.

"Jenn'll whip something up, then we'll go upstairs and change for the party. You don't mind if we use Simon's room, do you?" Rubicon took a bottle of cava out of an ice bucket and began twisting the cork off with waiterly expertise.

"Oh—well, perhaps . . ." Mark had no idea of the state of Simon's room, and it occurred to him that perhaps the boy kept something in there that it might be . . . unwise to have Rubicon find. Perhaps the boy kept a journal? Mark knew his son wondered what he thought about that night. He'd caught the boy looking at him surmisingly in the months the two had spent since Arabella's death, in the cold war between widower and adolescent. And now, thought Mark wearily, he'd have to pick up Simon's room, put away his computer.

He should never have had a party, save for the need to force life back into a semblance of normalcy. Also, the cava, Mark felt, was profoundly inappropriate—but serve it he would. The shed was full of the stuff since Arabella's last car trip to Spain.

What a fool I am, thought Mark again. God, I wish someone would tell me how to manage all this.

Meanwhile, the blond Yank was bustling around his kitchen with a sort of clattering competence, pulling out trays and knives not used since Arabella's death. She unboxed a brie and began wrapping it in phyllo dough. Everything she did had a complacent certainty to it, an unembarrassed self-satisfaction. Mark watched as Rubicon poured glasses of cava.

Jenn refused hers and began issuing instructions to them both, clearly unaware of the black rivulets of mascara streaking her cheeks, creating marionette lines down her jaw to her short bull-like neck. To Mark her body seemed block-like, sexless beneath that thick fleece jacket.

She pointed a manicured finger at his chest. "You'd better go up and get changed, Mark. Rubi said people will be here in half an hour, right? So I'll get this organized, and then Rubi and I'll get all dressed and make a late entrance. Like prom in the old days. Right, Rubes?"

Mark had thought he was already dressed for the party. Looking down, he realized the bossy American thought he should put on a tie. So he would.

"I never went to prom," Rubicon said.

As he left the kitchen, Mark looked around to see Rubicon leaning on the island drinking cava as Jenn poured a can of tomatoes into a saucepan (followed by a full stick of butter). In minutes, a comforting smell of rich tomato sauce wafted upstairs to Mark, who busily removed any notebooks, notepads and portable computers from Simon's room.

Then he went to his room, just across the narrow hallway, and put on a tie. It was the one he'd worn to the funeral.

4

THE PARTY GUESTS WERE THE usual cast of characters found in the leafy suburbs just southwest of London. There might be artists, but not radical ones—more journos and media people, also doctors with or without a holistic bent, lawyers and lady accountants who were beginning to plan Botox events in their off-hours. Teachers married to failed writers (one or the other had family money, or they wouldn't be in Richmond), very successful retailers or mid-level actors, business executives who vote Labour and drive Swedish. Richmond, there at the end of the District Line, halfway between the heaving enlivening filth and disparity of London and the immaculate Christopher Wren chocolate boxery of Windsor.

The guests had arrived. It was 7:30 on that dark rainy night, and Mark milled about filling glasses. He now wore a blue silk tie over his white shirt and drab olive corduroys, and moved about in a sort of vague daze, as if he had wandered in from the street into a local gathering. How odd to have people here again. How odd, and what a blessed relief, not to be alone with Simon.

Since Arabella's death, Simon and Mark had lived in a silent standoff.

But tonight the boy was staying with friends, and Mark had removed all traces of a fifteen-year-old's adolescent paraphernalia: the video games, the dried tea bags on countertops, the hoodies tossed on the floor and the torn messenger bags slung over chairs. Mark found it odd that signs of Simon's life here were considerably easier to remove than those of Arabella's.

She was everywhere. The tea-light holders she'd bought at Habitat in the post-Christmas sales. The fairy lights that Rubicon or her friend had wrapped around the ficus tree. The glazed bowls containing the food Mark had bought—his barely warmed samosas and the gourmet crisps—were the color of gleaming peat. Arabella had excused their egregiously high price by saying that the bowls had been hand thrown by a celebrated Cornish vegan potter, who had dyslexia and an adopted Sudanese child.

Mark loathed those bowls, but there they were. Thank Christ the American hadn't put out the fruit knives. These were made by a one-armed but legendary swordsman in Wales. After ordering a six-piece set (and concluding her two-month affair with said swordsman), Arabella had felt that perhaps small sharp cutlery embossed with her family crest were actually rather bourgeois. One of those knives, never found since, had been used to kill her.

On the bookshelf Mark saw there was still one picture up of Arabella and himself, and someone (probably not Rubicon, Mark thought) had placed a tea light reverently before it, so that the eyes in his and Arabella's young faces seemed to twitch feverishly from left to right.

He wished Rubicon would come down, or even that friend of hers who'd made herself so comfortable in his kitchen. At least they would talk to people and look as if they didn't find it a torture, at least they wouldn't have memories of how each person at this party had changed toward them after Arabella's death.

And of course they'd all come, the neighbors who had avoided Mark for a while after the body had been found, after Simon had been sent to his grandparents while Mark was questioned by the police. Soon Mark's deep depression since Arabella's death had touched them, that and his apparent devotion to Simon—the way the two had just burrowed down, always at home alone together. Never a noise could be heard from the Everleighs' house—unlike the old days, the Arabella days.

But now Mark was re-emerging, and about time too! It was the lead-up to the holidays, a time of putting the year behind you, of donning party clothes and getting booze in, of rushing about importantly and greeting neighbors with a harried, bustling friendliness. Everybody felt sorry for Mark now. They had all seen him walking to his surgery in the mornings since the murder, always dressed in those rumpled old corduroys, his shoulders slumped, long grooves of anxiety by his mouth. A new year was coming and perhaps it was time to remember what a tiresome cow Arabella had always been, anyway.

So they all came. Free food and drink, that drawing in of nights which still seems exciting at the beginning of the winter, the American election and Christmas coming and the new findings of those robots on Mars, plus the fact of Simon—only fifteen—living near them without a mother, a silent reproach to the community. A new year is coming, 2005, imagine! So people came to bask in the glow of the Habitat tea lights, to hear the satisfying suburban clink of wine glasses against wedding bands, to feel enlivened by the slightly outdated pop music coming from the stereo speakers, to talk about holidays and schools, renovations and EastEnders, and those dreadful track suits everyone was wearing. Velour! A new word that year was Chav. Track suits were for Chavs.

Richmond was not, which made everyone feel lovely and serene. A sense of superiority: the perfect condiment to any party. Also conducive: A crime scene.

Because of course it wasn't just the canapés on low tables and crudités on high, or booze, or the darkness of a long winter's night seeping through the long French doors of the kitchen, that gave the guests a frisson of satisfaction. It was the knowledge that there—just *there*, behind the island—was where the body was found. There'd been diagrams in *The Mirror*.

And Kylie sang, *I Just Can't Get You Out of My Head*.

"ARE THOSE SAMOSAS VEGETARIAN?"

"Who knows, mate. Aren't all samosas vegetarian?"

"Rather depends on whether you consider lamb a vegetable."

"Oh, I do. As long as it hasn't still got teeth or hooves on. Have you met Anne-Marie? Where is she? She was just—anyway, I'm hoping to get stuck in there tonight."

"I think she's just behind you, Hugh."

"Hallo."

"Oh! There you are, Anne-Marie. Found yourself a glass of wine, have you? Excellent. This is Daniel Jameson. Tell him you're enchanted to meet him, then let's piss off outside for a crafty fag."

"I don't smoke."

"Good lord. Don't you?"

"Hallo, Daniel. I've only recently met Hugh. He is my daughter's school chum's father."

"Very nice to meet you, Anne-Marie. My condolences at your having to put up with this old reprobate tonight. He's not quite so bad once you get to know him."

"Do *you* have any children, Daniel?"

Hugh Fairleigh offered Anne-Marie the bowl of samosas. She ignored him and beamed up at Daniel, who had attractive salt-and-pepper hair and an air of humor and solidity.

"God no," Hugh stepped in briskly. "Caro and Daniel have a *life*. Lucky buggers."

.୨୧.

UPSTAIRS, JENN STOOD IN SIMON'S small room, beneath the eaved ceiling but above the party sounds of murmurs and music and clinking glasses. Rubicon had just left, telling Jenn to come down when she was ready. Rubi had removed the scrunchie and brushed Jenn's hair. She'd also insisted on doing Jenn's makeup and had actually taken her blue eye shadow away.

"It's not a Duran Duran video, Jenn. People don't wear so much makeup here."

Jenn had managed to keep hold of her *Coral Chaos* Maybelline lipstick, which she'd hidden in the cleavage of this faintly tight foundation garment. She'd apply the lipstick soon, with a slow circling focus.

But for now she stood looking out of an English boy's window. Lights from the party were dancing reflections in the blackened yard, and at the end of the grass, she could dimly see the outline of a large, hobbled tree. The sky above was streaked with swiftly moving clouds, sweeping over rooftops made of what looked like broken flower pots. Above most chimneys a many-pronged aerial stuck up, like the skeleton of a trapped bird.

Jenn closed the blinds, and breathed in deeply. The musky, almost feline stink of an adolescent boy's room was exciting to her and reminded her of high-school parties, of trembling hands reaching around her waist as a slow dance began, of boys' agonizing attempts to hide their erections within their pleated trousers, while she'd knowingly, accidentally, brush up against them.

A new song started downstairs —unfamiliar music. It seemed funny to her that a doctor would play this type of song. A husky voice asked *What's Your Flava? Baby What's Your Flava?*

Jenn bent over and softly brushed her hands along the English boy's bed pillow, smoothing it to perfection and wondering what his life was like after his loss. With mother and child, Jenn knew, the loss never ended, never faded, except in others' minds.

.୨ଓ.

As for Rubicon, she had descended the stairs knowing that she didn't look her best—or anywhere near it. Jenn's presence in the shop had dampened her friend's usually acute sense of style, and now Rubicon found herself wrapped in a cocoon of crushed velvet, which had seemed a jewel-toned burgundy in the shop but now was clearly the color of dried blood. As the dress warmed to Rubicon's body, the smell of another person's sweat began to come up. The whiff of cheap deodorant and sulfur. The stink of someone else's night out in this velveteen nightmare. The dress was intended to be a sort of ode to Dior, with its high bodice and long glowing skirt, but the excess of fabric made Rubicon's slenderness seem bony and spinsterish, rather than enviably chic.

She wished she had some Febreze with which she could douse her underarms.

Walking into the room, Rubicon saw Daniel and Caro talking to a stranger, a small dark anxious-looking woman who had her back to Hugh. Women often did, thought Rubicon, as she waved to them and grabbed a glass of cava. Since his divorce he'd become even more manically laddish; poor Hugh, turning into one of those blokes who thought women only like married men because he'd begun lunging too much since the divorce. When married he had been less desperate, less needy.

"Rubicon!"

"Thank God you're here, Caro. You wouldn't believe—I nearly had to go to Harrods today." Caro was married to Daniel, designed the displays for Harvey Nicks, and was wonderfully chic with bobbed, hennaed hair and dramatic silver jewelry.

"Oh dear. How ghastly—why?"

"Friend from the States. She's sweet, actually. And an embodiment of every American cliché; it's almost staggering. We went to Pandora's and I bought this. Isn't it horrible?"

"It's brilliant, but you're absolutely swimming in it! Beware of friends who put you off your style compass. They're always bad'uns. Joking, darling. Where is she?"

Hugh stuck his graying leonine head into the conversation and whispered piercingly, "Caro, I believe my girl is about to give your husband a hand shandy, which would be a sad misapplication of her talents and of Mark's cava. Step in, would you?"

"Oh, do shut up and leave the poor girl alone, Hugh. It's far too early in the night for your rudeness. Daniel, take Hugh to the garden for a fag, would you? And run some of his energy off, like an aging Labrador."

Daniel threw an intentionally heavy arm around Hugh's shoulder and led him protesting out the French doors. "That mouthy cow Rubicon will tell Anne-Marie terrible things about me, mate!"

"Well," said Daniel reasonably, "you should've thought about that before going on about hand shandies. And what's to stop us from having a fag and saying terrible things about Rubicon?"

"Good point, that." Hugh opened the French doors to the back, and the men stepped outside—but not before the whole room heard Hugh's next comment. "She looks like a wet weekend tonight." As Daniel closed the doors behind them, Hugh added, "Rubicon had better watch out, some buxom nurse will catch Mark's eye and he'll be off—again!"

Mark flinched as the French doors again shut out the darkness and Hugh's voice. He wished he was like Daniel. A military man, comfortable in his body and competent at managing people.

As for Rubicon, her face flushed an unattractive mauve color and her speaking voice became louder and more abrasive. Suddenly it was a mid-Atlantic shout, the Mockney/Illinois hybrid she'd used in her *It's Pants!* days. She cawed out to Anne-Marie.

"Wot're you doing with *Hugh*, you daft cow? C'mere and I'll tell you about the time he gave his wife a blazing dose of the clap."

An anguished cry came from the garden. As she'd intended, Rubicon's voice had carried through the closed doors to Hugh.

.ᕤᕤ.

UP IN SIMON'S ROOM, JENN stood examining a poster hanging next to the mirror. It featured a hugely buxom, half-naked young blond woman whose direct gaze contained more hostility than promise—the name written in pink cursive beneath was "Jordan."

Slowly, Jennifer veered her eyes to her own reflection. Holy crow! If Rubi was this good with makeup, why didn't she wear some herself? Jenn couldn't recognize the person in the mirror—she looked like a rich Chicago lady, the kind who strolls down Michigan Avenue with a yappy dog in her purse. Her eyebrows had been brushed with a brown powder; they looked like the ones she'd had in high school, but fuller, *groomed*. Her eyes seemed bigger (though less blue) without the aqua liner she'd used for decades inside her lower waterline. Her lips were muted, and that needed fixing. Rubi'd spent a lot of time on them and they did look sort of full and oddly gentle, but let's face it; Rubi couldn't be expected to really know how to make the most of Jenn's type of looks. And maybe, just maybe—she didn't want Jenn to make too big of a splash.

Jenn pushed that unkind thought away, saying to herself, I honestly didn't mean that.

But she pulled out that hidden *Coral Chaos* and thickly smeared the bright orangy-pink color around and around her lips.

Bass notes pumped rhythmically up through the floorboards.

Jenn reached for the dress Rubicon had made her buy—she'd wanted the pretty lavender Laura Ashley dress with the smocked top, but had mystifyingly been told it was for "deranged Sloane Rangers." Rubicon had instead insisted she buy this wrap dress in midnight blue, shot with silver stitching along the neck and along the sleeves. The sleeves were long and widened toward the wrists, fluttering out over Jenn's small but thick hands, disguising her grasping fingers. She'd barely seen it on—Rubicon just said, "That's it. You're built for a wrap dress." And it was bought. Ridiculously expensive for something that's not even new, though Jenn didn't let Rubi know how shocked she was. But $200—for a used dress?

It was the first time she'd really looked at herself in years. Too much sun damage on her cheeks and chest. Her neck was shorter than she thought, and kind of thrusting. She pulled her chin back. Better. She'd felt fat and short and small town next to Rubi, whose face was skinny and seemed to make no effort to retain the memory of adolescent fullness, the impenetrable cuteness of a high-school beauty. But then, Rubicon hadn't *been* a high-school beauty. Aging obviously wouldn't frighten her.

Jenn hadn't realized how long she'd felt invisible, unviable. A sense of power only dimly remembered began coursing back through her veins. It was exciting.

The music downstairs got a little louder, the voices more boisterous. People would be wanting her good normal food, she realized. You can't drink champagne with potato chips—c'mon. Those weird-looking chips had made her worry about what that doctor Mark had been eating, and feeding his son, since their loss. She'd noticed Mark's slumped shoulders, and his muted greeting of her friend. It'd probably never occurred to Rubicon to get some food in for these boys, do some cleaning, bring some feminine energy and *life* back to this house of sorrow. To impose it for their own good.

Jenn remembered you put the dress on like a coat, pull the left sash through a right-side slit and the right-side sash around the body, then tug both tightly together. Midnight blue and silver silk slithered and gathered around her bust, slid whisperingly over the foundation garment, then pulled into a neat V. She could see right off that the fabric draped lightly over her powerful thighs. She knotted the sash and looked at herself in the mirror.

She'd just lost fifteen pounds.

She looked . . . she looked *expensive*.

"Hello," she said aloud to the mirror. It sounded a little abrupt, like she was a social worker about to hand out questionnaires. All those years waiting on Mike—of wrangling with Medicaid and Mike's constant suspicions—had left her sexless, she'd thought. She touched her waist again and suddenly remembered the richness the world had seemed to contain, back when she'd been the cutest Pinekillian of her generation, when she'd had to be super-nice to people so they wouldn't say she was a snob because of her looks.

Standing up straight, remembering to tuck her chin down, Jenn spoke again. "Hi there," she murmured, watching as the muscles in her throat rose and fell. "I'm Jenn. Could you help me with this plate? Thanks, sweetie . . ."

Perfect.

THE PARTY DOWNSTAIRS SETTLED INTO the usual. Getting louder as the men began taking the piss, and the women discussed holiday preparations while denying each other's friendly accusations of weight loss. Daniel and Caro were, as always, the most at ease and therefore the most liked. Each had the gift of being interesting without bitchery. It helped, both Mark and Hugh thought, that they hadn't had children.

Also at the party were Thom and Lydia, in their forties and unhappily dating. Lydia's pale pudding of a face became more depressed every year by Thom's lack of commitment and concomitant dedication to telling the same joke (about a donkey and a masturbating boy) at every party. Jack Brayson and Vanessa were somewhat subdued, having had an enormous row before they left their house; as they were getting dressed, Jack had stupidly mentioned that he thought Mark was a jammy bastard, living a woman-free life the last year—footie on the telly, takeaways every night— just him and Simon.

Vanessa had silently clipped heavy gold knot earrings onto her lobes, and then said, "Nonsense." She was simultaneously wishing that her chest wasn't quite so bony and remembering how Jack had often looked at Arabella's décolletage with the blank gaze of a man lost in a spot of fantasizing. "That lovely man has been through absolute hell since her death."

"Absolute hell? He's had Rubicon dancing on a string for eons, and God knows how many patients have been making sheep's eyes at him—"

"Is that what you honestly believe a widower's life is, Jack? Choc-a-bloc with lonely women panting for a fumble at your rather tired equipment? What a sad little man you are."

Jack had drawn himself up to his full height, and loudly intoned his opinion of Vanessa's fumbling abilities. The argument continued as they walked down the street toward the party. Jack liked Mark. Mark had done him a massive favor during that ghastly time Jack got that girl from Lymington up the spout and had been absolutely terrified that Vanessa would learn about it somehow. Mark had put them onto a friend of his, no waiting about at the Stopes clinic, just a job well and quickly done. Thank God. All blokes together. Apart from the girl, obviously . . . what was her name again? Anyway, all's well that ends well.

And Jack had been able to do Mark a good turn the evening Arabella died. He'd been in his kitchen washing dishes when a high-pitched scream came from the Everleighs'. Jack had frozen for a moment, Fairy Liquid in hand. He was just about to resume his task again when there was another scream. This time it was deeper, ragged.

"Oh, Mummy!"

Jack heard scrambling sounds and saw Simon climb over the fence separating the two properties—he'd done that since he was a child retrieving an errant football. At first Jack thought the lad was wearing makeup. The boy leaped down from the fence, staggered over toward the house and paused to lean on Jack's precious hybrid grill for a moment, gasping for air. Jack went out to the garden, saw that it was a smear of blood on Simon's face, and shouted out for Vanessa.

So 999 had been called, and then Mark. They arrived to find Simon in the Braysons' house, weeping in Vanessa's arms. Upon Mark's entrance the boy had fallen silent. And Jack never mentioned to Vanessa the curious, appraising way Simon had looked at his father. She hadn't seen it—but he had, and so had that police inspector.

.ᘒᖇ.

ONCE AT THE PARTY, THE Braysons ignored each other and began drinking too much on empty stomachs (they shared an expensive taste in food and separately recoiled from the puckered samosas, the margarine-rich mini-quiches). Vanessa's fine-boned face was stern but serene as she spoke to a new neighbor named Sam, a shy pockmarked man rumored to be an artist and to own a house in Normandy. There were several more neighbors, new arrivals to the neighborhood or casual acquaintances who'd been lured by the holiday season, by Mark's pale notoriety and his flowing cava.

Daniel and Caro, Lydia and Thom, Sam and the Braysons. Hugh and his shock of graying ginger hair (both given a new unnatural luster since his recent divorce), and of course his date Anne-Marie. Hugh's boorishness was making Anne-Marie melancholy, which bad dates and holiday parties on winter nights can often do. Winter's darkness encroaches and single people head out to the celebrations, clutching a hostess-gift bottle of wine by its neck, chilled by the festive realization that one is utterly alone.

Nonetheless, Anne-Marie began concocting plans to leave early. A faked emergency would save on babysitting money and minimize her losses—she had been curious about Rubicon Baines (she had watched *It's Pants!* on the telly after school as a teen), and wanted to actually chat with potential murderer Mark Everleigh.

However, they'd both turned out to be disappointments.

Mark was possibly the least sinister person Anne-Marie had ever met, with his sad brown eyes, sagging corduroy trousers, and unimpressive canapés. Rubicon Baines was still loud, tall, and birdlike, with flying hands and whorls of dark-red hair pointing toward the skylights—but she was also brittle and hard to talk to, and kept one eye on the host at all times. And she whiffed too.

Disappointing. Such cheeky stuff she used to wear in the '90s—tutus and artfully torn turtlenecks, eyes flashing beneath jaunty bohemian headdresses. Now

Rubicon seemed rawboned and insecure, too bony for the stiff raspberry velvet dress she wore.

On some cellular level, Rubicon realized that Anne-Marie had once been a fan, and she found herself acting a tired revival of her *It's Pants!* persona. This involved being tediously opinionated and shouty and telling people what to do. Now emboldened by wine, she danced over to Hugh and Anne-Marie, her hair gleaming like titian meringue points beneath the track lighting.

"Hugh! Hugh—before you get completely arseholed, promise to be nice to my old friend Jenn when she gets down here. She's fresh from rural Illinois."

Hugh's red nose twitched, and he held his champagne glass by its stand, as if it were a tea saucer. "Oh lord, must we have yet *another* Septic slapper bouncing about the place?" He placed his arm around Rubicon's shoulder, and their glances met eye to eye, his practiced and lustful, hers warily defended. "More bloody Yanks? The whole lot of you, if you're not busy being born, you're busy buying—usually pies." Anne-Marie stood nearby, watching Hugh's thumb rub intimately along Rubicon's collarbone.

Rubicon was bored by his predictable touch and stepped away. "Ah. A fat Yank joke. How original! Watch out—Jenn's pure American, unreconstituted. Voted for Dubya, I bet. Quite possibly has a Glock concealed on her person."

"Now Rubicon . . ." Mark stepped out from behind the island. "She seems lovely and clearly adores you—she calls her 'Rubi.'"

Hugh asked, "You've met her then, Mark? Is she dangerously obese or merely fat-arsed and bulgy?"

Mark ignored him, though privately thought the latter description more accurate.

Jack, who'd been gulping down Bombay Gin and tonics as a gesture of rebellion toward Vanessa and her beloved bloody Cabernets, strolled over looking a bit bleary. He leaned back and rubbed his cashmered belly, saying, "'Rubi'? Who adores our little Rubicon?" Jack winked heavily. "The ladies are hoping you might do that, Mark."

Vanessa rolled her eyes—she never should have told Jack that Rubicon had hopes of Mark.

Hugh grinned wolfishly and looked between Mark and Rubicon.

A flush appeared again on Rubicon's narrow, jaunty face.

"We *all* adore her," Mark said firmly as he picked up some empty wine glasses. "That's why she's Simon's godmother." A bell went off in the kitchen, and Mark wandered off again, after a chilly glance at Jack.

Rubicon darted back toward Caro. "Oy, mate!" she cried. "You haven't told me about the Christmas windows at Harvey Nicks yet!" The two of them settled down on the sofa near the fireplace, chatting. It didn't occur to Rubicon to help Mark refill drinks or to check the bell that had just gone off in the kitchen—not her thing.

Hugh and Anne-Marie were left under the drunken, rather benevolent gaze of Jack Brayson.

"Rubicon and Arabella were old mates," said Hugh to Anne-Marie with a wink.

Her pale almond eyes opened wide. She hadn't expected people to openly talk about the dead woman! Perhaps, she thought, the night would be more interesting than the canapés and Hugh's bombastic lechery indicated.

Jack began eating the greasy samosas, because he really was starting to feel a bit pissed. His stomach would be in bits in the morning. He plaintively caught Vanessa's eye, but she looked away and continued talking to some bald wanker about renovations to his farmhouse in Normandy.

Turning back to Anne-Marie, Jack nodded solemnly as he filled his hand with mini-samosas. "Rubicon and Mark—she was a bit smitten with him, don't you know." This came out sounding like "Donsh-no," but Jack heard it and pulled himself together. "Don' you *know*, years ago. First-date type of thingy. Took him to a party. Introduced him to Arabella, and he never looked back . . ."

"Oh really," Anne-Marie said. "I—er—expect she—well, an old friend must have been of some help when—" She hardly knew how to finish, but Hugh leaned forward with a wicked smile.

"I rather think she wanted to help Mark in *any* way she could." He winked, as if his words had been too subtle for comprehension. "But he wasn't having it. Rubicon would ring the bell and wait by the door like a sad little bunny, but no joy. Mark absolutely holed up for the duration—just himself and Simon."

Lydia, who was found dull by Caro and Rubicon and knew it, had been eavesdropping on Hugh, Anne-Marie, and Jack while she watched Thom, her ersatz "boyfriend," prowl the party, waiting to tell that ghastly joke of his again. Lydia glanced around to see where Mark was. He was standing by the oven, his broad shoulders hunched as he blankly watched the timer slowly count down, a wine glass dangling from his fingers. Realizing Mark wouldn't overhear, she jumped into Hugh's conversation.

"*Terrible* for the boy, I thought it." Lydia spoke with quiet relish, thinking of the fun it had been to see one's street in the *Daily Mail*, which also noted the enviable property values. "The boy has been completely isolated apart from school, and of course missing poor Arabella." Lydia had loathed Arabella, who'd alternatively mocked and ignored her, and, according to Thom, had once told him he could do with a proper shag.

"Now, Lydia," Daniel said, "The tabloids were everywhere, and Mark didn't want them talking to Simon—"

"Or vice versa," said Hugh as he put his arm around Anne-Marie in the same territorial and thumb-rubbing way he'd just done with Rubicon. Anne-Marie hated it, his coarse thumbprint whorls pressing on her collar bone. "One has to wonder what the boy thinks happened that evening."

"Ah," said Jack with a solemn hiccup. "I believe he—"

"Oh, do shut it, Hugh. You're drinking the man's champagne." Daniel drew the line at accusing one's host of practically decapitating his wife.

"I don't think Mark bloody *did* it—though I did for a while—can you imagine the absolute hell of being married to Arabella? All that money and so little sense. One of those posh birds who thinks it's shocking to discuss buggering."

Far on the other side of the island, Mark bent over to open the oven door. A gorgeous soft smell of garlic, butter, and tomatoes wafted through the room, and Jack put down his fifth mini-samosa. Apparently there was better to come.

Anne-Marie looked over Hugh's shoulder at the artist Sam and wished she were here with someone like him. Thom had buttonholed poor Sam and loudly launched into his joke, while one of the new neighbors turned the music up, then up again. With a fluttering birdlike whirr the CD player settled on another song.

Over the speakers Pink threatened, *I'm coming up so you better get this party started.*

Lydia spoke to Anne-Marie in hushed tones as she nodded toward Rubicon. "She introduced them, you know. It was love right off." Lydia laughed mockingly— then realized her enjoyment was inappropriate, and sighed deeply. Anna Marie was still looking at that poor artist, trying to evade the boor, and didn't realize they were still discussing Rubicon.

"Who introduced who?"

"Whom," said Hugh, stupidly. (You can correct someone's grammar or you can get in their pants—to do both is not possible for most of us, and certainly not for the Hughs of the world.)

Anne-Marie shrugged his arm off her shoulder, looked at her tiny wristwatch and decided right then to leave early. Spend good babysitting money on this man? No. A night in with crispy duck and Poirot repeats was infinitely more appealing.

"Rubicon introduced Mark to Arabella . . ."

"Oh yes, I'd heard."

Lydia continued, unhearing. "They were an item at the time, but of course Arabella swooped in and eclipsed her. All that money, and that sweet little face of hers."

"And the fact that she could suck the chrome off a Bentley's tailpipe." Hugh again.

"Possibly a factor," Lydia agreed tightly, turning to Anne-Marie. "Arabella was a rather *sexual* creature, and she simply bowled poor old Mark over. Next thing you know, Arabella has a baby bump and Rubicon . . ."

"She's a bit of a cold fish, our Rubicon—a bony one, at that."

By now, Anna Marie was disgusted with Hugh. "Don't be stupid," she said stoutly. "Or are you one of those tedious blokes who think all small-chested women are frigid?

"No," said Daniel, crinkling friendly blue eyes at Anne-Marie. "He's one of those blokes who thinks all women who refuse to give him a go are frigid."

"Ah. Then no doubt that's what you'll be hearing about me."

The two of them laughed. Lydia smiled tightly, and Hugh thought Anne-Marie was more attractive than she'd been earlier.

From the other side of the room, Sam, who was patiently listening to Thom, looked over and thought the small dark woman laughing with Daniel looked rather sweet. Who was she?

Rubicon and Caro called out over the music, telling Mark to stop fussing in the kitchen.

"It's not like you're doing anything useful, for Christ's sake!" Rubicon shouted. "Jenn'll take care of it. It's her baby, after all!"

Mark smiled wearily and thought that if that bossy blond wasn't down in five minutes, he'd send Rubicon to rout her out. This party of his was foully depressing. It was making him feel more clumsily isolated than ever. He missed his son, and at the same time was relieved Simon wasn't there. What would he do about him, about their life together now? Arabella had simply broken the boy with that cruel combination of demands and indifference. The boy needed love. As for Mark, he was so tired, so bloody weary, he almost missed Arabella too. For all her faults, at least she had to some extent *looked after* things, despite her constant rageful whinging.

Caro's kind eyes met his and offered sympathy. "Do come join us, love—How are things at the surgery?"

Mark went to the fireplace and began talking to Caro and Rubicon.

Lydia noticed that the artist listening to Thom was slowly backing away from him, with a frozen smile glued to his face. Why on earth did she stick with Thom, anyway? It was the first time she'd wondered that. Hmm. Lydia stayed with Anne-Marie, wanting to talk more about horrible Arabella, who frankly had bullied her for years. "We all knew Arabella engaged in some dodgy behavior, but we never expected . . ."

"Poor Arabella," said Hugh, glancing toward the kitchen from where the aroma of delicious garlic tomatoey hors d'oeuvre wafted. "She lived as if life were a *Carry On* film—but a humorless one, with full penetration. The woman was incapable of leaving a workman alone, I hear."

Daniel admitted, "Caro stopped recommending tame men to help Arabella out with the odd job. It got a bit embarrassing for her."

"*Black* boys too!" Lydia whispered to Anne-Marie. "Anyone, really."

"Which is why," Hugh intoned. "The police thought Mark might've . . ."

"But I thought they decided it was some man from the rehab house on the Kew Road? Or some stranger. Looking for drug money, I heard."

Hugh said nothing, but Daniel nodded. "Yes. That's how it looks. Poor old Mark."

There was a long silence. From across the room, over the music, you could hear Thom loudly speaking to poor Sam. "So the boy says, 'I'd love a donkey ride, grampa.' And the tinker led her around the garden . . ."

For the third time Sam stepped back from Thomas, but the back of his legs hit the sofa.

Without hesitation Thom moved a step forward and continued with the joke. "You *listening*, mate? Right . . ."

Sam sighed.

Caro watched Rubicon and Mark as they chatted and noticed that each seemed to be presenting their weaknesses tonight. Mark, though a lovely man, looked more slumped, even more passive than usual. And Rubicon seemed more manic, unsettled and insecure. Could it be from spending the afternoon with this old friend of hers? One never knew with childhood acquaintances. If this American said anything admiring of George Bush or this preposterous war he'd got them into, Hugh would start roaring about stolen elections and Blair and hidden weaponry, and it would all be very tedious.

From across the room, Daniel looked at Caro. He thought, for the thousandth time, that he adored her agreeableness, her bright whiskey-colored eyes, and her open smile. Agreeableness sounds like a boring quality, Daniel thought, but the fact that they both had it made life much nicer. He caught Caro's eye and winked at her.

Rubicon kept talking loudly, her voice filling the room and her eyes on Mark. She so wanted to put an arm around him, perhaps her head on his shoulder—but her consignment shop dress smelled more and more oppressively of a stranger's sweat.

Hugh plied Anne-Marie with more cava, but she refused it.

Vanessa walked over to stand next to her husband, their shoulders touching.

Jack was relieved; the argument was over. He already wished he'd never touched those samosas.

No one had eaten the gourmet crisps.

Suddenly the oven gave off a series of musical dings. *Ding Ding da . . .* Jenn's appetizers were ready. Mark didn't know what to do. Should he take that dish out? Perhaps not, as Rubicon's mannish friend had seemed very bossy, and you never knew with Americans. They were very peculiar, never seeming to take proper offense, yet constantly (and loudly) telling you exactly what you have done wrong.

If you were listening, which only Mark was, you would've heard a door open upstairs. A tapping sound heading along the hallway, then heavy steps down the stairs.

The bell had clearly been Jenn's signal to join the party.

At that moment, just after the fifth bottle of Arabella's Cava had been opened, just as Vanessa Brayson firmly took Anne-Marie over to be introduced to Sam (it turned out that she had been born in Normandy, and within an hour the two would be drunkenly snogging in the garden while Hugh fumed indoors), just as the stereo system began whirring with that flutter of birds' wings to settle, with a self-satisfied click, on a new song, Jenn joined the party.

I've never seen you look so lovely as you do tonight , the singer claimed.

HUGH, WHO WAS JUST BEGINNING to notice that Anne-Marie might be paying too much attention to that artist chap, was the first to see Jenn. His arm, which had by now twined its way around Lydia's surprisingly obliging waist fell away quickly.

Then Daniel clapped eyes on her, raised an eyebrow, and looked toward Caro. Their glances agreed that this promised to be interesting. Jenn sailed through the dining room and Vanessa saw her next. She looked sharply toward Jack, who had been pinching his nose while gulping water from a crystal glass in an attempt to get rid of the hiccups. Through the kaleidoscopic crystal, Jack saw a blond, blurred vision in midnight blue and lowered the glass slowly, with his damp mouth slightly open.

Thom was still keeping Sam pinned to the edge of the sofa. "So now's when the grampa says, '*first* you want an ice cream, *then* a donkey ride, *and then*'—Good lord, who is that?"

Jenn shimmered by Hugh and Lydia and Jack. She glided straight toward the kitchen island, put on an oven mitt, and waved one sparkling midnight-blue arm toward the room. Some eyes followed the graceful billowing of her sleeve, while others noted the immobile blond hair, the high-colored cheeks, the profound competence verging on the bossy. "Mark." She smiled. "Sorry I'm a little late. I'll just get these apps out of the oven."

Mark didn't reply. Was this the same woman?

The first person who spoke was, of course, Hugh. He was what the rap artists were calling "old school." Hugh only needed a single, joyous eyeful of the full body and slender waist, of the round and solid thighs whispering beneath blue silk for him to respond with the inevitable growl. "Ding dong!"

"Who's that—with the massive—?" This was Thom, whispering loudly to Sam.

From across the room, Lydia answered him thinly, loudly. "Perhaps she's the help."

Jenn pulled the first dish from the oven. It was brie wrapped in phyllo dough, to be served with raspberry compote. She turned toward the room and held the hot dish just below her cleavage. How wonderful she felt to feel power again, the power with which the male glance had long ago infused her. Male stares like warm caresses.

It had been so long.

"Mark," she said with happy bossiness, "I'll get all of this organized—just tell me where you want it set up! Or do you want me to decide?"

Silence. Rubicon looked at Mark.

He gazed back at her blankly for a moment, as if at a stranger, and then his glance swung toward Jenn again. "Please," he said hollowly. "You decide." Oh, the relief of it. The oven mitts on her hands, the billowing of her skirt, the sheer unstylish reassurance of her petite full-figured body.

Jenn spoke to him as if to a sweet but dim child. "Right. Just can you tell me where the serving dishes are? Then I'll be all set, sweetie."

Mark just stared at her.

Rubicon felt a leaden sulfuric emptiness in her stomach she had felt once before, only once. A horrible thought came to her: that men are more romantic than women because they *can* be. Because, for men, there's always another treat around the corner. Always another sweetie.

Hugh took a quick step forward, but commanding tones stopped him.

"Leave it, Hugh." Mark spoke like the host, like the man of the house. He stood arrow-straight for the first time in months, years perhaps. "I'll help Jenn."

"Lucky bugger," said Hugh. But he saw the bright, dazed look in Mark's eyes and thought it might be extremely interesting.

Rubicon also saw Mark's eyes. For the first time in seventeen years, she broke her eternal diet and ate after dark. Her long bony hand reached out and clutched three mini-samosas.

Was it just to Rubicon that everything seemed to happen with slow inevitability? No. That's the way Mark saw it too. He walked toward Jenn, a figure of competence and bounty. On the whirring CD Chris de Burgh kept singing—he sang everything Mark was feeling and had forgotten he could feel.

There's nobody here, it's just you and me.

Jenn's appetizers were a great hit.

She and Mark married twelve weeks later.

II

THE
MARRIAGE

5

Daniel and Caro said they'd love to look after Simon for the fortnight. For Simon they were, frankly, a delightful respite after a year of having Mark's dark glance upon him whenever he (inadvertently) laughed, or left the house, or even played a little Panzer Dragon on the Xbox. The *mildest* video carnage would cause his father to flinch, with an expression of pained sorrow that made the boy yearn to smack him hard with the game console.

Daniel, however, was all right. He didn't quiz Simon about what he had eaten that day, how he was feeling, or where he had been. Blessed bloody relief. Unlike Arabella, Caro didn't make horrible sexual innuendos; unlike Jenn, she didn't ask silly questions about girls or who Missy Elliott was. And after ages of awkward sequestration, it was wonderful not being the focus of Mark's intense, silent gaze.

From the minute he rocked up at Daniel and Caro's doorstep after Mark and Jenn had fucked off to Florida, Simon began to feel almost normal. Walking into the small foyer of the house, he'd hesitantly put down his rucksack. He expected nervousness and clucking from Caro and sheer unwelcoming taciturnity from Daniel. Instead, Caro merely smiled and kissed his cheek as she headed out to work, then Daniel rustled the *Times* and said, "Ah there you are, old man. Fancy Chelsea's odds on Saturday?" This made Simon feel both grown up and deeply comforted.

Even the furniture at Daniel and Caro's was easeful—none of Arabella's Swedish arse bruisers or weird constructions that could be either stools or sculptures. Just overstuffed, oversized armchairs with cats sleeping on them, and lots of little round-top tables with shaded lamps that emitted a low golden glow. On the odd occasion when Simon came home late from school or from one of his mysterious adolescent jaunts, Daniel and Caro scarcely seemed to have noticed. But there would always be a hot meal warming on the hob and some crusty bread on the counter.

So Simon exhaled a bit during Mark's absence. A muscular boy with his mother's freckles and his father's glowering gaze, he again haunted the high street—occasionally even laughing in a nervous soupy gulp as he lounged outside the Tesco with his friends, or as he rode his skateboard along the village green with the grace of a caffeinated giraffe. He could wear his hoodie and no one complained. Caro even apologized after her cat Apollo was sick on it!

Simon didn't care. Simon was happy. For the first time in his life, he was free, free from Mark's anxiety and Arabella's tedious vacillation between obsession with and indifference toward him. She'd thought hoodies were vulgar. Simon had just bought a second one. (Jenn had secretly loaned him her new English bank card before leaving on her honeymoon. He hadn't thanked her, but he did pocket it. It was his father's money anyway.)

But he didn't just spend on himself. Simon bought Caro flowers from Waitrose, twice, because he'd been flattered by how her whiskey-colored eyes had lit up the first time he did it. He'd swelled with pride when she later pointed the lilies out to Daniel, saying, "At least there's *one* man in this house who appreciates my lovely ways!"

"You're making me look bad, old man." Daniel lightly punched Simon's shoulder, a casual gesture of male camaraderie that was beyond Mark's self-doubting nervousness. "Swift pint down the pub?"

"Don't be ridiculous, Daniel. He's too young."

"Bollocks. At his age I—"

"I've got homework," said Simon. Really (as Caro knew) he wanted to watch *EastEnders*, because Zoe might tell her mother about Anthony tonight. She was the only one he liked on that show; the other females were all demented slappers. Behaved as if they'd chop it off as soon as look at it. But Zoe . . .! So he liked watching *EastEnders* with Caro, and they'd usually split a fruit & nut bar. Daniel would head off to the Warwick Arms while Simon settled down in his comfy chair, reading the T2 section beneath the glow of soft yellow lamp shades as Apollo kneaded bread on his lap. The soap opera's theme song swirled to fill the air, familiar and meandering as the curve of the Thames.

Such happiness couldn't last.

After two weeks, Mark and Jenn returned.

.യ.

THE HONEYMOON HAD BEEN A roaring success, more so than even they (and hugely more than anyone who knew them) had anticipated.

Really, Mark and Jenn both agreed, with the astonished smugness of middle-aged lovers, they were just so *suited* to each other! How wonderful and easy it all was and would continue to be. They each had lived alone for years, they agreed. Married but alone. The loneliest way to be, Mark had said quietly. This somehow made Jennifer laugh, she surprised herself by laughing, and then she snorted. Mark seized her warm, full body, the flesh around her ribcage soft and swollen as new-risen brioche, and laughed with her. He whispered to her about doing something naughty she'd never done before.

Mark had never wanted to go to Florida in his life, despite the proliferation of property shows on telly. The place had looked ghastly to him, with its candy-colored brightness and the bleached, oversized modern buildings bulging with every feature money and tastelessness could provide. The eye-searingly bright ocean views appeared denuded of nuance or subtlety, the streets unnervingly identical, and every 100 yards offered the opportunity to buy a chemicalized foodstuff that gleamed the same glazed brown as the people who bought it.

But Jenn had really wanted to go there, and Mark had been in such a state of perpetual sexual arousal that to refuse her whims was unthinkable.

Jenn would not sleep with him before the marriage. Unbelievable, but true. They had kissed, at the beginning sweetly and hesitantly. The first time was the night of the party, after Rubicon had gone drunkenly (angrily) home, and Mark had said he would drive Jenn over later. Jenn and Mark had sat on the sofa, holding empty wine glasses as Jenn softly told Mark how sorry she was for his great loss— how she knew loss and pain and that his son must be a great consolation to him. "And a worry, right? How you must worry." She'd known this.

Mark almost wept from relief.

Simon *had* always been the greatest worry. First, the shocking news of Arabella's pregnancy and her refusal to have an abortion—she was fancying herself as an Earth Mother at that time. That had worn off quickly after the constant bouts of thrush, the bloody birth, Simon's colic and his sleeplessness. Arabella used the child from the start, had used Mark's surprised love for the child against him. How could you win a battle of wills when your own is weak? How could you shock a person into sense when they pride themselves on their fascinating unconventionality? From the start Arabella had treated Simon with the casual, jocular contempt some women reserve for anyone foolish enough to fall in love with or, even worse, need them.

Mark had watched his son's face as it changed from unmarred adoration of his mother to confusion and then to wistfulness and ultimately, disgust. Her faddish whims and affected graces, that thoughtless cruelty combined with the endless posturing and postulations of beliefs she never actually understood, much less held dear.

But Jenn was different. Couldn't be more so, really. They were engaged within ten days, but she would not sleep under his roof until they were married—so (once Rubicon made it clear there was no room for Jenn at her place) Mark rented a room for her at the Richmond Hill Hotel. For three months. It was expensive, but her virtue was worth it.

Mark had never met anyone so conventional, or so unapologetic about her conventionality, as Jenn was. It made him feel a bit worldly and devilish. He was touched by her sexual inexperience; that side of her married life had never existed. She was also incredibly obliging—no, bloody *gagging* for it—once he did manage to get her into bed. After their first night together, Mark stood in the bathroom of the Blue Top Inn in Key Largo, beneath the amber glow of the post-shower heating lights and next to the Steri-Fine toilet seat cover dispenser, and thought of Jenn in bed.

So different from Arabella, whose disappointment with Mark's sexual prowess had been emphasized by a sort of bright-eyed chattiness—about the water bill, the organic camembert at Waitrose, some teacher of Simon's who was rather moreish despite his tedious Barbour jacket, what Jacobi the waiter had done to her with his mouth under the table during that holiday in Switzerland. Mark would labor away on top of her, grimly holding on, as she chatted and bounced, utterly, utterly bored by it all.

But now here was Jenn. And it seemed to poor Mark that he'd never really felt like a proper man before. A proper man. He'd always thought that even the phrase was idiotic, though he'd looked at men like Daniel and even that old bore Hugh with envy. They were men with single-minded vision, who knew what they wanted. Jenn had turned Mark into one of those men. After all those months of her sweetly bossing him about, telling him he had to wait while worrying he wouldn't, those gorgeously frustrating nights in his house, with Simon snoring away upstairs as his father was downstairs enacting teenage rituals. Trying to get the bra off the blond without her noticing, gently pressing his mouth against her protests as he proceeded toward what she called 'the downstairs patio'—his long surgeon's fingers being swatted away from the brass button of her jeans. So she'd kept him waiting, but he knew she wasn't doing it from manipulation but from fear. Fear of being used, fear of losing love, fear of everything good being just a short moment of mirage. Even, it appeared, fear of God.

He'd discovered on their wedding night that his wife prayed. He'd never seen anyone do that before. Her powerful neck bowed, the heavy blond hair tumbling forward like a modesty curtain to give privacy to her pleas.

Now Mark looked at himself in the bathroom mirror. A proper man, for once in his life. He'd done the right thing, seized the day and the woman when she came along; had he not? If he hadn't, he'd still be in those sagging corduroys, plodding to and from the surgery. Everyone looking at him as poor sad Mark, under Arabella's thumb even after her death. He'd surprised them all.

He'd surprised himself.

He felt movement again as he thought of Jenn's eyes in bed, shadowed by the yucca-leaved wallpaper in the Bridal Suite and the stripe of blinds she insisted upon closing. Blue eyes darkened by half-closed lids and an expression in them of passion mixed with a sliver of dark challenge. But he had done what he wanted, and she had yielded, had turned her head away, "No . . . oh, what are you doing?" but kept her body with his. That astonishing body which had never known a diet or a moment of worry about its power or its health. Pale, curved, warm weight of flesh that smelled of soap, skin that was marbled on the thighs with blue veins that mapped the river of her bloodstream. He wanted her again. He was gratified by her appreciation and her silence as it all happened. Oh lord, to silence a woman. He'd never done it before, not really.

Mark took his toothbrush from the holder and wet it. The water spewed out toward the granite sink bowl in a foamy burst. He squeezed tri-colored Aquafresh on the toothbrush and stuck it in his mouth.

"Mark?"

Jenn's voice from the bedroom.

Mark smiled. He spat in the sink and regarded himself in the mirror. Perhaps he should get his teeth whitened while he was here? Licked toothpaste from the corner of his mouth and squared his shoulders, raised his chin.

It had been such a while since he'd had real pleasure. His life had for so long consisted of people feeling let down by him. Arabella's cool bemusement; Simon's blank desperation. Emphysematic patients wheezing blue-lipped curses; drinkers swollen with resentment at his inability to provide them with kidneys pink with the fresh flush of youth; ham-ankled cardiac patients who'd worked all life for their pensions and now knew, deep in their fluttering hearts, that Mark's surgery was their entryway to the world of the sick, from which they would never be released.

But here was Jenn. Miseducated into judgment and prudishness, she acquiesced and then, delightfully, lapsed instantly back into shocked prudishness, so he would always take her for the first time, always gain power from the hesitation and astonishment in her eyes.

And he was going to do something new to her, right now.

This time something he thought was possibly illegal in the southern American states. Hmm, he thought. Perhaps that's why the Yanks are always so bloody bossy and judgmental. Demonizing sex makes the descent into the flesh much more pleasurable. Unlike we Brits for whom (after a bit to drink) nothing is forbidden, apart from being a bore. Yanks offer that surface of smoothly certain mundanity, while beneath they burn with denied urges and violent contradictions. God and guns, indeed.

But as for now . . .

Mark marched into the bedroom, his naked body shaded against the sun's bleaching glare. Shadowed by the yucca leaves, atop a black bedspread decorated with golden pineapples, his wife gleamed in the shadows, blond hair swirled around her head. Her ankles were delicately crossed, as were her both arms over those full breasts. Starry starry night, and a woman shyly waiting for him.

Right, then.

"Let me see you." Mark spoke decisively. After a pause, Jenn unwrapped her arms. She was silent, but Mark could hear quiet fast breaths from within the shadow of the yucca leaves, he could see the bedspread pineapples tremble at Jenn's movement.

"Turn over, love," said Mark.

Jenn's blue eyes widened. Then she turned over onto her belly.

"My husband," she said reverently, her voice muffled by the bedspread as he fell upon her.

.༚ཊ.

But what about Rubicon?

Where had she been during Simon's cozy nights in front of the television, and Mark's storming of the American citadels of prudishness and calculated acquiescence?

Well, she'd been having a pretty shit time of it.

At the exact moment when Mark told Jenn to roll over on the bed, Rubicon awoke gasping from a vivid dream. She was in the *Big Brother* house in South London, standing in the oval yard at night. The yard was smaller than it looked on TV, but she could hear the shouts of an excited crowd and the cawing shout of *Big Brother* host Davina McCall's microphoned voice.

"I'm coming to get you, Rubicon!"

Thousands of people stood out there, thousands, cheering for her. A few booing. The sky was an azure blur behind glaring production lights, and as Rubicon lifted her head toward those lights and the brassy volume of Davina's voice, she was also trying to smoke a crafty fag, hiding it within her cupped fingers. The production lights kept getting brighter and hotter and sweat began to blur her eyes. The crowd became louder, more emotional.

"Roo-bi-CON!" they shouted.

"Roo-bi-CON!"

Rubicon was about to be the last person released from the *Big Brother* house, the crowd couldn't wait to see her. Davina would come and get her any minute— she had won! That meant huge media deals; it meant the public loves her again. It meant radio, the cover of all the tabloids. It meant telly, getting papped, quite possibly a hosting job. Rubicon drew deeply on her cigarette and then flicked it away. The ember arced like a star in the night sky—she was back, praise God she was *back!* Tonight she'd dine at the Ivy. After replays of her highlights on Channel 4, and a full hour of being interviewed by Davina, watched by millions. Millions.

But why was she wearing this goddamn velvet tracksuit? And in pink, of all colors?

And, in that sudden dreamlike way, she realized the tracksuit was damp. Odd.

Rubicon turned her back to the cameras and the cheers, and looked down at her body. The tracksuit pants were wet with her blood, darkly saturated from crotch to knee. She touched the blood and it was cold, so cold. "You don't expect blood to be so cold," someone said. She turned toward the voice, expecting Davina. But it wasn't. It was Mike Bellwether, mangled and dangling from a car's windshield. The crowd's cheers rose as Mike pointed a swollen finger at Rubicon. "Waste of protoplasm," he said. The cheering reached a hysterical level as a velvet tracksuit cord around Rubicon's neck slowly slid and tightened and turned into a noose.

That's when Rubicon gasped awake.

She stuck her hands down her pajama pants.

Both hands came up soaked with blood. So were the sheets, down to the mattress below.

It had begun again.

Rubicon walked to the bathroom with her hands cupped between her legs, pulled off her soaked pajama bottoms and tossed them in the trash bin along with her underwear. She cleaned herself with the shower hose, but blood kept pouring out of her as she stood in the shower. Finally, after a few largish blobs, the bleeding slowed down and Rubicon was able to get herself clean. She opened a packet of tampons and inserted two, then put a maxi pad in some fresh underwear. Then she unfurled a large stolen hotel towel over the wet stains on her bed, and lay down. This bleeding had begun about three months ago. Just after Jenn's arrival in the UK, actually. Rubicon's periods had become fifteen, twenty days long; blood seemed to pour from her as if from a tap, leaving her pale and trembling. But that wasn't the scariest part.

Oh God. In the isolated dark, with shadows shifting in her mind while the sulfuric streetlight slivered and crept along her walls, Rubicon's eyes were too dry to weep. She ran long fingers through her short hair and tried to feel something other than fear. Oh God all those years of casual health, and now so alone, so poor. And always tired. Why hadn't she looked for the security of love or money? Why had it always just been attention? How she hated women who had found them, love and money, who had found and held both so easily. How had they done it? How had they *known* to do it?

Against her will, Rubicon placed both hands on her lower abdomen. The lumps were still there. Was it her imagination that one was just a bit smaller since this last bit of bleeding? Both lumps were hard and smooth, roundish and muscular.

The large one, on the right, felt like half of a firm mango beneath the skin. The one on the left was smaller, rounder, harder and slightly lower. Between the hipbone and the pubic bone.

She couldn't remember exactly when the lumps had appeared. The bleeding had come first, Rubicon thought, as she turned to her side and watched branches scratch against the window panes like some fine calligrapher's tool.

She lay in the silence of 3 a.m., hands down her underwear, staring at the lamplight glow on the far wall of her studio flat. She lay there for half an hour, listening to those branches scrape against the large filthy windows of her flat. The tree outside was leafless, perhaps having died over the winter, and Rubicon would have no shade next July. Southwest London smelled like countryside at this time of night, this time of year. Damp earth and seeds and dormant roots coming together to push plants forth, to fill the air with soft oxygenating seedlings. Daffodils' hardy arrival was soon, late February—just after this horrible shame-making, ridiculous wedding of Mark's.

To Jenn.

Oh God it hurt. It hurt physically, knowing they were together. The pain moved in a figure eight around her heart and the lining of her stomach, like a great hunger and fatigue all at once. Only food and sleep stopped it. And sleep wasn't reliable.

With a sigh, Rubicon sat up. The branches nodded slowly, welcoming her to the enviable silence of other people's sleep. The only people up now are the addicts, who shrink behind curtained windows, the lovers who shift and murmur like fallen leaves beneath our moving shadows, and people like you. The overlooked.

Hunched at the side of the bed, Rubicon noticed that she had other new bulges on her belly. This was just plain old fat, brought on by depression. She grabbed a roll of fat and it felt like one of those hotdog rolls at Pinekill school barbeques—so white and yielding you had to squeeze it hard. Oh God. She had to stop eating. She didn't think she could do it. The bleeding made her tired, so she *had* to eat more.

Over a stone in the last few months. Around twenty pounds. Nothing fit anymore, nothing worked, nothing looked right.

And the timing couldn't have been worse.

Rubicon flipped her mobile phone open. A small still image of a cassette tape showed on its screen, meaning she had a saved message. The message had been there for ten hours now.

Rubicon heaved herself from the low, grief-rumpled bed and walked to the bathroom. She'd listen to the message again in a moment. After drinking cold Thames water from the tap, she wiped her mouth with the back of her hand and looked in the mirror. Hair like trembling stick insects. Coarse gray zippering along her roots.

That was easily fixed though. Possibly Truffle still worked at Le Salon d'Or. Maybe she could get a freebie for a mention? Very likely. Rubicon leaned forward and pulled heavily at the skin on her neck. A bit gray too. Maybe a loofah would sort that out. Maybe a goddamn sandblaster would do the job. Her face . . . even beneath the humming fluorescent light of the bathroom mirror, it wasn't *so* bad. Still had the cheekbones, a bit, and there'd been some recent sinking in at the temples which accentuated them. Plus, there was the new Photoshop thing (whatever that is) which people are always accusing actresses of doing. But the body? Holy crap. Talk about needing a sandblaster. This body, her mother's body, had just been waiting to catch up to her. Waiting for a crack in the facade, to be puttied in with fat. Soft slabs of fat, margarine curves.

Within the arc of the faux-marble green breakfast bar that separated the kitchen from everything else in the studio flat, there hummed a thigh-high refrigerator. Rubicon opened the door. Cold light angled across her legs, and the small flat filled with the odor of cheap wine and stale onion. From the frost-encrusted freezer, she pulled a Dr. Oetker mini-margarita pizza.

The diet begins tomorrow. Tonight she needed a carb stupor, or she'd never get back to sleep.

After placing the pizza in the mini-oven, Rubicon (for the ninth time in the last ten hours) picked up her mobile, pressed the button to the answerphone, and tapped the speaker button.

She needed to hear the message again.

The branches searchingly scraped the windows; the fridge hummed indifferently; the oven ticked laboriously to the heat level recommended by Dr. Oetker as Rubicon listened again to these magic words, spoken by a young voice in a stranglehold between the pudding richness of entitlement and East End affectations.

Hallo——this is Evangeline Nepotis calling from Style Magazine at the Sunday London Times. I'm trying to reach Rubicon Baines? The one who hosted That's Pants! on ITV in the nineties . . . a long while back, innit? We are planning a feature on the ladettes. Sort of a where-

are-they-now piece. You know, are you a yummy mummy, all married and babied up like Zoe Ball? Or still just a sad slapper with a can of lager and a kebab? Just kidding, of course you're not! So we're terribly curious—Ms. Baines, where are you? We'd like to interview you, photograph you with some of the other ladettes, yeh? Zoe, of course, Meg, you know. Yer whole old lot. We contacted Tats Gripp; guess she was your publicist? She gave us this number and said she'd love to hear from you any time. So give us a call back, Ms. Baines. We'd appreciate hearing from you as soon as possible. Peace out and all of that. Byeee!

A margarita and pesto smell began to emanate from Rubicon's mini-oven. *Style* Magazine couldn't have called at a worse moment, or at a time when she needed them more desperately.

Tomorrow she would call this Evangelina idiot and ask to be contacted by a grown-up over there at *Style*. Or maybe Tatiana might take her on again and she'd call the idiot. That's the way it used to be! "Call my publicist, darling."

And definitely, definitely get in some broccoli and start drinking hot lemon water twice a day.

The thought of buying broccoli made Rubicon feel better. A sense of hope releasing her from shame's grip (*Jenn* being chosen over *her?*) for the first time in five months. Just as she picked up a tea towel encrusted with coffee grinds, the oven set off a series of ticking noises, and then a loud *ding!*

It was time.

Turn your life around.

But might as well enjoy her Dr. Oetker pizza first. The Dr. provided mind-numbing solace to the lonely insomniac. Rubicon's crooked white teeth bit down on hot cheese and pestoed tomato as she stood by the oven and dawn silvered the darkness outside her window. The dead branches scraped and waved.

Broccoli tomorrow. Hot lemon water, 9 a.m.

And the other issue? Rubicon felt a clutch of fear in her chest and picked up another slice. It couldn't be—she didn't want to say the word: Cancer. Rubicon decided that if she heard that word in the next twenty-four hours, it would mean that God or the universe or *whatever* wanted her to go to a doctor and get it checked out. If she didn't hear it, well . . . she'd give it another month. Or two.

.๑ค.

"WELL, OLD MAN. IT'S BEEN a pleasure having you knocking about the place these last few weeks."

"Daniel, you know you loved having Simon here—finally someone to listen to you waffle on about Syfores—syfoe—"

"Syforests," said Simon, correctly pronouncing the name of the Chelsea Football Club owner.

"Well, whatever the tedious man's name is, I was tired of hearing it, and you've done us both a great favor. Please send your father and Jenn our best love. Have you got all your books? And your rucksack?"

"He can always walk the thirty steps back here if he forgot anything, Caro."

"Of course he can. Lovely. Come any time, Simon."

"See you down at the pub, old man."

"You've both been—well, I'll see you." Simon's dark eyes showed his reluctance to leave. Then he walked down the pathway, weighted by more than his rucksack.

Now he'd have to deal with Jenn. For years. Christ.

The boy turned back slowly, toward where Daniel stood next to Caro. Both terribly old, maybe in their fifties, but nice with it. Daniel with that daft bristle haircut and Caro's little face as always creased with a smile, ready to be enchanted.

"Thanks," Simon said. "You've been ace, thank you."

"You're all right, old man."

The door to the lovely cozy foyer began to close. One of the cats stood in the garden, its coral pink tongue determinedly grooming marmalade fur over its well-fed shoulders, with one paw dangling elegantly in the air like a bride who wants to display a ring. The cat utterly ignored Simon, though he bent to pet it.

As Simon straightened up again, Caro called out, "If there's ever a problem, do just come back here. For a chat. All right, Simon?"

"Right." Simon smiled wanly, fighting the urge to run and rest his head in the crook of Caro's neck and breathe in her consoling scent. A seasoned soft aroma young girls never seem to have. But if he grasped her too tightly he might begin to blubber, right in front of Daniel. Simon sighed, before turning his muscular back to them, and headed down the pavement toward home.

"That turned out rather well," said Daniel, as he settled down into his comfy chair and rustled the *Times* with the satisfied importance of a man who plans to be napping beneath it soon.

"Ye-es." Caro stood by the window, absentmindedly tapping two fingernails against her squarish chin. "I don't know why I said that, about him coming back here."

"Just being nice, I thought."

"I suppose so. It can't be easy, losing your mother—Arabella was mad as a box of frogs, but she was still his mother—then gaining Mrs. America as a replacement."

"Oh, he'll have a few fruity thoughts about her, but then he'll settle in nicely. I expect she's rather the maternal type, despite the page-three looks."

"Hmph. Let's hope she's a better mother than she was a friend to poor Rubicon. Well, we shall find out soon enough. The thing that makes me feel rather bad is . . ."

"Oh lord. What now?"

"I do think there will be a problem. To be frank, Daniel—I'm sorry to say this, but I woke up today glad that boy was going out of this house. There's an odd sort of . . . clinginess to him. Makes me feel terrible to say that—"

"You're barking. He was just bored, making the best of being stuck here with old buggers like us. Here's the *Culture* section—distract yourself, woman."

"I'm right, Daniel. That boy's never recovered from what happened to Arabella. But having him around began to make me feel nervous. He was too attentive."

"Daft. That's what you are."

"Poor boy," Caro said softly. "And poor old Mark."

"What about Jenn? She's the one who's got him on her hands now."

"Pfff. That one will be fine. She's the sort for whom things just work out."

The paper rustled and covered Daniel's face.

After another moment peering out the window at the cat outside, who also ignored her, Caro picked up *The Weekend* section of the newspaper and sank down on the sofa.

A companionable silence.

Simon walked to the corner, subduing emotion by counting his steps. Thank Christ he hadn't blubbed.

Nineteen steps.

Then he took a right, walked forty-three steps along Harrow Road, turned right again, and fished the latch key from the pocket of his red hoodie. The heavy door, painted a gleaming black that always looked as if it would be sticky on your fingers, opened. Simon walked into silence and the musty smell of damp.

Mark and Jennifer weren't back quite yet.

Simon knew his luck too well to hope for a long wait.

Simon had always loathed his mother's too tender public caresses and her cawing contempt for anyone else's opinions. The way she'd walk around the house in knickers and no bra, dismissing Mark's annoyance as sour grapes over what he no longer controlled. Her body. Her son had always known how she thought, though he wished he didn't. She'd never forgiven Mark for getting her up the spout and then that *fetus*, a lump of flesh like a hangover from a heavy feast, had grown inside her, trapped her . . .

Simon.

Men. Disappointments. All men, really. Mark and Simon, her family. Kept her free spirit nailed to the suburban floors of Richmond, surrounded by bores. Men and their traps. She'd complained bitterly about her family's stinginess with money, how her parents' miserliness had denied her trips to Ibiza, India, Rio de Janeiro. Any place where she could release herself from the suburban tedium of the Gin and Jag bourgeois life. But she was trapped by marriage, by Simon. Then, ironically, she'd sought relief through more men, more gin.

Well, Simon thought. She's released now. Poor old Mum.

Maybe if she'd had a sliver of artistic talent, she could've found a way to be less . . . predictably pretentious. Simon's throat constricted as he looked in the mirror. Maybe she'd been right about that, at least. A glance revealed that he looked awful in a hoodie. His sedately anxious eyes, so like Mark's, and the pale freckled skin inherited from his mother made the effort to look like he was from Brixton a complete joke. Fake. A spaniel trying to be a pit bull. He must never be fake.

No pretensions, thought Simon. No endless adolescence, not for me.

He turned the heater on, put water in the electric kettle, and rummaged through the cupboards. Time for a Hobnob. Unwrapping the chocolate biscuits, Simon looked around the kitchen. He knew Jenn wanted to change it, remove the horrible memories. But Simon didn't believe in wiping slates clean, had never in his short life seen it successfully done. And, though it might be weird to admit it, one of the few good memories he had of Arabella was of her in the kitchen, trying to clean those rubbish Portuguese tiles. (While eager to admit that marriage and motherhood had been a desperate mistake, Arabella was incapable of doing the same in regard to her crap design choices.) Simon flipped a wet tea bag out of his mug, where it lay on the tiles, seeping amber fluid.

He waited.

.♋.

THE DOOR BURST OPEN.

"Oh my God—have you got the Target bag?"

"It's still in the taxi. Hold on a tic, love."

"Hey, It's cold in here. My handsome husband—how come you look so great after that long flight?"

"Come here, wife."

"I'm so tired. I bet I look like a wet rag."

"You know you look lovely, and extremely moreish."

The sound of rustling, of giggling and kissing followed.

"Yikes! Your hands are cold. Where's the heater in this joint?"

"Right here, my love." More rustling, and a brief meaningful silence.

"Mark! Stop that! Simon might be here . . ."

"Oh bollocks, that's right. Simon?" Mark called out.

In the kitchen, Simon sighed and silently sipped his tea. Two years until he left for university.

"He's your son, Mark. Don't joke. I hope he likes the gifts I—"

"He'd bloody better. You'll spoil the lad rotten. He's here, all right. There's his rucksack." A briefer and more businesslike kiss followed before Mark spoke again. "Put the kettle on, would you, while I unload your ludicrous purchases from the cab."

"Right."

The heavy door banged shut behind Mark, and Jennifer ran her hands through her long just-highlighted hair (she figured she'd better get it done in the States while she still could). Ice Maiden, the frosty blond was called. She'd had acrylic nails done, too, which was expensive but made her hands look much less square and grasping. The nails gleamed and curved a full inch above the tip of her fingers. Prairie Rose. Mark had been silent when he'd first seen them. Said, "They wouldn't be much good in a garden." But later he'd shivered when she ran them up his thighs.

"Hey, Simon! We're back!"

Jennifer picked up her new Dooney & Bourke handbag (buy American), pulled out a lipstick and neatened herself up. Then she called up the narrow staircase. She'd have to get a nice cheery runner for those stairs—these bare floorboards were so darn grim!

"Simon?"

He didn't reply, then heard her sigh, "Ah, well," followed by a funny little chirruping noise that he later realized was a sneeze. Simon heard Jennifer rummaging through bags, and then her quick heavy step toward the kitchen. She was smaller than he'd remembered; the woman was bursting with so much energy she stuck in memory as filling the entire room. All yellow hair and white teeth and eyes so focused they seemed almost crossed with optimism.

"Well, say! There you are, kiddo! Why didn't you answer when we called you?"

Simon shrugged toward the French doors. "In the garden, wasn't I?"

Jenn stepped forward, clutching a red cardboard box. "Well, okay. It's great to see you! We missed you!"

"Right," said Simon, stepping back as Jenn held the cardboard box out like an offering to her stepson.

"Lipton tea," she said brightly. "I don't know why they don't sell it here. I got *boxes* of the stuff."

"Hmm," sniffed Simon. "Coals meeting Newcastle."

"No, you'll like it. And wait to *see* what we got you." Jenn spoke nervously, too loudly, while running hands through her Ice Maiden locks. She hadn't really dealt with teenage boys since she was young. "Anyway, I asked all these kids in Miami what was 'happening' now, and they told me—"

As Jenn nattered on, she filled the kettle and bustled about with confidence, opening her box of tea bags and putting them in a canister. She was saying something about how much Simon's father missed him, then something about that prat Robbie Williams. Simon stopped listening and just looked at her. Bustling about the place like she bloody owned it, those long fake fingernails of hers about as much use as a chocolate teapot.

The tea bags Jenn had brought all the way from America were tiny and less than half filled with what looked like powdered dung, and they had staples in them.

Daft! As Jenn poured boiling water into the teapot, the room filled with a peculiar odor like wet paper towels.

Jenn was still talking, talking, talking, as she fetched a towel and vigorously wiped Simon's earlier spill off the counter. "Tell me the truth, Simon—I swear I won't rat on you. Did you have any girls over here while we were gone? You kids can never resist an empty house . . . Honestly, I bet the girls around here are just crazy about you." Jenn looked at the kid's bent neck and thick chestnut hair and thought that he'd be cute if he'd just stop sulking for like a minute. Plenty of muscle on him. He just needed some joshing. A solid and sound family life . . . soon, who knows, she bet he'd be asking her for advice!

Jenn loved giving advice. And no time like the present! Start being a mom right away. "You know, you should take up the guitar again. Your dad told me you used to play—girls just *love* that. It's almost as good as football with them. Yeah, you do that and we'll have a party for you. Maybe hotdogs and popsicles, you can ask some kids over and just casually grab your guitar. Like you always have it lying around, waiting for you to noodle around on . . . It'd be so cool!"

Simon said, "I sold the guitar."

But Jenn waved that away and continued extending her plan. "Oh, I'll get you another. Anyway, maybe I'd do a potato salad. With tarragon, to make it fancy . . ."

She didn't notice Simon sigh again.

He was thinking of Caro.

How she'd just turn on the telly and silently hand him half a fruit & nut bar.

Now that'd been the life. Not having to impress anyone or prove himself—for once in his life he hadn't had to be someone's performing monkey. But this Yank had put paid to it.

Though he did rather like the firm way she rubbed the tiled counter down with a damp tea towel. You had to credit her with lovely baps, but Christ, did she *ever* shut that gob of hers?

A few moments later, Mark staggered in the front door with four suitcases, the Target bag, a new set of golf clubs, and a large box containing a new pedi-spa for Jenn which she'd picked up at Sharper Image at the Miami airport. He was just in time to see Simon's back as the boy headed up the stairs.

"Simon—how are you? Simon?"

The boy kept walking.

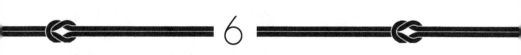

6

RUBICON CALLED TATIANA GRIPP THE day after she'd received that message from the *Style* section. She'd hoped Tats would call her (as she always had back in the day of Rubicon's celebrity—morning calls in which she'd reel off lists of parties and openings, appearance offers and chat shows, before descending into brutal and rather fascinating gossip). Their chats had always been informative, and usually profitable—until the offers stopped coming in. Then Tats had begun phoning later in the day or avoiding Rubicon altogether.

It'd been nine years since they'd spoken, but Rubicon's call was put through immediately.

"Oy, you bony arsed slapper!" Tat's Silk Cut cigarette growl came over the line.

"Hey, Tats. It's Rubicon Baines."

"Don't be daft, mate! I know who it is. Been waiting to hear from you since Wednesday. You talk to that posh slapper from the *Times?*"

"Nah." Rubicon lit a cigarette herself, thinking the casually cool gesture would help her maintain an offhanded attitude. Tats could perceive the stink of desperation in a heartbeat.

She also hoped her voice didn't sound fat. Tats hated fat clients unless they were male, of course. And funny, or very, very successful. "Nah, Tats. I thought

I'd call you first. See who's doing this and what the—uhm—angle is." It'd been a while since Rubicon had breathed in the entitled air that filters through the lungs of the successful. The effortless exhales of privilege that waft over the phone lines.

"Listen, you silly cow. Are you off your trolley? If you're interested, call them and grab it with both hands. No one's mentioned your name in . . . well, I doubt Google knows who you are. Have you been up to anything interesting?"

"Just working. It's kind of creative, though. Aromatherapy, mostly—"

"Sloppy oils in brown bottles? Sweetie, please. Who cares. Have you popped out any sprogs? Everyone's mad for yummy mummies and baby bumps now, God help us."

"Oh, no. No kids." Rubicon stubbed out her cigarette on the pizza plate that was still on the counter from the night before. She didn't see the paper napkin stuck there, nearly translucent with grease.

"I know. They're absolute bores, the yummies and the spawn that hang off their—but *Grazia* eats 'em up. Plenty of dosh in kids nowadays. But also—Hmmm, how did I never think of you for this?—we may be able to sell a piece by building up an angle on you and rehab. How much time did you put in at the Priory? Done a spell in Thailand to detox off charlie? We could get an angle on that, with the aromatherapy as a sort of happy ending. As bloody boring as it is, at least it's an arc."

"Never been in the Priory, or any rehab, Tats."

"Bloody hell. Are you kidding me? The way you used to put it back? I remember you straddling a toilet at Bagley's, snorting lines of gak the size of Tom Jones's willy. What happened to you?"

"Well, when I didn't get it free anymore I just . . . stopped." Rubicon wished she hadn't put out that cigarette so quick. At six pounds per pack of twenty, they should be smoked to the knuckle.

"You just *stopped*. Well. Aren't you PollybloodyAnna? Listen, unless you've suffered a resourceful bout with cancer or a *really* humiliating love affair with a sleb, you're simply out of luck, my love . . ."

Rubicon could hear impatience in Tatiana's husky voice now. She knew the publicist was grabbing her Chloe "It" bag and preparing to sidle off to the Ivy for a lunch of icy sauvignon blanc with smoked salmon and venomous tabloid editors, probably getting more dosh for Davina Goddamn McCall, she of the Garnier glossy hair and enviable rehab history.

"I mean, we might be able to sell a sad little piece about you to *StreetWise* or something, but if you really want to remake your career, darling, you'll need reality TV. It's a game changer, as you Yanks say, but you've got to have something to *sell* beyond candles that whiff of anisette and seaweed. Even if it's just a little bad behavior or a leaking bladder issue, it's got to be something to get the punters on their fat arses in front of Sky TV, clutching mini-Babybels before they go nighty-night."

"Hey, Tats—people still recognize me. Get me on a reality show and I'll make it interesting. Shit, I'll *say* I went to rehab, if that helps."

Tats spoke regretfully. "Oh, my darling, we can scarcely lie any more. Everything's provable now. Nothing's good without photos of someone falling out of a pub, wankered, with Ross Kemp's knickers on their head. No—just do this *Style* shoot, and enjoy it. I'll see if there's anything doing with reality TV, but I frankly doubt it, my love."

Just then the smoldering cigarette Rubicon had semi-extinguished on the pizza plate began to emit a heavy stream of smoke. The greasy paper napkin had caught fire and was producing an acrid smell of burning chemicals and fried cheese. Burning tissue strips wriggled as they rose to dance through the air in Rubicon's small flat.

"Tats—hold on a sec—I've got a grease fire started here—don't go." Rubicon grabbed a coffee grind-encrusted dish towel from the night before and waved it frantically in the air. Dying tissue embers fell onto the thin green carpet.

Rubicon grabbed the phone again.

"You still there, Tats?"

"Just barely, my love. If you do manage to burn your flat down, call me. There's news in arson—ITV's putting together something called "Celebrity Criminal Reform"—putting slebs through their paces with social carers in Wormwood Scrubs. John Barrymore is doing it, and they might have Boy George, if he doesn't wanker off again."

"Very funny, Tats."

"It's a real show, God help us. But it's not for you. One word of advice, Rubicon? Grab the *Style* piece with both hands, and get yourself Botoxed and babied up for it. All the other ex-ladettes will, you know. I'll take a look once the piece is published, and we'll see what I can do. But honestly, babes, interest in you wavers between slim and none. Byeee, love."

And Tatiana Gripp was gone.

Rubicon hung up and then called the *Style* section herself.

Just like a nobody.

She wished Tatiana hadn't mentioned cancer.

THAT NIGHT, JENN, MARK AND Simon had their first family dinner together.

While Simon had an unsatisfactory wank up in his bedroom (his mind was distracted by contradictory and frankly confusing images of Caro's solid knees crossed on the sofa, combined with the pale curve of underwire bra and heavy flesh on a girl he'd seen on the bus that day—but none of these did the trick until he added Jenn's face to the mix—Jenn's face looking up at him with her mouth wide open, then with her mouth filled). Simon exploded in a rush of shame and pleasure.

Thank God he didn't have to worry about Jenn busting into his room during these times. She seemed the type who'd always pop in for a bright and boring question. But Arabella had once slammed his bedroom door shut with such vehemence it now often stuck in its frame. Unwittingly, she had given the boy some privacy. And that privacy helped him feel that his secret, buried in the floorboard of his closet, was well-hidden.

.୨ଙ.

DOWNSTAIRS, JENN BUSTLED ABOUT, LISTENING to Radio 2 and setting the kitchen table while an aroma of roasting chicken filled the house. Simon found these sounds comforting, but somehow they also made him roll over on his bed and feel like weeping, just a little. Then he buckled his trousers and wiped his eyes. His father and Jenn were talking. You could hear every word in Simon's room, only slightly muffled, as if they spoke through paper towels.

"He'd really be happier with a chicken tikka masala takeaway, Jenn. That's how Ara—that's his favorite meal."

There was a pause in the soft clattering of stainless-steel silver on the pine table.

"Mark." Jenn's voice was quiet. Or quiet for her; it had a deep pointed tone.

Mark spoke quickly, with tame apology. He'd been well trained in apology by Arabella. Apologize often, apologize fast, before bad things happen.

"I'm sorry. You do as you think best."

"Sit down, Mark."

Simon heard his father cross the room and a chair scrape out from under the table. Only one chair, so Jenn was still standing. Simon looked over at the poster of Jordan, semi-naked and wrapped in pink ribbons, on his wall. Her eyes met his with hostility. Her ballooned implants swelled beneath stretched flesh like weapons she was painfully, resentfully smuggling.

"Mark." Jenn still spoke below in meaningful tones. "I don't mean to speak ill of the dead, or of Simon's mother . . . but she clearly didn't know how to love the boy. Didn't create a world of security for him from her hands and heart. That is what I want to do. That is what we do where I come from."

"I want that too." Simon almost didn't recognize his father's voice. Mark spoke in a strangled uneven tone. The boy heard Jenn move toward his father; he could almost feel his father's nose pressing against the buttons on her shirt.

"We have that, you and me. God gave us that through marriage and our bodies' worship. I love you so, Mark. Nothing can ruin our happiness except—"

"Except what?" Simon could barely hear this part, since Mark's face was deep in Jenn's chest, his surgeon's hands clutching her bottom.

"Except we must pull Simon aboard. He will be jealous of us if we don't include him—even if it's against his will. We're adults. We know better than him."

"I think you know better than me."

"Oh, that's sweet," Jenn said. "Yeah, I totally do." Then both Jenn and Mark laughed. Simon heard kissing and the scraping sound of a chair being moved, then the eloquent silence of bodies moving apart.

"Now could you haul that chicken out of the oven for me? I'm scared of breaking one of these fingernails."

"Certainly, you silly girl. And I'll open a bottle of Côtes du Rhône, shall I?"

"Oh no, Mark. It's *family* dinner. We drink what Simon drinks—milk."

Mark was so besotted that he agreed to it, foolishly setting a bad precedent.

TWENTY MINUTES LATER. JENN HAD dimmed the lights in the kitchen. There were green, red and purple napkins from Provencal on the table (bought by Arabella during a Haiku and Reiki retreat she'd taken two years before), and brown and gray stoneware plates (purchased in the sales at Habitat by Mark when doing his postgraduate studies). Three insulated plastic goblets filled with milk. The low brass chandelier softly gleamed and reflected the raindrops steadily falling outside the French doors. Night had descended, and the sky was low and safe, the stars hidden. Trees stood in dark benignment, watching from a distance. They were just beginning to bud again.

The chicken was on a china platter at the head of the table.

Mark sat there, at the head, Jenn to his right, and Simon to his left. As Mark picked up the carving implements, which were a Poseidon-pronged fork and a matching, gleaming ten-inch knife, he paid his compliments to the chef.

"What a lovely bird!"

"Thanks!" said Jenn, smiling.

"Right." Simon spoke quietly. Talk about feeling like Banquo's bloody ghost, he thought. Or *seeing* it . . . he felt he could see a shadow of Arabella in one of her knee-length cashmere scarves, rolling her eyes at the bourgeois largesse. Snickering at Mark's clichéd comments, at Jenn's placid self-satisfaction.

Jenn piped up, little knowing Arabella's ghost hovered over her shoulder.

"Shall we say grace?"

Mark and Simon had already picked up their forks, but now Mark dropped his like a snake. Simon calmly speared roasted spud. Nice crispy skin on, you had to credit her that.

Jenn bent her head to intone some Yank prayer of false humility, but in honor of his mother's vague apparition, Simon just popped the potato in his mouth.

"Grace," he said, through the floury mass.

Both he and Mark regarded Jenn to see how she'd take this subordination. For a flash of a moment, her narrow eyebrows drew together and lowered, so she looked like a well-coiffed but peevish hen. But, as Simon blandly kept chewing, a small smile appeared and then widened.

"Oh well," she said. "I'll learn you yet."

Jenn's small plentiful teeth gleamed beneath the brass chandelier as she tossed her hair. Blond bangs covered one eye flirtatiously, as she recited: "Through the teeth/And 'tween the gums/Thank you Lord/'Cuz here it comes!" Jenn bit into a roasted carrot with brown sugar and winked at Simon. Then she began telling him a suitably G-rated version of their honeymoon.

.੭੬.

LATER THAT NIGHT, AFTER THE dinner had been finished, the carrots wrapped up in plastic, and the leftover apple crumble put in the freezer so Jenn wouldn't eat it during a moment of late-night weakness; after they had watched a Pierce Brosnan Bond film where a big-browed girl with a quavering voice claimed to be a nuclear physicist despite not knowing how to pronounce "fission"; after Mark had awkwardly pulled Simon aside to ask if he was doing all right (to which Simon lied and said he was fine, just tired, just a bit knackered), they all went to bed.

But no one went to sleep.

It was Jenn's first night sleeping in Mark's house. *Her* house, now—her husband, standing by that funny knobbly dresser taking his watch off and winding it. She'd tried to get him to buy a watch at the duty-free, telling him he should get a fancy expensive watch, always reassuring to see on a doctor. But Mark had said he'd had a Rolex, a beautiful one from the 1950s called a Tudor Gold. It had a slight chip on the bezel but Mark had loved that watch. Arabella had given it to him—and it was stolen the night she was killed.

It was the only gift she'd ever given him that he had absolutely adored, he'd said.

And Jenn had smiled, adding, "Apart from Simon, of course!"

Now Jenn yawned. How funny he was, not to like a cool thing like a new fancy watch from duty-free. But he was funny that way. English people definitely were different. And what was up with their furniture not being painted? Looked so . . . unfinished. She'd change that, Jenn vowed. She'd cover all this pale plain pine in a satin finish. The place would gleam!

Then Mark turned toward her with that look on his face she'd learned over their honeymoon: the look where his chin lowered and his thick eyebrows dominated. His brown eyes hooded, made dangerous, by the shadow of the overhead light. He was a doctor and he knew things. He had escaped from a bad marriage, eluded its trap and now he was hers, hers. He gave her family and she would give him everything. God was okay with it, she knew. Jenn lay back in the bed, one arm curled up helplessly. She liked it when he looked at her like this, with that empty dark expression in his eyes. It meant he was going to grab her, and do what he wanted with her.

Mark walked toward his wife. Voluptuously clinging to the bed, exactly where Arabella used to regale him with stories of her conquests.

"Right," Mark said, as he stepped forward and threw the duvet to the floor. "Do you know what I'm going to do to you, woman?"

Jenn's trembling left hand gripped the headboard, and Mark could see the muscle of her white inner arm, the curve of her lightly stubbled armpit.

She giggled.

.୬୧.

IT WAS A LONG NIGHT for Simon, for when all the noise and the sounds of walking back and forth for glasses of water had stopped, after he'd heard Jenn walk downstairs, remove the apple crumble from the freezer and put it in the microwave, he lay in his small narrow bed and thought that perhaps he'd found a way to shake Jenn's bloody patronizing Yank confidence.

All that palaver he'd just heard? He'd do something about it.

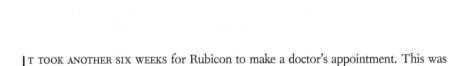

7

I T TOOK ANOTHER SIX WEEKS for Rubicon to make a doctor's appointment. This was a potentially tricky move, since her local NHS surgery was where Mark worked, but when ringing she'd requested a female doctor and been told that it would be no problem.

She'd cut Mark and Jenn out of her life, quietly and utterly, since their engagement. If Jenn couldn't figure out why, she was dimmer than she looked— which was saying a fuckload. And now they were back from their honeymoon. In Florida of all places. Mark, the idiot, was lucky Jenn hadn't dragged him to Dollywood, or Niagara Goddamn Falls.

Rubicon's bleeding had continued getting worse; her last period had finally ended after seventeen days, with blood loss to the extent that she'd had to buy a bumper pack of navy-blue towels and layer them on her bed before going to bed at night. Always two, sometimes three, tampons in at once, but still any slight tensing of her stomach muscles (which of course *were* always tensing nowadays) would release bubbling rivers of blood. Loss of iron, loss of fertility, loss of bright unthinking optimism about the future. They all seeped deep down into the mattress as Rubicon lay awake, in the dark, alone in the cold wet bed.

Who knew blood could be so cold?

And she had to stop pressing down on that muscle-hard lump which had formed on her abdomen, to the left of her hip bone. Pressing on it released more blood, but somehow the lump was getting bigger. The size and firmness of a mango, and growing, growing . . .

What would she do? She couldn't return to the US; no family anymore, no home. And, shamefully, no healthcare. Some country. War's a cancer the Red White and Blue will shell out big bucks for, but the other kind? The usual internal cellular riot? You're out of luck, expat. And the only trickle-down effect you'll be experiencing is the drip drip drip of your own rusty pipes.

If only she were still famous, Rubicon thought, she'd be so much less alone— she'd still have all that love—plus money. As the thin spigot of blood dripped from her womb, Rubicon realized for the first time on a conscious level that fame was *about* love. And it was such a safe love, since it didn't rely on one person but on many, so many, that none of them could hurt her and they couldn't *all* leave her.

Except, of course, that they had. Along with the money and the glistening illusion of importance.

So now she knew what she should've done. She should simply have told Mark she'd always adored him. Said the sappy (true) words even though they left her exposed. Should've pushed her own awkwardness and fear away and just loved him, just loved him without fear of refusal or rejections, because here she was, anyway. Just so for once she could have said something *real*, instead of relying on arrogance and nerve and their underlying structures of fear and insecurity.

It would have been a fun change just to tell him the truth. Even thinking about it pushed the terror away for a moment. But blood still leaked. Something real was happening right now to poor frightened Rubicon: she realized that she had never been loved, because she had always been too afraid.

And so here she was, in a pool of damp blood, at 2 a.m.

Fame, even the weak variety she had briefly savored, had taught her she didn't need to love. Only to get (attention, money). Now these dark nights undid that teaching. She found herself hoping that Mark would find happiness with Jenn. This sentiment astonished her and impressed her, and made her feel that, just perhaps, she wasn't as damaged as she had thought. She thought about wanting Mark to be happy, truly happy for the first time in his life, regardless of any feeling for her.

Not that she'd ever be friends with Jenn again.

.ᴥ.

RUBICON ARRIVED AT THE CLINIC twenty minutes before her 11 a.m. appointment. The surgery was a small shabby building that had once been a girls' school, and its overheated reception area was filled with the mingled scents of old bodies and Purell. An overworked receptionist sitting behind a low desk glowered as she examined Rubicon's NHS card.

"Yer early," the receptionist said. "There are chairs in the reception lounge, yeah?" She had powdery low-hanging jowls and short pineapple-yellow hair. Flicking the card back to Rubicon, she also handed her a piece of cardboard with the room number "7" written on it in a blue marker.

"All right. Oh!—" She saw someone walking along the corridor behind the receptionist, and Rubicon's heart tightened. Dammit! That familiar set of slumped shoulders had just walked into one of the numbered offices. Mark. Mark was here. Wearing some God-awful teal-blue jumper that could only have been purchased on his honeymoon. He hadn't seen her, but she could tell he was smiling as he closed the door behind him. And he was in surgery #7.

"Oh," Rubicon said. "Oh *crap*."

The receptionist took a sturdy bite from a Yorkie bar and peered dismissively over her shoulder. Rubicon leaned over the counter.

"Wrong doctor," she said. "I called earlier. I don't want to see my regular doctor. I want to see a female doctor today." The receptionist looked at her with a glance that was anything but receptive. An impatient cough behind Rubicon alerted her to a small muscular man in tweeds, clearly a retired military type, glaring from behind her. She knew how to shut him up.

Rubicon turned around and hissed, "*Women's* troubles, you see. Blood all over the show."

"Good lord," the small man muttered, dropping eye contact. He took a step back as if worried about catching endometriosis or a rogue case of menopause.

"Exactly," Rubicon agreed. "Tons of blood, like bubbling crude—and I want a female doctor who won't react like that, see?"

The receptionist drew herself up as if Rubicon had just spat on a soldier's grave or criticized Prince William's ass. "Dr. Everleigh is a *wonderful* doctor. Chopping and changing does you no good at—"

Goddamn it. Rubicon was so tired. She'd been eating mushrooms and spinach for the iron (and chocolate and ice cream and gâteaux for the hell of it) but she was always so tired lately. Tears welled up, but she brushed them away. Not going to cry for these people.

"I just want a female doctor, right? Is that so goddamn much to ask?"

"You'll get nowhere using language like that. If you want another doctor, you'll have to make another appointment, I'm afraid."

"Are you serious?"

"The next vacant appointment is in two weeks."

Rubicon was stuck, a weak willow wedged between two ageless rocks—great British glares coming at her from both sides. Just as she was preparing to sigh and make another appointment in a fortnight's time, the door to surgery #7 opened again and Mark emerged, briskly drying his hands on a blue cloth. His dark eyes softened as he recognized Rubicon up at the desk arguing with Lita. For five months his and Jenn's calls to her had remained unanswered. He registered her pallor and the unusual darkness beneath her hawklike eyes.

Rubicon turned and saw him. He looked stupid in that teal sweater. He also looked lovely, tanned and somehow taller, no longer hunched for an anticipated blow. Then, surprisingly, she found herself feeling glad to see him so happy. She felt kind of sad about it too, but a funny kind of sorrow that felt like there was wisdom in it. So. She really was pleased for him (though why did it have to be *Jenn?*) The corners of Rubicon's mouth began to turn up in response to Mark's smile.

Then she burst into tears.

Mark leaped forward. Over the receptionist's complaints, he immediately escorted Rubicon into his office as her tears flowed and she deposited a large dollop of snot onto the alligator logo of his new sweater.

BONDING WITH SIMON DID NOT happen the way Jenn had expected it to. At all. In fact, she was beginning to find the boy very disconcerting. It all came to a head on the same afternoon Rubicon was attempting to wipe snot off Mark's sweater with a crumpled (and probably used) tissue. Jenn and Simon were feeling out their way together.

In the weeks since Jenn's return from the honeymoon, Simon had been biding his time. One afternoon he returned from school to find her—as always—in the sodding house. She was always there. Cleaning or cooking or simply talking endlessly with that mad barracuda grin fixed to her face. Trying to be his friend.

That day—he spoke.

"I'm afraid I have a complaint to register, Jenn." Jenn was wearing a pink velour tracksuit with the legs cut short just above her calves. It made her arse appear enormous from behind, but slender ankles twinkled delicately above bejeweled flip-flops. The woman had no idea how to dress. She should be shopping. Why was she always faffing about the house, anyway? Painting and hauling splashing pails about, baking things and calling up the stairs to tell him what she'd made.

Jenn had just finished hoovering the sofa and was putting a single soft karate chop in the top of each decorative pillow to make it look artlessly plump, when Simon silently entered the room. This was the first time he'd called her by name.

"A complaint, Simon? Gosh, I'd kind of rather we discussed stuff than complained about it."

She beamed upon the stocky young man, and not for the first time it came into her head that Mike had been a mere year older than this boy when they'd conceived Lovina. Of course, he hadn't seemed like a boy to her then, with his meaty shoulders and the way his butt had looked in those baseball pants. She could still hear the sound of his cleats tapping against the linoleum of the gym hallway on his way out to the field. How wonderful she had thought he was, back then. Poor old stoic Mike, but gone now and glad to be so. By the end the only thing she'd liked about Mike was his stoicism, mainly because she never realized it was fed by a silent contempt for her. It's really not fair that people like Jenn can so often be loathed for their cheery competence (though Mark actually adored it. So far).

Anyway, Jenn sat down on the sage-colored sofa, blew a lock of blond hair out of her eye, and played a broad smile on Simon. She patted the sofa cushion next to her, but the stocky boy regarded her coolly, with brows so like his father's but with green sparkling eyes which she knew had been Arabella's best feature.

"Okay. Let's have a 'discussion.' I warn you, it will be rather awkward."

"Awkward, huh?" Jenn kicked her legs forward artlessly. What did he have to discuss? probably he wanted a car—or money. With kids it was always money for some little thing. She remembered how it had been.

"Yes." Simon sat quietly down. "I wanted to ask you something while my father was out. Since it concerns you rather more than him."

"Okay." Jenn waited patiently, mentally preparing to buy Simon whatever he wanted. Soon she'd be shaking her head while discussing him with friends, happily complaining about his busy teen life and how he always asked her for advice and called her for rides (to the movies and girls' houses, but she'd turn him down if he wanted her to buy beer). Mark my words, she thought. One day soon Simon and I'll be sitting on this very sofa, watching TV and splitting a package of cookies, laughing at *The Simpsons*.

Everybody likes *The Simpsons*, right?

If Simon had known what she was thinking, he'd have had three words for her.

Not. Bloody. Likely. (In regard to the biscuit-sharing, obviously. Not *The Simpsons*, which he'd watched since he was a toddler.)

As it was, the stocky boy inspected his fingernails for a moment, then spoke. "I wanted to request that you be a bit quieter when you're shagging my father. It's rather intrusive, you know, listening to all that screaming late at night."

Jenn's smile froze, and her face turned a raspberry pink.

Score, thought Simon.

8

"WHY ON *EARTH* HAVEN'T YOU seen someone about this before, Rubicon?"

Rubicon was exactly where she hadn't wanted to be. And she was thoroughly enjoying it, in the embarrassed way one can with attentive pity. This wasn't how she'd ever imagined this happening; it was infinitely better. She was lying on Mark's medical examining table, with her jeans unzipped and Mark's slender fingers pressing down between her hipbones, just beneath the elastic of her Marks & Sparks blue cotton underwear. It was surprisingly unembarrassing. A fan circled lazily above, casting slow shadows on the cheap popcorn ceiling. Rubicon crooked one arm behind her head as she craned down to see as Mark pressed down on the lump between her hipbones.

"I . . . it hasn't been going on that long. Less than six months. Since the last time I saw you."

"Hmm."

Mark pressed down again, his fingers now working down into the soft flesh of her stomach. Rubicon looked less knobbly than she had always done, he thought. And as for *this* . . . approximately 100 millimeters; a significant size. The size of a four-month fetus. The growth was already moving up, its top toward Rubicon's belly button. You have to credit Rubicon this, he thought, she's consistent. Takes crap care of herself in all ways, really. That flat of hers which I've heard is dire, her diet alternating between E-chemicals, Ribena, and semi-starvation. And she'd never seemed to gain an ounce, until now. But she looked better for it. Haggard and frightened, yes. Less fashionably bony, but her new softness made him feel comfortable around her, protective even.

"You haven't seen a gynecologist?" Mark stripped the gloves from his hands and leaned against the office sink.

"Christ, Mark. I already said I hadn't." Rubicon's eyes were large and dark in her face. "Just—I mean, I know it's not good. The blood. That's no normal period. And those huge goddamn . . ." She couldn't say lumps. Tears slid hot and slow down the sides of her face.

"I'm sorry I was so bitchy about you and Jenn, Mark." The words burst out of Rubicon. "Maybe it made no sense to me, but it wasn't for me to—"

"I understood, Rubicon. After all, Arabella was your friend too. It must've seemed too soon after her death, it *was* soon—"

They both knew why Rubicon had distanced herself from Mark and Jenn, refused their calls and their invitations. Rubicon had wanted him, though never had the nerve to say it or the vulnerability to show it. But she'd told Jenn, that day they met at Waterloo, and of course Jenn would've shared it with Mark (probably in bed, and definitely in a faux-concerned manner which underlined her own victory). And of course others knew: Hugh and even Jack Brayson had mentioned Rubicon's crush on Mark—but she'd never said a word herself. For years she'd waited for him like a schoolgirl at the gates, in fruitless silence.

Rubicon wiped one eye with the back of her hand and sighed. "No. That wasn't it, but you know that. You're being kind to me now. There's no point going into it, really. Just, please accept my apology."

He noticed she didn't say, ". . . and send apologies to Jenn too."

"Of course I do." Mark was moved by Rubicon's lack of front. He changed his tone to a friendly bluffness. "You've been a daft cow not to see me sooner, as a doctor, I mean. Of course you've been terrified—anyone would be."

She shrugged. "Well, it seemed a bit weird, so . . ."

"I'm happy to see you, Rubicon. And I'm very glad you came in." Mark's hand patted his old friend's thigh. "Oh, do yourself up again—" He turned to look out the window as Rubicon sat up and stuffed her swollen abdomen within the buttons of her low-rise jeans. Flesh bulged over the top button, pale as bread dough.

"Decent?" Mark asked. He winced as he saw a small boy in the park outside pick up a plastic shovel and hit his granny on the knee with it, hard.

"Yeah."

"Right then." Mark turned around. Rubicon sat with one hand up to her mouth, waiting to hear his verdict. "Well, you've been a bloody fool, Rubicon. This isn't cancer—at least, I'll bet my hat it isn't."

"What?" Rubicon said. "How can you be so sure?"

"How long did you say your periods have been heavy?"

"They started getting heavy like a year ago."

"And the lumps? A few months?"

"Yeah."

"If you had seen a gynecologist, you'd have been told that you probably have fibroids."

"Fibroids?"

"Yes. Benign—*benign*—tumors that grow inside the uterus or the fallopian tubes. They create extra surface within the uterus, which means the uterine walls hold more blood, hence heavier bleeding. So first you had that, and then the fibroids began to really grow. Probably a hormonal imbalance, as you age toward menopause. You are, in fact, a very silly *old* cow. But not a dying one." His dark eyes softened.

Well! He was throwing around a lot of words, including the dread word "tumors," which normally would've been all that she'd hear, but the fact that he was making rude comments about her age (when she was seven months younger than his goddamn wife, who was no child bride herself)—made Rubicon realize that she might be okay.

What a difference a little friendly rudeness can make.

"There are several things we can do . . ." Mark turned toward his computer and began punching the keyboard.

And in an instant, Rubicon's soul emerged from the darkening fear that had kept her up for so many nights, face deep in Dr. Oetker pizzas and Waitrose raspberry meringue roulade. A reprieve! She'd heard Mark talk before about the world of the sick, of the people who waited hopeless-eyed in that surgery day in and day out, unseeingly looking at old issues of *Grazia*, only dimly remembering what life had been like before illness and fear had marked them as theirs till the end. She'd thought that was where she'd be now, but no. And Mark was talking like a friend.

So Rubicon got lucky! Fear had marked her and then walked away, its assault unfounded, as it often is. Maybe these unfounded fears are there to challenge us to see past their shadows, Rubicon mused as Mark kept tapping away, the keyboard keys clacketing with reassuring competence. Perhaps, she continued, in this moment of ecstatic weightless relief, this fucking terror she'd been running from was *meant* to be connected to Mark. He was the perfect one to release her from it, so she could also release him. From all those years of her stupid hopes and expectations. All those years of her thinking how much she lurrrrved him, and meanwhile being so nasty, pleased by how miserable he was with Arabella. Gratified by that hunch in his shoulders, that graying of his skin. Because it was caused by her.

Mark was talking. He'd found an official-looking notebook and now glanced through it, then picked up the telephone and began to say things into it. Rubicon just sat there unhearing, grinning with the vacant ecstasy of a morning-show host.

What, she mused, was that thing the Buddha said—or someone—some guy's thirteen precepts. She'd heard about it in an aromatherapy workshop she'd sneered her way through. Something that made all Christian crap about the needle and a camel's eye look like a cub scout trick. Something about generosity . . .

Rubicon gazed at Mark as he talked on the phone. She did love him, but also she just *liked* him so. Oh! Now he'd hung up and was talking to her. He was mid-sentence, so maybe she'd better listen. Good old Mark.

". . . surgery quite possible, unless you're lucky and still can get an embolization. They're rather new but . . . after the sonogram we shall know better. At least one of the fibroids is as large as a second-trimester fetus. Either way, Dr. Segorad is expecting you to call."

He looked sternly at Rubicon. "And you *will* call, right, Rubicon?"

Rubicon's Rimmel-smudged eyes gleamed softly, and she nodded. Ah! Now she remembered. The Buddhist thing. If you want to be truly generous, release all expectations.

So maybe she could just let Mark have his life without her needing to be a part of it? Couldn't she find the generosity to be his friend, without wanting to grab for more? Rubicon nodded, yes, she'd call the doctor he recommended. And in her heart she released Mark.

Forgave Mark for not loving her, and even—a little bit, because, let's face it, it's a tough kielbasa to swallow for a chic brunette to forgive smart men their tedious weakness for big-titted blondes—forgave him for choosing Jenn. Forgiveness felt like a block of ice cracking in her chest, and she almost gasped at the power of the thawing. It trickled through her ribcage, melting the ice of self-obsession, of shame and oh, even of fear. Mark continued to describe potential treatments for these fibroids, but she interrupted him.

"Mark—" she realized, and said, "I should've helped you with Simon over the last year. I should've just stepped up and thought about you more, not about me." She shook her head in regret and stared out the window. A limping grandmother was dragging a screaming boy away from the playground.

Rubicon, for once, didn't seem jittery. She was calmer than Mark had ever seen her. He flashed back to twenty years ago, when they'd had a few dates (before she'd introduced him to Arabella). She'd been sharp and elusive, deeply sarcastic. While Arabella had come right out and grabbed—well, that certainly hadn't been the best choice he'd ever made. But all these years Rubicon had been so alone, maintained those defenses. It must have been exhausting, he thought for the first time. And he'd never thought of how alone she must also have been.

Mark realized he'd always assumed that Rubicon was with other people, as she'd been when they were young, all that time ago. But of course everyone had paired up and poor old Rubicon was alone, increasingly poor (for that aromatherapy thing can't be profitable, can it?), maybe even lonely.

"Oh Rubicon, I never thought it was your job to look after me—"

"No, but people do, don't they? Or they should. Look after each other. Like you're doing for me today."

Rubicon smiled rather sweetly, sitting on that metal table and swinging her calves from side to side like windshield wipers, while banging the sides of her Converse shoes together. She looked like a teenager. Shy even, with her dark hawklike eyes earnest.

If only things had been different, he thought for the first time. If only he had never clapped eyes on the candy-wrapped nightmare that had been Arabella. For the first time Mark was touched by the realization that Rubicon, so seemingly cynical and worldly, had felt such tenderness for him. Why had it seemed like a burden before?

But now he was with Jenn, and so happy.

He thought of Rubicon returning alone to her no-doubt dire little flat in Barnes. Of her endless wait through the NHS bureaucracy, of her waiting alone in metal chairs, being a number on a computer screen. Just another middle-aged woman, her potency and promise leaking from her drip by drip. And he knew how he could help.

"Would you like me to go to Dr. Segorad's office with you?"

Rubicon looked at him in surprise.

"Not for the exam, obviously, but I could ask questions and get things moved along for you. Be your advocate, as it were."

"Well—really? I'm sure I'll be fine on my own. I mean I always …" Do stuff on my own, she was going to finish. But that sounded rather sad so her words just trailed off.

"Well," Mark said. "Let's just do this together. It'll be an education for me, really …" He nattered on about how these treatments had advanced and he wasn't as up-to-date on them as he should be. But actually, secretly, he had decided that he would pay for Rubicon to get private care.

Rubicon's eyes glistened with tears again. "Mark, you really don't need to."

"I know that. But I will."

Mark felt like a proper doctor, and a proper man.

Neither of them mentioned Jenn again that day. She was outside of their reborn friendship.

9

SIMON HAD BEEN LOOKING FOR a big reaction to his request to Jenn, and he absolutely hit pay dirt. First that face of hers, usually small and brightly certain, flushed the painful purplish-pink. Then her lipsticked mouth opened but nothing came out. Well, nothing coherent. "You—"

"Yes, of course I hear everything going on. People in Twickenham probably do. They mightn't be receiving full benefit of the dialogue, but they've definitely been hearing the highlights of your union over the last few weeks. If that's what you were after, then well done."

Jenn's hands flew over her eyes, gleaming mauve nail varnish matching the mottled mauve button nose between her fingers.

Simon coughed quietly and examined the ceiling. "It's a bit rich," he noted. "A bit rich for me to have to listen to some woman in my dead mother's bed being buggered by my father, you know."

Jenn gasped as if she'd been slapped. "Simon, we honestly never did *that*!" Jenn lied. Then she sat up straight and began wringing her hands. "I want to say right now that I apologize. Oh, Simon, I'm so, so sorry. Your father and I *are* blessed by marriage, though—"

"I'm not!" Simon suddenly felt a thrill of anger. An apology already? This was unprecedented, and he'd *known* it would feel this good. Build on it. *"I'm* not blessed by your fucking silly marriage. Two minutes ago you were in the States and knew none of us!"

"Simon, but I know you now, I love your father and you—"

"You didn't know my mother and you don't know *me.* What you've got is an instant free house and my dad, I guess—but you don't fucking love *me,* Jenn." Something unexpected then shot out of his mouth. "My own mother didn't love me, why would you?"

These were the saddest words Jenn had ever heard. She sat back on the sofa, still with those painted nails over her lips but eyes filled with tears for this poor lonely boy.

She was crying! Simon thought. Oh it was wonderful. Bloody marvelous. Self-pity and righteous anger coursed through his body in a delicious brew, fermented by adolescent hormones and a lifetime of lost arguments. Arabella had never once offered an apology; she had always, always won arguments using her twin tools of contempt and indifference. Simon felt a powerful mingling of self-pity and joy as he stood over Jenn.

Funny he'd never thought of how small she was. Her certainty was so big he always thought of her as taking up the room, but this was his room now! He jabbed a finger toward her. "Why do you never ask about my mother? Months it's been, of you trying to buy me milkshakes or telling me your promcoming bloody boring stories."

Homecoming, Jenn thought, but not the time to correct the poor kid.

Simon continued, "Has my father told you? About what he did . . ." Simon paused. "I mean, late home as always, wasn't he? Leaving me to find her." He added weakly, the rage draining out of his voice. "Of course I was the one to bloody find her—he was never around, was he?"

The pain in this boy's voice made Jenn's heart ache. She realized that was why Mark told her so little about that night—he was ashamed. Ashamed of abandoning his son because he was avoiding his wife. Poor Simon, oh poor Simon, and poor weak Mark. Shame on him for not protecting the boy . . .

It was the first time she'd thought of her husband as weak.

Slowly, carefully, Jenn put her hands up and clasped Simon's wrist. She gazed up at him with such sorrow in her eyes—not rage, but sorrow.

He drew his thick dark brows together, which he thought would make him look commanding, but to her it was the look of a frightened boy.

"Oh, Simon."

The sad steadiness in her eyes made him feel funny. A bit silly, actually.

And Jenn saw that she'd been a bad mom. Here she'd been judging Simon's mother for not providing love, and what had Jenn done? Make the poor kid a couple of chicken dinners, and then turn his house into a freaking sex show. Though vaguely she felt that the last part was kind of Mark's fault . . . but as a woman the shame was hers alone. She held Simon's wrist tightly as tears filled her round blue eyes.

Well! This whole confrontation had proved more exhausting and thrilling and upsetting than Simon had ever anticipated. "Right," he said, not knowing how to continue. Those tear-filled blue eyes looking at him with all this emotion made him very uncomfortable. "Right. So. None of that noise in future, yeah? I just— well, it's very *upsetting*," he ended weakly.

"Oh, Simon. You poor brave boy. Never again." Jenn said this quietly. She tried to catch up to the terrible fact that she had not done her job, had not thought of Simon first, had behaved in the way Mark encouraged her to do (men!).

Men.

She'd been a fool; she'd been sucked into that *male* world of just doing whatever men want whenever men want it, never thinking about real priorities or what matters in the long term. Sure sex is fun, but it's not what matters—women know this, or should. Family and respect and his dead mother should have been her focus, and ohmigod the shame of it. Overwhelming shame. And the pity of his loss.

Parent and child. So sacred, so deep.

"Simon. I–I just cannot tell you how sorry and ashamed I am. I—how *terrible* for you. Hearing your father and me." Jenn half reached a hand up to smooth his forehead, but pulled it away in case he thought her a total whore.

She put her hand back onto her pink velour lap just as the boy thought how soft that velour looked. "Oh, well. I mean, it wasn't *terrible*." In fact, he'd been kind of turned on, and more so when he'd realized he could embarrass her by mentioning all that "Oh my GODing" and "You're my big BIG MAN"ing.

"No. Terrible." Jenn looked the boy next to her in the eyes and made a vow. "Never again, Simon. You will never hear that again."

"Well, if you don't mind. Though honestly" —Simon couldn't imagine why he was saying this, but apparently he was about to— "it sounded better than with my mum. She would just shout, 'BORING!'"

Jenn looked at the young man and thought, Jesus—what a life. She never even knew her parents had sex, much less graded each other on it. The kid lived in a harsh world. The thought made her want to cry again, but instead she hiccuped.

"Would you like a glass of water, Jenn?" Simon leaned forward, concerned.

"Oh, sweetie, no."

"Or maybe we should have a cuppa, and a few biscuits?"

"That'd be great! But I'll go get 'em." Jenn wiped her eyes.

"No, I can. You stay put."

"Simon." Jenn shot to her feet and looked at him with great seriousness. "I will make us tea and biscuits."

"All right, then. Cheers."

"Simon. What kind of tea do you like?" Jenn spoke in the meaningful tones of a woman who has accepted a solemn mission.

"Oh, workman's brew, please. Not the Lipton, though—sorry. I don't like it at all."

"You'll never get that again," she vowed.

When Jenn returned from the kitchen, she had a packet of ginger biscuits and a proper cup of PG Tips. She and Simon sat in front of the TV together, at first awkwardly. They opened the biscuit packet. Soon Homer Simpson made them laugh, and ease began to descend.

DID MARK NOTICE HOW SUBDUED Jenn and Simon were that night, when he arrived home for dinner? Actually, yes. Yes, he did, but he was relieved about it, because he also had something to be quiet about. Just this morning he would've thought that telling Jenn about Rubicon's need for surgery might've eased the way for a reconciliation between them and given Jenn someone to look after and Rubicon someone to talk to. But Jenn seemed calmer tonight, less desperate for connection. And Rubicon's medical information was her own to reveal or not.

So Mark decided, as he looked at his lovely wife with her pink flushed skin and strong neck and at his son who was so like him that sometimes seeing the boy move was like a warped mirror to the past, he would keep mum about Rubicon, her visit to the surgery, and her revelation. He would simply look after her himself.

Jenn had made something called Turkey Divan: a casserole that tasted like salty mushroom soup but was actually rather moreish provided one had a few glasses of water on hand. And a salad of grated carrots, scallions, avocado and raisins. The three of them sat at the table near the French doors, with the amber ceiling light creating a golden triangular arc over the triumvirate. Jenn was at the head of the table, with Mark on one side and Simon on the other. If someone had been lurking in the back garden, they'd have seen a quiet, contained family unit— pretty woman, affluent man, healthy boy. All calmly gathered around the family table beneath the glow of the amber light, in this leafy suburban spot at the end of the District Line.

In the garden the large dead tree trembled in the winter wind.

Simon was now sixteen. When was it time to call him a man instead of a boy? When do you know someone's a man, and not a boy? There should be a better word than "teenager" for the middle bit, really. For someone who hasn't yet grasped the power of a man's estate, but is working on it . . . working on it.

10

"RIGHT—YER LATE. EVERYONE'S GASPING for a coffee. Yer gear behind you, love?"
Crap, thought Rubicon. *I thought I was early.* "My gear?"

"Talent's got to be fed and watered. And so does *this* lot."

A tall man with full cheeks, sculpted brows, and electric-blue hair had thrown open the door upon hearing Rubicon's quiet knock. It was 9:30 a.m. and she had just arrived at a studio in Brick Lane for the *Style* shoot. The barracks of a room was bustling with the usual self-important mag hags (the phrase "fashionista" was newly popular). Camillas and Chloes bonily slouching about, arguing about backdrops and fawning on the photographer, an older Frenchman who wore a kilt, a safari coat and an air of affronted majesty. Racks of clothes, regiments of cruelly pointed shoes laid out, already that smell of warm flesh and aerosol mingling in the clammy air of the stone-walled space. Rubicon had been up since 5:47, eaten nothing but a clementine, and drunk two coffees and a Red Bull. She felt as if her heart was going to leap out of her eyes.

"I'm Charles. Hair," the man explained, as he leaned over a multi-bulbed mirror and critically examined his face. "Did I go a bit *mad* on the pencil this morning?" He turned and pointed to his eyebrows. "Do tell me. I don't want to channel late Joan."

"Late what?" Rubicon's jeans were so tight she yearned to shove a hand down the front and rearrange her underwear. All that Dr. Oetker fat was still on her ass.

"Joan . . . You know, darling. Crawford. As she aged her brows turned into hedgerows of rage. In her sixties close-ups she looks like an outraged Airedale."

"No. You look fine. I like your hair." Rubicon swept her hat off and showed him her short auburn locks, whose tips had been dyed an eggplant purple.

Charles ran expert hands through it. "Oh, I love! So bored with all this yummy mummy lot and their filthy extensions. Today's will be a particular nightmare, believe you me."

"Oh, do you think so? I'm—"

"These bloody ladettes all denying their HRT, God help us. Better get set up, you know." He looked at Rubicon more closely. "You look a bit peakish, love."

The Red Bull and the smell of the room, the early morning and the long sleepless night before all combined to suddenly overwhelm Rubicon. She was hot but felt her forehead and neck were oozing a cold thick sweat. Also, the bleeding had begun again; Rubicon hoped to Christ it didn't seep through the two super-plus tampons she'd put in. Dropping her heavy slouch handbag on the floor, Rubicon sat down heavily in front of Charles's mirrored table.

"Actually," she wiped her brow, "I'm one of the bloody ladettes. And I . . . I kind of think I'm going to *faint.*"

From there the shoot went uphill. First, Charles turned out to be a good egg. He apologized for the HRT crack, produced an orange juice and a half-eaten wholemeal scone, and then expertly tipped Rubicon's head over between her knees. Blood rushed to her cheeks, sugar entered her bloodstream, and soon after he tipped her back up, the room began to fill. Zoe and Meg and the others arrived. Rubicon pretended not to notice that cars had obviously been sent to pick them up, while she'd been told to take the tube. But the room began to ring with "Darling, where have you been?" and "You look fabulous!" and "Oh, it's been much too long!" (The latter said while the speaker was already turning away.) Stylists cajoled and preened, and the caterer finally showed up, complaining about bad directions and the sodding foul weather.

There was a moment's envying silence at Patsy Kensit's entrance—Kensit's *Emmerdale* bitch turn had recently reignited her career—before she was surrounded. Rubicon remembered a night she and Patsy had sat in a bathroom stall, hoovering up charlie and talking about men, pubic lice, and self-hatred.

Kensit ignored Rubicon's half wave as she passed, but Charles saw it, and felt for her. He didn't remember Rubicon's days of cawing and mocking on *It's Pants!*, but to him she was the only one of this lot who seemed a little lost, a little real (and wasn't Botoxed to the cortex).

"Come with me, love." Charles put an arm around Rubicon and led her to the makeup artist, a Scotsman the size of a jockey who wore a skull-emblazoned black angora sweater. "Sean, this is Rubicon. I want her to get the *full* treatment, darling. Make her look fabulous."

Sean was there only to work on the top girls but he rather fancied Charles, so he agreed to work his dark magic. In twenty minutes Rubicon's face was transformed into that of a tragic Gallic film star—enormous eyes in a pale cut-marble face, lips of mobility, expression and passion.

Rubicon began to have fun.

Nineties' Britpop blared over speakers as superannuated ladettes laughed, grimaced, or despaired as they tried on garments and shoved size 39 feet into 37 shoes. The air began to smell more and more strongly of the past to Rubicon, the lipstick, sweat, and aerosol smell that accompanied success, the kind of success which brings an enveloping glow of financial stability and smugness and, oh God, it had been so long since she'd inhaled such complacency. It was almost intoxicating, enjoyable, but . . . Rubicon realized that she had almost entirely lost belief in her separateness from the common woman; thought perhaps she was now a "civilian," a person on the outside of the fame experience.

No! she thought, as she was placed at the corner of the set. I'm just nervous, it's simply the early hour and . . . I still want this. This is my dream, she thought grimly, as she walked on set. And even Patsy now turned to her, said she looked divine.

The ladettes were dressed in the most ladylike styles of 2005, a year when the deconstructed tweed skirt was ultra-chic, cut close to the body with a slight tulip flare beneath the hips. On top they were enrobed in cashmere, great swathes of cashmere piled one atop another. No stockings but those cruelly pointed court shoes. They were sitting at a proper tea table in a pure-white setting, dressed as wealthy suburban matrons, but atop the table the silver tea service was upturned, and there were crumpled cans of cider and jettisoned flotsams of fast food along with piles and piles of classic cream-filled English desserts. All given pints of lager to grip in their manicured paws and encouraged by the photographer to throw food and drink at him and each other. The ladettes screamed and laughed and sank back into the ease of the nineties as the thronged fashionistas applauded and music bounced off the stone walls, the anthem of the old days. Pulp singing "Common People."

Rubicon got Zoe Ball in the ear with some Eton Mess, and received a faceful of raspberry ripple in return—brilliant! And Jarvis sang:

You'll never watch your life slide out of view, and dance and drink and screw

. . . as the photographer turned his lens on lager-and-cake soaked superannuated ladettes and snapped, snapped, snapped.

"I'M TELLING YOU, IT WAS great. Just fan-bloody-tastic!" This was Rubicon to Mark on the phone, after. He'd rung to leave a message saying her fibroid embolization had been scheduled for the following Monday. She should've thought that was odd, really. Rubicon had been in England for over twenty years. Did she think every aging woman on the NHS gets surgery on her tired old uterus with no waiting time whatsoever? No. She'd read the papers, she'd seen the pictures of doughy-faced Britishers who'd spent years on dialysis, waiting for transplants. However, as with the rest of us, good news never seemed inappropriate or unlikely to Rubicon. Mark said the procedure was scheduled, so that was how it was. Sometimes the NHS moves fast. Trust the journos to get it wrong.

But, of course, Rubicon was getting private medical care, though she didn't know it. Fibroid embolization was somewhat new to the UK, but Mark was mates with a fellow who did it, an American doctor with offices near Eaton Square.

After Mark spoke with Rubicon, he put his mobile back into his pocket and rejoined Jenn and Simon at the car-boot sale in Clapham, where Jenn and Simon were looking for new posters to hang in Simon's room. He hadn't been to a boot sale for years, as Arabella found them simply too grim, and they *were* a little sad, he conceded, if one goes to them alone. All that endless finger-dirty tat, the plastic now scratched and dimmed, the used clothes that took on the bulges and slouches of their (now dead?) wearers. But occasionally there was a treasure, or a lovable object looking for a home. Mark walked over to the open boot of a Honda Accord, and picked up a cassette tape from a tatty cardboard box. In green marker the label read, "Walking on Sunshine."

Ah! Katrina and the Waves. Marvelous song. One of the best of the eighties. And how long since he'd actually held a cassette tape? Five years? More. They'd seemed so cheaply made back then, and obviously they were; but now he looked at the tape, he admired its almost antique physicality. The tiny screws that held it together. The fragile film of the tape itself, its dark petroleum gleam. How many times had he put a number two pencil within the slotted hole of a cassette and wound it? How many times had he spliced a torn cassette together, its tape having unspooled in a river of stretched ribbon, before rewinding?

"Mark, why are you staring at that dirty thing? I think Simon's found a poster he wants."

Jennifer stood next to Mark, tapping her manicured finger against his shoulder. He put his arm around her and held out the cassette. Was it his imagination or did she stand more rigidly apart from him, no longer sinking into his embrace? He tightened his grip slightly. "Do you remember this song? It makes me think of summer festivals when I was young. We'd put it on when it was chucking down, and dance outside."

"Chucking dow—oh, raining, right?"

"Right, my love."

"I don't think so." Jenn glanced over at Simon and saw he was trying to haggle with the lady two Ford Escorts down. She fought the urge to snuggle against her husband and instead stepped slightly away. "How's it go?"

"Oh," Now it was Mark's turn to look over at Simon. The boy was holding up a framed poster and examining it solemnly. "It started sort of like 'duntduntduh, duntduntduhduhduntduhduh . . .'"

"No. We never had that in the States."

"Of course you did. It was a monster hit. 'Duntduntduh,' and then there's this kind of whoosh! And she starts singing, '*Used to think maybe you loved me, now baby I know*' —then more 'duntduntduhduntduntduhdudiliddle'" Mark bobbed his chin up and down solemnly, his eyes bright with remembrance of outdoor parties and endless afternoons, how it'd felt to wear hair so long it brushed one's shoulders. Bedsits with tea bags on the sink ledge and joss sticks smoldering in the corner. Before he'd started medical school, and married, and . . . Mark was trying to remember more of the words. He didn't notice Simon walking toward them, clutching the poster.

Jenn did, and removed her hand from Mark's arm. "I honestly think I've never heard that song."

"But you have. You must have!" Mark turned to the vendor. "*You* know this, right, mate? '*I'm walking on sunshine—*'"

The vendor, who had a mullet and wore his big belly high beneath a torn green sweater, said, "Ahh, Katrina!" He pointed at Mark and, in a wobbly tenor, also began to sing.

"*I'm walking on sunshine, Ohh oh—*" The vendor and Mark bobbed back and forth.

Simon stood next to Jenn, watching them. She was smiling. He wasn't. He looked around to see if anyone was watching. His father was making a fool of himself, though on a rather harmless level.

The vendor and Mark threw arms around the other's shoulders to finish the chorus, "*And it's time to feel GOOD!*" An older couple milling through the car park turned to look and smile.

"Oh, yeah! I do know that song!" Jenn said.

"Everybody does," said Simon.

"I don't care," said Mark, flushed and with his arm still around the vendor. "How much is this tape, mate?"

"Ah, I'd never thought it'd sell. Just take it so." The vendor had danced to the song, long ago in West Cork.

"No—here's a pound. That's a small price to pay for a lovely memory." Mark slipped the cassette into his coat pocket.

Simon had had about enough of dancing to the oldies. "Just take a look at this poster," he said. "It's dead cool. I reckon I'll take down the Jordan one and put this up—she's pretty naff."

"If 'naff' is kinda scary, I'll second that," Jenn said. "She's even scarier than this poster, for sure." Jenn thought that Jordan girl looked like the kind who'd rifle through your handbag at a disco, and then steal your boyfriend. "It's from a movie. *The Exorcist.*"

Mark stopped smiling, but when Jenn looked over, he said nothing.

"Oh sweetie," she said. "Everyone knows *The Exorcist*! It's super-scary. That's Linda Blair. She throws up pea soup."

Mark examined the poster silently. An inset image showed Linda Blair with glowing green eyes, her round young face filling the frame in a blood-streaked grimace. The majority of the poster showed a man paused anxiously beneath a dimly ominous street lamp, clutching a black hold-all. Mark didn't like it. He said, "Ridiculous, having that thing hanging over your bed. A recipe for bad dreams."

The three of them turned to the car. One of Jenn's wool-gloved hands was tucked through Simon's right elbow, and one through Mark's left. Cold, surprisingly piercing raindrops began to fall on the used goods and the vendors and the torn crisp wrappers and anoraked buyers milling through in the dingy muddy field.

Simon noticed people—men—gazing at Jenn with the blank surmisal in their eyes of a British male who sees a bit of all right. He felt that Jenn saw it, too, though she never looked directly at a man other than his father or himself. But her voice became brighter and her neck lengthened, and Simon felt his first thrill of being seen with a quality bird. It made him feel bigger, older. He wished his father wasn't taller than he was.

"Oh, Dad, don't be so bourgeois," Simon replied coolly. That was one of the words Arabella had frequently thrown at her husband. Mark shot a glare at his son.

Jenn disengaged her arm from her husband's and wiped a raindrop from her forehead as she examined the poster more closely. "It says here the movie won an Oscar, so it must be serious. Have a message and all."

"Christ," said Simon. "I hope not."

Mark fished his keys out of his pocket and opened the door of his Volvo estate wagon. Better to focus on the sociological implications, he thought. But once I get Simon alone—well, that *thing*—that poster will not hang over his bed. "In my opinion," he began, in the lecturish tone Jenn already knew drove Simon batty, "the horror genre focuses on our unconscious fears. I believe this film was about a fear of burgeoning sexuality. Of the, er, of the female kind."

"Well, you've neatly sucked the joy out of that potential experience, Dad." Simon sulked out the window as they drove through the crowded parking lot toward the exit.

"No, he didn't, Simon. Now I want to see it too! I never thought of scary movies like that. Like, as meaning anything." This was true. For Jenn, the culture of movies and TV was either boring or not; they didn't connect to actual life. She thought Mark's viewpoint made things more interesting, somehow. Plus, it was good for him to have someone listen to his opinions, the poor old sweetie.

"You're pretty darn smart, Mark." Jenn beamed at her husband.

"Mmph," said Simon to the window.

Still, he liked his poster. It was framed and all. And he would put it up. What could his dad do about it? Plus, Jenn really didn't like that Jordan poster.

.ଡ଼ୁ.

LATER ON, MARK DROPPED JENN and Simon off at the Blockbuster near the train station, while he went to Oddbins for a bottle of Pinot Gris and then to the Village Pizza for a large hot American (pepperoni, sausage, green peppers and onion). Netflix had been shutting down video shops everywhere, but since they wanted to see a movie tonight, there was no time for the DVD to be mailed. The two of them wandered through the empty store. Jenn saw The Exorcist and held the DVD up for Simon to see.

"You want to get this? So you know what's going on in your poster?"

"Yeah, but I don't think my dad'll be too happy."

Jenn put an arm around Simon's waist and winked. "You just let me take care of him."

Simon felt the warmth of Jenn's tightly packed flesh within her suede jacket.

"Ooh, Smarties!" They were at the counter now, and Jenn picked up the candy and some microwave popcorn. She held up a credit card and asked, "Simon, you want anything?"

"No." He looked into her round blue eyes. "No thanks."

Soon the two of them stood outside beneath the Blockbuster's blue and yellow awning in the dark and damp air, waiting for Mark to pick them up. Simon examined the DVD.

"Hmm," said Simon. "Made in 1973. That was before you were born, right?"

"Oh, sweetie," said Jenn. She might as well tell the truth, she figured, since she'd annoyingly had to get it printed in the paper here before her marriage, as part of something called The Banns. "I'm way older than that. I'm the same age as Rubicon, you know."

"You lot all look the same age to me."

Jenn smiled, and gently touched Simon's pale, firm cheek. "I remember feeling like that. But remember, us wrinklies are always here for you. No matter what."

Simon looked away. What she said made him feel silly and shy and ashamed of the stiffy he'd just got when looking at her. But also, a warm tendril of comfort and trust took hold in Simon's stomach. After a moment staring at the rain-slicked cars gliding by, he said, "No, actually you look younger than Rubicon does. You're much . . ."

Mark pulled up and saw Jenn clutching The Exorcist DVD and Simon glancing at Jenn's cleavage, which was visible above her shawl-collared coat.

The pizza was good, as was the movie in its way.

11

IF RUBICON HAD KNOWN THAT the fibroid embolization would involve so much vomiting, she'd have had it done before the *Style* shoot. As it was, she'd probably lost about five pounds in the last forty-eight hours. It was comforting, how it had all gone just as Mark had said it would. She'd shown up at the Marylebone hospital at the crack of sparrow fart, around 5.30 a.m. She'd had little sleep, no shower, and hadn't been allowed to eat since 10 p.m. the previous night. Mark met her in the waiting area. He looked as if he'd just rolled out of bed, with his hair sticking to his scalp and his eyes tired and slightly puffed beneath those serious brows of his. She'd never seen Mark's early-morning look, Rubicon realized. For some reason the gray-brown tuft of his hair made her think of a book she'd loved as a child. *The Velveteen Rabbit.* Rubicon and Mark hugged briefly, then sat on the low vinyl bench in the waiting room. They yawned companionably.

"The drive all right?" she asked eventually. She'd already filled out forms and given blood, and wore a stiff laminated bracelet with her name, age, and Mark listed as an emergency contact. Rubicon had not noticed that no one had asked for her NHS card.

"Lovely, actually," Mark said. "Not a jot of traffic. Now, no worries. It'll go like clockwork. Segorad's a good man, and embolizations are rather dull, really."

"Dull's good." Rubicon yawned. "In this situation."

"Right you are." Mark placed a reassuring hand on Rubicon's knee, and she looked at his long fingers, the reddening of his knuckles. She felt his warmth through her jeans but did not place her own cold palm over his hand. Mark continued, "In a few minutes you'll get an IV, and then a drip will administer the anesthetic. You'll feel absolutely nothing during the procedure, but you'll be awake, in a way. It's called twilight."

·୨୧·

AND THAT'S JUST HOW IT went. So comforting to know a doctor.

During the twilight sedation, as Mark's radiologist friend put a small slice in Rubicon's groin, she felt absolutely nothing. But she heard it all. Medical personnel chatting over her supine form as music played; *Hotel California* by the Eagles seemed an insensitive choice, but the radiologist sang along contentedly as he inserted a tube within an artery and began disseminating gritty blockages high within Rubicon's womb, blocking the tumor's rich blood supply. *You can check out anytime you want, but you can never leave*, he warbled along with Glenn Frey.

Afterward, again just as Mark said, Rubicon (who'd been hungry since 10:12 the previous night) found she couldn't stand the sight of food. Morphine, yes. Moreish, misty water-colored morphine, oh yes she wanted that. After a leisurely floaty bit when she was dimly aware of Mark saying something to the nurse and then subsequently being wheeled to another room, Rubicon slipped further into a warm and mobile reverie. She could see the inside of her head and it was a wood-paneled room. She'd always known it would look like that. It was a cluttered room, but nice. Very nice. Weird how she'd also known there'd be a window right there, above the reading chair in the room inside her head.

Rubicon looked around her head's room. It contained a large reading chair surrounded by closets of clothes and cameras; it was decorated with lavish velvet curtains of a royal blue, tangled with microphone cords that wrapped around her feet; then there were voices from another room, telling her to get on set, ten minutes, thirty seconds—better get on set! Rubicon complied, or she tried to, but the cords caught and held her, now by the abdomen in a controlling embrace which began to hurt, just a little at first.

It seemed decades, but after only one hour and twenty minutes, Rubicon began to climb from morphine's purple swirl. Slowly, she came to, moaning and repeating one word, over and over; the target she had to reach. Now her abdomen ached and clenched like a fist tightly gripping small wet marbles, too many marbles to hold. Inside her head she kept moaning and trying to keep a grip. The moaning helped her to do that. She wondered about marbles, why was she trying to grab them? Holding on to them required that she keep repeating the word, a monosyllabic moan about the only thing that had ever mattered to her next to the other thing, the lesser thing of fame.

Mark.

Mark.

Suddenly Rubicon pulled herself out of the swamp of unconsciousness and realized she was speaking out loud. Mark.

He was right there.

Sitting by her bed, softly napping with reading glasses perched low on his nose. The telly was on, muted, with Kilroy mouthing empty words to an enraptured audience of women. She looked back at Mark. Thank God, he hadn't heard her. She'd never seen him in his reading glasses before. When had he got them? When would she need them herself? Soon, she thought, soon. Rubicon lifted a heavy hand (how it looked like her mother's!) and tapped Mark on the leg.

In fact, he'd never actually been asleep. Just pretending, and he saw she was pulling herself out of the morphine swamp. He'd overheard it all; her morphine soft lips had repeatedly wrapped around the letter M, before with increasing infinite softness, they opened like a kiss in reverse, and she uttered the rest of his name. *Mark*.

So when Rubicon touched his leg, Mark pretended to suddenly awaken. Giving an actorly start, he opened his eyes and lifted his tortoiseshell reading glasses to his forehead. "It all went off beautifully." He smiled. "How are you, silly girl?"

" . . ."

"It's about ten now. Best if you eat something, really."

"Oh . . ."

Rubicon's eyes looked so large and liquid in that pale shadowy face, pupils pinpoints and her skin pale and powdery. Mark knew from his residency days how people differed when they came out of anesthesia. Men sometimes fought imaginary menaces, pulling IVs from their arms and clawing at stitches with bearlike gracelessness. Children lay stunned, still and seemingly boneless beneath the starched sheets' entrapment, trying to be good, thinking goodness will help them escape pain. Women . . . well, women. They know goodness doesn't stop pain, though some remember a time when they believed it would. Women are either weepers or doers. The doers leave the weak netherworld of anesthesia behind them disdainfully, as if it was a shameful postcode they'd driven through on their way to an important meeting. They begin to make to-do lists, they plan renovations, spring cleanings. They try to chat with their doctors as if encountering them at a cocktail event, and are vaguely annoyed when treated like patients. The weepers— and Rubicon looked like a weeper—found release in weakness. Sometimes you could feel the sheer relief of yielding to helplessness stirring the air around them.

However, as his wife (the first one, naturally) had often told him, he was too fanciful. She'd been a doer, and, he suspected, Jenn was one too. Odd, that he'd never before thought of them as alike in any way.

Mark leaned forward to straighten Rubicon's sheets and rumple her matted hair, and she smiled ruefully. Then he shrugged as tears filled her dark eyes. They brimmed over and streamed down her shadowy cheeks, and she touched her face in mild surprise at their effusion, saying, "Well, this is stupid."

And then she really began to blub.

"Not at all, not at all. You'll feel better after." Mark patted her warm shoulder.

After handing her a few tissues, Mark pointed at a beige plastic tray nearby which contained a Tesco raspberry yogurt and two salted crackers. As she reached for the yogurt, Rubicon saw her mother's hand again, the one she'd so often seen stringing beans on their Pinekill porch as WGN transmitted the Cubs game over transistor radio. It was her own hand, of course. Rubicon had never before noticed how the bones and veins had risen from her flesh. She examined the yogurt through thick morphine tears. Its pink plastic image of raspberries and splashing cream was disgusting.

Then suddenly the pain in her abdomen centered and rose, and she threw up.

Mark hadn't warned Rubicon about that. What would be the point? Her body, like every woman's, would try fiercely to reject the blocking of the fibroid's arteries, to restore the life-giving, fetus-feeding blood. The fibroid tumors, the muscle babies nurtured by Rubicon's aging, hormonally-imbalanced womb, were being starved out.

Rubicon threw up for nine hours, between moments of exhausted languor.

Mark stayed with her.

It was, he told himself, the least he could do. He did not tell himself that he enjoyed doing it.

.ઝલ.

BACK AT THE EVERLEIGH HOUSE early that evening, Jenn examined a packet she'd accidentally bought at Waitrose. It had been in the meat aisle, next to rows of ground beef and lamb and pork. She'd been planning to make a nice beef and noodle casserole with maybe a little goat cheese to fancy it up, but now she realized that what was in this packet looked like meat, but it wasn't.

It was some junk called *Quorn*.

It looked just like beef, but kind of grittier and more pebbly. She turned the packet over and read the label—it was made from some kind of mushroom protein. Good Christ. What growing kid wants to come home from school and be told, "Here's some chewy mushrooms—eat up, buddy!"

Maybe after dinner the makers of this stuff thought she'd offer Simon a few broccoli cookies, or a slice of whipped tofu and carob pie.

Not likely.

For half a moment, Jenn thought she might as well just cut the thick plastic package open, just so she could have a taste of the stuff—but then she heard the front door. It could've been Mark coming home from work, but she knew it was Simon. Mark always pushed the front door open slowly, as if half-sure there was something behind it that would leap out to frighten him. Simon opened the door with a sudden bang, then closed it with exaggerated slowness as if to say, "See? I'm being careful." Teenage boys are so cute, thought Jenn affectionately.

"Simon?" she called out. "I've got a question for you."

"Dad called," he replied.

She could hear Simon's progress through the foyer and sitting room, the sounds as he dropped book bag and gym shoes (the latter went one by one with heavy clonks on the wood-paneled floors). The soft rustle as his coat was tossed on a tabletop. The boy rounded the corner, flushed from the cold, but not looking nearly as pinched and peaky as when she'd first met him.

"Simon, do you eat 'Quorn'?"

"Dad's not coming home till late."

They laughed, having both spoken at the same time. Then Simon saw the Quorn package. He rubbed the back of his head unhappily. He'd been eating Quorn since before he could remember. There were pictures of him on his highchair, wearing a Bosnian hand-woven bib and spooning up bits of warmed

Quorn from a pile of mashed (organic, locally farmed) potato. He'd eaten Quorn in vegetable-protein, spelt-roll burgers, on wholegrain, artisan quinoa pizzas, and, most disgustingly, pulverized in wheatgrass, Quorn, and carrot smoothies during a time when Arabella thought they were all far too smugly plump and Westernized. It had been like a summer spent drinking meadow vomit.

"No, Jenn. I do *not* eat Quorn. In fact, I steadfastly refu—"

She raised a plump, manicured hand. "Kid, I'm with you on this. So your father's not coming home?" Jenn stood up, shook her long blond hair over her shoulder, and carried the Quorn package over to the freezer. She opened the door and tossed it in dismissively. Maybe she'd feed the stuff to some vegetarians, one day.

Half a gratified second passed before Simon replied, "Yeah. I don't know why he didn't call *you*. He never usual—"

"He maybe just wanted to hear your voice, Simon." Jenn smiled.

This hadn't occurred to him and sidetracked him from the point for a moment. Had his father wanted a chat? He didn't think so.

After Arabella's death, the two of them had sloped, stunned, around the house. There had been little chatting but lots of questioning silences.

"He's at the hospital," Simon said. "Don't hold dinner 'cos he doesn't know how late he'll be."

Simon and Jenn looked at each other, both thinking it was a little awkward. Inevitable, but awkward. The two of them alone together for an evening. At night Mark was always around. Jenn had become used to soothing the tension between the two of them (which always emanated from Mark, she disapprovingly noted) with lots of bright chatter.

So Jenn and Simon regarded each other over that Portuguese-tiled kitchen island. Sure, nowadays they sometimes watched telly together, but more often he went off with mates after school, mainly because Jenn was always busily repainting all the pine furniture that was in the house, or going to B&Q for plants, or looking at ideas for a new kitchen island, or any one of the endless busy things Simon sometimes worried she did specifically to avoid him.

"So . . ." he said. "No Dad."

"And no dinner. Well . . ."

Jenn thought: It's good. For kids to see that sometimes your plans don't work out, but that you must roll with the punches. Turn dinner into a treat! Makes them feel secure and loved. Jenn flashed a bright smile, and her round rouged cheeks glowed beneath the expensive track lighting installed by Arabella.

"I've got a how-about," Jenn said.

That's what she called an idea, and that little phrase was beginning to get on Mark's wick, while Simon, who had at first thought it was naff, now didn't criticize.

"How about we go to that dumpling place you like?" Jenn said. "The one near the movie theater?"

"Seriously? You said they didn't put enough ice in your coke."

"Kid," Jenn spoke with a meaningful grievance, and her V-tweezed brows lowered. "*No one* here does. I'm going to have to find a way to manage that. It's only frozen cubes of water I'm asking for, for goodness' sake. Not . . . uhm . . ."

"Plutonium?" Simon suggested. "Roc's eggs? Or the Shroud of Turin?"

"Exactly. Awesome examples. So you want to go there?"

Simon looked at Jenn, who was still wearing those weird short trousers she liked, but belted so you could see her curves. And that thick blond American hair that never looked dirty, the whites to her eyes like a child's.

"Maybe we should have a burger?" Simon's downy cheeks flushed in the blotched peachiness that only occurs in youth. "We can go to Burger King, and then . . . well, there's a Will Ferrell showing at the cinema. If you, er—we could . . ."

Jen's eyes sparkled as they hadn't since Mike Bellwether kicked the field goal that'd crushed the Byron Seminoles in the '80 homecoming game. "Do you honestly want to be seen in public with your old Stepma?"

The boy shrugged. "I don't mind."

"Cool! Let me do up my face while you get the movie schedule. Do you know where you do that?"

"Chff. Been doing it for yonks."

"You'll have to show me sometime." Jenn climbed the stairs to spritz herself with *Charlie* (she'd been wearing it since the seventh grade, on and off) and to find her lipstick.

Simon sat down and clicked at the computer to look at the Odeon Cinema's website. He felt rather competent.

They left the house ten minutes later.

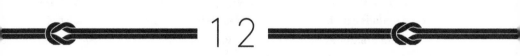

L ATER THAT NIGHT, IN BED, Jenn and Mark had their first real argument.

Before dinner in town, Jenn had bought Simon one of the new mobile phones that had advanced texting capabilities as well as email and internet service. Mark was appalled at the cost of the thing, plus that it involved an enormous bump in monthly payments to Virgin Mobile. He had arrived home late, and very hungry, to find the house empty.

Twenty minutes later, as Mark was sitting on the sofa dutifully eating Ryvita with hummus, Simon and Jenn burst loudly into the house, giggling. The boy was taking pictures of Jenn as she pretended to be a television game-show dolly waving languorous arms at new cars. Mark was silent as Simon showed him the Nokia's capabilities, listening as he tried to tongue Ryvita gunk out of his back molars. Jenn had also bought the boy a Chelsea Football Club phone case and rather expensive but delicate-looking earphones. Simon thought Jenn was brilliant and, Mark knew, next time he wasn't around, the boy would expect her to buy him something again.

Now Mark and Jenn hissed at each other in the bedroom. Lately, Mark noticed, Jenn had been very, very quiet in there.

"Come *on*, Mark. Loosen the purse strings! The kid's had an awful rough year and this was just a little treat. Why're you making such a big *deal* out of this?"

Mark sighed. Here, apparently, was another thing Jenn had in common with Arabella; not only did they both incessantly improve the house, neither of them seemed ever to understand his point of view. And both resented that he thought they should even try.

Mark sat on the corner of the bed and looked at his wife. "Because now *I'm* going to have to be the wanker here. It's going back to the shop tomorrow. A hundred pounds a month so he can impress his friends? Do you have even a clue as to the amount of knife crime in London over these things? You're begging for him to be robbed on the tube one day."

"C'mon. He's a smart boy. He'll keep it in his pocket. You need to give him more credit."

"It's an unnecessary risk, Jenn. From now on, no more major purchases—or signing contracts—for my son until you and I have spoken about it."

If Mark had not been up for sixteen hours, he would never have been rude enough to use the exclusionary words, "my son." But he never would have anticipated their effect.

"Oh. Oh that's how it is, is it? It's *our* son when I'm caring for him the way you want, but *yours* when I'm not following some invisible set of GD instructions?" Jenn sat straight up, and the mango-orange duvet slid down her chest. The blue and white stars on the bodice of her red nightgown were heaving up and down. Mark had never seen Jenn furious before. Her whole face seemed to shift lower, to resettle itself down upon that strong jaw, which drew forward as her eyes darkened.

"Now Jenn, obviously that's not what I—"

Jenn set her teeth and leaned forward. She fixed her husband with a chilling, empty stare.

Suddenly (it was foolish, he thought the next day, foolish for him to have felt this way about her) Mark was frightened. Somehow the anger made her massive, no longer feminine and curvy, but an immutable block of flannelled American Rage. Humorless, with a willed narrowness of understanding that made her seem terrifying, unappeasable. What could she possibly do to him? Mark asked himself later. He didn't know—but suddenly he saw that Jenn was capable of completely unexpected responses.

"I don't give a darn what you *meant.*" Jenn's vowels broadened. "FYI, *Doctor:* I'm not just an equal member of this family—I am the only mother he has now, which means I AM his family and it's sacred, and my voice means the same as yours." The trembling grew in her voice, extending so the hair on her head, the dough-soft flesh on her arms, the folds of her patriotic gown quivered. "In every way there is. You—"

"Jenn, I am merely trying to explain—"

"I am flesh of your flesh, and that means of Simon's too. If you try to remove this God-given blessing of motherhood . . ." Her eyes examined him with such contempt that Mark fought not to drop his own glance.

"Well, of course you are," he said uncertainly. Mark patted his wife's ankle, plump beneath the duvet cover, but she froze him with a glance, and so he stood up, moved to his bureau, and picked up a comb. He could hear her breathing, deep and fast, and remembered how someone had once said that to dismiss Americans as childish was only to half-understand their dangerousness. But that's absurd, of course, with Jenn. It's just that Yanks are weirdly totemic about family. Not Rubicon, but normal Yanks. And they're not the first, when one thought of it. "Flesh of your flesh" was a rather tasteless concept. "I just don't want the boy spoiled."

"People aren't spoiled by love, Mark."

Jenn's patronizing, cool tones now made Mark angry. What a fatuous thing to say! People are spoiled, absolutely ruined, by love every bloody day because others call their warped possessiveness, their angry self-protection, their violent delusions, love.

Take a bloody stand, Mark told himself. Jenn needed to learn that through idealizing Simon's youth, she lost sight of him as a person. Arabella had often asked Mark, "Are you a man or a lapdog?" He realized now he had so enjoyed living without a leash's curbing pull.

"You can see, can't you, that the situation with Simon is a little more complicated than most? And the boy was just using your pity to his advantage?"

"So what?" Jenn shouted in reply. "Let him! I don't care!"

Mark somehow knew that Simon complained about him to Jenn, and that she encouraged it as a form of "bonding." He picked up his cheap watch, the plastic replacement for his much-loved Tudor Rolex, and began over-winding it.

"Thank Christ it's only two more years before he's off to uni," Mark said. "And believe me, my girl, by then you'll be glad to see the back of him." How had he gone from arguing with Arabella about her disinterest in her son to assuring Jenn of her impermanent interest in the boy? Christ.

Jenn stared at Mark as one large vein began to pulse, jagged as a thunderbolt, above her left eyebrow. She thought he was wishing the days of her motherhood away! At the top of her voice, she shouted, "You should be ASHAMED of yourself, Mark. ASHAMED!"

Then she switched off the bedroom light.

Mark stood silently in the dark. Being a man hadn't worked out terribly well. So he apologized. "I'm sorry, Jenn. I'm just knackered, you know. Cream Crackered," he added, for she had once liked it when he'd taught her Cockney rhyming slang. But now Jenn's back just twitched his words away.

After a long moment, Mark went downstairs quietly and poured himself a small scotch. Right, he thought. Bloody Simon—here he is, complicating things again. Mark had never been properly happy since Simon's birth—and yet, he loved the boy piercingly. The sight of his child's solemn face was a familiar ache in the chest, a feeling of always being caught between yearning and loss.

Upstairs Jenn lay awake thinking that never again would she let a man tear her family from her. Never. Ever. Again.

Of course, Mark and Jenn should've discussed Simon and their ideas on child rearing before the marriage. They'd had plenty of chances. But Mark had been dumbfounded by lust and astonishment at his luck, and Jenn . . .? Well, she'd assumed that others' standards of behavior were the same as hers. Since she was a child, she'd been told that her way of life was the envy of the world. Ridiculous for Mark to argue against that. Hence the situation they were in now, of them separately fuming, and Simon next door having overheard more than was good for him. He knew it had been weeks now since Mark and Jenn had had sex.

·೨೭·

TWO DAYS AFTER THE NOKIA phone argument, Mark stopped by Rubicon's flat.

He was carrying a plastic bag from Mark and Spencer's containing two mini-cheesecakes, free-range eggs, organic carrots, prewashed spring greens, a tub of low-fat garlic spread, milk chocolate digestive biscuits, wholegrain bread, Kerry butter, and ten daisies with an attached sachet of long-life preservative.

Rubicon lived on the Barnes High Street, above an Indian takeaway and the kind of hairdressing establishment that has time-yellowed pictures of eighties girls in spiral curls in its windows. An elderly lady wore a vinyl robe within the rain-splattered shop, her fuzzy cheeks cheerfully powdered and rouged, singing along to the radio and waving a ginger biscuit in the air as she perched in the hairdresser's chair. "*We're all going on a . . . Summer holiday, Summer holiday.*" The stylist whistled along as he expertly rolled the lady's fine damp strands of hair into foam curlers.

This was where Rubicon lived?

Not that living over a shop wasn't just fine, Mark told himself, as a Pakistani student carrying a pizza and four large Stellas let himself into the building and Mark trailed in behind him. It was just, well . . . *studenty*. As Mark climbed the stairs, a smell of curry powder and warm clothes dryers emanated rather comfortingly from the shops below. He wandered along the narrow hallway that led to Rubicon's door. Mark realized that until recently, he'd always assumed that Rubicon lived a middle-class life, as they all did. But on what? He asked himself, aromatherapy and memories of fame? Her chic clothes and jaunty bearing seemed a little poignant to him now.

Mark knocked on the door to flat 3. After a moment, he heard movement within and then the sound of Rubicon's voice, rising slow as a bubble from swamp water.

"The door's open . . ."

Mark seized the rather greasy door handle, pushed the thin wooden door ajar, and stepped into Rubicon's flat.

It was a marvel.

For one thing, there were no up-to-date granite counters. No track lighting, or fancy bloody tiles that cost the earth and chipped endlessly. There was no pale and immaculate wooden flooring. No expensive minimalistic window treatments or industrial cooktops or untouched cookbooks or double-tiered ovens or ceramic sinks with restaurant-style spray faucets in brushed steel. No archly retro sofas with oversized coffee tables, no halogen lighting leaking fluorescent grimness, and most divinely of all, no bloody stupid kitchen island.

It was like walking into the past. Into his own student days and earlier, when he'd come home for tea and his mother and Nan would be sitting at a proper kitchen table, with newspapers spread out amid used mugs and biscuit crumbs and orange peels. Light slanted in through bay windows here as he remembered it had back then. It was a dingier cozier kind of light than he'd seen in years, speckled from dirt on the glass.

"Rubicon?" he finally inquired. "Where are you?"

"Mark! What in the name of arse . . .?" Blankets on the futon moved, and Rubicon's pale figure emerged, pushing hair away from her dark-ringed eyes as she propped herself up on one elbow.

Mark just gazed around, blinking.

Rubicon looked around. Oh crap, she thought. It was hardly Vaux-le-Vicomte, was it? From her futon she could see: a large oriental rug on the floor, its colors muddied from overuse, a telly with a wire clothes hanger jammed into where the aerial had been; rather girly curtains, white with red cosmos, sun-faded past their first flush of youth; bookshelves loaded with paperbacks and essential oils, and the odd joss stick hanging out like long rusted nails; small two-ring painted cooktop with Brillo-scratches; a large wooden table clogged with papers and apple cores, and chairs pushed out as if invisible guests were still sitting there, digesting.

The door to the bathroom was open (she'd forgotten to buy a light bulb, so the door was always open) and Rubicon could see the lavender shower curtain and the toilet seat's green terry cover, so tacky but it got *cold* on there, in the dark. Rubicon was dazed with mild opiates, which somehow made it essential that Mark not see the toilet seat cover. She licked her lips and, with an effort, threw the tangled sheets and blankets to the bottom of the futon, and tried to rise to her feet.

Mark, however, thought the whole place was perfect. The most relaxing, comfortable, warm and padded, moreish, come home and take your sodding boots off-ish thing he'd seen in years. A proper bloody kitchen table. It was like time had stood still in Rubicon's flat, here alone in all the world. What utter bastard, he wondered, had come up with the idea of creating an oversized, overpriced wooden box and calling it an 'island' anyway? Suddenly Mark realized Rubicon was trying to stand, holding her stomach and bent over like a question mark.

"You daft—lie back down immediately!"

The dark eyes looked at him, clearly surprised. Then Rubicon gingerly collapsed back into bed and pulled the covers back over herself until only those eyes and that brush-like thatch of hair were visible.

"Right," said Mark, putting the M&S bag down on the table with a bang. "First I'll put the kettle on, and then we'll take a look at you." He gathered up four apple cores, six filmy yogurt lids, and a red wax Babybel cheese wrapper, and deposited them into the trash (which was a Tesco bag hanging off the sink cabinet. And what more does one need? thought Mark). Then he filled the kettle, put the food away, found an old jar and shoved the daisies in it, and wiped the kitchen table before putting the flowers on it. On top of a coaster, of course. Mark was a well-trained man.

"Now." He turned to Rubicon. "Are you hungry?"

"What crazy breeze blew you in here?" Rubicon wondered how much codeine she'd actually downed. "Er. You didn't tell me you were coming, or did you?"

"No. Rather a spur of the moment thing, really."

"Oh. Well . . . here's the old sock." Rubicon gestured weakly. "Be it ever so humble and all that."

"Yes," Mark said. "It's bloody *marvelous.*"

"Well . . ." Rubicon sounded surprised. "I don't know about that. I mean, it's okay . . ."

"No. It's fucking perfect," Mark corrected her firmly. "I thought everyone wanted their home to look like a Swedish hotel nowadays. This honestly is . . ." God, he thought, were there people all over the UK still living like this? Had this been a possibility all along, and if so, why hadn't Arabella, with her loathing of middle-class tat and privilege, never mentioned it? "This is marvelous. Now, do you want Earl Grey or a workman's brew? And I'll make you some eggs, shall I?"

"Oh, I don't want food."

"No—you should eat some protein."

"Okay. Okay. But first . . ." Her dazed eyes looked up at him, bright with a sudden plan she wasn't sure he'd like. The look somehow made Mark smile.

"What is it, you silly girl?"

"Well, could you sit and watch Countdown with me? It's *much* better watched with someone, I always think."

Mark's smile broadened. Then he threw off his cashmere tartan scarf and woolen overcoat and even, daringly, removed his shoes without asking. He made them tea, put the digestive biscuits on a plate, and reorganized Rubicon's pillows so she could sit up properly. Then Mark and Rubicon sat in the bed together with only their elbows touching and watched Carol Vorderman do mental math on the telly.

Mark had not felt so relaxed, so unweighted by expectations, in years. In decades. Ever.

He thought, perhaps one can only properly relax in a home with no children in it. And no sodding granite countertops.

13

A ND SO MARCH SOFTENED INTO April.
    Every year the early springtime daffodils had astonished Rubicon with their hardiness, the resolution with which they pushed up through the frozen earth, the tender, almost fluorescently green stems impervious to unwelcoming weather. Sideways they grew at first, buffeted by winds and angling low to stay safe, until the yellow flowers burgeoned and the stems suddenly swerved upright.

Jenn, of course, had never witnessed this before. It was her first spring in London. She drank her morning coffee and gazed out the French doors at the yard outside, toward the elegantly gnarled tree she'd first seen from Simon's room on the fateful night of Mark's party. Its roots had seemed strangled by ivy, but now daffodils burst around its base in verdant determination.

As for Simon, he simply settled in and blossomed under Jenn's ministrations, basking in her certainty. They shared breakfasts of Weetabix after Mark left for the surgery following family conversations as bright and thin as winter sunlight. Mark had begun to leave earlier each day, with a bounce in his step that Simon had never seen before and which Jenn thought was because of her.

Simon's favorite bit came when he returned from school and he and Jenn broke out the Nutella and toast. Over lashings of hazelnut chocolate spread, the boy taught Jenn about social media. He created a MySpace page for her and assured her she was now part of the wave of the future. He liked to watch her as she bent toward the computer with her thin brows pointed down, her warm round arms brushing against his. They put pictures of the house, of the two of them, on Jenn's MySpace page, and sometimes Mark was in the pictures too, glowering shyly in the shadows.

Jenn wanted to show Mark the MySpace page, but Simon said he wouldn't be interested, and, reluctantly, she realized that was true. Mark was working so late, so often, nowadays—the poor guy was tired out. He'd slouch in front of the TV and watch some lousy old comedy about men who sold junk to people. It was depressing how these characters lived—she'd have preferred something flashy with great clothes, like *Dynasty* back in the day. But she got this *Only Fools and Horses* stuff. Men like weird TV—everyone knows that—but Mark worked hard, and he'd given her this son, this house, this life. As she watched Mark chortle as Del Boy shouted at Rodney in their messy basement apartment, she thought *this is one funny country*—but she'd known that going in.

It struck Jenn as surprising, and it made her sad, that she hadn't found even one woman friend since she'd married Mark. She'd had boatloads of friends back in Pinekill. But here? When she ran into someone she knew, like that Lydia or Caro, all she'd get were the politest brush-offs ever. "Lovely to see you, *must rush—byee!*"

She assumed that Rubicon would come around eventually. *I mean, yeah.* It wasn't great that she'd landed a guy Rubicon liked, but if she'd said no, it didn't mean he'd go for Rubicon instead, did it? Plus, Rubicon never would've cared for Simon like she should. So really, Jenn had helped the universe care for one of its children. Which is as it should be, right?

Right.

She missed Rubicon. Weird when you consider how little time they'd spent together in the last twenty-five years. But she could feel, somehow increasingly, that her old friend was nearby. So she missed her and was often lonely.

During this time Simon also began to lift weights, and sometimes the ceiling over the living room would shake when he dropped them. Jenn clucked indulgently up toward his room. If Mark was home, he would give a start and swear. On the weekends, when Mark was filling out forms for the NHS, Jenn painted that plain pine bedroom furniture in gleaming whites and blues, or admired her new brocaded sofa covers and matching window treatments—the best and brightest the high street could afford. It would be cool if she had a friend to do that with . . . however. Best to remember that a husband's always better than a friend, and a family more sacred. Jenn knew these things. So she'd make tea for Simon, and let him teach her Halo. All those weapons popping up out of corners and from behind boulders! It was so stressful!

"They aren't real, Jenn." Simon laughed.

The boy had begun to lose that vague inward gaze, and days had fallen into a schedule with a sort of sweet normality he would never see again—though the concept of 'normality' is clearly an advertiser's construct, designed to make us feel excluded, willing to do (pay) anything for a sense of acceptance, of worthiness, it's nonetheless a powerful myth.

The normalcy only did some of it, really. Mostly Simon changed because he was thoroughly ravished by love for his stepmother. And this love made him do a very stupid thing. Mark had, we must increasingly agree, been very foolish indeed to marry Jennifer so quickly—and now his son foolishly decided to impress her. His actions were successful, in a way. They certainly brought Jenn and Simon closer. They also brought police to the house for the first time since the investigation of Arabella's murder.

THE BOY TOOK ACTION a month after Jenn and Mark's argument over his mobile phone had begun. They were discussing it again—the walls between the bedrooms were thin, and the boy listened intently. As he again heard his father refer to him as a child, Simon's jaw jutted forward. He was sitting on his too-soft bed, facing the closet. He got up, opened the closet door, and then sat back down on the bed. The bedsprings creaked. Simon continued listening to the *sotto voce* argument next door.

Jenn was treating him as a mate—meaning friend—and now his father was mucking that up by saying "the boy" would be mugged, knifed, in the tube. If he were Mark, Simon thought grimly, he wouldn't mention stabbing . . .

If only *he* could pay for the bloody phone. That'd shut his father up—if Simon could saunter up and tell his dad to keep his precious money, *he'd* manage it from now on. The boy pictured the three of them at dinner, familiar familial tension beneath the overhead dome light's honeyed beam. Jenn's hair gleaming. Mark bollicking on, smugly thinking he could still lay down the law. But something about Simon's composure would make his father hesitate, eye him with mistrust. Simon would casually wipe his mouth on his napkin before leaning back to reach his hand into the pocket of his new Uniqlo skinny jeans (no sagging corduroy for *him*, ta very much). There'd be a pause as Mark and Jenn watched him pull out 120 quid. Or more. Which Simon would then toss on the table. The notes would slide, separate, and Mark's mouth would fall open when his son coolly murmured, "There's the phone, paid for. Now none of it's come out of your precious bank balance."

Simon basked in his vision of Mark's dismayed confusion. Jenn's face would break out into a smile of white-toothed admiration over Simon's coolness, his competency. He'd give her a wink—no wait, that's just Bruce Willis wankery—a chin tilt would be cooler. Then, as Mark would quickly think of another objection, Simon would be ahead of him. "And obviously I've arranged for the monthly statement to be sent to me. From now on. So let's hear no more about it, right, Dad?"

Ah, imagined victory! Mark sputters, Jenn glows, glows firm and admiring and peach-like.

It would take only money to achieve this vision. Simon had no idea of how much privilege was wrapped up in that word, "only." All one had to do, in the mind of a boy raised within the green enclave of Richmond, was re-jigger some arrangements, make a few decisions, reach out one's hand and . . . there would be access to money. His mother' son as much as his father's, the boy was raised on cries of boredom at their bourgeois existence; but these cries had always been accompanied by the swish of Pucci silk, the solid jangle of Swedish car keys, the easeful movement of corks from bottles of French wines.

But actually, Simon was right. In fact, all he did have to do was reach out his hand, and money would be there.

He decided to get the ring out of its hiding space.

He hadn't looked at it, not properly, not since he'd put it in the Braysons' garden after Arabella's death.

Simon rubbed his head, stood up, and closed his bedroom door. He stood still for a moment, listening to movement in the house. The television still blared the faux-somber music from a repeat of *Trigger Happy TV*, meaning Mark was downstairs. The accompanying sound of water rushing through pipes meant Jenn was still in the kitchen, merrily scrubbing something down.

Simon went to his closet and got to his knees. He began moving items out of his way: the fifteen kilogram weights, a deflated football, the toolkit that contained shoe polish, and a naff porn magazine he'd found at a bus stop. His thinking had been that if someone (Mark) were looking for guilty items in the closet, the lads' mag might qualify and the search would be completed. But really, old Tits McGee lying there with her tramp stamp and legs spread was a red herring.

Simon pulled out more items—the Ikea shoe stand holding twelve pairs of old trainers, dress shoes, and sweat-warped slippers. Two felicitously fallen jumpers that covered a deep crack in the pine plank floor at the back of the closet. Using a pen, Simon gouged dried brown candle wax from the crack and pulled out a tiny saran-wrapped packet the size of a pound coin.

A sudden loud "HA!" came from below, and Simon froze—then realized it was his father's dry lone laugh from downstairs. Dom Joly's tired antics, no doubt. Then the blare continued, as did the pipe noise.

Simon tore open the wax-smeared wodge of plastic wrap and pulled out its contents. The rest of her jewelry was gone, God knows where, but here was Arabella's engagement ring. A platinum band with a big oval emerald surrounded by small diamonds. How she'd hated that ring! Simon wondered, not for the first time, why she'd worn it every day.

14

THAT SUNDAY MORNING RUBICON ROLLED over in bed and stretched her long legs out, letting her toes fan and tremble in luxuriant anticipation. Today was the day! She'd rested her dark head on a crooked elbow, short hair sticking up like bird's beaks, and noticed that lush green leaves were finally unfolding on the young tree outside her window. Only buds so far, bright ruffled buds brushing up against the glass. Six a.m. clouds like shreds of cotton candy moved with proud delicacy across early-morning skies, above the friendly round smokestacks of Southwest London. Rubicon thought that close nearby, probably even on this street, some lucky bastard was strolling home late from a post-drunken shag right now—and stopping for a paper.

All over this country, people were picking up the *Times*. There were cups of tea and becrumbed breakfast tables, the telly on mute, necessary Nurofen downed before they crack open the paper, flip through, and comfortingly choose their favorite section, the same every week.

Rubi kicked the duvet down the bed and leaped to her feet. She nearly wiped out on a pair of velour sweatpants she'd left on the floor, but found her footing again and struck a triumphant gymnast's pose. Arms up! She'd crank the radio and make some brekkie and postpone the pleasure of the newsagent. Eggs over easy and Flora-soaked toast, rashers and sautéed mushrooms. Hey, time to celebrate!

She was back!

A crow landed heavily on a slender branch outside Rubicon's window; the branch dipped beneath the sudden weight. The bird emitted an outraged squawk and flew off awkwardly, like a widow's veil seized by a rude gust of wind. Rubicon laughed, saluted the complaining crow goodbye, and danced toward toast and Flora.

By now, Rubicon had entirely recovered after her surgery, though the endless post-procedure vomiting had not stripped her body of her post-Jenn fat. That's what she called it—Jenn-related pudge. The fact is that, having once given in to her appetite, Rubicon found she could no longer go a day on just a banana, or a night without the delights of a consoling Cadbury finger.

But finally Rubicon could put hands down her tight but still-silky pants and feel the knotted fibroid lumps beginning to shrink. The scar by her groin was just a pink exclamation point. All those arteries inside that had been pumping blood to enlarge the tumor, the phantom muscle baby her womb had been determined to feed, were now blocked. Huzzah! Or, in the language of my people, thought Rubicon, *Fuck yeah!*

Biting into a contemplative piece of toast, Rubicon dreamily thought that she'd like to give her remedied interior works a tryout. Find some way to organize a crafty shag so she could make sure all was copacetic on the inside. Chance would be a fine thing.

But then again, sex had always been so overhyped. It looked so, well, *sexy*— and the buildup to it actually was. But when *in* it, unless extremely drunk or practically crowbarred by coke, the intimacy of the act brought a rush of fear which always undid Rubicon. She'd had to leave, get out before the guy did the same, or before he saw through her and realized . . .

Rubicon never knew exactly what someone might realize.

And anyway, who cares! *Style* magazine was out today! People right now were flipping open *The Sunday Times,* still in its proper broadsheet format (the weekday issues had recently gone to tabloid style; pure heresy, though admittedly easier to read on the tube). Grayish white pages were being curled forward, section by section. Front Page News, News In Review, Sport, Business (who cares), the Magazine, the Arts—and finally lovely slender glossy *Style.*

There she'd be. With all the other ladettes from the good old nineties, when the stock market was boom and everyone still hated South Africans, not Americans. That sweet niche of time when political correctness made it perversely allowable to say anything. *Men Behaving Badly* and oh Christ, how the women did too! Girls like her who drank pints and smoked unapologetic fags and mocked and earned all that wonderful dosh. Oh, the grunge-glimmering smoke of adulation!

It had seemed it would go on forever. Like she'd gotten someplace safe, a lauded perch.

Outside, the air still had nighttime's chilled spice to it, but was softening at the edges with springtime sun. Rubicon turned up the end of her road and began climbing the hill. To the right she could see a long lawn sloping down toward the river, stretched out like a *belle époque* beauty draped over an undulating bedspread. All overlooked by the church spires, the low square satellite-dished roofs of council houses, surprisingly near the iron gates of rock stars' homes.

A wonderful land, packed so tightly with people and history and dissent and debate all leavened by humor.

A balding man turned the corner up ahead and headed toward Rubicon. She recognized him from a successful Richard Curtis rom-com, in which he'd played the joyously gay friend of a closeted toff. Now the actor wore a haggard expression and a worn leather jacket. His lower eyelids sagged like the weave of a worn hammock. He was a father, pushing one of those thousand-quid, featherlight baby prams that wheeled the infant beneficently upright like a drooling pope. Resting in the front basket of the pram was *The Sunday Times*.

All over the country, Rubicon reiterated to herself. Hell, even the queen will read about me today, see my picture. Probably not Philip, but the queen will, and Judi Dench and lovely Stephen Fry and Joanna Lumley and . . . ha!

Jenn will too.

As the weary actor passed Rubicon, she could not stop herself from speaking to him. "I'm in that today!" she said. "The paper, I mean. *Style* mag."

"Good on you," he said, and kept moving. The child belched benevolently, and a rivulet of milky fluid shot out of its mouth.

Yuck, thought Rubicon, as she continued climbing the steep pavement and turned onto Friars Stile Road, just at the Chinese takeaway. Next to that was the newsagent's with a sign out front advertising the *Telegraph* (a.k.a. *Torygraph*) and Aero bars and ice-cream coronets. There were notices in the big glass window of things for sale locally: roller blades and cleaning services, language lessons and a coconut shy in the churchyard next weekend.

Ah England, thought Rubicon. Odd how she'd been dreaming of Pinekill again, so vividly, so frequently.

Rubicon swung open the newsagent's door and rickety bells rang. She stalked past the ice-cream freezer and dusty card displays, past the cans of baked beans and tiny sausages, past the lad's mags and *Grazia*. Right up at the counter, in front of a small Pakistani woman with a dark furrowed brow, were the papers. *The Observer*, *The Independent*, *The Daily Mail*, *The Telegraph*, *The World News Weekly*, and the greatest paper of them all, *The Sunday Times*.

Rubicon picked the paper up and held it in high observation, as if it were a firstborn child. It had a wonderful wobbly weight to it. Should she get three? Looking down at the pile, she saw there were only seven there. Maybe she should get five. But first . . . oh, she couldn't wait any more.

Ladettes to Ladies: When Bad Girls Grow Up!

"You must buy paper if you read." The woman behind the counter had a surprisingly harsh voice for one so tiny and somber-shawled.

"Oh, I'm going to buy it! I'm going to buy *loads* of them. I'm just looking for—I'm in this!" Rubicon waved the magazine flag-like and then reopened it. Contents: Going up/Going Down, Miss Mills, Ask Sally . . . ah! "Ladettes: Where Are They Now?"

Page 36.

Rubicon flipped the pages eagerly. Various celeb party shots—she'd be there soon—snarky blind-eye gossip bits, more on McQueen's hoof shoes, every goddamn week with the hoof shoes . . . and Page 35.

She turned one more page. Ah!

There they were! The famous blondes and glacéed brunettes from the shoot. Leaning on ladders, wearing tiaras, throwing pieces of white-frosted cake at one another (though not at Patsy; no one had been allowed to throw anything at Patsy). Hoisting pints, hoyden grimaces despite their enforced kitten heels.

But . . .

Rubicon scanned the picture again and again, not believing it.

She'd stood right next to Denise Van Outen and her new lip job—right on the second rung of that ladder. Rubicon had held a pint glass and a fag, made the devil's horn with her fingers, stuck her tongue out.

But there was only Denise. No one to the right of her, though the ladder mysteriously remained. Unoccupied. The bulk of the newspaper slid to the floor from beneath Rubicon's arm.

"Pick that up!" ordered the woman behind the counter.

Rubicon didn't hear a thing. She tremblingly flipped *Style's* pages back and forth, her suddenly sweaty fingers sticking to the magazine's thin glossy sheen. One paragraph was dedicated to updates on all the ladettes, on all included in the piece.

Which Rubicon hadn't been.

And nobody had bothered to tell her. Rubicon stepped unseeingly over the dropped newspaper and staggered out of the newsagents, still clutching *Style*. The woman behind the counter banged her beringed hands down. "You pay me now, you horrid thief!"

But Rubicon had already walked around the corner. Gone. I am done, she thought as the woman's shouts retreated behind her. And oh, I am so stupid. So stupid to hope like that.

She went home, drank a bottle and a half of cheap plonk, vomited, and took to her bed.

.ᕲᕤ.

SIMON WAS LATE COMING HOME from school the following Monday, but Mark arrived home on time, an increasingly rare event. Jenn felt that with all her men in the house, her blessed family, she should make a proper dinner. It all probably would have come down the same in the end, she thought—but later she wished Mark had not been present, that it'd been only Simon and herself. She learned too much about her husband that evening,

The evening began so well too; it was even idyllic, if suburban idylls are your thing. The three of them, a modern blended family, sitting around the teak dining room eating a meal of smashed sweet potatoes with marshmallow, roasted lamb, and Waitrose's finest frozen peas. Jenn felt haloed within the domed beam of the overhead chrome light. It rendered the back yard invisible, apart from that warped tree which absorbed cloudy moonlight. As always, Jenn pictured an audience outside admiring the perfect family. The stocky boy, the work-weary man, the gleaming blonde.

If you looked closely, however, or at least without vision blurred by tele-wishful clichés, it would have been clear the atmosphere was already tense.

The ongoing mobile-phone argument had started up again after the Nokia in Simon's pocket began pinging, an echoing underwater sound. Simon slid the phone from his pocket, shot his father an expectant look, and silenced the phone before re-holstering it.

Mark responded as if on cue (which it was; Simon had set the alarm to go off at this time). "Madness. One hundred and twenty quid. I was never given any toy that costly as a child—"

"He's not a child, Mark—" Jenn scooped peas, smug with butter, into her mouth.

"It's not a *toy*, Dad. And actually . . ." Simon wiped his mouth with a napkin, leaned back, and felt in his back pocket. Nothing there. Shit! Panicked, Simon checked the other one.

"—I actually had to *work* before I had expensive things, so I apprecia—"

"I keep telling you, Mark, it's like jeans when we were growing up. You *have* to have the right ones or people think you're a dork. I remember one girl, you won't believe it but her name was Hilary Hamburger. She wore—"

Alas, Jenn's Hilary Hamburger reminiscences will remain forever unshared, for Simon had located his wodge of money, which was so large he'd had to put it in his hoodie's kangaroo pocket. Tightly rolled, it was about the breadth of a shot glass. He pulled the money out, raised the roll above table level, licked a self-impressed thumb, and began counting notes. Jenn's words trailed off. Mark put his fork down.

"Fifty. A hundred. And . . ." Simon pulled a final note off the back of the wodge, and tossed the money on the table. "And twenty." Jenn had never seen fifty-quid notes before; they were very large and curling, like rectangular cabbage leaves. From the front of the house came the sound of someone opening the gate, but the Everleighs didn't notice.

Mark looked from the banknotes to his son, who returned the gaze defiantly, kind of. Simon gulped, so actually the look came off as nervous. Jenn, however, was impressed.

"Simon, did you get a job?" Gleaming white American tombstones flashed between lipsticked lips. "How great of you!"

"Jenn," Mark said. "Please. Where did that come from, Simon?"

Simon strove for a Bondian cool while realizing that he really should have expected that question. But still, in for a penny . . . He saw that Jenn was looking at Mark through narrowed eyes. This gave him confidence. "I've arranged for Virgin to send the monthly bills to me. So it won't affect your precious bank balance any more. It's been set up so—"

BANG!

Jenn nearly jumped out of her seat.

BANG BANG BANG!

Mark and Simon froze. They recognized that sound, the righteous insistence of that knocking. Jenn, who didn't yet associate it with ignominious nights in a holding cell or intrusive questioning, nonetheless realized that this was something serious. Definitely not someone dropping by with a neighborly casserole.

"Metropolitan Police!" A brusque voice echoed through the house.

Mark looked at Simon, and suddenly his heart seemed filled not with blood but with liquid dread. His son's ruddy face had gone ashen. And as his eyes fixed on his father's in shame, the defiance drained . . . but something else was there. A plea. Oh God, thought Mark. Oh God, it's come.

Mark felt the chair scrape the hardwood floor beneath him. He was standing. His heartbeat pulsed within his ears—did that mean others could hear it? Hard and fast.

"Stay here, you two."

Mark threw his napkin down. It fell over the money lying there.

BANG.

"I'm COMING!" Mark shouted. He turned his head, finally releasing his son's gaze.

Simon seemed to see a flickering on the deck behind Jenn. It wasn't candlelight. It seemed more a twilight shadow, a flickering of irritated laughter: Arabella as she used to pace the deck outside, rings on fingers, resentment in heart, wine in hand as she fumed over her trapped bourgeois existence. She should be in Morocco, smoking hookahs; she should be in California, guruing film stars.

She should be anywhere but here.

As Mark walked away from the table, Simon looked down at the lamb shank on his plate, fat pearlizing between gray muscle. When he raised his eyes again, that complaining shadow was gone. Only the hobbled tree was there, at the end of the yard, branches swaying like sleeves on a torn garment.

BANG!

Mark paused just before he left the room. That look on Simon's face. He had to ask. "Simon. Is there anything I need to know?"

Jenn's eyes narrowed again. "Mark, what are you asking him?"

"What?" Simon's voice was high. "Why are you asking me that? I haven't done—I *swear*, I haven't done anything!"

"I'm sure your father doesn't think you did!" Jenn leaned toward the boy, put out her hand.

Mark looked at them, then left the room.

"It's the police," said Simon unnecessarily. They were here a lot, right after Mum . . ."

BANG.

Jenn heard Mark open the front door. She walked over to Simon and put her arm around him.

She realized that her stepson was trembling.

1 5

MURMURINGS FROM THE HALLWAY. THE sound of feet (how many? it seemed like a lot) being wiped on the doormat with grim thoroughness. Jenn pictured Mark standing there holding the door open in his stockinged feet. Somehow knowing he was shoeless while watching, *allowing*, this intrusion, highlighted weaknesses in him. He should be protecting their precious family; threatening to get on the phone to some lawyer, standing up to these (gunless) flatfoots, not watching them rub their soles on his welcome mat.

Anyway, Mark did not stop the cops from coming in, or call a lawyer, or even raise a word in protest against the intrusion. Instead, he padded sock-footed back into the room with a clutch of cops behind him.

"Don't worry, sweetie," Jenn murmured to Simon as she squared her shoulders. "Whatever's up, I'll handle it." Someone had to reassure the kid, for Christ's sake. (Not to get all blasphemous, but if Mark didn't man up, who would? Jenn would, she vowed. Jenn always would.)

She discerned a deep voice approaching from the hallway, muttered replies from Mark. A woman's voice, often interrupted by the man. ". . . information received . . . a pawn shop on the high street in Twickenham . . ."

Simon shot Jenn a fearful glance. There were sudden haggard bags beneath the boy's eyes. The contrast between his youthful skin and those haunted eyes made him look like a boy in a French movie. Jenn leaned against him supportively, but he was frozen. She'd learn him. He'd come to trust her fully. He thought she smelled like a combination of apples and antiseptic.

Mark was saying (*bleating*, thought Jenn), "I'm certain he's never been there. And this is an incovenien—" Simon pulled away from Jenn.

"I should go upstairs. I need to—"

"You're not going anywhere, kiddo. We go through stuff together. Hello!" This last was to the cops.

"Mrs. Everleigh?" Two police officers, just like on TV. The man was rumpled, in a dark overcoat, black jeans, a virulent yellow shirt. His shaved head might've given him a tough guy appearance, but it was ruined by pink bobbling jowls around damp rosebud lips. The woman next to him was more official-looking, if only because of the exasperated gleam in her small eyes. She was taller, dishwater-blond, in black trousers and a buttoned-up blue shirt.

"Yes. Hi. You guys realize you're ruining our family time, right? It's the middle of dinner and—"

Isabelle Stoddard, the policewoman, didn't like the look of Jenn from the get-go. First, Jenn's blouse had sprung a button when she'd put her arm around Simon, so there was a gaping expanse of ruddy cleavage bulging from a blue lace bra. Second, well, where to start? Dyed blond, the seeming rows of sharp white teeth, the page-three-girl pink lipstick. Men, supposedly educated men, are endlessly predictable. No surprise to Stoddard that her colleague stepped forward eagerly, his hand extended to Jenn.

"Inspector Drape. You all righ'?"

"I'm fine." Jenn's cold hands with their strong fingers wrapped around Drape's. "I'm assuming this is kind of important, for you guys to interrupt us, right? So maybe I should get on the horn to our lawyer?" (I hope Mark has one, she thought. He must, right?)

"Oh no no, no need for that, I mean for a lawyer, Mrs. Everleigh. It's only—"

Drape's eyes flickered downward, making Jenn realize her shirt had come slightly open. She fixed the button but remained firmly by Simon's side.

144

"Simon." Mark edged forward. Why on earth, he wondered, was Jenn talking about lawyers so soon? It shouldn't presume guilt, of course, but it *does*, dammit. "Simon. The police say you sold jewelry at a pawnbroker's today."

Jenn, Simon, and Mark all made a palpable effort not to look at the money under the napkin, near the platter of congealing lamb, on the dining-room table.

Stoddard thought they were hiding something.

". . . to a what?" Simon asked. "I never—"

"They have CC footage. Of your son outside the store."

". . ."

"So?" said Jenn, when Simon was silent. "That's not illegal, right?"

"It is, actually," Stoddard smiled tightly. "Minors are not permitted to use these establishments. Which is why Simon paid a homeless man twenty quid to sell a ring for him, while he waited outside."

Phwoar, Drape thought as Jenn's white smile clicked back into action. The doctor had a bit of all right there. It didn't look like he could handle that sort of acreage, but then he was a deep one. Fair dues. Drape adjusted his trousers.

Simon's eyes narrowed.

STODDARD SPOKE UP. "THE PAWNBROKER, a Mr. Huston, rang us this evening." Her voice was soft, but authoritative.

Mark and Simon both wondered if she'd been to the same posh girls' school as Arabella

"Oh yeah," said Jenn. "I told him he should do that." Simon looked at Jenn in astonishment. "I mean, what good is jewelry to a kid, right?"

"That's not quite the issue, *Mrs.* Everleigh." Drape and Mark could tell that the emphasis on *Mrs.* was an insult in some unfathomable feminine way. "Mr. Huston belatedly realized that the ring Simon pawned was on a list of stolen items."

Jenn was silent. Uh oh, she realized. The kid was in hot water.

Mark muttered, "Jesus."

"Actually." Drape was never happy when Stoddard got to say more than a few sentences in a row, particularly when a saucepot blond was in the room. "It was among the items Dr. Everleigh reported as missing after his wife's murder."

The liquid dread feeling Mark had experienced earlier returned. However, the dread was blood no longer frozen but coursing fast and heavy through his veins. Everything seemed to be happening in slides, an old-fashioned slide show, as Mark turned his head click click click to look at his son.

Oh Simon, what have you done?

Jenn raised her chin, tightened her grip on the boy, and prepared to fight.

Family.

MARK'S FACE HAD ALREADY TRAVERSED from a blustery red to pale, shocked defeat, so Jenn had to think quickly. "Oh—I think I messed up! I'm so sorry . . . it's all totally my fault. Honestly, I just spaced. See we found this ring last week and—"

"Jenn," said Mark. "No, we didn't."

Jenn's mouth hung open. How dim was her husband? She stared at him, standing there in his stupid stockinged feet. Now's the time to *fight*, not let the cops walk all over you. Her round blue eyes sent an imperious get-on-board-fathead message to him, but he just shrugged.

Like he didn't even want to try to help his son out!

Thinking fast, smiling hard, Jenn fell on the dumb blond sword—a trick she'd been using since junior high. "Oh my God! Mark—did I forget to tell even *you*?" She placed a hand against her forehead. "Lordy, I am such a goofball sometimes! See, we found this ring last week—it was last week, right, Simon?"

"Yes." Simon said. "Five days ago, actually." He couldn't believe Jenn; never in a million years had he expected this. Just look at how she stepped forward, chin up. America to his rescue!

"Right! It was in the like safe hiding place your wife left it, so I guess it never actually was stolen. I didn't know you thought it had been! Anyway, I just thought, well, it's probably Simon's now and you know how kids can always use money . . ."

Drape watched closely as Jenn prattled on. He could detect the outline of her nipples beneath that blue shirt.

Stoddard, whose arms were crossed over her own chest, interrupted. "And where did you find the ring?"

"Well," said Jenn, trying to think of something plausible. "It was weird—we were making dinner, see . . . "

"We found it in the shed," interrupted Simon, who remembered seeing police rigorously inspect the kitchen inch by inch in the aftermath of his mother's murder. "In a flowerpot. Behind the wine."

Drape pulled his eyes away from Jenn's frontal development. "Really?" His voice was wary, skeptical.

"Oh that's right!" Jenn said. She gave a comic smack to the side of her head with her hand. "I'm such a *spacehead* sometimes. He's right. I was planting some impatiens under the big tree out there, and Simon helped me—"

Mark could feel Jenn sending waves of instruction to him—*back me up; stand up and fight; find your game face, come* on! No idea what kind of trap she might stupidly be creating for herself—and for his bloody son. He groaned silently and stared at the ceiling. Fists clenched within corduroy pockets.

Yes. He'd finally said it, to himself at least. She was stupid—and so confident she didn't know it. The dangerous kind of stupidity.

"Interesting," said Stoddard.

Drape pulled out his mobile and pressed some buttons.

Jenn's white smile with its gleaming incisors encompassed both officers. "So I was like, hey, Simon—"

"Hold on a minute, Mrs. Everleigh," Drape said. "I'd like to double-check something."

Jenn said, "Sure, come on back tomorrow some time and—" But she heard the front door of the house opening again, and heavy footsteps approaching. *More of them?* Jenn thought, *Didn't even wipe their feet on the mat.* "Seriously, guys? We're in the middle of dinner—"

Two uniformed police officers walked through the sitting room, wearing those funny little curvy hats with black-and-white checks on them. One was a petite dark woman with a pale mouth like an inhalation of the word "Oh!" The other was a beefy Irish man with a wide smile and dead eyes. His uniform was too small; ham-hock shoulders tested seams with every gesture.

Drape interrupted Jenn, nodding to Stoddard. "Ask him," he said.

Stoddard thought turned toward the constable and said, "Didn't you search the garden last year, O'Donnell? After the death of the former Mrs. Everleigh?"

"Certainly I did," said the constable. "That was after the detective sergeants examined it."

"Including the shed, isn't that right?"

"Oh yes. Everything examined."

Uh oh, Jenn thought. Just bluster through. "Well, all I can tell you is the ring was there, just, you know, in some *dirt*—"

"All bags of soil and boxes were emptied," the constable implacably continued. "Poured out. All items examined. All bottles of wine and liquor."

And Christ there'd been a lot of them, O'Donnell remembered righteously.

He was a teetotaler and found the British attitude toward drink shocking. The shed, with its thousand pounds' worth of intoxicant, was in his opinion a monument to godlessness.

"Well, clearly you guys missed something—" Jenn fought on, despite Simon' silence and Mark's refusal to meet her eye.

"We emptied the shed, examined the ground, re-examined every removed item."

Drape (who'd walked off with a rather nice bottle of Meursault the day the shed had been emptied), said, "Could you have missed a small item of jewelry, O'Donnell?"

"Oh no, not at all. Between myself and the detective team, no."

Jenn tried again, "Well, nothing's certain in this world, guys—"

O'Donnell's wide smile vanished. His mouth set stubbornly beneath those dead eyes. "It was a systematic and complete emptying and examination, Sir."

There was a pause. It was long enough so everyone heard a noise from the back of Jenn's throat. A loud click. O'Donnell examined Jenn. Small and curvy and hand-reared, he'd wager; he liked looking at her, but knew it was for the wrong reasons. His eyes met Stoddard's. He didn't particularly like looking at her, but there was nothing wrong in that.

"Right," said Drape. The atmosphere became businesslike; no more conferring with the Everleighs.

Simon felt the entrance of the constables had pushed him from the center of the scene, and he skulked miserably behind the dinner table. He stuck his index finger into the platter of cold lamb. The meat was cool, yielding, like the flesh of someone's cupped palm. He put his finger in his mouth.

"I'm quite certain," said Stoddard, "that you did not find that ring in the shed, Mrs. Everleigh."

"Really!—"

"We do need your permission, however, to question Simon. As he's a minor."

"Well, you're not going to get—" Jenn began stoutly.

"That's fine." Mark raised a silencing hand toward Jenn. "You can question him." The flecks of gold, that Arabella gold, stood out in Simon's eyes as he stared at his father, wondering what he was playing at?

As for Jenn, she hated Mark at that moment.

Why were men so *weak*?

.৯৫.

IT WAS A LONG NIGHT. Mark and Simon left for the police station, where Simon would, Jenn knew, crumble like feta cheese under questioning. She remained at the house, listening to the two constables pull Simon's room apart looking—for what? She wondered. For the first time in her life, Jenn opened a bottle of wine and drank a glass alone. She stood on the deck outside the French doors, flat-footed in her on-trend velour sweatpants and tightly-buttoned blouse, staring out over the moon-dappled garden with the sway-limbed tree at the end of it. The flowers she'd planted beneath it had wilted from lack of direct light, from the ugly tree sucking up what little nourishment was in this tired city soil.

She'd hire someone to cut that tree down, she thought. Or, even better, pay Simon to do it. Always good for a kid to have a job.

Inside the house the constables moved from Simon's room to the kitchen, again, pulling everything out of the cupboards, moving the appliances from the walls.

Whatever they were looking for, they didn't find it.

.�૭ᙖ.

AT THE POLICE STATION ON Kew Road, Mark and Simon sat in a small oblong room with Stoddard and Drape. A tape recorder (a remnant of the analog age, plastic and rectangular, with grudgingly hard-to-press buttons and a window which displayed the slick spools of cassette tape as they ticked around) sat on the table between the two sides: Mark and Simon, Stoddard and Drape. Drape was chewing a candy that stank of chemical banana flavoring, and there was a framed poster of a Corfu sunset on the wall. Public service posters hung on the wall stating the hazards of binge-drinking, the potential dangers of bombs hidden in left-luggage on the tube, and the increasing frequency of knife violence relating to mobile-phone theft.

Mark looked pointedly at the last poster and then at Simon, who pretended not to notice. Much of the wind had been taken out of Simon's sails by the absence of Jenn, Mark felt. He was right about that, in a way—but only for a moment, only for this moment. For Simon had discovered one tremendous fact that evening: in Jenn he had a champion, an anchor, a source of solace and definition.

And he would protect that, whatever happened.

Anyway, we've all seen it. The police room, the clicking on of the cassette recorder, the police stating the time and date of the interview, the people present. Ever since *The Silence of the Lambs* had block-blustered female slaughter, thousands of television episodes had featured cops questioning folks about their actions on the night of some woman's blood-splattering demise. The interview process had seemed almost comfortingly familiar to Mark and Simon right after Arabella was slaughtered, but for a while afterward the two of them avoided crime telly. However, in the ensuing eighteen months, they'd again become inured to the rituals of female killing and questioning of suspects. There were simply too many to avoid.

By this time, a year and a half after Arabella's death, no one had ever found the weapon, Mark's beloved vintage Rolex Tudor watch, or the other jewelry stolen. The pawning of the ring awakened police attention to the Everleigh household. To both Mark and Simon, this evening already had a dull dreamlike quality; they had been here before . . . the questions, the story spouted then retracted.

As Drape dislodged a particularly large wedge of banana chew from one of his molar teeth, he nodded to Stoddard. She began the dialogue.

"Mr. Everleigh, we have your permission as your son, Simon Everleigh's guardian, to question him about a ring pawned at 4:35 this afternoon at the Huston pawn shop in Twickenham?"

"Yes."

"This is a ring belonging to your late wife, Arabella Everleigh?" Stoddard placed a small plastic bag on the table, containing the platinum and diamond ring.

"Yes."

"And you have remarried since that time? Your current wife's name is . . . Jennifer Everleigh?" Drape's damp rosebud mouth savored his juicy tropical sweet as he mused upon the doctor's second wife, who bore a strong resemblance to the greatest of the eighties page-three girls, Samantha Fox. Legendary.

Mark nodded glumly, then, remembering the tape recorder, he replied, "Yes."

"Right. Now, Simon . . ."

Mark felt tension vibrate through his son's body, saw the boy rub his sweating palms on his jeans. Was Jenn right? Right to defend the boy without question or reserve? No, Mark thought—only half-listening to his son identify himself for the tape recorder—that was absurd. It was lax, lazy. She was wrong to think that's parental love.

And for Simon to be found with that ring! Mark had spent hours creating a list for the insurers of exactly what was missing after Arabella's murder. What would the boy say about where—and when—he found it?

Mark mused passively on, asking himself how other people seemed to know when they should act, and when they should be silent. Proper *blokes*, men like Daniel, seemed to know these things instinctively. Mark had wondered this many times in his life. When Arabella told him she was unsatisfied. When it became clear first, then again and numbingly again that she'd taken lovers, each a temporary Band-Aid over her miserable dissatisfaction with Richmond, with Mark, with the soullessness of English suburban life. Mark now kept contemplating, trying to identify exactly where and when he had become so feeble that he simply didn't care anymore, scarcely paid attention . . .

Wait, what had Simon just said?

The dour businesslike feeling in the room suddenly crackled with energy. What had he missed? Mark leaned forward, wishing he could hit rewind and listen to the last few moments of the cassette.

"Why didn't you tell us that last year, Simon?" Drape asked.

"I don't know. I simply . . . I was kneeling there on the floor—I'd tried to stop the blood. She was dead but I was *trying*. I realized I was kneeling on something small but lumpy. And it was the ring."

"Simon," Mark said.

"Please, Dr. Everleigh."

Mark stared at his son, appalled. (By the way, Mark's male ideal, Daniel, would absolutely have stopped the questioning at this time, and found the kid a solicitor. Mark fell silent.)

Habit, eh? Don't fight because there's no point turns into can't fight because you don't know how. Mark had become so comfortable in his semi-dissociation that he realized he'd lost the ability to spring into action. He could even *feel* where that ability had been, somewhere in the back right corner of his mind—but now that cluster of neurons was flabby, useless from long-enforced paralysis.

"Let's unpack that statement, shall we, Simon?" Stoddard spoke calmly, but could not hide a slightly excited warmth in her plummy tones.

The doctor sat pale and gray-faced, staring at his son. Simon's fists were clenched, and thick tears stood in his eyes.

As for Stoddard, she no longer believed Mark had killed his wife, and had never believed it as fervently as Drape and the constables had for a while. To her it was neither revelatory nor particularly shocking that a husband would tolerate his wife's contemptuous philandering—perhaps that's a class thing, or simply a glimpse into Stoddard's background.

But the son? Hm.

"And you've had the ring since then?"

"Uh huh." Simon wiped his nose, ran his thumbs along his eyes.

"You knew that it was extremely valuable and reported as stolen, along with other items. Why did you not tell us you had it? Or tell your father?"

Simon's face reddened in blotches as he tried not to sob. "I dunno. I'd just found my mother on the floor, dying. Maybe whoever did it was still in the house. Or the ambulance people would stomp on it or *I don't know*. It's just, if there's a diamond on the floor, you pick it up, yeah? So I put it in my pocket and called out to the Braysons, then a hundred police came in and I got taken next door."

"Your house was searched that day."

"*I* wasn't," said Simon. "And when you took my clothes to look for the guy's hair or DNA or—I mean the guy who killed Mum—I just moved it over to the new clothes." This was a lie, but Simon didn't want to implicate Jack Brayson.

"Did you?"

The boy hadn't been searched after finding his mother's body. The day of his mother's murder, Simon had been out with friends skateboarding near the Tesco's, and then they'd all gone to the Odeon Cinema. These friends had vouched for him, and he'd been briefly visible on the CCTV mounted outside the store—his thick shock of hair differentiating him from the clutch of other loose-jeaned, hoodied boys circling awkwardly around, their £200 skateboards revealing the sullen gangsta-rap swaggers as the posings of privileged offspring. The Odeon also had footage of the boys buying tickets and messing about near the pick-and-mix before going in to see *Elf*.

"Yeh. I mean yes. I didn't remember it till later when you lot asked about missing jewelry. Then the penny dropped. I realized—maybe it's bad that I had it? So I hid them—it—in the Braithwaites' garden for a bit."

Drape made a solemn sucking noise as he wrote a note for his constables: dig around that garden, have someone ask a few questions of those neighbors. Then he yawned and picked his teeth with his pen. A glob of candy dislodged from his molar, which Drape examined and then returned to his mouth. Stoddard watched this with horrified fascination. Mark regarded it dully.

"Another question, Simon." Stoddard rang a bell on the table, and a bright-eyed officer immediately swung the door open as if arriving at a surprise party.

"Sir? Ma'am?"

Drape passed the note to the eager constable, who held it aloft like an Olympic torch. The door shut behind him.

Simon had a sudden image of the constable sprinting down the hallway, his tongue lolling like a Labrador's.

Meanwhile, Mark was looking again at Arabella's engagement ring, which rested in a plastic bag on the table. It looked expensive and slightly shabby. He felt no emotional connection to it whatsoever. "Simon," he asked. "Are you certain this is the only thing you found?"

"Good question, that," Drape said. "I was just about to ask it."

Simon nodded miserably. "Yeah. I mean, the guy—whoever he was—didn't drop anything else. Not that I found, anyway."

Mark refused to give in to the impulse to put his head in his hands. He realized he'd just heard Simon use the word "them" when talking about hiding the ring, which could be a slip of the tongue or could mean he had hidden more than one item.

What a fucking shitshow this all was.

And suddenly, sitting in the police station with his clear-eyed son beside him, Mark blamed this all on Jenn. *She* bought Simon that sodding mobile. Everything had been fine, died down since the gruesome time last year and now—here they were again. Fluorescent lights and tape recorders, crap coffee in Styrofoam cups and the smell of fear and Vim.

Mark now—and always later on—saw Jenn as he first did that night when Rubicon brought her to his house. That complacent heaviness as she emerged from the rain. The peevish, self-satisfied tilt of her plucked eyebrows—that was what he'd noticed first, before the hair and the lips drawn back in a smile of pink acquiescence. The sweet unpleasing scent of cheap cosmetics and antiseptic. In a completely new country, but it never occurred to her—not for an instant—that perhaps she was wrong . . . For her smug coddling of his son, for her showing the boy how to lie to the police, to twist the truth with an unreserved certainty that it was the right thing to do because it was the *winning* action to take.

Mark cleared his throat. His voice emerged, squeaky as it had sounded in his younger years. "I'm ending this questioning now. It is well past—past my son's bedtime."

Stoddard's beady, algae-green eyes looked at Mark musingly, but the interview ended.

16

Back at home, the boy didn't even look at his father. He dropped his coat on the newel post and headed upstairs. The sound of running water came from above—Jenn showering. Simon closed his door quietly. Jenn's shower immediately switched off.

She knew they were back.

Mark walked into the lounge, turned on the telly (some "reality" faff about fourth-rate tabloid celebs living on a desert island, dating, gossiping and arguing while courting melanomas), then hit the mute button. He heard Jenn's steps above, heavily padding along the hallway. She paused at the top of the stairs. Mark, who was thinking of pouring himself one of his increasingly large whiskeys, paused too.

He heard Jenn turn away from the stairs.

Mark put ice in a glass.

.ᴔꙶ.

Simon lay on his narrow bed, beneath *The Exorcist* poster. He looked up to see the inverted image of a priest standing on the abandoned street beneath a full moon. A tap sounded on his door. Jen, with her bustlingly humble awareness of a teenager's need for privacy, rarely ventured into Simon's room. But now she tapped on the door, entered, and sat on the too-soft, narrow mattress next to her stepson's reclined form.

He shifted aside to make room for her to sit.

Simon closed his gray-green eyes, the slightly oily lids almost opalescent with fatigue. Jenn was in her bathrobe and smelled of chemical green apple shampoo.

"Hey, pal." She reached out and smoothed his hair.

Simon's lids flickered, but he said nothing. For a long moment, neither did Jenn. A creak came from the staircase, then silence.

"You poor kid. I just want to make sure you're okay." Leaves tapped against the bedroom window, and in the garden, the dead tree outside twitched beneath low-passing clouds. "It's always seemed to me like you had to grow up real fast." Jenn's voice thickened but her fingers still gently, ever more gently, smoothed Simon's hair. "Me too . . ."

Jenn lowered her voice. "When I was just a hair older than you are, a death made me grow up fast too."

"Someone died?" Simon's eyes opened, but he kept his head still, so she wouldn't take her fingers from his hair.

"Yeah. I'll tell you about it all, someday, maybe. See, these things sort of become bookmarks, you know. Like these permanent bookmarks in life of before and—after."

"I dunno if an 'after' ever really comes, with stuff like this. Dad thought it did, but not me." His eyes closed again, though the room was shadowy, lit only by the moon outside. He felt like that lone figure on the poster, paused before moving up a jagged hill.

Jenn's voice oozed pity and compassion. "It comes. Things are not the same as before, but it does come. And it's not as tough for your father as it is for you. It's different, with mother and child, when one loses the other."

The hallway was silent. Jenn continued speaking in a low voice. "What you and me have been through, it's kind of like riding a wave of pain. It goes, but then it comes back at times. At the darndest times." She sighed.

Simon realized that Jenn had been a mother. He should've known that, from the way she'd feast her eyes on him sometimes, when she thought he wasn't looking. Poor old Jenn.

"You learn to ride the wave," Jenn continued. "And you're doing great. Tonight will turn out to be not a big deal. We'll come apart, and we'll come together again, that's how family works." Simon grunted disbelievingly, and Jenn grasped his firm arm with strong, manicured hands. "Don't forget you've got me now. Whatever happens."

The boy shut his eyes, and a silent sob swelled inside him. It rose and shuddered within his chest, but he didn't cry. Instead the sob broke, like ice cracking within his breastbone, into a flood of joy.

.୨୧.

MARK STOOD OUTSIDE SIMON'S HALF-OPEN door, quietly listening to their conversation. Simon and Jenn remained, unmoving, in the darkened room together. Then Mark walked away, down the hallway and into his room, where he lay on his own bed.

The bed he shared with Jenn, rather. He lay down like an old man takes to a gurney—stiffly, adjusting his body so he is lying straight. After a bit, Mark began repetitively to rub his sweat-soaked palms on the duvet cover, an orangey Habitat pattern called "Mangoes Manana," which Jenn had bought and he disliked enormously.

Ten minutes later, Jenn pushed the bedroom door open. She wore a blue sateen robe and a microfiber turban that pushed her eyebrows up into a Croyden facelift. After husband and wife regarded each other silently for half a moment, Jenn turned and left the room. Soft slippers padded heavily down the stairs.

Mark turned his head to look out of the window, at the clay-pot roofs along the street, ugly television aerials stabbing low clouds in genuflection to the great god media. Eventually, realizing that no one was going to comfort him, Mark went downstairs to finish his drink.

.୨୧.

JENN STOOD IN THE KITCHEN, listening to Mark's footsteps as he descended. What was his problem? She'd just given him a chance to not have a fight tonight, and he was coming down after her? She'd planned to sleep on the sofa, but soon Mark's bony butt would be on it as he sucked on some booze and stared at the muted TV.

But then, maybe he wanted to apologize. Or needed some advice.

She liked giving advice.

But when she padded into the lounge and saw Mark's face, with the television's kaleidoscopic mediocrity flickering over his grim expression, Jenn knew that advice was not on the menu. He didn't look at her. Not fair! Jenn thought. *She* was the one—the only one!—holding things together for his son. She was the one confused by what was going on here but finding the courage to move forward on faith alone after what she'd seen of Mark that night. She deserved some support, some comfort—but wasn't dumb enough to hit the bottle for it! (Apart from that glass of wine she'd had earlier, but that's kind of European or New York-ish and not the same as hard booze).

Anyway, men were supposed to comfort their women. Or hadn't he heard? It comes right after "protect your kids" on the list of Obvious Rules for Real Guys.

Meaning, guys with balls.

Mark glanced at his wife, briefly, then turned back to look at the telly. He thought her velcroed turban and quilted sateen robe gave her the look of a peevish barmaid. She stepped forward and stood between him and the flickering rectangle. A looming figure, some character from an eighties nighttime soap; one who is dangerously certain, blunderingly intrusive, with judgments based on sentiment and self-willed provincialism.

In short, an American.

But Mark knew one who wasn't bad at all. Who didn't need the defense of that unquestioning certainty, the armor of all those identical, culturally-demanded possessions.

"Mark," said Jenn, her voice too loud for such a silent, flickering room. Hardcover books sentineled in the sedate oak bookcase seemed to flinch reproachfully. Mark felt so bloody tired again. Just like last year.

"Not now, Jenn. It's been a long evening." Mark waved his drink, indicating that she should stop blocking the telly.

Jenn stood her ground, of course. "I need to talk to you."

"I said not now." Mark spoke quietly, heavily, as he took a sip of the peaty fluid in his glass. Too cold. Why had he put ice in, anyway? He never had done before going to Florida. Mark abruptly stuck his fingers into the glass and fished out opaque crescents of ice. He tossed them into a lead crystal bowl of potpourri near his seat.

Jenn's mouth tightened further. The potpourri was new. Springtime Scentsations; it had a cute strawberry patch smell and now was probably ruined. Her muscular hands tightened on the blue sateen hips. "Listen. I don't want Simon to hear us, so I'll keep my voice down."

"Right." Mark drank deeply, adding, "Very important, that."

Jenn frowned, wondering about his tone and whether he might be mocking her. Probably not. What was there to mock? "I'm going to point out a few things you need to hear."

"Oh, excellent," said Mark. He considered refilling, but instead put his glass it down on the coffee table, with careful reluctance. "Would you like to begin immediately or shall we have a sing-song beforehand?"

"First ..." his wife began.

Mark thought what an odd word that was. Wife. *Wife* wife *wife* wife . . . a swiping sound like windshield wipers when you're driving through a storm. An unbalanced percussion that comes at you faster whenever the going gets worse. *Wife* wife *wife*.

"Are you listening to me, Mark?"

He looked at her blandly. The tight microfiber turban held her brows up into a crosser V than usual. Or maybe her face was doing that.

"*First,*" she said, "I don't get why the heck you assumed Simon had done something wrong, accusing him before you'd even answered the door."

"Ah, Simon."

"Yeah. And then why didn't you protect the poor kid? You just let the cops drag him out like some . . ." Jenn didn't want to say it. Criminal.

"Excuse me, Jenn. Does it not strike you that there's an inherent contradiction between those questions?"

Hands back on hips. "What?" The television projected blue and green digital flashes onto her back but Jenn's eyes were in darkness.

"I was wrong in thinking he'd done something potentially illegal. Yet I'm also wrong in not helping him avoid questioning. For something I was not supposed to believe he'd done."

"Exactly!"

". . ." Mark stared at the robed Valkyrie looming above him. "Jenn. The idea that a sixteen-year-old boy has been up to something foolish is a fairly normal assumption for a parent to make."

"Not this parent."

"Really. It didn't occur to you that teenaged boys generally don't have great rolls of money to show off at the dinner table unless they've been up to something dodgy?"

"Excuse me, sunshine. You don't seem to get this pretty straightforward fact: I know how parents act, and how they feel too. Or how they *should* . . ."

On the last word, Jenn darted her face toward Mark's seated figure, and the word snakelike came to his mind. If one could imagine a turbaned snake with a downy bleached mustache.

". . . instead you just sit back and let them haul that kid in—your *son*, your sacred responsibility—like you're some kind of pantywaist." She loomed above him, padded and muscular, immobile and righteous.

"Jenn." Mark had never heard the word pantywaist before, but he got its meaning. It was dangerously near something Arabella used to tell him all the time, all the sodding time.

"I never thought I'd say this about you, Mark . . ." Jenn paused. Hands on hips, leaning forward, just where Arabella had formerly stood, saying—don't say it, Jenn, Don't say it. And she did pause, looking into the sudden flicker in Mark's eyes that did not come from television or the whiskey. Some long-dead illumination.

Mark spoke, his voice as casually sharp as a straight razor. "Were you about to say 'useless,' Jenn?"

Neon televisual lights rising and falling within dark oak walls, sentineled books in baited observation, over-padded ottomans crouching low, Mark and Jenn regarded each other. Mark waiting, waiting—Jenn considering.

Some words, she knew, get turned against you. Women shouldn't use them or men will instinctively beat you down with one or more of the big five: fat, slutty, crazy, ugly, bitchy. Words that teach women they're not enough (or too goddamn much). But Jenn at heart was a scrapper, a fighter in the name of family unity.

"Yeah, well, if the word fits. At least he has me for a mother. Because you're being a *useless* father! Useless. And that's worse than none at—"

Mark roared to his feet and suddenly his empty glass of whiskey hit the opposite wall. Had he thrown it? He had! The crystal shattered like a frozen snowball. Jenn flinched and he—*he!*—was hissing in *her* face. By God, it felt wonderful! "YOU ARE NOT HIS MOTHER, you stupid bint!"

Jenn gasped, but recovered quickly. Right in each other's faces, breath to breath, they stood. She didn't yield an inch of ground. "I am. And thank God he's got me, bec—"

Mark stepped toward Jenn so she was forced to lean back. "No." He spoke as if talking to a slow-witted dog. "Because—and here's the nub of my argument—you *are* stupid. Utterly delusional to think you can confront a situation with lies and bluster."

"It's better than—"

"Profoundly stupid to think you are really anything to a boy you met just last year."

Jenn hissed and drew herself up.

Mark continued speaking, but her momentary silence calmed him, and he made the bad decision to turn dismissive. "One day, when you know what you're talking about, we can discuss this further. Let me know if that day ever comes, won't you?"

In a flash, Jenn kicked the ottoman out of her way with one bare foot, planted her hand in the middle of Mark's face, and shoved him back hard. He fell onto the sofa, his brief spurt of fire fading, the wind sagging in his sails. Mark stared, appalled at Jenn's fury-swollen face. Her neck bulged with veins, and her chin jutted forward, and she roared in a voice torn between a choke and a scream. In Mark's fall he'd landed on the remote control, and the TV volume blared a raucous addition.

"TONIGHT!" a canned ITV voice blared, "ON CELEBRITY LOVE ISLAND . . ."

"When *I* know what *I'm* talking about?" Jenn asked. "I'M the only parent that child has EVER had, you douchebag!" Jenn bent over Mark's sprawled form.

He put up one hand, trying to push away the wall of insensate sound, the bulk of American fury trembling over him. Her eyes. There was no humanity in them, only implacable certainty and righteousness.

It was terrifying. And yet . . .

"I know a goddarn sight more than you think," she said. "I'm a freaking encyclopedia of emotional smarts next to you, *doctor*." She jabbed a steel-hard finger into his chest.

He'd never realized how powerful little Jenn was, the muscularity that bulged beneath that blue quilted robe.

"WILL TWO CELEBS MAKE A LOVE CONNECTION, KELLY?"

"You don't catch *me* cowering when I'm needed. I *act*. I know how to take charge of a family, how to face trouble without whining that I'm so *tired* of it."

"Jenn—" Mark's hand remained upheld.

"OR WILL THIS WEEK'S LOVERS END UP IN OUR SOBERING SANDSTORM?"

"You have the nerve to say *I'm* stupid? When all I want to do is protect this family, do the job you should be doing?" Jenn's eyes were slits of rage. She knocked his upheld hand away.

Mark dropped his glance. He couldn't bear to face this ferocity. He felt the shame that fear of a woman brings some men.

The manicured finger was shoved right in his face, again. "I know more than you think I know, *mister*."

Mark was just wondering what she meant by that when a sudden banging sound from upstairs made Jenn stand upright. The sound was Simon, closing the bathroom door. Jenn took two steps away from Mark and took a few ragged breaths. Rage drained from her face, but Mark felt he'd never see her suburban prettiness again, never regard her homilies as amusing. She stood with her robe half open, legs wide like a wrestler, slightly bent as she listened for more sounds from above. Silence. Simon was not coming downstairs.

Mark flicked the TV off.

Silence, and now the room was dim. Jenn retied her robe, a gesture of modesty which further defused tension.

But Mark couldn't stop staring at this woman he'd married. How did he have the nerve to call her stupid, when he'd acted so impetuously, so selfishly? He could still feel the pressure of Jenn's hand hard on his face and realized his whole adult life had been him either waiting for, or receiving, punishment. He didn't know why that was.

Soft sounds trailed down the stairwell. Simon was playing on Xbox. Radio One muttered in the background. Jenn raised an arm and released the microfiber turban from her hair. It fell, half-dry to her shoulders. The chemical smell of fruity shampoo.

Slowly, Mark rose to his feet. Dinner seemed a long time ago.

"Right, it's late," Jenn said, feeling suddenly dog-tired, knowing it would be an awkward night ahead, with her and Mark in that bed trying not to accidentally touch each other in any way.

Mark turned away as his wife left the room and began climbing the stairs. He heard the bedroom door shut softly. For a minute, he stood still, head tilted as if listening to a snatched refrain of an old song playing from a long distance away. He examined the room around him, the house. Looked through the sitting room to the open-plan dining room and kitchen, through the French doors to the enormous, hobbled tree outside, which shook in a mirth of wind.

Then Mark walked to his front door, put on his coat, and left the house.

.ᴑᴇ.

HE WALKED ALONG THE HUSHED nighttime street and met no one he knew. He simply had to move, get away from any neighbor's curtain-twitching. Mark wondered if the police were watching his home, if they'd seen him leave. Heading away from his street, he turned left down a cul-de-sac road. Post-war architecture reflecting humbled ambitions. There was a low wall in front of a new, semi-finished construction. A sulfuric yellow streetlight muttered above. Mark sat on the wall. Concrete pebbles were cold and damp beneath him, the sky overhead darkened with low-weighted gray clouds.

From somewhere above a starling breathed a low liquid moan and then fell silent.

Mark began to weep. He held a hand over his eyes and tried to hide the tears. Failure again; wrong again; trapped again. Unwanted. He attempted to reason with himself, asking what had really changed in the last few hours?—but something had, radically. Within him. As for Simon, what had he been thinking? It seemed all of the boy's life Mark had felt a guilty sorrow for the boy, along with that love for him that was like a painful, tethering cramp. Now he simply wished the boy were gone, or never had been. He didn't mean that, of course. He just felt it.

Mark wept for a while. He felt tired, with his heart fluttering within him like the wings of a frightened bird. Finally he wiped his eyes and stood up beneath the feeble beam of light. Across the street a bone-thin fox stared intently at him. The fox had matted fur and sharp, wary eyes that held no fear, no expectations. The noise of a drunken fight taking place somewhere nearby, of threats and pleas, echoed down the road. Mark and the fox ignored these sounds and regarded each other beneath the sulfuric street lights for a long time. At least a minute, ages long for an inter-species gaze. Then the fox noticed a sparrowhawk circling overhead. It turned and slunk away into the bushes. High-shouldered, bony, and outcast.

Mark suddenly knew what he would do next.

After watching the fox's tail disappear, silently enfolded within the bushes, Mark headed back up toward the main road. His home was two blocks to the right. He turned left and began to walk with a purpose.

1 7

RUBICON REALIZED THERE'D STILL BEEN a few comforting vestiges of youth clinging to her perception, which were now utterly blown away since the *Style* debacle. The loss of hope changes a person. She had seen it in the tilted mirror that hung in her bathroom. Overnight, aging had crept from the recesses of her uterus into the center of her face, wrapping its loose coarse grip around her eyes, narrowing her neck.

For so many years Rubicon's olive-skinned, hawklike appearance had remained the same, for so many years deluding hope had enlivened her complexion, brightened her glance—but now hope was no more. Well, actually, it had been over for quite a while—but like a damn fool she hadn't realized it until now, hadn't felt its absence.

Rubicon curled her legs beneath sweat-heavy sheets. Time to give in, say uncle, like they'd had to do when losing fights in Pinekill. Time for thick waists and sensible legwear, for the stone-colored, immobile helmet of hair that indicates the acceptance of invisibility. Move along, people. Nothing to see here.

Would the loss of hope be less acute if she were still in Pinekill? Would imminent invisibility feel so complete there, the town in which her dreams had been born and which she'd shed for her chance at the brass ring? For a moment Rubicon saw the shadow of her mother seated on the wicker chair here near her bay window. Her mother's belly resting like a soft sandbag on the low waistband of her poly stretch trousers. Broad veined hands, eyes hooded evasively. Then the chair was empty again. Rubicon gazed at the clouds sulking outside her bay windows, silver on the top but weighted with an iron gray. She fell asleep. A muttering dream pulled down the corners of her lips, her hands twitched, and she scissored her legs around the bulk of her duvet.

Branches scraped along bay window glass, the quietly buzzing streetlights seeped softly through the branches' burgeoning leaves. Shadows and light and sleep relaxed Rubicon's expression from its usual chary guard. A small smile played on Rubicon's chapped lips, then one of her hands began to clasp and release her pillow. Clasp and release, over and over.

Just after midnight.

In the darkness, a lock turns. Just a soft *fuh-click* sound, and the door slivers slightly open. Dim light from the narrow hallway slants across the floor. Rubicon rolls away from the light; the duvet twists within her scissored grip. And Mark steps into the apartment.

He'd been here often in the time since Rubicon's embolization. The two ate takeaways and watched daytime telly while he skived off work. He had never seen this place so late at night before though. It looked to him like a treehouse designed by Van Gogh. Slanted surfaces; wooden, rickety, *humble* furniture. Yellow light and bowering leaves, shadows of table legs stretching at unbalanced angles across a chipped wood floor, the sheer blessed fairytale shabbiness of the place. It smelled of red wine, bergamot, and boiled egg. Mark sighed and a great calm passed through him.

Rubicon muttered, then was silent again.

Mark sat at the kitchen table, only feet away from her bed. He bent over to unlace his shoes. Broad, tan, rubber-soled, with a certain Germanic functionality. He removed them and placed them neatly next to each other beneath his chair. He removed his Barbour jacket, rolled it up tightly and put it on the floor. Then he just sat back for a minute, listened to Rubicon's regular breathing, and rubbed his eyes. He saw an opened bottle of Tesco plonk on the table. He uncorked it with his teeth. Mark dropped the cork on the already wine-splattered tablecloth, then drank from the bottle.

Then he spoke. "Rubicon."

She stirred. ". . ."

Mark drank some more and looked at his stockinged feet. Rubicon's thin duvet slid down, and he could see a pale shoulder blade, sharp but unprotected, gleaming in the shadows. Mark regarded the glistening vulnerability as he finished the wine. Cheap tannins coated his tongue like grape-skin burlap.

"Rubicon, wake up."

One thin, unmanicured hand released the duvet, and Rubicon wiped her eyes. Then she turned and saw Mark sitting at her table, hair tousled, his brow heavy, serious. His eyes were red, exhausted in a pale drawn face. One long toe stuck out from a hole in his sock.

"Mark?" She had to be dreaming. The toe, she thought, was a convincing detail. Funny how dreams do that stuff so eloquently. Mark began to unbutton the cuffs of his shirt in the vulnerable, wrist-up gesture that can be so beautiful in men. The veins of his wrists were mapped beneath the pale, moon-soaked skin.

The streetlight shone with ragged tenderness through the branch-scraped windows as Mark stood and began to unbutton his shirtfront. His movements were heavy, meaningful.

Rubicon put her head back down on the pillow and regarded him with calm wonder, eyes like a little girl listening to a favorite bedtime story. The branches continued to brush against the bay windows while Mark pulled his belt off. As he hung the belt and the shirt on the back of the chair and its legs scraped the floor, Rubicon thought, *This is real.*

So she spoke. "What's going on?"

A sigh.

He felt as if he'd been sighing all night, all year, all his bloody life over women and money and love and duty. He'd figured none of them out, not for a moment, and he was done trying.

Oh God the relief of being done trying.

Mark whispered, so as not to disturb the quietude of this moment, in what he believed was the middle of his life and knew to be the acceptance of this apartment's nocturnal embrace. "I'll tell you in the morning." He unzipped corduroy trousers, removing his holey socks. "But first—"

Rubicon stayed very still. Her hawklike eyes gleamed. Any movement could ruin this.

"May I stay?"

He stood before her in Marks & Spencer Y-fronts, hands outstretched.

Rubicon slid over in the bed and threw the duvet open. She was naked. Her body looked so young, straightforward, uncomplicated, when compared to that wry defended face of hers.

Mark slid into bed and took her in his arms.

He'd never thought she'd feel so soft.

·�·

THE NEXT MORNING DAWNED FINE, with soft air and hard, determined springtime earth. Jenn stood on the back deck and inhaled deeply before stepping back in the kitchen to tell Simon that Mark had left early for the surgery.

"Honestly," she said brightly, round blue eyes sparking in the glassy manner Simon already knew meant she was lying. "I don't remember *why* he had to go there so early."

Simon nodded, his mouth full of Weetabix. He took a slug from the glass of Ribena nearby. He didn't give a toss as to where his father was; he was just thankful to be spared a rehash of the previous night's drama and happy not to be asked again about Arabella's missing engagement ring.

Breakfast with Jenn was cool. His mother had loved creating chaos out of her married life and flaunting it to anyone nearby—which often meant to Simon. He'd felt weighted to the spot; his reception of her chaos gave purpose to his existence. As a young child he had pressed triple-ply tissues to Arabella's freckled, tear-stained cheeks as she lay on the floor bemoaning her lot in life. He'd brought her Rollos, unwrapped their golden foil and pressed them to her mouth. Chocolate, to make her happy, to make her stay. Arabella refused the candy. Instead, she told him that soon she'd leave for good—to India, to Ibiza, to the flesh-colored sands of New Mexico. Richmond was too bourgeois for her, didn't he *see?* Or was he as stupid as his father? Motherhood was too, too dull, and her husband—ha!—an utter flop.

Young Simon, aged three, aged five, aged eight, would sit cross-legged beside his mother, solemnly listening while chewing the refused Rollos.

But of course, those had been Arabella's down moments. When up, she could be fun! Before Simon learned it was always really for a new lover, another dream of escape, he'd rather enjoyed the shopping sprees, the outfits she'd try on for him as he waited outside dressing rooms eating salt and vinegar crisps as she'd tell him about her upcoming trip to Paris—the boutique hotel where she and (here she'd giggle and wink) would stay—how lovely Paris was, how once, at Shakespeare & Co., naughty old George, the owner, had taken her upstairs and tipped her over a pile of books to enter her from behind. It had been seamy, filthy, delicious! Arabella laughed, ivory teeth gleaming as she recounted how George's daughters had waited downstairs, determinedly oblivious.

And so Arabella had chatted away, occasionally emerging from behind brocade curtains to show her son a cloud-soft caftan made of llama's belly wool, or maxi boots of pure unbridled snake. But at nine, Simon had had enough. He stopped buying Rollos and also let go of the little respect remaining for his father, a tattered remnant of his babyhood. And by ten years of age, when Arabella took to the floor weeping, Simon would simply step over her reclined form and go upstairs to play videogames.

Simon now watched Jenn bustle around. Tightly rolling the Weetabix wrapper within its box before placing it back in the cupboard and quickly aligning it with the other cereal boxes. Busy, bright-eyed. And true as an arrow, she'd turned out to be.

Simon almost smiled. Instead, he nodded. Poor old Dad. He thought of his father's face last night, mouth slack like a camel's. Of his father's protests and ineffectual blusters; the poor old sod didn't know how to look after him—Simon had always known that. And he didn't know how to protect his father.

But now he had Jenn. Who really, in all ways, had turned out to be a bit of all right. Simon chewed. Sunlight filtered in through the French doors. Daffodils trembled in the soft breeze outside. Suburbia wasn't bad.

Simon watched Jenn as she clattered around the kitchen, wiping down those Portuguese tiles as if they'd insulted her, pouring vinegar through the coffee maker, chomping multivitamins with those tombstone teeth of hers. Action action all the time, keeping on that determined cheeriness. It was restful, having someone do the worrying for him.

Another spoonful of Weetabix. Jenn's whole body shimmied while she scrubbed hardened tomato sauce from the cooktop. He'd finally got a bit of luck. Terrible, of course, about his Mum and he'd probably need a course of psychology to recover from all of her nonsense but . . . *all's well that ends well*, thought Simon, with the platitudinal complacency he was learning from Jenn. It was tremendous actually, to feel the lightness of his life since Jenn began relieving him of the burdens he'd been carrying for so long. He was tired of gluing together the torn seams of his family. Let her do it!

So Simon stood up and did something new, out of gratitude. A couple of things, actually. He put his Ribena glass into the empty Weetabix bowl and carried both to the kitchen sink. Then, rather nervously but also with a damn-the-torpedoes casualness, Simon put a hand on each of Jenn's shoulders and swiftly kissed her on the cheek. Just above where the end of her lipsticked mouth turned up. She stiffened in surprise, then trembled slightly. And looked ready to mist over, the silly moo.

"Cheers for breakfast, Jenn." Simon swiftly picked up his rucksack and headed out. "I'll see you later."

"Simon—wait!"

Bloody hell, the boy thought as he reluctantly turned to face her. She was going to tell him all about the argument, about his father leaving. She'd probably get all smeary with weeping like those fat women on Oprah do.

But Jenn wasn't weepy. Instead there was a dazzling smile. All those little, very white teeth she had. No more sign of tears.

"Just hold on a minute!" Jenn reached into her pocket and pulled out a crumpled note. "Here, get yourself a Big Mac or a CD or something after school." She handed him some money and winked. "Or add it to your money roll. You're a good kid."

"I—" Simon looked down and saw it was a twenty-quid note. "Brilliant! I mean, are you sure?"

"Sure I'm sure. Have fun. Now bust a move, kiddo. I'll take that back if you're late for school." She hugged him firmly, then pushed him away.

Oh the smell of her. Green apples and antiseptic and security.

⊷

JENN EXPECTED MARK BACK, AND soon. He wasn't the type to stay away, was he? He liked his home comforts, his couch and his TV, his nightly stroll around the rectangular garden, his set bedtime schedule. Remove sweater, shirt, and that day's corduroys; fold clothes over chair; scrupulous dental routine (though his teeth never lost that pale English taupeness). She wouldn't lower herself to call him. He'd be back today.

Jenn's certainty wasn't just because she still had the pretty girl's confidence in her charms. There was something else too: Jenn had never been left before (since

Mike Bellwether's flagrantly unsuccessful attempt on that long-ago night of the car crash), and it's a thing that takes getting used to. Tough at first to wrap your head around the fact that you're a disposable attribute to someone's life, like a magazine subscription or fresh-ground pepper. Some people learn this cruelly early, and often. Some lucky fuckers never get the lesson and lead blithe and blindered lives. But Jenn had lost, so far, only to death. That's no shame; we all play in the shadow of death's house and the house always wins.

So Jenn squatted in a springtime garden in the Southwest of London, patting impatiens into the ground and thinking of how weirdly comfortable it was to be in Mark's house without him. She'd thought he'd be the world to her, a tired old world into which she brought energy, optimism, cleansing certainty. She sipped Lipton Iced Tea mixed with Crystal Light lemonade, and thought, "I've given everything to him."

But deep down, she knew that it was Simon who was the world to her, and whom she would empower. However, when Mark returned, she would forgive him.

Jenn had no doubt it would happen soon. And as Jenn's life, unknown to her, was recouping for another act, another season, another springtime growing within, she decided to forgive. Which means she'd use the handy trick of pocketing her resentments to later transform them into coin.

He had betrayed his son the other night, with his weakness and his half-voiced suspicions that verged on accusation—she would spend the coins of resentment to ensure he never, ever, did that again.

And, she added, pressing her square palm into the scrabbled bark of the half-dead tree and rising to her feet, she would love him too. Or rather, them.

Simon and Mark. Family.

She could almost feel Mark's relief in knowing he was forgiven, in learning what she'd do to keep her family united.

"JENN?" A DEEP VOICE CALLED from inside the house.

Ah! Two days, just as she had thought. Jenn ran iced-tea-cold fingers through her thick hair, fluffing sweat away in the soft multicolored breeze. She hoped she had an endearing smudge of dirt on her face.

"Out here!" she called, raising a hand over her eyes and trying to see over the deck, through the French doors. "In the garden." She nearly added "Sweetie," but no point in giving it away too soon. The figure moved in the shadows behind the French window, began to open it.

"Were you expecting—"

The door opened.

"—the Spanish Inquisition?" Simon stepped out onto the deck, grinning, rolling his eyes at his naffness. He and Jenn had watched one of Mark's favorites the night before, his old Monty Python DVD.

"Oh!" Jenn's hand fell. "Oh, cool. How was school, Simon? Are you hungry?" A shadow crossed her face as she picked up the bag of potting soil she'd bought with the impatiens. A moment's anxiety flipped her stomach.

Then Simon said, "I'll get that—half a mo'," before stepping lightly off the deck. He flexed broad shoulders beneath the hoodied, low-slung garments of modern youth.

It was too early in the day, Jenn thought, as she brushed dirt from her hands. Mark would still be at his surgery.

Simon hoisted the weight one-handed onto his shoulder.

·ೞ·

MARK WAS NOT AT HIS surgery. The previous morning he'd rung the office saying he was riddled with bacterial conjunctivitis. That his eyes were creaking with infection and profoundly contagious. Very sorry and all but . . . any questions, please ring him on his mobile, not the land line.

But of course, Mark was healthy and in Rubicon's bed. Just as Jenn plunged a fistful of impatiens into the earth, Mark was crooking his arm free from beneath Rubicon's pillow. Rubicon continued sleeping as he turned and lifted a glass of water from the floor. No nightstand, thought Mark. No coaster!

The air in the room was close, some might call it stifling. Shag-stink and stale sheets, dust motes hovering, and only the merest crack in the window admitting bird call and street sounds. Mark could see the entire flat from where he reclined. The messy bookshelf with much-thumbed paperbacks and a creased photograph of Leigh Bowery wearing a veiled skull on his head. The door to the loo, where he knew there was toothpaste stuck to the sink and a single, slightly whiffy, navy-blue towel hanging nearby. The round table with two unread newspapers, breadcrumbs, room-temp smears of butter and an open bottle of long-life milk. His clothes were still hanging from the chair. His socks? Mark looked around. Where were they?

Oh, who cares.

Mark drank the water. It was also stale, and tiny oxidized bubbles clung to the inside of the glass. The water tasted sweet to him. He returned the glass to the floor, his head to the pillow. Mark's eyes traced a diagonal crack along the ceiling as he thought for a while, in a leisurely dreamlike way, about kitchens and coasters and children with conjunctivitis, about middle age and the modern martyrdom to fear of failure and to possessions and where these martyrdoms entwine. Eventually Mark lifted his head again and cleared his throat.

"Rubicon?"

". . ."

"Are you awake?"

A rustling as he turned toward Rubicon and poked the top of her head gently. Once, twice, three times.

Rubicon kept her eyes shut, but smiled. He could feel her smiling.

"Rubicon."

"Mmm?" She reached back, took his hand, and wrapped it around her waist.

Mark pressed his lips against the back of Rubicon's head. Then he spoke seriously. "I've a question for you."

He felt a tightening, just slightly, beneath her ribcage. Mark would be the first to say he understood nothing, nothing about women—but that was an exaggeration. He knew a statement like that, in a circumstance like this, would prompt a certain anxious review within from Rubicon; a shuffle through the Filofax of the mind, an instant re-perusal of events to reinterpret them in the face of potential outcome. Women are with reinterpretation like drunks are to another binge: however often they tell themselves they're not going to do it—it happens. He knew that, and knowing that he knew it, was right about that, made him feel happy.

Rubicon turned toward Mark. Readjusted the sweat-softened sheets. "Okay," she said, warily. "Out with it." Not a question, a get-it-over-with. Accompanied by the solemn directness of a pillow-shared glance.

"No," said Mark. "I cannot ask you this if you are looking at me like that."

Sheets pulled as she turned away from him again, toward the window. The fabric of her camisole slid warm and yielding beneath Mark's fingers. He loved the feel of her belly. Despite Rubicon's boyish figure, Mark had discovered that she now had a firm little pot belly, like Madonna used to flash in the early eighties before veganism and privilege tautened her form.

It was remarkably sexy.

"All right," she said. "I'm not looking at you. Shoot."

Mark's left arm remained crooked above her head, and he gently tugged at the pointy locks of hair she hadn't washed in days.

"What?" Mark asked, ("Whot?"), knowing full what.

"Shoot. Meaning, go ahead. Say your piece. Lay it on me, daddy-o." Oof, she thought, as she looked at the light dappling in through the dirty bay windows. Shouldn't have used the word "daddy," because that'll make him think of Simon, which'll make him think of—she reached back and pinched Mark's side. "What's your query, mate?"

Mark actually hadn't thought much about Simon at all the last few days. At first he'd carefully kept himself shag-drunk, but then things began to change. Things deepened and the time in this Barnes studio flat, each generous easy moment inhaling hair dye and turmeric from the shops beneath, relaxed something inside him that hadn't unclenched since his student days. Possibly not even then, for he'd already been bookish and anxious and queasily uncertain. He'd forgotten completely that people had times like this—days and days of shagging and dozing and eating pasta out of the pot at midnight, of watching half a video, then kisses lingering, lengthening, as the whole lovely cycle starts again.

"My question." Mark coughed. "Hmm. Well, I'm rather nervous."

Rubicon didn't want to hear the question. It was bound to be disheartening and send them back to earth with a bump. A nasty Jenn-shaped reality bump. For Rubicon, too, these last few days had been precious—but unlike him, it didn't surprise her. She had a sharper knowledge of how fleeting and rare these shag-drunk days are. Rubicon sighed. Yank off the Band-Aid.

"Don't be nervous," she said to the speckled sunshine. "Out with it."

"Hmph. Easy for you to say." Mark kissed along the base of her neck, and his words were muffled. He wanted to keep drawing out this cocooned time, to tease her, to say something too. "What I have to ask is important, woman. It concerns something which exerts a powerful, symbolic influence on our lives."

Symbolic, eh? Rubicon thought that can't be Jenn. She's far too straightforward for symbolism.

"But one must know these things, before—moving forward. Rubicon?"

"Out with it already, goddammit." Now her voice was tight. Oh God, don't let him go, don't let it end. Was he going to set ground rules? Was he carelessly, blindly ending this deep, delicate time between them?

"There are things we need to discuss; we cannot remain in this halcyon futoned state forever. The first must be this . . ."

Rubicon waited.

After a moment he peered at her inquiringly, thick eyebrows raised. "Rubicon, I must know. Do you like hummus?"

". . . that's your question?"

"Yes. Rubicon. Hummus. Your opinion, please."

She exhaled with relief, fumbled for a small pillow, and hit him with it. Twice. Mark yanked the pillow aside, pulled her body against his, and held her compliant arms over her head in a tight grip. Their heights exactly the same, their bodies hip to hip, nipple to nipple.

"I loathe the bloody stuff," he murmured into her ear.

It tickled.

"Who decided a dingy plaster of ground beans and lemon should disfigure every fucking table top? Why is this pulp so vastly represented in modern life?"

"I don't know. Never thought about it." Rubicon was relieved their golden time would continue, for now. "I mean, I eat it if it's there but I've never thought, oh, I *hope* there'll be hummus tonight."

"And yet, every time one totters into a bloody party, there it is—squatting like birdshit on a table, surrounded by limp crudités. People wearily eating the excrescence like it's a menial chore they've taken on . . . why? What on earth is wrong with pâté?"

"It's expensive, pâté is." Rubicon spoke consideringly, as if determined to be fair to hummus. She released her arms from Mark's grasp and ran a hand down to the small of his back, where she'd discovered that if she stroked him just at the indentation at the base of his spine, he would tremble a bit. He did. "And hummus has fiber."

Outside the sun-dappled window, a springtime bird made a throaty "tuwit-tuwhorl" sound over and over as if anxiously guiding a fledgling home.

"Don't defend the hummus, woman. It will go badly with you if you do."

Rubicon stroked again, and he trembled again. She whispered, "Also, important minerals."

Mark slid his right hand down Rubicon's clavicle, chest, ribcage. "Let's have none of it, Rubicon." As Mark held her ribcage, he slid down to inhale the scent of her. Musk and cigarettes and butter somewhere, too. He lifted her softly crumpled midnight-blue camisole, but kept talking. "In our lives, no hummus. No dinner parties. No objects bought to impress neighbors or, worse, ourselves—" His mouth trailed lower but he spoke urgently.

Rubicon closed her eyes as outside the bird called out with soft springtime insistence. Our lives.

"—no puff pastry, no talk of property values, wheat intolerance, or rice steamers; no cobblers about hi-tech mobiles, or multi-culti world music. No God-bothering, no school runs, no reading of articles that tell us we're past it—"

No school runs? What was he planning to do about Simon?

His chin paused to rest on her soft firm belly, inches up from the sturdy but shrinking fibroid knots. Rubicon placed Madonna-calm hands on his head. "I can live with that," she said. "But I will occasionally need to discuss Dot Cotton."

Dot Cotton was Rubicon's favorite character on *EastEnders*. An elderly Laundromat worker, Dot was a helmet-haired, chain-smoking, scripture-quoting and avidly gossiping character whose son was constantly trying to kill her.

"Well, Dot Cotton, obviously. I'm not an animal."

Rubicon's long, always slightly grubby fingers combed his hair.

Mark's eyes closed. "But now the hummus is out of the way, we can address other issues."

"Obviously," Rubicon noted. "There's Corrie, and *Emmerdale,* too."

"Myself, I'd draw the line at *Emmerdale*, but we can discuss that another time. Now I must tell you." He tried to smile, but she saw a nervous flicker in Mark's eyes, a tension to his mouth. "You see, I did a shambolic, foolish thing." He shifted, so she could only see the top of his head on her belly— that slight Velveteen Rabbit thinning on his crown.

Mark had given Rubicon a weary, brief summary of his night with the police. Suddenly she had a surprising thought: had he lied to them? Was that the foolish thing he'd done?

"Mark—you don't need to—"

"You see, I married another woman."

She said nothing.

"Well . . . that's it, really. That's what I did."

Tuwhit, Tuwhoo. So he was planning to go home; he was tendering her up to make it easier for him to walk away. Rubicon felt a staggering in her heart, but what had she expected, what else, really, could he do? Jenn would win; the wives always win—the house always wins.

Words dredged up through a pumice of disappointment.

"What's to discuss." Rubicon shrugged. Again, not a question. Stoicism, loneliness, and age had endowed Rubicon with a weary valiance.

"We are no longer young," Mark said.

Rubicon didn't move. Best not to move.

Mark lifted his head and smiled into those dark, hopeful, wary hawk's eyes of hers as he continued speaking. "We can't muck about, anymore; I've made enough mistakes. I want to get a divorce; I want to be with you."

Rubicon turned her head, then her whole body away from him in the relief of love, at last, and thin tears slid down her face onto the worn bird's egg-blue sheets. Mark consoled her with his body.

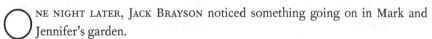 1 8

ONE NIGHT LATER, JACK BRAYSON noticed something going on in Mark and Jennifer's garden.

He'd had a slash and was doing up his trouser buttons while casting a stray glance outside the bathroom window when Jack saw a small orange light moving in the shadows of the garden. Evenings were drawing out again, but shadowy dusk had fallen, and the darkening air was lively with pollen. Surprising, Jack thought, how that old dead oak at the end of the Everleighs' garden had sprung leaves for the first time in several years. He didn't want his view blocked. Just now the branches had only the filliped bright buds of springtime, but if they continued in their encroachment, they would soon shade and obscure the view.

The movement Jack saw was that of a single light—perhaps a firefly? Or too early in the season?—zipping up and down erratically. He realized it was actually the tip of a cigarette, being raised and lowered surreptitiously, sometimes half-masked by a cupped palm. As Jack kept peering through the space between his bathroom window's cream-colored House of Fraser curtains, his eyes adjusted, and he realized a hooded figure stood in the garden, darkly dressed, slender but full-shouldered. At first, Jack thought it was Mark, but then the person moved, the light shifted, and he realized that, of course, it was Simon.

Smoking a crafty fag in the garden as teenagers have done since time immemorial.

Oh! How Jack wished he could smoke again, but Vanessa would render his life absolutely miserable if he did so. The woman was a lunatic, practically American, on the subject.

And the boy certainly looked as if he was enjoying it. Lifting his head and blowing plumes of gray-blue smoke toward the canopy of burgeoning leaves. The sudden squeak of a small animal's dying cry came from nearby, then a banging from within the Everleighs' house. Alerted, Simon turned his head, and Jack also froze. Something about the boy's watchfulness, about the turn of his neck, made Jack think, enviously, that Simon was nearly a man now. He'd known Simon since birth and always found him rather a nervous, sniveling child—well, that *mother!*—but now Simon had crossed the magical border and soon would be a young buck out raving in London, fumbling with young girls in alleyways and on borrowed sofas. Young girls' bodies, still porpoise-firm, with that velveted down on their thighs.

Oh God, to be young.

Simon turned his head back and resumed his smoking.

Jack did remember, dimly, how miserably insecure he'd been when young: he wished he could go back and do it again, with a little welly this time. He'd learn how to fight, and then how to walk like those men do, the ones who know how to fight. He'd find a small, dark, slim girl, one with full lips, as unlike Vanessa as possible.

But wait—something was happening. Simon suddenly threw the still-lit cigarette away and leaped forward in an attempt to quench the spray of embers. He moved like a bad dancer, with feet stomping randomly around him, hands trying to break smoke apart in a weirdly incantatory manner.

A thin voice emerged from the house. "Simon?"

The boy, young man, finished the dance of the embers and turned toward the house. "Just coming in, Jenn. Half a tic."

"No . . ." The voice so thin and distant, making one think of old phone wires coursing beneath the Atlantic Ocean, beneath coral and fish and the wreckage of ships. "No, I want some air. Let me . . ." Here the words trailed off indecipherably. Jack thought she could have said, "Let me get what's mine," but that didn't make sense. Then there was the clatter of a French door opening, the smooth scrape of a screen door sliding, and Jenn's glowing blond head emerged from the house.

Wine. She'd said wine. Jenn was clutching a large glass of it. And even from this distance and odd angle, he could tell she didn't look as she normally did.

Swiftly, Jack looked over his shoulder, hoping bloody intrusive Vanessa wasn't coming up to check on him. No, he could still hear her below, washing up after dinner. Jack moved a little further toward the crack between the curtains.

Something . . . what was different about Jenn? Jack realized that she looked a bit scruffy, which was normal among his English friends, but not Jenn. Usually she appeared scrubbed to a pink plasticine buff, every hair wet-combed or otherwise bullied into place.

Tonight she was different. Her redoubtably American teeth were not bared in a smile. She looked more like a Brit, albeit one with famous frontal development, but that chest was covered by a large depressive cardi which she clutched shut with one hand. Her usually immaculate Garnier Fructis blond hair was lumpily pinned back, her strong-ankled feet shoved into some matted fur slippers. Wssh wssh wssh, the sound those slippers made moving across the gray deck wood.

That was the sound of a woman at loose ends, Jack knew. Vanessa had a pair of furry slippers. He suspected every woman does, after a certain age. The age when, in private at least, women give up the battle to remain sexually relevant.

It didn't occur to Jack that women of all ages would be more interested in coziness than in his opinion of their sexual relevance. Thank God I'm a man, he thought, sucking in his stomach and taking a broad-legged conqueror's stance (from behind the frilled beige curtains). The old inkwell never dries up, he thought, not really, not for us blokes.

"Simon?" The nasal American voice called out to the dark garden. Jenn shuffled over to the deck lights and flipped them on.

The boy stood out on the lawn blinking like a rabbit in the dim fluorescence. The scene had the air of outdoor theater, and Jack had balcony seating.

"Jenn I was just checking the bins, making sure they won't draw foxes and erm—"

"You were smoking, Simon."

". . ."

With a sigh, Jenn added, just at the moment the wind changed direction, so the sound reached Jack's ears like the near rustle of dried leaves. "It's just so bad for you. I never understood why people *do* that."

Simon stood on the lawn, gazing up at Jenn as if in sulky supplication. "I dunno. It gets you out of your thinking, just a bit, like gives you room to view things from just a few inches above the top of your head. I took it up after . . ."

After Mum died. The words didn't need to be spoken. The oak tree's branches trembled as the wind switched again.

"Oh," said Jenn. "I never knew that. I thought people only did it to get skinny or look like James Dean."

Simon, still staring up at Jenn illuminated on that deck, cardi wrapped around her body, hand wrapped around the wine glass, shook his head. "No. It gives you a bit of space, in your head."

A long pause, during which Jack could hear that Vanessa was now in the sitting room. She was changing channels on the telly downstairs, blurts of one meaningless sound following another.

Jenn's voice trailed through the night air. "Can I try one?"

Simon sounded reluctant. "Seriously? Best not, really."

Jenn gulped some wine and then said, "I know they're expensive. I'll buy it off you."

"That's not it at all. It's a naff thing to do, starting smoking at your age."

"Give me a cigarette, Simon." Jenn held her square hand before her like a queen, like the queen of the deck in her fuzzy slippers, the wine glass as her scepter.

Jack was not surprised that Simon stepped forward, drew a cigarette out of a packet of Silk Cut he carried in his hoodie pocket, and placed it in Jenn's palm.

After examining both ends of it, Jenn placed the filter between her full pale lips and bent forward toward the young man's outstretched lighter. She held her bangs away from her face in an unconsciously humbling gesture as the fire from the lighter flickered high, then low, as she pulled in flame. Jenn stood straight and exhaled as Simon lowered the lighter and looked guiltily, interestedly, up at her.

In silence, Jenn puffed away. Coughed softly, just once. Then she delicately took the cigarette out of her mouth, examining it as if an instructive message might be written on its side.

"So, Simon." She spoke with careful casualness. "You get that something's going on here, right?"

Jack had known it! There was something in the air between these two that spoke of familial tensions. The wary energy of people emerging from their retreated corners. He leaned forward as Simon spoke.

"You mean with my father?"

Ah!

Jenn nodded. "Have you spoken to him?" She continued to hold, to examine the cigarette, and Simon to regard her from his lowly lawn position.

"No." At hearing this, Jenn puffed again at the cigarette.

Both Jack and Simon watched, fascinated, as it illuminated the center of her face in a totemic way—the tiny nostrils and pointed brows dark above flame-lit flesh.

"Well," Simon added. "I rang him."

"At the surgery?"

"On his mobile. I got the answerphone."

"Oh." Jenn examined the cigarette again.

Simon continued. "I tried the surgery. They said he was sick. He hasn't been to work."

The two of them, boy and blond woman, stood silently listening to the sounds of leafy Richmond in the night—distant televisions and quietly bypassing cars, muted shouts from nearby pubs, rustlings of wary animals scraping a living from human castoffs.

Hmm, thought Jack. Trouble in paradise for Mark. Poor sod can't keep them happy.

Suddenly Vanessa's voice called loudly from downstairs. "Jack! Wherever are you? Michael Palin's on Parky!" Palin meeting Michael Parkinson would be a coming together of two kindly, cashmere-scented national institutions.

But just a minute more . . . Jack stayed peering out the window, hoping Vanessa would shut up.

Jenn was speaking, still holding the cigarette. Its ash burned tremblingly long.

"We had a fight."

"Well, yeah."

Simon sounded annoyed that she thought he mightn't be aware of that fact. Jack wondered what kind of fight it was, and if that's what had brought the Old Bill around the other night. He'd seen Stoddard and Drape knocking on Mark's door.

Simon continued, "And you told him to bugger off for a bit. Happens all the time, really."

"Does it?" Jenn reached down and handed Simon the fag end, which was down to the filter.

In a sweeping move so graceful that Jack at first thought the young man was bowing, Simon bent over to extinguish it in a pot of marigolds.

"It's never happened to *me*."

"Well, but the bloke you were married to was crippled, yeah?"

Jenn nodded once in the moonlight and gulped down the last of her sauvignon blanc.

"Poor bloke. But kind of hard to do a runner." Simon paused awkwardly. "I mean, not that he'd have wanted to."

"Are you saying your dad did this with your mother?" Jenn's voice was almost a gasp of relief.

"Oh yeah," said Simon easily. "She was always handing him the keys to the street. Sometimes he'd leave and sometimes he'd just ignore her."

"But where would he go? How long would he stay away?"

"Well, you know, not long . . ." Simon looked through the treetops, toward the wispy clouds filtering the night sky.

Jack thought the boy might see his shadow behind the curtained window, but Simon's eyes slid back to Jenn.

She spoke quickly, quietly. "As long as this?"

". . ."

"Simon. Did you expect him back by now?"

"Jenn, he'll pop up soon. He's hardly the type to—"

"Do you know where he's staying?"

That, thought Jack, is the question: Where has Mark got to? Hardly the type to have some obliging totty stored in a pied-à-terre, he was probably bunked down in his office or alone in some pay-by-night Pimlico hotel, hand-washing his kaks in an undersized sink.

"Jack?"

He didn't hear Vanessa call, or the subsequent sound of her footsteps on the stairs behind him. Jack continued to stare down upon his neighbor's flood-lit garden, musing on Mark's whereabouts.

Simon's voice floated up to him, "Jenn, he's probably at the surgery. He's a sulky sod—"

"Yeah, I know he can be. But—" Jenn replied.

Vanessa rounded the corner of the upper stairwell. The bathroom door was closed, the light off, but there was quiet movement from within.

Inside, Jack craned his neck to hear Jenn's next words. "Simon. I'm your mother now, and I should be strong for you. I—oh Simon, I'm scared. When will he come back?" When her voice broke, Simon stepped up onto the deck.

Jack again saw how grown the boy had become; he was exactly Jenn's height.

The boy awkwardly, tenderly, took his full-bodied stepmother in his arms— just as Vanessa Brayson threw open her bathroom door and found her husband standing in the dark, spying on his neighbors.

.୨୧.

DURING THE BORING BITS OF Parky, Vanessa got Jack to tell her exactly what he'd overheard. Hmm, thought Vanessa (though she claimed to be appalled by her husband's voyeuristic intrusion). Hmm, she thought, savoring the thought of Jennifer's comeuppance.

It's always gratifying when an interloper finds they bit off a bit more than they can chew, even with those barracuda American teeth. She couldn't help but wonder what Arabella, with her freckles and tiny hips and posh vowels, would have made of Jenn. Arabella, who constantly invited young tradesmen, tame men hired to do menial jobs, into her house for seduction followed by a spot of dishwasher repair. What *would* Arabella think of Jenn, all alone with that boy? Even in his arms!

Vanessa decided she would call Caro tomorrow, to see if perhaps they might lunch together soon.

19

MARK RETURNED HOME TWO EVENINGS later.

Jenn and Simon were sitting on the sofa, watching *Emmerdale*. When they heard the fumble of Mark's key in the front door, they froze and looked at each other—Jenn's eyes wide and glassy, Simon's youthful brow furrowed. By the time Mark entered the sitting room, they'd both turned their faces toward the door and were looking at him with remarkably similar expressions. Mouths slightly open, eyes blank and gauging.

"Erm—hello," said Mark.

He stood there less apologetically than one might have expected. Less hunched than usual. The mechanism of Mark's rusted passivity had been eased, oiled and finally loosened by the bohemian enclave he'd shared with Rubicon. By her grateful delight in him, the humility and the wit with which she acknowledged the love she'd always had for him—how time and hopelessness and other men hadn't killed it, but made it quietly stronger. Undemanding and unexpectant, yet endlessly patient. If it hadn't been for those fibroids of hers, those fake muscle babies—would she ever have come to him?

The sheer undemanding shabbiness of life in Rubicon's dusty studio flat and the tenacious fiber of her long love for him worked on Mark like a tonic.

So now Mark stood straight, regarding his wife and son together on the sofa, with a half-smile on his face. It was a moment that would embed itself in Mark's memory. Not that Mark would need to remember much, for much longer.

He was certain now. He wasn't going to be weak.

Of course, that's one of those statements which is easier to determine than to enact, without cruelty, at least. And Mark was not a cruel man: things would have gone far easier for him if he had been.

And so.

"Erm—hello," as he cautiously walked into his home.

Simon slinked away from Jenn and off the sofa like a dog who'd made itself too much at home. But as he left the sitting room, he bumped his muscular young shoulder against his father in passing. Mark flinched, feeling Simon's solid hostility and noticing for the first time the rank scent of his youthful potency.

"Right. I'm off," said the boy to Jenn.

"No," said Jenn. "Don't go, Simon. Please. We're going to have family dinner." Jenn's muscular hand with its perfectly painted fingernails reached forward and dropped a crumpled Kleenex on the coffee table as she drew herself up to her full height. Blond hair greasily gleaming, bullish neck tense, and her body wrapped in that pink juicy "couture" velour sweatsuit she'd bought in Florida.

She looked ridiculous to Mark. But as he noticed a spiky dark hair growing from her chin, he also thought *She's human and therefore more fragile than she looks.*

Simon slouched by the door, not knowing what to do other than scowl.

Mark said, "Perhaps it's more important that we talk now, Jenn."

"No," she said. "First we'll all have dinner." Family is sacred. And she would not lose it. "Right." Jenn clapped her hands together in hearty brittleness. "Twenty minutes to spaghetti with meat sauce. Mark, there's a new bottle of whiskey on the sideboard. Simon, is your homework done?"

"Bugger," thought Mark and Simon simultaneously. So that was how she was going to play it.

Jenn left the room with head held high, a crooked smile playing on her tight lips—but once she turned the corner her mind began racing. She should've showered, shouldn't have eaten all those GD chocolate pavlovits or whatever they were called—but she had to stop "should'ing" all over herself and seize the freaking reins. Control was hers to take back so she could move forward.

Here's what she had to do, and now: Wash her hair under the kitchen tap.

Filth is a sign of weakness. Put water on for the pasta to boil; add a lot of salt like how Mark likes it. Wash lettuce, take Jamie Oliver tomato sauce out of freezer, heat it, make garlic bread—what *is* it with men and garlic bread? She wondered distractedly as she turned the kitchen tap on and stuck her head beneath the cold chill of water. Whip together a vinaigrette since Mark doesn't like normal salad dressing like Thousand Island.

Jenn fumbled for the shampoo and conditioner she kept under the sink for when she did her roots. The shampoo bottle was old. It farted as she squeezed it, and a chemical stink and de-coagulated pink pus emitted from the bottle. Even goddamn *shampoo* goes wrong in this country, she thought.

Keep cool. Keep going. She rinsed shampoo from her hair, slicked semen-colored conditioner through her hair (good lord, what had brought that image to mind? Yuck!) As she rinsed that out, she thought, Oh crud! I don't have ground beef in the house. In Pinekill, of course, she could just run over to a neighbor's and borrow half a pound no problem. But here . . .? No.

Maybe she could find something in the freezer.

Remember that you have the power here. You are the wife and sort of—no, Jenn corrected herself, as she rubbed her hair with a dishtowel—you *are* the mother here. The heart of the house, that's you. Now Simon knew that he needed her and the blessed normalcy to which she connected him, and Mark would relearn it too. Probably already had.

There are many lessons God needs us to relearn, thought Jenn sanctimoniously. She combed her hair, put pasta in the now-boiling pot of water, and decided to skip washing the lettuce. But just in case, she also threw together a quick appetizer for her boys.

As she strode, wet-headed and radiating an enforced calm, into the sitting room, Jenn was surprised to see Simon still there. Mark was on the sofa, watching TV, as his son leaned against the doorway sulking. She gave him a quick, cheery wink as she placed the hummus and pita plate down.

"Dinner in twenty, boys!" Jenn trilled determinedly.

Mark murmured something, but Simon remained silent.

She found that old packet of Quorn in the freezer, stuck it in the microwave, and as the brown plasticized lump twisted slowly within the radiation, Jenn thought thankfully of Simon glowering in the doorway. Children were such a blessing, sometimes in such unexpected ways.

The microwave pinged. Mark came into the kitchen. Something in Jenn's gut lurched as he cleared his throat, then said nothing—just got himself a whiskey glass, and walked out again with an empty half-smile.

She didn't want to be alone with him just yet. The tomato sauce simmered and smelled powerfully of garlic and earth and steel. Thank God Simon wouldn't leave her alone with Mark. She needed the ballast, right now, of his adolescent sullenness, to produce a sense of normalcy.

IT WAS THIRTY-FOUR MINUTES later but, as Jenn brightly said, "Who's counting?" when the three Everleighs sat down to dinner. Had it really been less than a week since they'd last eaten around this modern rectangle, with its coolly enrobing overhand light and view of the darkening garden? Jenn and Simon had been eating dinner in front of the television, then splitting an Aero bar.

But now they were all back in the same spots they'd sat in on the night the police arrived.

"The days are getting longer," offered Jenn as she passed the garlic bread. It looked almost fancy, she thought. But too bad how the paprika had bunched into red dusty clots like that. Focus on the salad. Avocados look prettier sliced when they're nice and hard. Focus on that, and on Simon's sulky face opposite.

"Mmph," said Simon, stabbing romaine on his plate.

"Yes," agreed Mark. "It's nice. When that happens."

Long pause.

Two small sparrows hopped along the deck outside, chortling merrily. Simon glared at them.

"Well, Mark," Jennifer said. (Bull by the horn, she thought; Simon deserves to know where his father's been.) "I have to ask you . . ."

Mark wiped his mouth with the soft woven napkin Arabella (and now Jennifer) always reserved for "best." God, the stupidity of it, the terrible self-importance. Rubicon simply stole napkins from Caffe Nero and used them for everything, from paper towels to loo roll. Sensible.

"Yes?" Mark said calmly.

He turned serious eyes, with those dark brooding brows lowered, toward Jennifer.

Simon did the same, but there was a small, hopeful smile playing around his face.

The two looked so similar. Man and boy, thought Jenn fatuously. Family. Flawed and full of uphills and downhills, like a field that must be respected, nurtured. Honestly, Jenn thought, I think things will be all right. (She didn't, no she didn't—there was something about the way Mark looked at her now that made her nervous. Kind of the blank way you look at a rerun before changing the channel.)

She decided not to ask her husband where he had been.

"So Mark—can you tell a difference in the spaghetti tonight?"

Mark blinked and felt the urge to shrug, but he was too polite. "No. Should I?"

"Of course you should!" poor Jenn crowed nervously. "Guess what I put in it?"

"Erm. I can't imagine."

"Broken glass? Cyanide crystals?" suggested Simon, as he examined a forkful of spag bol.

"No, silly! I put in that Quorn stuff. Can't believe it but I did!" Her tones echoed brightly, falsely, and Jenn speared a sauce-covered chunk of Quorn.

It was extremely chewy.

The sparrows outside emitted final playful chortles and flew away together, dancing an entwined connubial flight.

Simon pushed his pasta aside.

And from the front right pocket of Mark's thick corduroys a muffled vibrating sound began to reiterate. He made no move to retrieve his mobile.

"Aren't you going to answer that?" Jenn asked, eyes narrowing.

"No," said Mark. "Not just now."

.இ.

BACK AT HER APARTMENT, RUBICON put her cell phone down on the rickety kitchen table and gazed at her empty bed. She hadn't left a message. What was there to say?

He would return, or he would not.

But as she looked at the soft blue sheets, almost dove-gray from too many washes and recent overuse, she knew that Mark would return.

Rubicon pulled the sex-scented sheets from the mattress, yanked the dirty old pillows from their gentrifying cases, and she felt nothing but calmness, competence, trust.

Last night had been somber, for they'd known he would be leaving today. They'd lain in bed and watched *Raging Bull* on BBC2, because Rubicon wanted Mark to see and admire the single shot of blood thickly dripping from a boxing ring's rope. So much beauty in unexpected places. This morning he had left, telling her he would return soon, almost immediately. But what to do about Simon?

There had been a darkness in Mark's eyes as he'd asked that question.

I guess this should be all wrong, Rubicon thought as she stood with hands on hips, looking toward a pink-daubed sunset illuminating clay-pot roofs, but it's not. It's the righting of an imbalance, really. That salty sip of fame she had so early left her thirsty as hell for more—when it wasn't good for her. It helped her forget how to be normal; it was only how to be cool and oh man, that shit calcifies you. Now Mark knew she loved him, and she knew she could love like a normal person, and all the things that got so kinked up, so long ago, could be straightened out. Arabella, who took him from her first with that privileged sluttishness of hers. That bullying marriage that malformed Mark. Then Jenn swept over the horizon. With her overweening confidence and emotional simplicity. Poor Jenn.

But still.

Jenn would go back to where she belonged, to Pinekill's waiting embrace. Rubicon didn't consider that to be the punishment she once had, for since hearing Jenn's story of Lovina's death, she had begun to dream of her childhood home almost every night. At first it had been painful, but then she remembered and recreated a noble starkness to the place. She hadn't remembered that about Pinekill, not in years. Was it normal, this nightly return to her hometown? Did entering middle age awaken a sifting through adolescence, was this analysis the last hormonal upheaval? Who knew.

In Rubicon's covert nocturnal embrace of the girl she had been, of the land she'd run from, Pinekill's ugliness turned to beauty through kaleidoscopic montage. Of childhood falls on cracked cement and hugs from neighbor ladies with soft, fat, powdery arms like underbaked bread, of Dixie cups and homemade ice pops held up by scanty toothpicks. Memories, sifted and churned through decades of absence, of her girlhood sense of the stark noble land Illinois had once been and which still lay, dormant but dark with fertility, beneath the stone of strip malls weighing its once serene prairie, the illuminated signs blocking its endless expanse.

From the bottom rack of the bookshelf wedged in her closet, Rubicon pulled out a second, even older, set of sheets. She could see her long fingers through the maize-colored cotton. Rubicon stretched her arms high and wide, and the pale fitted sheet billowed like a spinnaker sail above her head, just as the Everleigh family finished dinner two miles away.

FAMILY CAN GET THROUGH ANYTHING. Honestly . . .

Jenn's optimistic—or frankly delusional—catchphrases weren't working, and now, as she scraped hardened tomato sauce off their dishes, she found herself brushing away tears.

Dinner had not been a success.

Ever since Mark had left the house, Jenn's mind had refused to organize itself as usual (I mean, not having ground beef in the house? C'mon!). It flitted exhaustingly from topic to topic, settling on none. This mental circularity made her bone-tired and ratcheted up an almost physical anxiety in her usually quiescent mind. Her stomach did funny flips at odd moments, too, like it was half-remembering something scary. She found herself having tremulous imaginings, unprecedented for Jenn, who was nothing if not practical. The thoughts had begun the first night Mark had left, and the only way she could soothe them had been through a combination of food and keeping very, very still. So lots of TV watching, with Simon.

Right now she kept examining, and thinking about, the Quorn. Which was really nasty stuff to scrape down a swirling sinkhole; the little brown pellets of vegetable protein looked like dried scabs in the sauce. And since the sauce had that freezer-burned metallic smell, it was bloodlike itself. Yuck.

Jenn scrubbed faster, but her mind kept musing. She'd never thought about this before, but hamburgers, particularly the fast-food ones, look like scabs too. Like thick scabs picked off an elephant's knee or something. And fast-food hamburger onions look like sautéed baby toenails.

Well, that's disgusting! As she bent her head and scrubbed the Brillo pad, blue-gray and foaming, against the clotted saucepan, Jenn had her first inkling of why someone would become vegetarian. It's eating someone's ground muscle, muscle that's been trapped in plastic like a coroner's exhibit. Like maybe Arabella had been . . .

There was something funny about Mark tonight.

MEANWHILE, MARK WAS BACK IN the sitting room, watching TV. He was surprised that Simon hadn't sulked upstairs and barricaded himself in his room. Instead, his son slouched in a nearby chair, broad shoulders hunched, arms crossed, as if letting Mark know that he was keeping an eye on him. Mark wanted to ask about Drape and Stoddard; had they been back? Had Simon told them the truth?

In silence, the father and son watched *Couples*.

And suddenly, Mark could bear it no more. Why had he eaten that dinner? Why had he remained a minute longer than necessary, even out of kindness, in this smothering pile of shelves and tasteful "focal points" and throw rugs and blanket-filled baskets, of expectations and fucking Jesus the bills piling up like paper manacles? He slid his mobile from his long linty pocket (Rubicon had washed his trousers at the Laundromat; they were wrinkly and blessedly free of Meadow Scented fabric softener). With his son watching, Mark swiftly sent a text, then jammed his phone back in his pocket. After a moment's thought, he stood up abruptly and strode into the kitchen.

His mobile, however, had been badly repocketed. It slid from the corduroy depths onto the sofa, where it now chirruped three times. Simon leaned forward and picked it up.

"JENN," MARK SAID.

"Mark!" She hadn't heard him re-enter the kitchen. Hair was stuck to her brow and she went to brush it away, but she accidentally knocked the spaghetti dish (hand-painted by a Neapolitan astrologist) to the ground. It shattered into porous shreds against the hardwood floor. "Oh no!" said Jenn.

"I never did like that bowl," replied Mark.

Jenn got to her knees and began pushing the pieces into a pile, while Mark fetched the dustpan and brush from a hook on the cupboard door. Jenn held the dustpan while he brushed. In quiet unity they gathered the scattered fragments together.

"Well," said Jenn, too loudly. "I guess that's one way to get out of doing the dishes!" She leaned back and wiped her brow with the back of her hand.

"Jenn," said Mark, still on his knees. He took the dustpan from her and looked at the porous fragments within.

Jenn saw that his hand trembled and he looked at her with tears in his deep-set eyes.

"Jenn, I am so sorry. But I made a mistake in marrying you. I am so very sorry . . ."

Jenn's glassy eyes opened wide, whites visible below the blue pupils.

"Jenn, I'm leaving tonight, now, and for good. We can talk later about Simon. And further arrangements."

Poor Jenn stared at him and waited for words to come, but instead only a surge of self-loathing rushed in. Failure.

Mark left almost immediately, only packing a swift suitcase. He found his mobile on the sofa in the now empty sitting room, then went back upstairs to knock on Simon's door. He wondered, would his son come with him? Should Mark ask?

Did he even want to ask?

But Simon didn't respond—and his bedroom door was wedged firmly shut.

TEN MINUTES LATER, SIMON DESCENDED the stairs with trepidation. He'd recently heard that numpty Laurence Llewelyn-Bowen say that the kitchen is the heart of every home—if so, Simon thought as he rounded the corner of the sitting room, this house had a chronic cardiac issue, an ongoing arterial clot. Just over there was where he'd found his mother. And now standing by the enameled double sink was Jenn, wiping a long strand of saliva from the side of her mouth with the back of a strong shaking hand. Strands of hair clung to the sides of her face in vein-like rivulets.

Simon said nothing for a moment. He simply stepped forward, grabbed a dishtowel, and gently, gingerly, began to wipe the near side of Jenn's face. Her hair hung down and he had to brush it away. It was still damp, and smelled of garlic.

Jenn was trembling all over. After a moment, she turned toward Simon and showed him her other cheek. He wiped the sweat and saliva from that, and from her brow, as well. Then, carefully, meticulously, he held each of her hands and wiped them clean and dry. Jenn stood with her head down, her face hidden, like a weary, shamed child. Still in silence, Simon took a glass from the cupboard and filled it with a gasp of aerated room-temperature water from the tap.

He held the glass as Jenn drank deeply with her hands at her sides. Her eyes were still down, his on her face.

"Thank you." Jenn's voice was quiet, toneless.

Simon carefully put the empty glass in the sink, wiped his hands on his low-rise Uniqlo skinny jeans, and told his stepmother about the text message his father had just sent to Rubicon.

I'm coming back to you, if you'll have me forever.

And the reply had been, simply: *Come.*

The boy held out his arms to console Jenn, who'd emitted a sharp birdlike cry. But she turned away from him and vomited into the sink.

III

THE
DEATH

2 0

I S IT MORE INTERESTING TO read about love or about failure? Do readers prefer stories bobbing with the discovery of joy or ragged with heartbreak and loss? A little of both, ideally, but we all know that others' joyous discoveries can get a bit . . . samey.

So we'll stay away from Rubicon and Mark for a bit. Too much quiet contentment going on there at the moment, which is even more self-congratulatory than joy. For the next little while, they are burrowing ever deeper into the phase of a relationship when the outside world is nothing but passing traffic noises while inside it's the usual orgasms and pizza delivery, childhood stories and the proud, shy conferring of nicknames.

Jenn's got more to offer in the drama department. She was feeling her failure acutely (the locus of her pain didn't burn over the loss of Mark; it was around her failure to *keep* him—a different thing altogether). Within a few days of Mark's brief return and abrupt departure, all of the neighbors noticed the change in Jenn's appearance. As Vanessa Brayson put it when she ran into Caro in the organic produce aisle at the Waitrose, "The cracks are beginning to show, and in a very *American* manner."

Jenn herself now shopped at the Tesco, where she'd see fewer of Mark's friends and there was a better Mexican food selection. She remembered Mark commenting on their honeymoon, over a hubcap-sized plate of nachos served beneath the preen of a flamingo-hued sunset, that Mexican food was to Americans as Indian food is to the Brits. The food of the vanquished and the colonized. Jenn craved it now.

She roamed Tesco's slightly dirty aisles, leaning heavily on the handle of her cart, wearily tossing in plastic packs of over-stirred guacamole, sour cream, Doritos Cool Ranch Chips and the store's hottest salsa, which wasn't very damn hot. Jenn grabbed some red pepper flakes too. She bought Tesco's Finest frozen burritos and enchiladas, and hoisted pillow-sized plastic packs of soporific cheddar into her cart. Five cans of refried beans, stuff that looked as much like squashed shit as her life felt now.

Soon Jenn found that even chocolate is very good with a few hot pepper flakes on it. Anything, anything to burn the deadening taste of failure away; there was both comfort and distraction in the burning pain.

Surprisingly quickly really, Jenn developed an acid reflux regurgitation that made eating difficult, but she powered through. But Simon seemed to thrive on the Mexican food and rubbed his strong young hands together before every meal.

What Vanessa meant by the cracks showing in an American way was, of course, that Jenn was getting fat. Properly fat, not just the full-bodied, bursting with health way that had so diverted the men at Mark's party. Jenn's waist thickened, and her strong square jaw softened lumpily. Well, anyone in her position would plump up, wouldn't they? Someone who had long assumed the benefits of a blithe small-town beauty, losing to a rival who'd been on the shelf since Wham!'s *Careless Whisper* hit number one. It was humiliating; it was unfathomable —that was the word. Jenn stuffed herself with cheese and hot sauce to smother the galling unfathomability of it all. Mark had had decades to be with Rubicon. Why now? There was insult in the now-ness of it, and shame, and the slime stench of failure.

After just a few days of this diet, of wearing her pink velour Juicy Couture sweatsuit night and day, of not showering, and of belching jalapeño tears while consoling her affronted body with the heat and grease it craved when entrenched in front of the TV, Jenn lost her impervious polished gleam. When she hoisted herself up, her pink velour ass sagged like an elephant's. Even the glassy brightness of her round eyes seemed to fade, just slightly, as each day dragged by.

She. Had. Failed. Simon.

Because when you thought about it (and despite the staunch availability of capitalism's numbing distractions of processed food/entertainment, Jenn did think about it incessantly, particularly at night, when the grindings and twitchings in her Doritoed gut were at full blast), that Simon had been hurt the most by her failure.

Oh the dark, shadowed torment she felt each night, hearing Simon snore in the next room, knowing how alone he'd be again without her. Rubicon wouldn't love the kid, not properly. Mark couldn't, *that* much was clear. Plus, he was only a dad. It was a mother's job—to look after Simon, to be the nurturing source of consistency, constancy, unwavering absolute love. All she'd ever wanted, she said to herself, was to be the oak around which a tender vine could wrap. Her strength would protect it, her breadth providing strengthening shade, her solidity would nourish its strong-rooted hardiness despite life's icy winds.

She might be a figure of fun, our Jenn, and she might not have a complex worldview, or a trenchant wit, God knows. But, to herself at least, she *represented* something both new and timeless. Having always assumed that all mockery was envy, she believed down to her fluorided, Flintstone-vitamined bones that family and the importance of family values needed relentless protection—and that it was her job to provide it. Yet when she had finally been given the chance to mother, after so many years of losing Lovina and of listening to the rasping of Mike's sleep apparatus as she lay in the dark—she had somehow let this great opportunity slip away.

God had left her.

She felt so tired, she who had been defined by her blinkered buoyant energy. And far, far older than she'd felt even eighteen months ago as she stood watching Mike's angry reaching for death. Older than she'd ever felt, with the single exception of those long-ago days after Lovina's loss, when doctors told her that she'd never have a kid and she knew all her prettiness (thanks to the Bruiser's moonlit impact) had just become a barren show.

Jenn was further humbled by the weird fact that Simon seemed to harbor no grudge against her, in fact seemed to have no concept that he should. Instead, this young man with the muscular back and short pug nose had become someone she could herself lean on. But was that fair, she asked herself?

Maybe that's how atheists felt. That there is no fairness, no right, preordained order in the universe, in relations between people. It was the first time Jenn had thought anything like this, and it did not cheer her up. Instead, she became sullen, as people do when lies are revealed.

.9℃.

EIGHT DAYS AFTER MARK HAD left, Simon and Jennifer sat in the sitting room, watching an unshaven man talk to ostriches on TV. It was another episode of that year's compelling but debased programming, *I'm a Celebrity, Get Me Out of Here!* Jenn slumped on the sofa in her now grayish and stained sweatsuit. Simon had just returned, rather proud and self-conscious, after checking to make sure the home's doors were locked. He plumped down on the overstuffed cushions next to his overstuffed stepmother feeling about as manly as he ever had in his life. He threw a casual arm around the back of the sofa, near Jenn's hunched back. She was nibbling dully on a Mars bar, eyes enlivened only by the flickering neons of the telly.

After regarding her for a minute, Simon poked Jenn in the shoulder. Her eyelids flickered, but she ignored him. The show was back to the love story that had been packing in the viewers this year, a compelling but surprisingly hostile flirtation between a sweet, passé Aussie singer and a misandric British model.

Simon poked Jenn again. She stopped chewing, but still kept her eyes on the screen. He pointed at the TV and said, "That Jordan's a bit rough nowadays, isn't she?"

Jenn hadn't realized that the misandric model was the same woman she'd seen on that poster on Simon's bedroom wall on the glorious night of Mark's party.

"She wants to be called Katie now," Jenn muttered into her Mars bar. "Her real name. She's a *person*, Simon. She's not just . . . boobs for rent."

"Well," said Simon mildly, "then perhaps she should stop getting her tits out for money. Not that I obj—"

"*Perhaps*," Jenn interrupted sharply, "someone told her that's all she's got to get by with. Maybe she knows that even if men leave, money sticks around. Could be that's why she takes off her top." Jenn stuffed the butt end of the Mars bar into her mouth for emphasis, and dropped the wrapper to the carpeted floor.

Simon reached down to retrieve it. The carpet around Jenn's spot on the sofa was embedded with broken tortilla chips, bits of Flake bars, a few withered pieces of tomato, and a cracked half-slice of American cheese. Simon put the wrapper on the coffee table, picked up the remote and muted the TV just as the Australian singer retreated to his hammock, gazing at the glamour model.

"I was watching that," Jenn said.

The Australian watched Jordan as she stood beneath a makeshift shower, her mighty breasts straining against a crocheted bikini. Each was the size of a baby's head. The singer sported a semi-erection and the eyes of a beaten dog. The model twisted, arched her back, and pointedly ignored him.

"Jenn," Simon said. He put his smooth young hand on her veloured thigh.

Simon's fingertips were long and spatulated, like his father's—but unlike Mark's they were untouched by time and expertise so they also reminded Jenn of Mike's hands. Mike's hands as they'd looked all those years ago in Pinekill, when he'd rested his hand just where Simon's lay now. That possessive touch during school assembly had let the world know she was claimed.

And the word had gone out like wildfire, Jenn remembered. It was like being famous—the quarterback had chosen, as he should, the prettiest bounciest cheerleader. Tradition, wasn't it? But Rubicon's group back then had probably rolled their eyes. Rolled eyes greasily lined in Wet N Wild midnight kohl from Walgreens. All sneering at the stupid cheerleader who had believed it had meant something, something almost mythic, to be chosen thus.

But Simon was saying something . . .

". . . wasn't best pleased, at first. I mean, you just seemed like some fit loud Septic—sorry, American—suddenly in my house. But you're the best thing that's happened in yonks, and my dad's off his trolley not to see that you're bloody lovely, you are." The boy stammered, looked down, and removed his hand from Jenn's leg. His face flushed, and in his high color Jenn could see where there had been apples to his cheeks when he was just a child.

Her face softened. "Oh Simon, I'm sorry. I'm not being good for you right now. What's going to happen to you? Only sixteen and you've lost two moms. It makes me feel—" Jenn's eyes filled with tears. The TV flickered, flickered alongside the dim lamplight.

In the ensuing silence, Jenn noticed that her nail polish had chipped; on her thumb there was now a fuchsia outline, a flat-topped blob the same shape as Illinois. Back there she'd have someone to talk to, someone with defined beliefs who'd know what to do. Unlike the lipless jerks in this dilapidated country the size of a closet: people who waffled along and you never knew what they meant! "Not bad" means good, "interesting" means you just said something dumb, and "family"—*marriage*—for God's sake, was something disposable. No one here seemed to believe in it. Not even the ones who said they did.

Simon was also lost in his own thoughts, but when he raised his eyes to hers, they were dark with determination. "I haven't lost you, Jenn. And I won't. *He's* the one who naffed off. *He's* the one who left us here alone together, which is lovel . . . who cares if he pisses about with that bony slag?"

"Now, Simon, stop with that," Jenn said disapprovingly, hoping Simon would continue.

"They deserve each other, right? And we can stay just like this. It's really much nicer than when it was just him and me."

Oh it hurt her heart. To be loved by this kid, and know she was just temporary felt like a cramp. "Simon. Facts are facts. He's your father, and your relationship with him is for life."

The boy reached over and pulled something from Jenn's hair. It was a tiny shred of lettuce. "Unbloodyfortunately, I reckon that's true. But so are you. *You're* for life for me, too, yeah? I mean—" Suddenly his face tightened within the cavorting neon light of the telly. "—I mean, no one ever looked after me before."

"Simon, of course they did. Your mom might've been a little weird to deal with, but I'm sure—"

"My mum hated me," the boy said it bitterly.

Well, one would say it that way.

"No she didn't, Simon. She couldn't, it's not in nature."

"She *told* me so. That she hated how I'd stare at her from my cot. *Needing* her."

"Of course you did!"

"She found being needed very boring. She liked being wanted, but not needed. You're different, yeah? That kind of . . . it doesn't make you run away, or not look at someone." Simon pulled himself together. "I mean, it seemed like when you married my father you really took me on too."

"Yeah. I really did, Simon." Quietly.

"Right." Simon exhaled like a decision had been made. His nose was a bit snotty, and his eyes felt dry but they could move on from here. "Well then. So we carry on. And I'll look after you too. Apparently you need help with keeping lettuce out of your barnet." He gestured toward her hair and Jenn laughed. "So Dad can bugger off. We're sorted." He leaned back on the dark tweed sofa and grabbed the remote with the air of a man whose job is done. The sound of tropical rainfall and birdsong filled the room as, in the celebrity-ridden jungle, a supposedly famous gossip columnist was eating a long-horned beetle as part of a challenge.

As the sound of a cracking exoskeleton filled the room, Jenn set her jaw.

Yes. Simon was her family now and she would pour herself into undoing what his parents had done to him. To her (and to Simon!) if not to his father, the marriage vows had truly made her the boy's mother. Jenn's sorrowful heart unclenched and began to swell with a satisfying self-pity. She would sacrifice herself to motherhood. Even sacrifice her country, her American way of life. She didn't quite know what that meant, but politicians always said that and it seemed to mean pickup trucks and friendly hellos and firecrackers and, of course, being the envy of the world. It looked like maybe—almost certainly—this was what God wanted for her.

Jenn took the remote from Simon's hand, patted his cheek, and turned the volume even higher up. A bird screamed in the televised jungle as the royal gossip columnist failed his challenge. He belched loudly and, against his best efforts, began to gag.

"Right," Jenn said. "Enough." She began to rise from the sofa. It was time for her to take a shower.

2 1

T HE NEXT NIGHT WHEN DANIEL stopped in for a swift pint on his way home after
work, the telly was also on in the Red Cow at the top of the road. As he pushed
open the pub's door and was greeted by a welcoming swirl of cigarette smoke and
the competing lures of colorful fruit machines and comfy booths, Daniel couldn't
for the life of him remember why he so infrequently came here. It wasn't the beer—
they pulled a lovely pint at the Red Cow. Anyway, he thought, as he examined the
amber nectar before taking the first (and always the best) sip, he should ring Caro.
She might like him to collect a takeaway on his way home. Some crispy duck and
perhaps some of that rather moreish satay chicken. Daniel lit a Silk Cut and pulled
out his mobile. The idea of banning cigarettes in pubs was ridiculous, he thought—
no pairing in life is quite as lovely as a pint and a fag.

As Caro's mobile rang in his ear, Daniel saw Jack Brayson crookedly slouched
in a back nook of the pub. A bag of golf clubs propped against the wall next to him,
and a half-read *Telegraph* sat on the table, next to several empty whiskey glasses.
Jack's slouch was so crooked, Daniel realized, because he'd fallen asleep. Now
Daniel remembered why he'd stopped dropping into the Red Cow—Jack was
always here, waiting, like a lonely old dog. Always anxious for a long natter and
trying to buy another round. Daniel decided to drink his pint quickly and leave.

He turned his back to Jack just as Caro picked up. "Oh yes, please!" Her tube was stuck on the District Line, and she thought a takeaway was a wonderful idea. "You marvelous man. I'm at Baron's Court—God knows when this bloody train will move again. Let's have some prawn toast as well, shall we?"

Daniel said he and the prawns would be at home in half an hour or thereabouts.

Daniel was just ringing the Dragon Inn when, from the corner of his eye, he saw Jack give a start. Clearly he was waking up. Jack emitted a mighty snort, stretched, then rubbed pink, loose-skinned fingers down his face. They looked like uncooked sausages. Daniel turned further away and began trying simultaneously to finish the takeaway order, extinguish his fag, and down his pint.

No joy.

"Daniel! Over here!" Jack waved both arms like a man lost at sea. "Grab a pew, mate!"

Bollocks. Nothing wrong with Jack, of course. Fine man. It's just that ever since the poor sod retired and found himself at loose ends, he'd begun gossiping like a schoolgirl—a schoolgirl stuck on a repetitive and oddly geriatric loop. Daniel waved to Jack, pointed at the phone. He'd be with him in a minute.

After finishing his call, Daniel sighed and headed toward Jack. As he pushed through a cluster of men at the bar, a tall man with paint-smudged clothes suddenly stepped back and spilled half of Daniel's pint down his arm.

"Oof—sorry, mate. You all righ'?" The man was in his thirties perhaps, and stood scratching the top of his ginger head while blinking in a sort of Stan Laurel manner. A dried fleck of blue paint hung on his cheek like a teardrop.

"No worries," said Daniel. "Happens. Would you just hand me a few of those napkins?" The painter reached over the bar to grab a towel, then began dabbing at Daniel's sleeve.

"Should've been watching myself," said the man, dabbing away. "Let me buy you another one."

Later, Daniel thought that he noticed the watch because its elegant gold face gleamed incongruously beneath another fleck of paint. He'd tried not to find it surprising that a working-class man would have a watch like that; his own father would have described a vintage Rolex Tudor as a "gentleman's" watch. Embarrassing, outdated idea.

"That's kind," said Daniel. "But I'm just saying hi to a mate and then popping over to the Chinese. Lovely watch, that." The man stopped dabbing. He turned away to throw the towel back on the bar. Daniel noticed the watch had a slight chip on the bezel. He'd seen that watch before, somehow.

"Daniel!" Jack called again, while drumming his fingers on the table.

Daniel muttered under his breath, and the painter, who was about twenty years younger than he, rolled his eyes. Clearly, Jack Brayson was the pub bore.

"Righ' you are. But if you change your mind . . ."

Daniel smiled and nodded. He moved off, and the younger man turned toward his mates to resume a discussion about when that wanker Prince Harry wore the Nazi uniform to a fancy dress party.

As Daniel approached Jack's nook, he saw that he had somehow managed to get another double whiskey for himself.

"Can't stay long, old man," Daniel said as he sat down. "Picking up a Chinese for Caro."

"Quite right," said Jack meaninglessly. "How're you?" Jack was very drunk indeed, despite his brief nap. His bottom lip hung in a wet pouch. It transpired that Vanessa was visiting an old school chum in the Cotswolds until tomorrow, and Jack had been taking full advantage of his freedom.

"Din't want to go bloody Cotswolds. Ladies eatin' salady muck, gossipin' about ol' friends—and any school friend of Vanessa's would *have* to be old, y'know." Jack tossed back half the glass of whiskey, then wiped his mouth with the back of his hand.

"Go easy, Jack. So you got some golf in today, I see?"

"Pfff." Jack glared at the golf bag like it was an eavesdropping intruder. "Mate, d'you remember? When you n' Mark n' I would pop round here for a pint every night?

"It's a fine old pub," said Daniel.

"Course, that was before he remarried." Jack waggled shaggy eyebrows.

"Naturally," said Daniel. "Haven't seen Mark much of late."

Jack leaned forward, winked heavily, and lifted a thick sausage finger to point at Daniel's face. "Wonner why you haven' seen Mark, do you?" Jack wagged the finger. "Trouble in paradise, mate. Ol' Jack had a bird's eye view. Mark can't keep 'em happy . . ."

"Vanessa's back tomorrow, you say?" Daniel had no interest in what Jack was trying to tell him.

"That ginger bloke you were talkin' to knows about it. Mark not keepin' 'em happy. One of Arabella's bit of roughs. Bits of rough." Jack focused his bleary eyes. "I mean, they shagged."

Daniel turned to look at the painter who'd spilled his drink on him. The man did resemble a fit, ginger version of Stan Laurel. He was laughing hard at a friend's story, and it looked considerably more fun than being stuck here with Jack's sausage fingers, slurred innuendos, and dust-covered golf clubs. Daniel suddenly realized Jack had brought the golf bag to the pub on the sad pretense of having done something today other than getting arseholed.

"How'd'you know that?"

"Oh, his mate said a while back. Said she gave him money too. Tidy chunk of it. Bought a used van with it. White van man, y'know. Painter. Ha! Arabella wasn't too old to get the painters in. Ha!" Jack laughed at his Wildean wit, and then added darkly. "N'like Vanessa. She's past it nowadays . . ."

"When was this?"

"Mate, she's been on the HRT for years now—"

"No, not Vanessa. I mean that bloke and Arabella." Daniel began to understand why Mark mightn't visit the pub more often, given that any pint-drinking odd-jobs man in the Richmond and Twickenham area might've shagged his dead wife.

"Dunno, mate. He must've given her a proper seeing-to though. F'r her to give him the dosh for *that*." The sausage finger pointed outside the pub's long street-facing windows to where a mud-spackled white van was parked. Its side read *Thos. Halp Painting Services, est. 2004. Eggshell or Pearl, Give us a Whirl! 0208 079 7326 5622*

Jack's wet pouch of a mouth constricted as if pulled by a drawstring. "Wait—around autumn half-term time. Apparently Arabella got a bit shirty with him, 'coz he di'nt want to come round for a shag when Simon was home from school."

Daniel considered. "Autumn half-term last year was just a few weeks before—"

Jack stuck out his lower lip. "Few months ago I tried to get him over to paint our fence. Help me out, y'know—get Vanessa off my tits about it. He din't want to. Prob'ly doesn't have the bottle to run into Mark. I tol' him—"

"JACK."

The color drained out of Jack's face, and a little whiskey leaked from his mouth.

Daniel turned around and saw Vanessa standing behind him. She was clutching the handle of a rolling suitcase and glaring icily at her husband.

The table was wedged too far in so Jack half-rose, staggered, and collapsed back into his seat.

Daniel, meanwhile, stood and gave Vanessa a kiss on the cheek. "Hallo, Vanessa," he said.

"Lovely to see you, Daniel," she said. "Jack, you *ridiculous* man. Stand up properly and take my bag. I told you to pick me up at the station this evening at six."

As Jack struggled simultaneously to release himself from the booth, pick up his golf bag, and explain to an increasingly contemptuous Vanessa that she was back on the wrong night, Daniel looked over at the ginger Stan Laurel. He and his mates were grinning openly at Jack as he accidentally buffeted a nearby girl with his golf bag, then meekly followed his wife's pointing finger toward the exit.

"Good bye, Daniel—tell Caro to call me, won't you? Jack, wait THERE."

Jack stopped by the door, eyes downcast like a scolded Labrador's. Then he followed his wife out of the pub.

Daniel's takeaway meal was definitely ready by now, but he caught Stan Laurel's (or rather, Thos. Halp's) eye. Perhaps a pint was in order.

Halp raised his glass, and Daniel walked toward this new acquaintance with a friendly smile on his face and a thoughtful look in his eye. He knew where he'd seen that slightly chipped Rolex before, or one remarkably like it.

Later that night, after arriving home late and eating cold crispy duck and sodden shrimp toast, he called an old friend of Caro's who happened to be rather high up at the Met.

MEANWHILE, OVER IN THE TINY plank-floored flat in Barnes, Rubicon and Mark's love affair felt anything but adulterous. There was none of that shadowy intensity or guilt-ridden drama. They were too old for histrionics and too young for somber realizations of the future being entirely used up. Instead, as they lay in the late-afternoon sunlight filtered through the dirt-grimed bay windows, these two simply basked. How right that old beet-eater Shaw had been in saying that youth is wasted on the young. How precious to be middle-aged and feel again a promise and potential in life along with a savory, time-humbled sense of gratitude.

Rubicon lay on her back and gazed upward at motes of dust suspended within the speckled rays of sun. Mark was drawing a long doctor's finger along the line on her clavicle where sun-exposed skin met the pale flesh that lay beneath the neckline. How glorious the contrast; how remarkable to find this softness beneath Rubicon's hawklike defenses.

He lay on his side, facing her. She did not look at him, but was warm with the knowledge that she could. She could turn and gaze deeply into his serious eyes, his gentle shame that he hadn't come to her sooner. And beneath it, a dawning ferocious will to protect their love. Finally, Mark willing to fight for something— and it was her!

Such happiness. Rubicon would remember this afternoon forever.

With the ruthlessness of successful lovers, they barely thought of Jenn (or frankly, Simon) at this time. They ate: Rubicon made a rather mealy kidney bean tabbouleh, but she also produced a brilliant, butter-saturated yet crispy garlic bread; Mark loved the combination. They shagged (Mark gripping Rubicon's boyish ass in a fervor of appreciation). They walked and laughed and did errands and snuck out to matinees at the Richmond Film House while patients all over Southwest London suffered longer waits at the surgery.

We all have these times which later evolve into vague memory montages. If we are very fortunate, we experience them more than once. Rubicon and Mark were so lucky, until they weren't.

It's not often one knows with complete certainty the moment when these dreamlike times ended. Usually the languorous intensity deflates, slowly, slowly, over time. Eroded by work schedules and transport delays and Thames Water bills, depreciating through nightly flossings and weary morning silences.

Later, Rubicon did know the exact moment.

It's soon.

2 2

TWO EVENINGS LATER, THE POLICE came to Rubicon's door. Mark had been sitting alone at the battered kitchen table, wearing boxer shorts and Rubicon's silk kimono as he read *The Guardian* and smoked a Marlboro Light. He'd started smoking again, and wondered not only how he ever quit, but *why?* Blue-gray smoke curled from the cigarette tip, coiling above his head like a plume of freedom; lung-rinsed white smoke streamed from his mouth and nose in exhalations of ease. Ten years later the young (including Simon) would be saying YOLO. But in 2005, for a brief moment, Mark was living that way. He liked smoking and pottering about and working part-time and Rubicon. She would be back from the shops in a bit, and they would eat leftover pasta while watching telly and taking the piss out of Tony Blair.

Tomorrow perhaps they'll stroll to the cinema together, share a drink beforehand. It was all so wonderfully unstructured.

The door downstairs banged, followed by heavy steps on the stairs outside. Not Rubicon; she walked quickly, lightly. Mark assumed the steps would keep going up, but no, instead they stopped on his level, followed by the paused muttering of people finding the right door. And then the kind of knock Mark immediately recognized.

Bang bang. BANG!

A copper's knock again. The loudest bang was a heavy boot-kick, a don't-fucking-not-answer knock. The easeful cigarette trembled between Mark's fingers. He paused, then with slow regret, stabbed it into the bottom of an old mug.

"I'm coming."

Mark didn't tie the kimono. Just put the newspaper down, stood up, and opened the door.

Drape and Stoddard stood in the hallway. He was holding a bag of Liquorice Allsorts; she was wearing her usual tight-arsed head-girl smile. Drape dislodged a liquorice from his left rear molars, and shifted the saliva-thinned black mass to the right side of his mouth. They both looked Mark over, a little surprised.

Mark leaned against the doorframe, hoping there were no piss stains on his boxers but nonetheless facing the cops head on. Drape chewed open-mouthed and the smell of saliva and anisette filled the air.

"You're a difficult man to find, Dr. Everleigh." Drape had always wanted to utter a sentence like that. It sounded dead cool.

"I've moved." Mark shrugged.

Stoddard said, "We've been trying to contact you. Left messages on your mobile, and through your work, and at your . . . former address. Your receptionist mentioned you might be here."

"Well, she was correct." Mark was rather enjoying this, though he wished he still had the cigarette in his hands to use for bohemian ease. Then he thought: *Oh good lord, what if they're here about Simon?* And his heart sank.

"We'd like to talk to you."

Mark turned and walked back to the table, where he lit another Marlboro. The police stepped into the flat and closed the door behind them.

23

THINGS HAD REALLY GONE TO shit for Jenn the night before, in just the way an ex-cheerleader should have predicted.

And it all started with such good intentions! Simon had insisted on making dinner for them both. He'd never cooked anything beyond beans on toast or assembling the stray Ribena, but she honestly (Jenn said, blue eyes wide open) thought it was a super-sweet idea, and she'd love watching TV while listening to that kid bang around the kitchen. Breaking things and messing them up and leaving her with jaggedly stacked piles of dishes to do later. While watching *Friends*, Jenn winced when a particular loud crash rang from the kitchen. After Simon popped his head into the sitting room to ask where she'd put the candles, Jenn thought maybe she'd get herself a little gussied up; show the kid she appreciated his effort.

And she really had only one flattering dress.

So a scant ninety minutes later, when dinner was finally served, Simon gulped when his stepmother walked into the kitchen wearing proper clothing—a dress, in fact! A blue dress shot with silver. And she'd put gold earrings in, and her hair was clipped up in the back. Her heavy locks were covered in so much hairspray they gleamed like clear shellac.

Simon suddenly felt embarrassed, in a pleasurable, jumpy way. Waving an abrupt arm at the table, he spoke too loudly. "Right!" he said. "I did Jamie Oliver's chicken."

Jenn felt a little uncomfortable herself. (Remember the last time you wore this dress, Jenn? Remember Rubicon and the pigeons circling beneath the stony sky as you emerged from the tube that day?) She noted Simon's pink face, the chaos of a kitchen, the mingled smell of smoke and burned skin.

"The table's so pretty!" Jenn said.

Simon regarded it with dubious satisfaction. He'd put lots of the stuff on the table that his mother had hated. The family silver, Buttercup pattern. Each piece had the balance of a sterling weight in the hand, and was whorled with heavy flowers and leaves. The china was Minton, the napkins were linen, the crystal glasses had been bought in the atelier of a Parisian glass blower. Arabella *had* liked these, but allowed no one to use them. Each glass's stem was a delicate art nouveau representation of a naked woman, whose head was replaced with a tulip-shaped wine glass. The flame of a fat brown candle reflected in the darkened French doors which led to the deck. The candle flickered with weird wildness as if an emphysematic ghost was gasping to blow it out, and it emitted a kind of hippie stench.

Ugh, patchouli, Jenn thought.

At the center of it all sat a covered silver dish.

For the first time in his life, Simon took a seat at the head of the table. Jenn sat at her usual seat as he picked up a bottle of red wine he'd unearthed from the shed and poured liberally. The naked ladies' crystal heads filled with berried Beaujolais.

"Well—to the great British roast dinner!" said Simon, placing the bottle down with a loud bump. He regarded the covered serving dish. "A bit scared to take that lid off, though. It doesn't look quite right."

"Oh, honey, I'm sure it's fine," said Jenn earnestly, trying not to wave that sweaty patchouli stink out of her nostrils. "Simon, are you old enough to drink wine?"

"Over here we all do, Jenn," Simon said airily, downing a double gulp. He'd had a few Stellas while the bird roasted too. He lifted the lid from the serving platter.

Ah geez, thought Jenn. Oh boy.

Simon regarded the contents with bafflement. He would freely admit that he'd overboiled the potatoes and the beans, but why did they look both burned *and* boiled? But it was the chicken that really confused him; only the top of the bird appeared cooked—the skin was black and curling there, while the legs and wings were sort of a putty-pink. And leaking.

Jenn's heart warmed. Male incompetence can be endearing, if they're young, if you need nothing from them. She really did have stuff to teach him, guessed she really was of use there. "Well!" she said. "I can't believe you did all of this. At your age too!"

"I'm not a kid, Jenn."

Something about that simple statement made a sliver of amused recognition rise within her again. "Oh I know, I know that, Simon." The wine tasted like fermented Gatorade. "It's just that I had a boyfriend once, in high school, back in the olden days . . ."

As he listened, Simon started slicing meat from the bird. Burned skin slid up and down with the plunging knife as oozings of pinkish sweat trickled down the nearly raw thighbone. Jenn hoped she wouldn't hurl.

"All I ever got for dinner from him was a Big Mac, once. And it was cold. It wasn't nice, like this . . ." Her voice trailed off. Jenn was glad she'd dressed up for the event, but she didn't remember this dress being so *itchy*, making her feel so hot. The smell of the candle mixed with the burned chicken skin. The scents mingled, clashed with her *Charlie!* perfume, reminding Jenn of long-ago disco keg parties and the way her morning-after clothes would stink of other people's sweat and cigarettes. Jenn wiped her brow.

"Hmm, well . . . I dunno." Simon regarded the pale muscle and pink-rimmed bone against his knife. Slowly, he stopped carving.

They both regarded the severed thigh there on the plate, the bloodied pink and green potatoes. Simon drained his glass of wine, which tasted like blackberries and seemed to go down a metallic pipeline straight to his stomach.

After a moment, Simon quietly covered the dish again. "It's horrible," he said. "What shit that Jamie Oliver is."

"Oh sweetie," Jenn said, simultaneously wiping her skirt with a napkin while internally celebrating this release from salmonella. "It was a totally great effort! I just think . . . like . . . maybe you turned the broiler on instead of the oven?"

Simon looked at her blankly. "I don't know what that means. What utter *balls* I've made of this." He could imagine Arabella's contempt for his failure at such a bourgeois pastime, how Mark would say it didn't matter but examine him with those dark brows lowered like he was trying, for the nine thousandth time, to put his finger on exactly what was slightly *wrong* with his son. Simon drank more wine.

"Cool down on the drama, kiddo." Jenn smiled. She poked the platter with an inquiring, hot-pink fingernail. "How 'bout we just skip to dessert? And as for this . . ." Jenn got up from the table and opened the French doors. Cool wood-scented air rushed into the kitchen. "Let's just give it to the foxes!" Jenn removed the top from the serving dish, walked out onto the deck, and hurled the chicken dinner, potato-bean mess and all, into the air. Bloodied chicken and potato sludge flew in a perfect arc and landed on the springtime lawn. Jenn held the dish in her hand and regarded the mess.

"Jenn!" Simon was shocked.

He'd spent ages trying to make this!

But his stepmother flashed those preternaturally white teeth at him, her eyes were bright and kind, and next thing you know, Simon was laughing, and his laughter made her realize again how young he was, how unlike his father. The meal was scattered on the grass, looking like small-scale carnage, and Simon laughed.

She really was on his side, he thought. Simon blurted out, "Jenn—you know . . . about that ring . . .?"

Jenn smiled and walked back into the kitchen. "You don't have to tell me anything, Simon." Jenn pointed one finger up, schoolmarm-style. "I know you didn't do anything wrong."

"I didn't, actually. But I got scared when I saw her, on the ground and—she was staring. I hadn't realized how different people look when they're dead." Simon sat back down at the table, and looked up at Jenn. "I mean, her eyes were empty, but it was how her *skin* looked all wrong. And the blood."

"Oh God, Simon. I hadn't realized it'd been like that." There was a silent acknowledgment that Arabella's body had been found here—in this very room. Simon picked up a napkin and began smoothing it repeatedly.

"I tried to run but I slipped in it, I think, the blood—and I felt something hard under my knee and it was her ring. So I picked it up." Simon began talking quickly. "I figured the . . . the robber had dropped it. Then I thought he might come back for it so I should get out of there, but *then* I thought the police might be angry that I'd touched it! I jumped over to the Braysons and dropped it in the coals of their outdoors grill. Then I found them and told them Mum was dead." Simon put the napkin back on the table. He stared at it for a moment, before adding. "And all the cops came. But now I'd mucked everything up and couldn't tell anyone. I don't know why I did it, Jenn."

"I bet you were scared out of your mind, finding your mother like that." Jenn stood behind the boy and put her small, warm hands on his shoulders. "I mean, anyone would wig out! Oh!" Something occurred to Jenn. "And then those cops began searching your house and the shed here."

"Yeah, Jenn. So then I saw they thought . . ." Simon didn't complete the sentence. "I mean, I was fucking—I was really messed up and I wasn't thinking clearly. A few days later, Jack Brayson came up to me and handed me the ring—he'd seen me hide it."

"Really?" said Jenn. "How weird."

Simon shrugged. "Oh, he's all right really, Jack Brayson. I was scared at first, but he said it was just between us. That it wasn't anyone's business."

"Hmm," said Jenn. "I kinda think he did tell someone. But it's no big deal." She walked to the hob and examined the cold potatoes still left in the pot. "Anyway, let's eat some of this before we hit the cake. And Simon—"

"Yes, Jenn?" Simon couldn't believe how easy she was to talk to.

"You're just a really good kid, you know."

It was naff, but his eyes filled with tears. Simon looked toward the garden, dark beyond the windows.

.୨୧.

IN THE END, THE TWO of them ended up eating boiled leftover potatoes and carrots. They drank the Beaujolais—Simon was very assiduous about filling glasses, particularly his own. The two of them, middle-aged American and adolescent Brit, slumped easefully back over their chairs and laughed over when they first met. How Simon had sulked! And Jenn had actually brought tea bags to England! Then they made cheese sandwiches and did the dishes together, and decided to eat dessert in front of the telly.

Simon thought Jenn would like Parky. "All the oldies do," he said.

Jenn slapped him on the arm. While Simon searched for ice cream, Jenn took two big slices of black forest gâteau to the sitting room. She just felt so good; she hadn't felt this happy since . . . again she saw the pigeons over Trafalgar Square and her old friend Rubi's coat swinging in the breeze.

Simon stayed in the kitchen just long enough to drink another Stella. Or two.

.୨୧.

HALF AN HOUR LATER HE went quiet next to Jenn on the sofa. She should've gone on alert. There's a texture to certain silences, in particular those that are masking profoundly inappropriate thoughts, as any former babysitter who's been driven home by a booze-bleared husband late at night knows.

Flickering lights, a hyper-awareness of bare legs beneath chaste skirts, the nocturnal forest-path lure of these thoughts equals weighted silences. A woman should be more alert, the mags of the day would've told you. But inside Jenn's head, that'd be an absurd idea! She'd had a lovely time with her boy, who actually had a GD heart of true gold despite his God-awful, messed-up parents. She was doing better by him, she thought, as she lifted a triple-layered chocolate cherry forkful to her face. For what is a mother, apart from an inviolable fortress of thereness? She was there, loving him, appreciating him. From the side of her eye, she could see Simon. Silent in the flickering television light, seemingly watching as Lauren Bacall told Michael Parkinson the mythified story of Bogart's death. Jenn didn't register many things through her filter of idealism. One of them was how ragged the boy's breathing had become.

She looked down at her dessert plate. "Say, do we have any more of that ice crea—"

And Simon lunged.

At first she thought he was reaching for the remote, but it sure as sugar wasn't in her bra and holy Moses, the kid's face was on her neck. All wet and chewing at her skin.

"Oh God, Jenn you're fuckin' lovely, you're—"

His voice was thick and she realized Simon was absolutely hammered.

Also: hard.

It was so quick! His hands were all over her, fumbling around as she tried to figure out a way to stand up. He twisted her right nipple like it was a radio knob, and she dropped her cake plate in shock, so melted ice cream smeared in a cold patch on her lap. Jenn knocked Simon's hand out of her dress, tried to stand up again, but he grabbed her thick wrist. The kid was *strong*. He held her hand back against the wall behind the sofa and then twisted his stocky body so he was on top of her. His breath was of beer and black cherries.

"Stop this NOW, Simon!" Jenn gasped.

"Jenn, oh please . . ."

He was trying to grind his still-clothed pelvis against hers, rubbing against the ice cream while he pleaded into her face, her eyes, her neck. Jenn almost managed to slide away from beneath him, but then he grabbed her other hand and began trying to push it toward his erection. She twisted her arm away, hit him in the face, but he caught her wrist again.

She wouldn't allow his hand to guide hers, she wouldn't touch him.

"Please," Simon said again, "All those nights I heard you and *him*."

"GET OFF ME, YOU JERK!"

Tears filled Simon's eyes, and he released her hand, the one he'd clamped against the wall, but only so he could hold her face to make her kiss him, make her love him, get from her what her body and her kindness made her uniquely qualified to give, and he'd be loved; finally someone would love him entirely.

But releasing both of her hands was, Simon instantly learned, a big mistake. While his strong young fingers gripped her face like iron, trying to turn it toward his, she rolled those big blue eyes of hers desperately to the side and saw what she was looking for.

The lead crystal bowl filled with Springtime Scentsation potpourri. Jenn's hand touched it, fumbled, seized the bowl just as Simon gasped, "You must've known I love you; I'll never be like him, oh, Jenn oh . . .!" He wept as he grappled with her.

And she hit Simon with the crystal bowl on the side of the head just as he orgasmed. Jenn was reintroduced to that musk potent smell of adolescent semen, though the boy's pants were firmly on, thank Christ. Simon released a small, almost silent "O," and slid to the floor, groaning. A little blood seeped out from his cheekbone. It looked much darker than the chicken's blood had.

Now the room was silent, except for their breathing. The television had somehow been turned off in the tussle. Jenn stood up slowly.

She was shaking all over, a deep trembling she'd experienced before.

She'd felt it the night she'd lost Lovina.

As Simon sat up, put his hands over his eyes, and began to weep for shame, Jennifer realized something terrible. On that night, the night she'd lost Lovina, she'd lost something that was hers, would've always been hers.

Now she saw that tonight was different. Simon had never, never, really been her son or her family. God she'd wanted him to be, so very much, but he was just a messed-up kid she couldn't help. Simon moaned and turned away from her, then slowly stood and walked toward the door.

"I'm so sorry," he whispered, wiping tears and blood and shame from his young face.

As he left the room Jenn thought that it'd all been one huge lie. A huge lie she'd told herself, and them, and no one believed her, and they were right not to. Just love isn't enough, just trying and having ideals isn't enough—you need that bond of blood.

She dropped the crystal bowl on the floor. I'm a stupid joke to them, she thought. A stupid, big-boobed joke.

.୨୧.

JENN CLIMBED THE STAIRS, HER shadow illuminated by the hall light. It stretched jaggedly before her. She heard Simon weeping as she passed his bedroom door. She began to cry too, not in his ragged and guilty gasps, but in a soft weeping.

Tears like the endless siftings of rain in this fucking toenail of a country, where no one's allowed to show a little enthusiasm. The whole place barely bigger than Illinois but with a tiny little sky, low GD limits, and secret codes of behavior masked by fake liberal squawking about *inclusion.*

I wasn't included, not really. Not ever.

Jenn found her passport in the pocket of the garment bag in her (not "their" anymore) bedroom closet. She pulled it out and sat on the bed, her bed, on the duvet she'd bought to replace Arabella's. Jenn looked around at the bedroom walls she'd painted the soft lilac of a Pinekill sunrise, the one that hid behind the many billboards' promises of more, now, better, eat, and don't miss out.

Holding the dark-blue passport in her hands, she bent it back and forth. The silver writing on the cover, the pages clothlike, soft. The stamps from Paris, from her honeymoon, from that day at Waterloo. She thought of Rubicon bringing her here for the party; she remembered coming through the door from her honeymoon, laden with tea and a foot massager and TJ Maxx bags and a meaningless marriage— she hadn't known it was all crap, though. She hadn't realized it was all disposable.

Jenn wiped tears from her face, and then remembered she had another Aero bar in her bedside table. She ate it, then resumed bending the passport in her hands, back and forth.

Now there was silence from Simon's room. As for his father? Back and forth the soft passport cover bent, softly back and forth. This time—it wasn't like Mike. She'd let Mark leave her. She felt tired, empty; she'd lost the motto-like ideals from which her energy sprang. She wasn't special. God wasn't on her side.

There was no reason to fight. It was time to go home.

2 4

THE NEXT AFTERNOON, MARK AND Rubicon were at the Waterman's Arms opposite the Richmond Filmhouse. They sat at outdoor picnic tables surrounded by hanging baskets of purple flowers that dripped with a sticky nectar. The Filmhouse had a matinee on that day, *Laura*. Mark and Rubicon sat beneath the spring-sapped flowers and a low oyster-colored sky, each nursing a soda and lime. A packet of salt and vinegar crisps splayed open between them. Rubicon squinted in the direction of the river. Mark blinked up toward the narrow brick road that descended from the high street. A companionable silence.

Mark had been pretty taciturn when Rubicon had returned last night; he hadn't even smiled as he usually did when she'd imitated Cheri Blair's mad grin. And Rubicon had put lipstick on her teeth and everything. The flat had smelled funny too. Like liquorice and bad breath.

But things seemed better now. Rubicon leaned back. "I think I might need glasses."

"Ah," Mark nodded. "It comes to us all." He touched his loafered foot to hers.

"I can't tell if those are small gulls or large pigeons."

" . . . "

A single raindrop fell on the table. Mark rubbed it in with his fingertip.

"I don't suppose it matters much though." Rubicon mused. "Pigeons or gulls."

"Not unl—oh *bugger*!" Mark's heavy brow lowered, and he grimaced. He glanced quickly at her and then back up the street before plastering a rictus grin of welcome on his face. Rubicon turned and saw Daniel and Caro approaching them. Delightful! Daniel wore khaki trousers and a tweedy green sweater; Caro was also dressed in walking garb, her bobbed hair freshly hennaed a gleaming burgundy.

"Caro!" Rubicon waved. "Hey—over here!" Out of the corner of her eye, she saw Mark looking trapped, still with that weird grimace on his face like something had a hold on his throat. Weird, thought Rubicon. Or maybe not?— first time we're out together publicly. But who better to see than Daniel and Caro? Rubicon got up and kissed her friends on the cheeks.

"Where are you elegant folks going?"

"Hello, mate." Daniel shook Mark's hand as he looked from Mark to Rubicon and back again. Rubicon was surprised that he didn't smile. "We're going for a walk up the river. Pub lunch near Pembroke Lodge, then back for a bit of a snooze, I suspect." Mark stood next to Daniel now, but wouldn't quite meet his gaze.

Unlike her husband, Caro didn't require a moment to put her thoughts together. The gleam in Rubicon's eye met hers, and Caro knew Rubicon was telegraphing, "He's mine now. I got him! I'm so *happy*!"

Fabulous! Caro's eyes telegraphed in return. *As it should be!* Aloud she said, "Rubicon—do come look in the Oxfam window with me. There's a creamer in there I think might actually be Royal Doulton, but Daniel says I'm off my game."

Daniel noticed as Rubicon touched Mark's arm with calm possession. "Be right back!"

The two women headed up the narrow brick road and stood chatting with their heads together, one brilliant henna and the other dark and tousled. They ignored the Oxfam window.

Daniel and Mark were alone. Which was exactly what Mark did not want to happen. He knew he owed Daniel: Drape and Stoddard had told him last night what Daniel had seen in the Red Cow, and what they'd later discovered in Thomas Halp's flat. But he also felt ashamed of himself. Leaving Jenn and Simon like that; it was shabby of course, but he wasn't going back—not for a minute would he go back to that life. Mark didn't know what to say to Daniel, and struggled against his usual passivity (not easy, since living with Rubicon had taught him to accept that he wasn't a go-getter. Why go? Why get? So much better to live like a student, and just drift on. He wasn't doing anything wrong; well maybe the Simon thing but . . .)

He'd only married the wrong American. Could happen to anyone, really. And didn't he deserve to be happy, after Arabella? Didn't he deserve to feel loved after all that time?

Mark sat back down. "Well, Daniel. Everything tickety-boo?" Christ. No need to sound like a sodding Mitford novel. He lit a cigarette, and as usual found the things were composure godsends.

Daniel sat in Rubicon's seat and watched Mark exhale. There were lines of worry in Daniel's tanned face. "So, mate . . ."

"Watch Arsenal yesterday, Daniel?"

"No." Daniel had, but wasn't going to be deflected. "It's none of my bloody business, but the coppers have been looking for you."

"They found me. Last night. I owe you thanks, I suppose." Mark sounded churlish, even to his own ears. But somehow he knew in his bones that the revelation from Drape and Stoddard would mean the end of his isolated dream-time with Rubicon—that they would have to face the world now. He hated the thought. Mark watched as Caro said something to Rubicon that made her toss her head back and laugh. He could make her laugh like that, he'd discovered. Marvelous feeling.

Daniel tapped a thick fingernail on the table to draw Mark's attention back. "I saw your watch on his wrist. They told you that, right? Turned out he went to your house that day—Arabella had, well—"

"Requested his services," Mark finished coolly. "The coppers came to Rubicon's last night to tell me last night they'd arrested who'd killed her. Found her checkbooks, jewels in his flat. And a knife that . . . fits."

Daniel began to say more, kept tapping that finger on the table again like the judgment of God, but Mark wasn't listening. He smoked and continued gazing up the street at Rubicon and Caro, who'd clearly settled in for a long natter. Caro had been Daniel's only wife. Trust the jammy bastard to get it right the first time. Plus, no kids. The unfairness of it all, the fucking unearned simplicity of it, didn't bear thinking about.

Up the street, Rubicon checked her watch, saw that it was still twenty-five minutes until the film began, and continued telling Caro about when Mark came to her flat late that night. About his holey socks and red-rimmed eyes and outstretched arms. From the corner of her eye, she could see Daniel talking, talking earnestly while Mark looked only at her. His gaze was unblinking, like a daguerreotype camera's slow aperture recording an eternal moment.

"Mark." Daniel drew his attention back. "What about poor Jenn, with this Rubicon business?"

"I'm not leaving Rubicon, and I'm not going back to Jenn."

"And Simon? Are they ready for the journos who'll be back at your house, wanting quotes?"

Mark blinked twice. Bugger. He'd told the coppers he'd tell Simon about it, and he would, eventually. Soon, of course. Eventually.

Daniel waited, but Mark said nothing. "Christ. You haven't seen either of them?"

"It'll sort itself out, mate." Mark glared. "There's time."

Daniel stood up. "That's your son, *mate*. You can't leave him to face this alone with a woman he's only known for six months. And does Rubicon know you're doing sod-all about this—?"

Mark fiddled with the ashtray, aiming for a Brando-esque cool but instead looking sulky. "She doesn't know about it yet. I decided to wait. The coppers said nothing would be released to the papers just yet . . ."

Daniel began to reply—but Rubicon and Caro were walking back toward them, arm in arm, smiling and strolling with the ease that a spring morning confers. Rubicon's defensive awkwardness was gone, calm grace had replaced it, and Mark knew that his love had done that. Her dark eyes sought his.

The sun burned a diffused dazzling light from behind the oyster clouds and a gray sense of oppression began to envelop Mark. He'd been trying to push it away since last night. Pubgoers' voices swirled around him as he tried to see a way to make escape from his old life permanent. He sipped his flat soda and lime and fought the cobwebs pulling him to the past, to the loneliness, to the joyless duties. Parenthood.

Daniel clamped a muscular hand on Mark's shoulder. The gesture matched the grim promise in his eye as he said, "Tell Rubicon. And look after your wife and your son, Mark. Not just yourself."

Daniel looked at Mark's blankly stubborn face. What was wrong with the man? Then he realized Mark didn't want to care for Simon. That's what he was using Jenn for now. Now that he was tired of shagging her.

The women were getting closer, Caro's little birdlike hand softly resting on the crook of Rubicon's long arm.

Mark spoke under his breath. "Daniel—I'll lunch with Simon in a few—"

"No. You married Jenn. You can't treat the woman like some international babysitting service—"

"I'm never going back. *Never.*" Mark felt the deadening cobwebs tighten around his throat. He knew Jenn, knew her connection with his son. She'd look after him better than Arabella had or he could. And Simon, Mark's resented, beloved weight, was better off without Mark in the house right now. And there was nothing Daniel could do, anyway.

Daniel saw the thought. "You straighten it out, or I'll bring Simon to Rubicon's. Tonight."

Impossible. The bastard. The three of them in Rubicon's glorified bedsit?

Mark stared at Daniel speechless. He thought of all the times he'd had the man on his surgery's stainless-steel table. How he'd told him to forgo pork pies and the curries. He'd put the man on blood pressure medication for God's sake!—but now the women stood next to them again. Rubicon's eyes sparkling, sweetness mingled with pride of possession.

"Absolutely not Doulton, Rubicon says." Caro slipped her arm into Daniel's. "Pure tat. Can't imagine what I was thinking . . ." Caro glanced between the two men. "Are you quite all right?"

"Absolutely." Daniel smiled at his petite wife, her lovely honest face. "Let's start, shall we? If you girls have faffed about quite enough?"

Caro and Rubicon laughed, kissed each other goodbye. As they did so, Daniel spoke quietly to Mark. "Get it sorted."

Mark seized Daniel's arm and muttered "Give us till tomorrow, Daniel. I'll go in the morning."

"Right," Daniel said, "I'll be there later to see you did."

"Not that you don't trust me."

Daniel didn't reply. Mark felt the inevitability; if he didn't return to his home tomorrow, Daniel would bring the boy to Rubicon's doorstep, and he knew, it was fanciful, but Mark knew in his tired, tame bones that he'd never escape again.

DURING THE MOVIE MARK SAT in huddled misery. At least he'd bought time till tomorrow. That meant something, anyway. Mark felt he deserved today, one more day of student life with Rubicon. Poor old Mark ended up paying dearly for this procrastination.

·ᴔᴈ·

AFTERWARD MARK AND RUBICON WALKED along Richmond High Street through herds of rugby drunks; they plodded past the Waitrose, its carpark teeming with BMWs filled with organic yogurts and cheeses and tender grass-fed meats and non-sulfate wines and all the soul-sensitive self-aggrandizing delicacies at the top of capitalism's food chain. They trudged by lilac-festooned, oddly dead-eyed houses flickering internally with media but where no people were visible. Twice during this journey, which had seemed a quick stroll a few hours ago, Rubicon tried to chat—but the sound of her voice made Mark flinch, made him retreat further from her, not physically, but within himself.

His shoulders were slumped forward again, his heavy brows burdened with a turgid shame, his eyes confused, trapped. He looked just as he had in his Arabella days.

Night was creeping in. Rubicon's great love walked next to her, to her flat, as if he were being pushed forward by a dread hand. What had Daniel said?

Had Mark somehow decided *she* was trapping him? Is that how he worked? Oh God, would she have to re-shoulder the terrible strength she'd become used to in the years of her loneness?

And what if, having had him for a while, she could never again find the brittle contentment in living alone?

The green carpet, worn in spots to a brown burlap, of her building stairwell. They climbed the stairs in silence but Rubicon began to feel the percolations of rage increase with each step.

Mark had said he'd loved these stairs, loved their complaining squeaks and wooden wobbly rails. Now with each step they said, fuck him fuck him.

Silently Rubicon turned her key, opened the door and then half-shut it in Mark's face—screw his male sulks and the bullshit self-questioning they prompted. Had she done something wrong, something rude, something needy? Had she been too available, too remote, too small-titted, thin-skinned, knobby-kneed, old? In short, too *human?*

She put water in the kettle and clicked it on. Then Rubicon banged into the bathroom and closed the door with a slam. Mark flinched. He looked around at the dirty bay windows, those branches always trying to scrape their way in. At the old translucent curtains that cast dancing shadows on the walls and the rag rugs flattened and color-drabbed by years, decades, of Rubicon's lovely light duck-walking weight. At the single table with its water marks and orange peels and wonderfully mismatched chairs.

The kettle began to mutter in the little kitchen like a ragged ship's galley. Mark sat at the table and put his head on his hands. Soon, the kettle began to screech and kept screeching; its turn-off mechanism had fallen off years ago.

Rubicon emerged from the bathroom. She sailed past him, but tossed a damp hand towel at his head. Then she snapped the kettle off and made herself a cup of tea. She didn't offer him one, and why should she? She could do sullen silence as well as he; she wasn't going to beg him to say what was wrong, what had clearly gone wrong when talking to Daniel.

Was Mark ashamed of her? Was she someone you'd be ashamed of?

But I was fucking famous!

Well, kind of. Kind of famous.

And now Rubicon knew love was like fame: a little is never enough. Probably a lot wasn't either, though she wouldn't know about that. Both gave you expectations of a world that's rosy-fingered as the dawn, but both are just as goddamn fleeting. Rubicon thought again of Pinekill sunrises, their prodigious promise and compromised beauty. *Man*-compromised beauty, *man*-compromised promise.

She flipped the telly on, flopped down on the futon, and glared angrily at the *EastEnders* Sunday omnibus. Sharon's new man was fit. Too goddamn bad he was her secret brother and all. Well, that's life.

"Rubicon," Mark spoke quietly. He didn't look at her.

She didn't answer.

"Turn that off, please." It wasn't a question. He spoke heavily.

"Nope. Oh, and Mark?"

"Yes?"

"Bite my ass." Fuck him. Don't even look at him. Just look at plump blond Sharon and her pink lips, which twitched like Marilyn Monroe's whenever she got stressed.

"I *beg* your—" For the first time in hours, Mark looked straight at her. "Turn it fucking off, I said. I need to talk to you."

"And I said NO." Rubicon placed a long finger on the remote and sent the volume soaring. Sharon huskily yodeled to her father, Dirty Den. ". . . *But I fink he's dangerous, Dad!*"

Mark stepped in front of the coffee table and tried to seize the remote from Rubicon, but she twisted and held it away from him, pressing up on the volume button. She was surprisingly strong.

"Ow! Give it over, you silly cow, I want to tell you something!"

Mark pulled at Rubicon's arm and began trying to unfurl her fingers' grasp on the remote, but she let go suddenly, his balance was off, and he fell backward onto the Ikea Iktap coffee table. The table cracked beneath him; the remote hit the ground and its batteries sprang out. The TV shut off.

Silence. Rubicon fought the urge to laugh, but she wanted to weep too. Her table was broken and Mark lay like an overturned turtle in its wreckage. But also, and still, there was this: fuck him. He shouldn't have given her hope. She knew what he wanted to tell her.

Mark lifted his hand, looked at the empty remote, and dropped it on the floor. "Christ." He shoved a jagged piece of the broken coffee table out from under his shoulder, then lay back down. He stared at the dirty crown molding on the ceiling.

"If you broke that remote." Rubicon sat forward on the futon and rubbed her wrist. "You and your fucking bimbo wife are going to buy me a new TV. Asshole."

"I *beg* your pardon?"

"You heard me. I know you're planning to leave. Daniel said something to you about sticking to Jenn or something. The fucking traitor."

"No." Mark sat up. Wood bits shifted around him, and he shoved them aside to rub his bum. He was bloody lucky he hadn't fractured his coccyx. But he didn't feel tired anymore, he didn't feel that cobwebbed passivity. He looked at Rubicon, whose eyes were fierce and, he realized, frightened.

"No, love," he repeated, quietly. "Or well, actually, I suppose yes, but it wasn't how you mean it. It's different—"

"Oh it always is, isn't it?"

"Rubicon. It is. I didn't tell you—but I need to go back to settle—"

"See? It's always the cocksucking same—"

"I honestly do not think that's the case here." Mark spoke grimly. "I've been a shit parent, Rubicon. And I was wrong, utterly in the wrong."

"—the woman in the weakest position gets *fucked*."

"Jesus, would you listen? This isn't *about* you, this isn't about me leaving you! Just *listen for a minute*, for fuck's sake!"

"Why should I? When I know what you're going to say?"

"You don't. Unless——" Here a thought struck Mark and he lay flat down on the floor again, heavily. He considered something for a moment. "Unless Caro told you? About the police?"

"Told me what?" Confusion suspended Rubicon's anger, but her eyes remained wary.

"The police. They——somehow Daniel actually found the man who killed Arabella. The police confirmed it. It's quite certain. Tom Halp. I remember him treating the deck after we put it in." Mark's back hurt, and he was pretty sure there was an Ikea wood shard embedded in his elbow.

"It's certain? But that's . . . isn't that good?" It was beyond her why Mark didn't seem relieved.

Mark put an arm over his eyes. "Oh yes," he said vacantly. "Very good indeed. And, you know, funny . . ."

"Funny? Funny how?"

Mark raised his head. He slowly sat up again, surrounded by wood fragments and splattered tea, and looked at Rubicon calmly. "Because, of course, I thought Simon killed Arabella."

Rubicon was silent.

Let's be honest. That idea of Simon's guilt had also occurred to Rubicon, but then the kid was proven to have been with his friends at the cinema, plus had been home for mere seconds when he found her body. Plus *lots* of people had thought that about Simon, and about Mark too.

Now she wondered if Simon thought his father did it. He must have at least considered the possibility.

And perhaps this thinking had become normal, in a world where half of our conscious hours are spent in the flickering reflection of murder, too often the same murder. Again and again a woman, a wife, is slaughtered between commercial breaks. It's the titillation that never sates, watching a woman get offed by someone she has enraged through implacability or unyieldingness or lust or, simply, her existence. And this image drip drip drip of dead women reminds the living ones, the ones watching on the sofa with babies or cats or a simple slice of pizza on their laps, of their flagrant mortality.

Arabella had never felt that fear. She should've been admired for that.

Rubicon continued, "Well, yeah, everyone has passing thoughts, when terrible things like that happen, but——"

"Oh, I was certain. You see, Jack told me Simon hid some jewelry in his garden, just after she died. But it seems now that . . . that actually meant nothing, just a stupid adolescent impulse. And now I'm supposed to go back there, face my son . . ."

"Go back for good, you mean." She still expected to be left.

Mark rose to his knees and leaned forward to put his arms around beautiful haggard Rubicon, whose hair was a shock of question marks, whose hands always smelled of lavender and cigarettes and onions. He wrapped his arms around her torso, placed his head on her lap and sighed, no no no.

"No. Just go there to talk. I hate the thought of going to that miserable house again, even for a minute."

Relief made her twine her fingers through Mark's thinning hair, almost pulling it with loving possession.

But there was something. At the back of her mind.

"Daniel says I must, though. Tell Simon before the papers come 'round."

Rubicon leaned over and kissed Mark's head softly, rubbed her nose along his ear. "So you call him tomorrow, tell him you'll meet him at Pizza Express. It's the mecca of divorced fathers having awkward conversations with their offspring. I've seen it a million times."

"Oh God yes—you're brilliant. It'll kill me to go back to that house. Took so long to get me out of there. But poor Jenn, good lord, what will I do about that?"

"Poor Jenn . . ." Rubicon repeated. She realized that was what had bothered her. "Wait a minute." She sat up, her hands stilled in his mouse brown-gray hair.

"Don't stop," Mark closed his eyes. "I adore your long dirty fingers."

"Okay." Absently Rubicon stroked his hair again, scratched his scalp. She gazed blankly at the curtain's fluttering shadow on the wall. It moved in the shape of a tattered veil, a Miss Havisham veil. "Mark." She didn't want to ask; why ask?

"Hmm?" He sighed, and breathed fully for the first time since seeing Daniel and Caro that morning. Pizza Express. Rubicon would go with him tomorrow. She'd keep him from getting pulled back in, somehow, to that dead domesticity.

"Did you really think Simon had killed her?"

"Oh God yes." Mark shrugged. "The way he was always watching me, after. And she was so horrible to him. Taunting. Vicious."

"She was that way to you too. Maybe he thought you did it? I mean, people did . . ."

"Who knows?" Mark closed his eyes. It scarcely seemed to matter.

"But Mark . . ." Goddamn it, she didn't need to know; don't ask the question, Rubicon. Don't you know yet, at your age, how precarious happiness is? How much it depends on delusion and keeping the blinders fully in place? "So you married Jenn, thinking that he'd actually . . .?"

Mark didn't even open his eyes. "I knew he was starving for affection, and she'd give it to him. He'd never hurt her."

Rubicon's hands kept working through Mark's hair, oh so gently now. He couldn't see her face, the shocked disillusioned eyes. "And you left her alone, in the house with him these last few weeks. Thinking that, about Simon."

"Yes, but Rubicon." Mark placed a warm reassuring hand on her ankle. "I was wrong."

And so was I, Rubicon thought as she bowed her head and her hands finally stilled. Outside, a car alarm began to blare repeatedly through the darkness. Something shifted in Rubicon's love for Mark. She saw Jenn again as she'd first seen her at Waterloo—the ridiculous patriotic T-shirt, the eyes so eager they almost crossed. What Mark had done to Jenn was shabby. So passive and selfish. Her fingers smoothed Mark's brow, and she waited to feel her love for him change, to shift to something more minor. It didn't happen.

Poor Mark. But also yes, poor Jenn and poor abandoned Simon.

2 5

THE MORNING AFTER HER STRUGGLE with Simon, Jenn awakened at 5:07 a.m. She'd been in the middle of a confusing dream in which she was back home in Illinois but had to take the tube to the dentist. Unfortunately, she didn't have the proper currency, only dollars. Consequently, she'd had to ride on the top of the train, crouching low when reaching underpasses, with her skirt hoisted up high so her rubbery thighs could grip the train's roof. She was speeding toward a low bridge, too low, Jenn was sure, and she pressed her head down, gripping tightly with thighs and fingertips and every fearful ligament—there was a sudden pulling lurch in her stomach as the crash was imminent . . .

Jenn's blue eyes sprang open.

Richmond.

And Simon.

And complete defeat of this life she'd tried to make, of the peace she'd tried to bring to this small broken family. What a fool.

Hard rain outside like the scrabble of dogs' clawed feet, leaves rustling as they tipped jet-fueled rainwater off, then flexed back up eager for more liquid filth. Just as Jenn was about to roll over that pulling lurch seized her again, but this was no dream. She threw back the covers.

Jenn barely made it to the en suite bathroom in time to be violently sick. It was bile, mostly, that she vomited, bile mixed with Aero chocolate oils. Then with her throat raw and ragged, her stomach aching with emptiness, Jenn placed her sweat-soaked forehead against the porcelain seat.

It was nice and cool and solid.

Jenn remembered throwing up once after a kegger in high school, and the toilet seat had felt nice and cool then too.

High school.

Jenn froze. Big round eyes staring straight forward, wide and unblinking. Her sweat turned cold.

Then another heave seized her, and she spent the next two minutes lurching over porcelain until her knees were tile-creased and her fingers shook with exhaustion. Another five minutes with her head pressed to the toilet, to make sure it was all over. Her head was bathed in sweat.

Don't move. Breathe, but don't move. She'd had a thought.

After a while, slowly—oh so slowly, as in a tai chi ascent, Jenn rose from her knees. She gently plucked a navy hand towel from the O-shaped rack. She wiped her face on the towel, folded it, lay it reverently down near the marble basin.

Moving toward the bedroom as if a vase were balanced on her head, Jenn remembered her weird thoughts lately, the giving-up thoughts and the illusion of defeat, her fatigue and the plaguing need for those Aero bars.

Outside, rain had softened to an earth-patting caress.

As if the focus of a solemn and public procession, Jenn moved to her (their!) bedside table and took out her date book.

She'd dyed her hair three weeks ago Tuesday.

Her last period was seven weeks ago.

Hope rose within her like a clenched fist.

·ᥫᩭ·

MARK ALSO AWAKENED BEFORE SIX, but he stayed in bed. He loved these early mornings in Rubicon's rickety futon, her body curled toward his and the opalesque vulnerability of her closed eyelids. He lay there with thoughts wandering cloudlike through his head; at this time of morning they hadn't yet hardened into fear. He thought of the love he had seen waver in Rubicon's eyes the evening before, when she knew what he'd thought of Simon. Mark never wanted to see the warmth, the steady affection gone from those dark eyes of hers again. He must make sure of that, most of all.

Of course Rubicon wondered how could he have thought that of his son—but how could he *not* have thought that? He himself had wanted to strangle Arabella; he himself had dreamed of knocking her over with his car, repeatedly, satisfyingly, feeling her bones splinter beneath the Volvo's tank-like frame.

But he hadn't done it in real life. And now he knew that Simon hadn't either. Mark realized that Simon had almost certainly made the same wrong assumption about him.

Christ, what a mess he'd made of it all. But the long shadow of his wife's murder was finally retreating. Just these few final hurdles. These he would try to clear with a little honor. It wasn't too late to try.

At ten, he'd call Simon to suggest lunch.

JENN LAY ON HER BED. She had remade it, very carefully, by pulling the duvet up and smoothing it with her hands gently, over and over again until the cotton seemed warm and was softened by the oiled warmth of her palm. Usually she'd just hoist the damn thing up, this stupid duvet (what's wrong with sheets and a nice separate quilt instead of these loose sacks the Brits call bedding?) and let it fall slouching onto the bed but now . . .

She had to be attentive. No weight. No lifting. No stress or negative thoughts.

Duvets were just fine really, she pretended. Honestly they are.

Breathe. Don't think or react or respond just yet, not quite yet. Just lie in the morning light, surrounded by the nourishing unthinking rainfall outside her window. She was as the earth upon which it fell.

So Jenn lay there perfectly still, hands crossed over her chest like she'd done when in junior high and playing "Light as a feather/Stiff as a board" during sleepovers. After two hours and seventeen minutes of stillness, she quietly got up, combed her hair, and left the bedroom. The pharmacy would open at eight.

She paused as she passed Simon's room. All was silence within. Jenn lay a gentle hand on Simon's bedroom door. She held her hand there for a minute, wondering if she was going to be able to teach him about love, after all.

Then Jenn descended the stairs, walked to the pharmacy on Sheen Road and bought a pregnancy test.

2 6

THE PHONE RANG AT 8:40 A.M. It was a jarring sound within the stillness of the Barnes flat. Mark was back asleep, and now Rubicon was awake, curled up like a prawn while reading a Molly Keane book.

The old landline sat right near Rubicon on the floor. An outdated umbilical reached from its back and toward the wall, and another cord curled toward a separate answering machine. After three unanswered rings the machine kicked in and the caller spoke to the room.

It was Tatiana Gripp. Herself, not a minion:

> *Hallo, cherub! I received your messages. Of course you're gutted by that "Style" debacle. I told you, it's all yummy mummies and their bloody baby bumps these days, God help us. But perhaps you have a little update on that friend of yours? The one who was murdered a while back? A little birdie told me you might know about some developments . . .*

Rubicon was listening, now with the book flat on her chest and her head tilted so it touched the warmth of Mark's slumbering shoulder. So the jackals were beginning to circle. Perhaps she and Mark should rent a cottage in Port Isaac. The best idea would be—and here's an idea Rubicon never would have had six months ago—that they bring Simon with them. Yeah, he's a kind of intense kid, but get him away. Lord, Tats was leaving a long message.

> . . . *We might get you a little attention for that, sweetie. Also, Rubicon my love, I was wondering if you're free tomorrow morning. Of course you are. One of the Boo Radleys was supposed to exhume himself to do this, but no such bloody luck, so why don't you come to All Saints Road to open a new vinyl shop? Very vintage, like you, rather hip—no pay but perhaps some lovely coverage—*

Mark turned in his sleep and rubbed his face on Rubicon's shirt, feeling the bony ribcage beneath it, and the beating heart it contained. He wished that horrid-sounding woman would stop screeching into the answerphone.

Rubicon put her arm around him while listening to phones ringing in the background at Tat's office, girls chatting and laughing, computer pings. That life she'd led, the lolly and lunches and lovely dosh and the almost chilling manipulation of reality. The media had obviously heard about the arrest of Arabella's killer, and Tats was moving in.

Still holding Mark, Rubicon reached over and picked up the phone. "Sorry, Tats," she said. "I'm no longer into getting 'coverage.' If that changes, I'll give you a bell. But, y'know, probably not. Byeee, sweetie." She hung up.

"Mark." Rubicon touched the top of his beloved head, moved as always by the small whorl of thinning hair at the crown, Mark's crowning mortality. He raised his heavy brows, looked up at her with a look of such gratitude that it resolved her. She might be a flake. She might be "vintage." She might be a husband-stealing ex-fame whore who still lived like she was a rather stupid eighteen-year-old, utterly confused by things like tax benefits and pension schemes and estate planning—but she realized she was still, at heart, a girl from Illinois. She wanted to be good.

"Mark," Rubicon said again. "Today's the day. You sort things out with Simon, and we'll deal with poor old Jenn later."

Mark rubbed his ear and yawned. "That's what I was thinking earlier. But also: fucking hell."

"Yep."

"What a mess it all is." Mark stretched. "But I was thinking this earlier too.

We're probably through the worst of it. I mean, it's still a fucking shambles, but now it's just the usual shambles people make of their lives—not a Hammer horror film."

"I guess that's true." Rubicon kissed that Velveteen Rabbit spot of his without knowing quite why she felt sad. His heavy, trusting, middle-aged warmth was in her arms, which was all she could ask for.

.୨୧.

AND OF COURSE THE TEST was positive. Jenn was surprised at how easy and how certain it all was. Not like the old days at all. You didn't even have to use the first pee of the day, thank God, like you used to. And although the little sticks were as flimsy as straws, apparently they're right like 99 percent of the time.

So she peed.

Though she knew already, anyway. The quickening.

Jenn shook her head in humble amazement. How silly she'd been, not to know that God would work for her, know that her body would heal despite the insult it had been given so long ago. She'd thought her depression and fatigue were just, well, kind of how things *were* here. Look at everyone else here, on this island. Terrified to mold the world to the way it should be. No one wanting to seize or support what is, or should be, theirs. This place had got her all confused; she'd forgotten that she was never tired, or down in the dumps. And that she never walked away from duty.

But now God had reminded her.

So. The Everleigh family. Well! It was a good old challenge, all right. But now she was equipped for victory. For the first time in decades, since Lovina had been scraped from her womb, Jenn got properly to her knees and thanked Jesus. He'd given her the ammo she needed to keep this family together.

Rising to her feet, Jenn moved the pee stick with its absolutely positive positive (++!) to a safe spot at the side of the marble sink and walked to Simon's room. She would awaken him, talk to him with God's wry wisdom, and then maybe make the two of them some banana pancakes.

No! She'd be making all *three* of them pancakes!

She decided the baby would probably like a few chocolate chips in there too.

Down the hall with her hand on her belly, her footfall as light as her heart, she tapped on Simon's door.

Nothing.

Oh teenagers! Jenn gave a fulsome chuckle. How they do *sleep*! She tapped again, harder, but in an upbeat staccato. Nothing.

Jenn cracked Simon's door open and saw that his unmade bed was empty. So she called down the stairs. "Simon?" she chirped. "Hey kiddo, let's have some breakfast!"

But the front door was open. Simon had snuck out while she was upstairs peeing on the stick. She'd just wait for him. It'd take a little while but eventually he'd be thrilled about the news.

Now she really *was* his family.

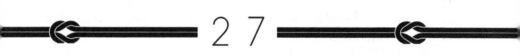

2 7

AFTERWARD, RUBICON THOUGHT ABOUT HOW casually she and Mark had begun the morning. They dressed as they always did during the brief time they shared, just slid on any old trousers, pulled T-shirts off the floor.

Mark pulled on his pen-marked, biscuit-colored corduroys and a white shirt with the sleeves rolled up. Rubicon always remembered what he wore, what they ate (toast crumbs would sit on the table for weeks. Mark's toast crumbs). That they nervously discussed what to say to Simon about the arrest of Arabella's murderer and the impending media attention. What to say to Jenn about a generous divorce arrangement.

Mark wondered how he could apologize to Simon for the thoughts he'd had, the decisions he'd made. He hoped the boy had wondered if Mark himself had killed Arabella—had also wondered until the assumption seemed an obvious truth—because then at least they could share the guilt. If guilt it was.

·ᘒ·

AT 9:30 A.M., JENN HEARD SIMON return home. The front door squeaked open slowly, like a tomb opening in a Vincent Price movie. There was an almost silent shuffle, an inheld breath, a muted click. The boy, young man, whatever—there should be a word for being sixteen: "adolescent" is too clinical, "teenager" too market-angled—had endured a rough night. But even the dark circles under his eyes were blooming with youth, the self-pitying curve of his shoulders riotous with testosterone, the dodgings of his mind hormone-swamped with inexperience, love, and confused self-preservation.

In short, all the kid wanted was to sneak back to his room unseen and shut the door, possibly forever.

"Hey Simon!" It seemed like Jenn popped up out of the bloody floorboards.

He stared at her with dead, reproachful eyes. He was bloody humiliated, and there she was, chipper as fuck, looking like she was about to milk a sodding ox or something. Eyes aglow, not a shred of normal human embarrassment.

Slowly, Simon walked by her and climbed the stairs. He did not look at Jenn again. She heard him move down the hallway, re-enter his room. The door was closed with quiet firmness.

Jenn wished he'd banged it shut, even though that door sometimes stuck when he did that. A slammed door would have been easier to dismiss as adolescent sulks. But then she caught a glimpse of herself in the front hall mirror, and she smiled.

Her beauty had re-blossomed, like a peony luxuriating in sun-toasting warmth... This, this is how she was *meant* to look, not all quiet and sedate in midnight blue, like poor old Rubicon thought. Jenn was supposed to be firm, be grounded, to flourish in the brightness of her mind and God's great kindness to her.

She could win Simon over.

He would be moved, she knew, by the knowledge of the baby inside her. She pictured it as the size of a lima bean but fully formed, with soft hair gently waving in amniotic fluid as it bobbed and nestled in the cavorting fluid of her womb.

It changed everything, everything.

Because of course now, to Jenn, even to have thought of leaving seemed to stink of the weakness of retreat. Silly even to have considered it, when obviously (hadn't God made it super-clear?) it was all up to her. The decisions about and the definition of this family was up to her—and Jesus of course—she added hastily, emptily, just for luck. This baby, this little bean inside her united them all forever. It was her own internal American ally! She'd let it have a little English accent, though, because just imagine being called *Mummy*.

Cool.

This one was a boy, Jenn knew, and she was happy with that. Boys just have things so much easier in this world, Jenn nodded, as she sifted ingredients together. She'd decided to make banana chocolate chip bread instead of pancakes. Bread would last till Simon's sulks were over. Easing a sunny lump of butter into a bowl, she then added a quarter cup of brown sugar and a quarter cup of white. Then, as her hands worked the fat and the sweet together, as sugar-grained welts of butter oozed white then warmed to translucence between her fingers, Jenn thought of how lucky boys are. How they don't even know it, but there it is, luck. In their lives every single day. From the beginning, a woman (her!) willing to sacrifice for them. All through their lives, boys can go bald or get glasses, be rude or even mean, eat every single thing they want and then not even think about it later.

Someone will always care for them. A woman. Maybe not fair but the way it seems to be.

And I will always care for *him*. Jenn looked up to the ceiling, toward Simon's silent room, clasped sweet, buttered hands together, and promised, "God. Let me care for both my children, teach them how to love. Let Simon, please let Simon be my first and oldest child."

Within her the bean flipped, the quickening occurring again like a sudden fillip of joy, and she knew it would happen.

Sifting flour, smashing bananas, flicking in chocolate chips, Jenn decided that when the bread was in the oven she'd go talk to the kid—sit down next to him and stroke his dun-brown hair. He'd be embarrassed by last night, at first, sure. But he'd learn. And hey, they could talk about babies' names! Maybe they could name him after that perfume of hers that Simon liked so much. *Charlie.*

Jenn thought that was such a cute idea.

And then the phone rang.

.୨୧.

"HELLO!" SHE ANSWERED THE CALL with a voice bright as a bell.

"Uhm."

"Mark? Is that you?"

"Hallo. Jenn—"

"Hey! What's up, Mark? Doing okay?"

". . ."

"Sorry, are you there?"

"Yes, Jenn. I'm here. I'm—good. You sound—good."

"Thanks! I'm doing great!" A moment's silence. Then they both spoke at the same time.

"I was going to call you—"

"Jenn, I was won—"

"Ha!" Jenn chortled.

"You first, Jenn. Absolutely." Over in Barnes, Mark looked at Rubicon and gestured toward the phone. He made a face to indicate that Jenn, under the circumstances, seemed bizarrely happy.

Rubicon had no clue what his grimace meant.

Mark shook his head impatiently and put his attention back toward Jenn.

"Mark. Come over," said Jenn, and her voice changed to a ripe fulsomeness.

"Jenn. I'm terribly sorry about all of this, but we need to make arrange—"

"Oh, Mark." If he could've seen her, Mark would have been extremely irritated by the patient, saintly look on Jenn's face. He would also have been intimidated by the certainty and power of her meaty, oiled hand as it rested on her hip. "Mark, don't worry about that. It's in the past. Nothing matters but your family needing you. Nothing matters but the future we create."

"Er . . ." His sigh reached down the line. "Well, Jenn, that's very pretty but, you know, sometimes the, well, our personal needs can oppose . . ."

"Mark. C'mon over. I'll expect you in an hour, okay?"

"Wait! Is Simon there?"

"Of course he's here! And he'll be so happy to see his dad! And Mark, remember—"

"What?"

"Everything's ahead of us . . ."

Then she hung up quickly, giving him no time to reply.

MARK TOLD RUBICON ABOUT JENN'S weird confidence during that call, but he didn't say how much her optimism felt like bullying— he didn't need to. She got it. Rubicon had been born with the type of mouth that sifts downward in repose, and consequently had borne decades of men telling her, "Smile! It may never happen!"

So of course she knew what Mark was not saying: that Jenn was talking to him like men talk to women, like Bush talked to Blair, like victory talks to history.

In short, he was just there to agree. To reflect a worldview back to its source.

Neither Rubicon nor Mark could wait for the day to be over, for the connection with Jenn to be snipped.

JENN THOUGHT, RIGHT! CHARLIE'S DAD'LL be here in an hour, so I'd better manage Simon now. By day's end we'll all be united. It's totally doable; everything is so easy when the universe is working with you and you know what's right. All that had been needed was certainty.

How she had missed it! But now it grew within her.

Men, Jenn thought affectionately, after she put the banana bread in the oven and climbed the stairs to Simon's room, do really have life so easy. I guess that's why they love to make things complicated! That's why we women are here. To show them what's right. To say, 'Keep it simple, stupid.'

Jenn smiled toothily and knocked on Simon's door.

2 8

"WELL, AT LEAST SIMON IS there, so I can talk to them both."
Rubicon gnawed on a fingernail. "Wait. I thought we were going to
take him out to talk."

"I don't know . . . now I think—" Mark paused and grunted. He'd just bent
over to slip on his battered black shoes, so old their stiff gleaming leather had
molded to the shape of his long, flat feet.

Rubicon, of course, had no idea it was the last time she'd watch him do this.

"—that I should talk to Simon alone, about his mother . . . and then to Jenn."

"Okay . . ." Rubicon stood behind Mark, who was now adjusting his sweater.
Wrapping her arms around his neck, she inhaled the woodchip scent of his flesh
mingling with the chemical odor of Tegrin shampoo. Her words ticked his ear.
"Better not to have the new woman around till you've closed the chapter with both
the old ones?"

"Something like that." Mark turned and looked into her haggard dark eyes.
Such sweetness there. How had he ever found her brittle, needy? But then, Mark
thought with pride, maybe I've changed that. Maybe what she needed was *me?*

Rubicon spoke into Mark's neck, but she could feel that smile of his, his long fingers on her not-so-taut waist. "Just get this over with, tear it all off like a fricking Band-Aid. Tell Simon about the police finding the guy who killed Arabella. Tell Jenn you're divorcing her and hiring an attorney today. After that, it's all just fallout."

"It's going to be truly horrible. Can we not just skip all of this and run away to Portugal?"

"Wouldn't that be great?" For a moment, they both stood, wondering what the hell they'd do in Portugal and wishing they could find out. Then they sighed and separated. Mark sat down to finish his cup of tea, to light another one of those very moreish cigarettes. Rubicon kissed the small bald spot at the back of his head, and went to put on some kohl eyeliner.

Twenty minutes later they left the Barnes apartment.

.୨ୡ.

JENN AGAIN TAPPED SOFTLY ON Simon's door. There was no reply, just the sound of Simon's bed squeaking as he rolled over. She smiled with affection and soft superiority (teenagers! Give 'em a glass of wine and they think they're Bruce Willis!), but she felt a little nervous as she tried the door handle.

It was unlocked. Gently, Jenn opened the door.

Don't let him upset you. You've got a baby on board.

But let him know he is loved; he is so needed—Charlie and I will really be his first family. And through us he'll learn to love properly, to protect like a man. He's a part of Charlie and me, forever and ever.

And Mark too, of course.

The room looked the same as the first night Jenn had ever seen it, with the eaves window overlooking that now-lush tree in the yard, those funny clay-pot English rooftops with the bird-skeleton aerials stuck on top. Tree branch tips had burgeoned, the leaves still that light inquisitive green of springtime. New life.

Ah! The reason this room looked so like that first night was that the poster of that topless model Jordan was back up over his bed, the movie poster gone. Jenn and Jordan again regarded each other, one insolent with mocking sexuality, the other condescending in her pity. That girl is just a slut, really, Jenn thought. She didn't know why she felt sorry for her the other day, on that TV show. Plus, Jordan was kind of *mean*.

"Simon?"

Simon was silent. He lay on his narrow bed with his back to her, his knees curled up and one arm over his face. That arm and his shoulders were firm and man-like, but the skin on his neck still had the oiled glow of a child's. What a tender time this is for a man, Jenn mused. Waiting for the power of the world to descend.

"Simon."

"Leave me be, can't you?" This reply was muffled in his shirtsleeve, and even after Jenn sat gingerly on his narrow bed to lean over him, she could see nothing more than a pink ear and square jaw. He did not move to make room for her.

"Simon. You were drunk. It's no biggie!"

He was silent, but his ear turned from pink to red.

"Plus, kiddo, we haven't had time really to become mother and son, so you'd really know it, really feel it down to your bones."

"You're not my mother. And you won't be. So why don't you just bugger back off to the States? No one wants you here."

"Oh, Simon." Jenn wasn't being condescending now. Being so close to this boy's pain—or perhaps it was the delicacy brought about by this life blooming within her—made her ache for him. It might just be crazy old hormones, but it goddarn *hurts* to feel shame at that age. He had to know how she loved him, that now they were utterly and eternally connected through blood.

"Listen, kid. I'm not going back to the US. I'm here for good. I'm gonna see you graduate from school, and I'm gonna help you pack for college." Simon didn't move; but he was listening. "And not so long from now, seriously, really soon—you're gonna look at me and think, 'I thought *that* was hot? That fat old Yank?'"

He didn't laugh but one finger reached up to rub his eye. That was good.

Jenn placed a cautious hand on Simon's back. She felt the warmth and muscle of it, and he didn't brush her away. Good. For a minute they were silent as Jenn gazed out the window, where the marble-like depth of England's low clouds swept through a sky blue and vivid as hope.

A deep calmness swept over Simon.

Jenn felt him exhale.

What a bounty life is. What a blessing is springtime. Yes, Jenn could be fatuous— but everyone's felt this way at times, and it's always too fleeting a feeling: in that moment we are redeemed just a bit, we are new for a moment, before a sound or an image pulls us back into the vacant business, empty busy-ness, of our blinkered days.

"Jenn." A tear-depleted voice. Monotone.

"Yes, Simon?"

"I know you don't feel the same." Long pause. "But I love you."

"Oh, kiddo. You don't, not really." She placed a hand on her stomach. "Plus, you know I love your father."

Simon rolled over and clasped her hand between his two palms, held it to his chest. He had his father's thick eyebrows but a square determined jaw which, Jenn knew, would look better as he aged and time coarsened his skin.

"You don't laugh with him like you do with me—Jenn, I just want to scoop you up and look after you. Properly."

"Oh." An old resentment, one she didn't know she still clutched to her chest, swelled within her. Was this what life could have been if Lovina, if Mike's accident, had never happened? Is this what college boys say to their girls, what young men are like before life has hardened them to their advantages? Imagine.

"God, Simon. You're going to be so wonderful for the right girl when she comes along."

His dark eyes glowered. He clutched her hand tighter. "She has—"

"When you're a grown-up."

Simon's dark eyes glowered, his hands tightened on hers and his voice cracked. "Mum said he'd never be a proper man, you know." Simon paused for a moment, then said, "I think that's probably why he killed her. She was always sayi—"

"Simon!"

Simon sat up and held Jenn by the shoulders, talking loud and fast, finally telling her what he'd always known. "—saying he was useless, a useless shag and a pathetic, limp, beige man, and the moment I found her, I knew—"

Jenn touched his cheek. "Simon. You know that's not true. And if you don't, you really should."

"It *is* true, Jenn! Who else? We spent a year here alone together. The way he'd look at me . . ."

"Simon. I'm going to have his baby."

Silence. For a moment she could hear the sounds of the house creaking, the abrupt flapping of birds' wings outside, the snap of a branch breaking. Jenn removed her hand from Simon's face. It felt cold without that contact. He must have felt the same, because Simon slowly leaned forward to gingerly wrap his arms around her, gathering her precious bundle to his heart. His arms were firm and warm.

252

"Oh, Jenn." He sighed.

"Simon, it's the best news ev—"

"Listen to me now." He spoke urgently. "It could still *work*. Us, I mean. *He* won't give a sausage, and it'll be a nine-day wonder for the neighbors, but then Jack Brayson and that lot will go back to their fucking riveting discussions about tax rates and Gordon Brown's eyebrows. My mum left plenty of dosh behind, we'd be fine—we could have this house and each other and," he touched his warm young forehead to hers, and she could smell sleep on his soft breath. "*And* that . . . baby. Let me look after you, Jenn."

She didn't know why she'd let him go on so long. She also kind of didn't want him to stop talking because it felt so nice in his—no—what was she saying? Jenn pulled back.

"No, Simon. You've got to grow up. This baby means your dad's going to come back home to us, and we will be a normal real family."

Simon looked at her pityingly from beneath those heavy brows, and then laughed. One barking, "Ha!"

Jenn stood up. "And he'll be here soon. So come down and have some cereal."

"Do you actually think he's going to tell Rubicon to piss off so you can play happy families? Best of British luck with that, Jenn!" Simon was caught between tears and anger. "He couldn't stand having *me*, and at his age he definitely won't like the news of another squirty little shit dribbler."

Jenn went pale. How *dare* this kid call Charlie names. Or Mark, of course. She walked to the door thankful that Charlie seemed calm inside her, not upset or trembling. He was just calm and certain and right now pretty pissed off.

She whirled back around and faced Simon again, her thin brows peevishly down, and one muscular hand on the door handle. "You owe me an apology for that, kiddo. You do *not* say stuff like that about my baby. *Ever*." Jenn glared from the doorway. "And just so you know, I'd knock down anyone who said junk like that about you."

The bedroom door slammed shut behind her, hard. So hard that two books, a Lynx deodorant, and an old Chewbacca action figure fell over on Simon's dresser. A few paint chips flew through the air as the door shook on its hinges. Neither Jenn nor Simon were aware of this, but the door had just jammed in its frame.

"Jenn," Simon called. "I'm sorry!"

She shouted back from the stairwell. "Your father will be home in a few minutes and we'll see what he says about that mean comment of yours!"

"I love y—" but Simon knew she could hear him no more. He got up to follow her, but just rested his head upon the shut door.

How could Jenn not listen to him? For so long, Simon had assumed that Mark had killed Arabella that it seemed a blatant, incontrovertible fact. The sky is blue, the dew is damp, Cold Play are naff, and my father killed my mother.

Simon would learn, too late, how wrong he was.

2 9

MARK AND RUBICON STOOD ON the pavement in front of his house.

A sparrow flew aggressively low over their heads—its nest was nearby and tiny birds peeped thinly from above, hidden within a magisterial wealth of swaying branches and burgeoning leaves.

"Right."

Mark's face was set and his skin grayish in the light of the morning. She didn't like letting him go in there on his own, but Rubicon agreed that Simon and his father should be alone when the boy learned about his mother's death and the arrest of that painter. Plus the least they could do for Jenn was give her some privacy while being dumped.

"I'll be out here. If you need the Marines." Rubicon held Mark's pale face between her long fingers. They stood a silent moment with their foreheads together, this middle-aged couple, just the same height. Around them the cul-de-sac road was at its most chintzily beautiful, green shoots of ivy and tangled roses beginning to rise, snails squelching up cement planters which emitted fetid marigold odors. And that black faux-iron mailbox with the attached magazine rack perched next to the door. It contained a single curling Oddbins flier.

Mark and Rubicon looked into each other's eyes and didn't think of wasted years or of the useless narrowing fear they'd each walked through before finally laying hands on one another. They just looked forward to later. Later, when there would be cups of tea and a recounting of what Mark said and what Jenn, what Simon, said in reply. There'd be Dr. Oetker pizza and *Corrie*, and desultory convo about where to get a new coffee table and what exactly to do with Simon, post-Jenn. There'd be life, in short, niggling and burdensome and brief; but also the blessed shared expanse of another person's mind to ease the clamoring of one's own.

"Right," Mark said. "Roll on, tomorrow." They kissed briefly, perfunctorily, and then he walked away, up the garden pathway. Rubicon stood alone on the pavement.

·9℃·

JENN WAS IN THE FRONT room when she heard Mark's key in the lock. She rubbed wet palms hard against the knees of her boot-cut jeans (Kate Middleton wore them, so they must be cool). As the door opened, Charlie gave a flip inside her. Hey kid, Jenn thought, you and me.

Mark walked in the room, cleared his throat, and without thinking clattered his keys down where he always had. Into an Ecuadorian bowl Arabella had once assured him was molded from dung. The sitting room looked lovely, but much too clean. The upholstery had been Febrezed, steamed, plumped; it seemed untouched by human ass. A plate was centered on the immaculate table, containing oversized croissants that looked like they'd been glazed with wood varnish. There was no vibrant mess in this place, though someone had opened the blinds on either side of the video console and morning light streamed in. Dust motes didn't dare dance through the air, though, not with Jenn around. The air was still and empty, sterile and dully paused in anticipation. He cleared his throat.

"Hey, Mark! Want some pastries?" Jenn spoke loudly.

He wanted to reply, "Indoor voice, please," as he had to Simon when he was a child. "Hallo, Hi—Jenn. No, thank you."

A sudden loud bang above told him Simon was in the house. Good. Mark had to be quick, even brutal; Jenn's determinedly bright face made that clear. Look at her. Welcoming the wand'ring husband home, dulling him with the flabby gloss of croissant consumption. At the same time, he could feel cobwebs of the past softly wrapping around him. This house, this miserable bugger of a house . . .

But he was kind, Mark.

"You look good, Jenn. Can Simon come down?" Mark took his old spot on the sofa and instinctively began to reach for the channel changer. Then he stopped—no channel changer again, not for him. Jenn curled down opposite him with her lips in a pink lipsticked smile and hands folded complacently over her stomach.

God the woman was irritating, and how shameful that he found her so.

"It's—oh, Mark. It's so good to see you. Just so so good. But Mark—"

"Or shall I go up to get him?"

Jenn raised an arch finger. "First I have to tell you, Mark. Our son just said some pretty mean things to me." Her thin brows drew down tightly. "I said you'd give him a talking-to."

She picked up a croissant and those tiny plentiful teeth of hers bit concisely through it, before chewing with flake-spraying incisiveness.

Another loud BANG came down from Simon's room and made Mark flinch. Why didn't the boy just come downstairs and sulk directly at him? God knows he'd done that often enough before. And why was Jenn behaving like Mark was just back from a business trip, as opposed to a wildly satisfying interval of shagging her childhood friend?

"Right, well—"

"You see, Simon's a really good egg . . ." Jenn said, still with the coquettish finger raised. "And with our love and help he will be super-happy. Because there's something you *need to know*."

Mark looked at her and thought, The woman's skin is poreless as peach-colored rubber; her eyes, her hair, even her silly pink ears seem to be made of a richly indestructible plastic.

And he felt the beginnings of that old dank weakness. My God, indomitability is wearying on those around it, and both Mark's wives had had it in spades. He leaned back, feeling the sofa re-embrace the slouch he'd formed within its depths over the years, the endless years of sitting there listening to one wife or another tell him *things he needed to know*. Another few minutes and he knew passivity would seep through him like an IV infusion. Unless he fought, fought now, he'd never get away. Never get back to the messy little flat with the kitchenette and the mismatched chairs and the tall woman with one front top tooth just slightly, adorably folded over another.

"Jenn, I'm terribly sorry . . . but I am proceeding with the divorce."

It was out! So why was she still looking at him with that pink beatific smile across her face. Why did she continue speaking as if he hadn't said a word? He'd said it aloud, hadn't he? Had he?

"The thing is," she said, "Simon's just getting to know that we are a family—a real family. And it *is* for real, it's beyond anything that you and Rubicon can do anything about."

Oh no, it bloody wasn't.

"You see, Mark . . ." Jenn leaned forward and patted his corduroyed knee. "I'm pregnant."

For a moment, Mark just sat there. He twitched Jenn's painted nails away from his leg, but then he just sat there. Breath taken, wife waiting, mistress outside gnawing her fingernails. Then a roar of defiance swelled through him.

"NO."

"But I am, Mark." Sharp white teeth appeared in a Cheshire cat smile.

"No. No, no no no." He dropped his head into his hands. Jenn moved to him, put her arm on his shoulder and tried to peer down into his face.

It was ghastly, the way she seemed to smell of nothing but chemicals.

"Oh Mark, we've been gifted with a baby who will truly bring us together." Jenn spoke with rapid excitement. "As a family, it's a freaking *miracle*, Mark! And Simon and you and I and the baby boy will be—"

BANG from upstairs.

"You said you couldn't get pregnant." Mark's voice was thick.

Jenn sat back, smiling gently, thinking, He's in shock, it takes a minute to accept miracles. "They told me I couldn't! That's why this is such a—"

Simon's muted voice came from upstairs. "Jenn! I can't get this sodding door open!"

BANG.

Mark shot off the sofa. His face was a mottled red, white around the eyes where his fists had been pressed. He spoke slowly, as one does when discovering an old, elusive truth. "You. Devious. *Bitch*."

Jenn shrank away. Mark's voice sounded like glass cracking. He looked around him, trembling on the verge of violence, wanting to shatter things, to break something, in refusal of her terms—but what to break? Slowly he turned toward Jenn. She recoiled into the sofa's depths, recognizing dark inspiration in Mark's eyes. Suddenly, he seized his wife by the shoulders.

"You cunts have all the same bloody unoriginal tricks, don't you?"

"Mark!" she sputtered.

"Doesn't matter what *I* want, does it, you smug cow? As long as you have your fucking way." He pushed Jenn back, hard against the sofa, and she screamed as her head hit the wall.

Simon, who had sat on his bed and was trying to text Jenn, *RU OK? My door is stuck*—paused. His thumbs poised over the mini-keyboard.

Had he imagined that scream?

.ෙ.

MARK LURCHED AWAY FROM JENN. He'd thought of something else he wanted to break; swinging out both arms, he cleared the mantle of its memories: Arabella's disdained, inherited Doulton china and her ashram-bought neti pots, Jenn's Florida trinkets. Shattered mementos of his entrapment. He hurled the Ecuadorian bowl at the television, but its weight wasn't sufficient to break the screen. So Mark yanked the TV from its stand and tried to throw it, but it was too heavy and only fell unbroken to the ground. Panting, disappointed and wild-eyed, Mark turned back toward Jenn.

.ෙ.

OUTSIDE, RUBICON HEARD NOTHING. SHE was scrabbling at the bottom of her handbag searching for a linty Ricola she'd seen down there a couple of days ago. Instead, she found her flip phone.

.ෙ.

WITHIN HIS TROUSER POCKET MARK'S cell phone vibrated, over and over. All he could see was that woman's pink lying face, those round blue eyes gratifyingly bloodshot with fear. Not enough fear.

"Get rid of it. Or take it to the States with you, but I am not doing this again. Another time I'm supposed to forget about *my* life? Well, I'm NOT HAVING IT, d'you hear me?"

Jenn did, because he had her by the shoulders and was shouting in her face. She shut her eyes in the face of his words. Mark roughly released his wife, strode over the broken china, and stormed over to the kitchen.

Upstairs, Simon was pounding on the door and calling out, but Jenn trembled on the sofa, hand over her mouth.

Mark began throwing open kitchen cupboards. The bint was off her fucking trolley if she thought he'd stay in this fucking duplicitous shamble of a marriage any longer. He'd get his laptop, find the deed to this house and put the whole fucking pile on the market.

"SIMON!" he shouted, hauling a laptop and a black acrylic duffle from a high cupboard. "Fucking get down here—we have to talk. NOW!" Mark began rifling through the high cupboards, looking for the deed, a folder, the fucking document file he'd carefully, long ago, put together. Looking for he knew not what, but he wanted everything necessary out of this house so he would never, ever have to enter it again.

"Mark." Again, Jenn had risen to her certitude. She walked into the kitchen, knowing he would have to calm down and accept the fate and the blessing that had been given to them. Men were prone to moods, rages—but she was rational. Her stomach didn't feel nervous or tight. It felt, again, as she'd felt so long ago when Lovina urged her on through Pinekill to go after Mike—but this time it was Charlie telling her what to do. Go to him, Mummy. Go to him, he needs you. She walked quietly up to the kitchen island, watching as Mark knocked ceramic pots and dish towels and candlesticks and a blender out of the cupboard. Plastic water bottles tumbled. A knife rack tipped over, and serrated and paring and butcher blades skittered and spun across the kitchen floor. Finally Mark seized a thick blue folder, dusty within the cupboard's depths. "Ha!" he said, holding it high.

Again the phone vibrated and hummed within his pocket.

The banging noises from upstairs also returned, but now harder and repetitive BANG BANGBANG pause BANG BANGBANG.

"Mark, you need to calm down." Jenn spoke quietly.

Mark turned to her again. God that smug face, that immobile yellow hair. He kicked aside the detritus from his search and shoved the folder in her face. "D'you see this, then? I'm going to sell this fucking miserable house—and you with it, if you haven't fucked off."

"JENN! Are you all right!" Simon's bedroom door began to splinter as he kept throwing himself against it.

◦◦

OUTSIDE, RUBICON HEARD SIMON SHOUT, and heard the banging sounds. Nervously, unsure of what to do, she moved toward the side of the house.

"YOU'RE SCARING YOUR CHILD, MARK." Jenn radiated calm. Crossing strong hands in front of her belly, she looked Mark directly in the eyes. "Both of them."

Mark slammed his fist on the island and his rage, the mad spews of saliva around his mouth, the clench of his jaw, made her flinch against her will. He thrilled to see this and held a fist up to that plastic face of hers.

"Do you think this is the first time? Are you actually *that* cringingly stupid, Jenn? Did you never stop to ask yourself why the *fuck* anyone would marry Arabella? 'I'm up the spout,' she said . . . and she was *laughing*, the cunt." Mark loomed over Jenn. His face was mottled, fist still clenched, forcing her to bend backward. "And I thought, daft bugger that I am, that a child would change things, make marriage worthwhile. Well, IT BLOODY DOESN'T!"

Jenn felt a moment's deep pity for him. It took courage, yes, but foolishness, too, for her to put a calm, placatory hand on Mark's arm. But then she went too far. She bestowed an oh-ye-of-little-faith half-smile. The tender pomposity of that look enraged Mark, and he seized Jenn by the hair. She screamed.

"Jenn!" Simon could almost fit his fist through the splintered bedroom door.

RUBICON FLIPPED HER PHONE SHUT. Why wouldn't Mark answer? Then she heard Simon's shout, mutedly, and she definitely heard a scream—Jenn's. She ran forward, looking desperately around. No people: only the bark of an outraged dog in the distance, the shimmering green leaves above, the rooftops' inert aerials which, as always, seemed to pierce the low, fast-moving clouds.

JENN'S FEAR WAS REAL NOW. Mark had bent her backward over the kitchen island, his hands gripping her hair. His nerves sang, his blood rushed delightedly at the sight of her terror and her high color, at the feeling of her pulse beneath his thumb, the sight of her flabby legs scrabbling for a foothold on the ground.

Jenn screamed again, piercingly.

In his rage, Mark decided that it was Jenn who should leave. He was almost weeping with frustration as he stared at her and considered his options. How had he ever thought he could manage her, her complacencies. How had he thought he could safely penetrate her buxom American fortress without consequences? He let go of her hair, intending to seize her arm and pull her upstairs to pack her bags, but she slipped out of his sweaty grasp, screaming, "You'll hurt the baby!"

RUBICON PEERED THROUGH THE SITTING-ROOM windows and saw the smashed china, the lamp knocked to the ground. She heard Simon's desperate shouting. Were they upstairs? Maybe she could get in through the French doors? While running toward the back of the house, Rubicon realized that Jenn would never break china. For a flashing moment she remembered Laverne, Jenn's mom, telling the two of them that a girl's purity was like china, once broken never mendable.

Just as Rubicon clambered onto the back deck, Jenn tried to pull away from Mark, and her foot landed directly on one of those knives scattered on the floor. She slipped on the handle, the blade spun, her fear-filled body twisted to the side, and with a scream she fell forward hard, slamming her forehead against the tile corner of that kitchen island.

Rubicon stood watching, aghast. She saw Jenn reach a dazed hand up to her temple and draw it down, bloody. Rubicon saw the scene through the garden's green reflection and thought about the ravines and Lovina, and that first day when she and Jenn had reconnected at Waterloo.

Jenn staggered. Then she slid to the floor.

SIMON'S DOOR WOULDN'T BUST, IT was prewar, unyielding as Churchill. Hot tears spilled from his eyes—Jenn had just shouted that he was hurting that baby, which meant he was hurting her! With a burst of rage and fear, the boy threw himself so hard at the door the hinges came away. He leaped down the stairs and ran through the shambolic sitting room. Jenn's last scream had fallen terrifyingly silent. Simon flew toward the kitchen, toward the sound of Jenn gasping, of ragged breathing. He didn't see Rubicon standing on the deck with her hands over her mouth.

.୨୧.

RUBICON SAW EVERYTHING. IT HAPPENED in a series of slides, just like a car crash. She saw Simon dash into the kitchen and skid to a stop. She saw what he saw, Jenn's bloodied body, Mark leaning over her with his back to Simon.

She saw the hope and fire die within Mark's eyes at the sight of his wife's blood. She saw that he stood above Jenn's limp but reviving body and how he gently found her pulse. She saw him see *her*—only yards away on the deck outside those windows—their eyes met and she knew what his glance of opaque hopelessness meant. Goodbye, my love, he was saying. I'm trapped again. She saw how slowly Mark sighed, how carefully he bent to put his hands beneath his wife's arms and raise her to her feet.

But that's when Simon seized another of the scattered knives. Because all he could see was Jenn, her face a river map of blood, and his father leaning over her. Rubicon stood on the deck with doom-haggard eyes as Simon rose, weeping, with the serrated knife held high. He shouted, "You—stop hurting her!" and plunged the knife deeply into Mark's back in a single scything motion. And two powerful Midwestern accents cut the air as Jenn and Rubicon each shouted, "No!"

The next few moments played out in silence. Mark staggered, and turned his head to see Simon trembling before him, already aghast at what he'd done. Mark's eyes contained shock but also somehow love, love and sorrow and a relieved, wry acceptance. There was no anger there. Then Mark collapsed forward with Jenn trapped beneath his body. Simon saw Rubicon standing out on the deck. The knife was still in his hands, but bloody now, its serrated tip chipped by one of Mark's ribs. The boy's mouth worked but emitted no sound.

Jenn struggled to escape the weight of her husband's dying body.

Mark's pain was a neon tunnel rushing forward to greet him. He tried to turn his face toward sunlight, toward the French doors and toward Rubicon, but with that single attempted movement, his body spasmed and he died face down.

To Simon, Rubicon's scream was silent. Defeated by double glazing.

But Jenn saw Rubicon's silent scream. She rose to her feet and the two old friends' eyes met, parted, and met again over Mark's body, across the soundproofed glass.

Simon released the knife. It clattered to the floor.

Jenn wearily raised her blood-soaked arm. With a limp movement, she waved Rubicon inside. Then she limped over to the kitchen tap and began to drink its thin aerated water.

The French doors had been unlocked the whole time.

ᘖ

RUBICON THREW OPEN THE DOORS and ran to Mark's crumpled body. She dropped to her knees on the bloody floor (it was Jenn's blood, mostly; Mark's wound bled comparatively little), and clutched him to her. His body warm, his scent of wood chips, the beautiful whorls of his ears and those sad, naff corduroys. She held his head on her lap and begged him, please don't be dead, please wake up—but something about his skin, about the movement of the bristles on his chin, told her it would never be. Rubicon had never seen death before, but it was unmistakable. There was no pulse—only his body's beloved wrapping, to which she pressed her face again and again, his neck, his scent, his precious empty self.

She fumbled with her phone, dialed 999. Why wasn't Jenn already doing this? "There's been—someone's been killed. Maybe not, maybe you can save him— please come—" her voice clutched. She gave emergency services the address and Mark's name, but suddenly the phone was pulled from her grasp by strong bloodied hands.

Jenn stood over her. She flipped the phone shut, ending the call.

Rubicon stared at her, but Jenn tossed the phone away. It hit Simon's elbow and skittered across the dining-room table.

"Sorry, kid," Jenn said. Then she did a funny thing, or so Rubicon thought. Moving slowly, like an injured wrestler, Jenn leaned over Mark's body, flattened the palm of her hand in the blood on the floor, and smeared it on her own face. At the dining-room table Simon was weeping, hitting his own head over and over with the butt of his palm. "Oh God, Dad, I'm so sorry, I take it back I'm so sorry Daddy . . ."

Jenn walked to Simon and put her bloodless hand on the boy's shoulder. "We need to figure something out," she said to Rubicon. "How long will it take them to get here?"

The boy's sobs filled the room. Rubicon said nothing. She clutched Mark closer, tried to cradle him but already it seemed that his limbs were becoming lankily uncooperative.

"We've got to talk about what's going to happen, Rubicon," Jenn said in loud, careful tones. Round blue eyes burned brightly behind her mask of blood.

"Why?" Mark's head was a dead weight in the crook of Rubicon's arm.

"Because you're going to have to help Simon," Jenn sat down heavily. "You'll probably have to move in here, take care of him. While I'm in jail."

Simon lifted his head from his arms. He looked at Rubicon, confused.

She couldn't bear his horrible, familiar face and just stared at Jenn. "What the fuck are you talking about, Jenn?"

"Simon, Rubicon saw me kill your father. You saw it too. He was hurting me, and I am going to have a baby, and it was my right to stop him before he hurt your brother. You understand? I killed your father."

"Baby?" said Rubicon.

"Yeah," Jenn looked at the knife, near her feet where Simon had dropped it. "That's what made Mark so mad. I'm going to have his baby. Simon's brother."

Then Jenn bent and picked up the knife. She gripped the handle firmly several times, then placed the knife on her lap.

Simon's eyes filled with tears, and he shook his head over and over. Over and over, but now he said nothing.

And as Rubicon held Mark, looking at the dead wonder of his long spatulated fingertips, she thought about that final glance he'd given the boy. About the enduring power and contradictions of his painful, flawed, tethering love for Simon. Riddled with mistrust and endless torn seams of resentment —but love it had been.

"Jenn. You are—are you insane? Simon stabbed him, you cannot lie—"

"I am ready to confess." Jenn set her heavy jaw.

With those words, Rubicon suddenly realized that Simon still didn't know who had killed his mother. She also realized why he'd killed his father.

Gently holding Mark's head close to her body, Rubicon told Jenn and Simon about Arabella's murderer. He'd been caught, and his apartment had contained Mark's watch, Arabella's checkbook, the rest of her jewelry. She told them that she knew Simon must have suspected his father of it, that his father had known that too. But he was innocent. She said nothing about Mark's own suspicions. Only that there were reporters who doubtless were planning to call today, soon, for quotes and responses and it'd be a shitstorm. A public relations nightmare.

Suburban House of Death. The headlines write themselves, really.

Simon went pale with shock as he listened to Rubicon—and now she could look at him, could see Mark's face there, so lost in hopelessness. She also felt the room filling with the power of Jenn's personality, of her certainty. And pregnant. Rubicon realized what Jenn had already understood: that as a pretty, blond, pregnant victim of domestic violence, she would probably get off scot-free in the end. It would be trial-by-media.

But what about her? That empty body in Rubicon's arms had been her only chance, not just her last but her only chance, to feel a full and formed life.

Though there was the other thing.

The old and shallow thing, the empty thing. Good enough if you can't get better. Jenn leaned forward, seeing a possibility of acquiescence in Rubicon's eyes, and her powerful, blood-smeared hand reached across the table. "You loved him, Rubicon."

And he loved Simon.

Rubicon filled with self-loathing as she thought about the next best thing to Mark's love that she had ever known. She leaned over his body for a final time, touching that Velveteen Rabbit spot of baldness, the turn of his ear. Then slowly, gently, Rubicon released him and stood up. Simon and Jenn watched warily as she walked to the table and picked up her phone.

"I think I'll call a friend of mine. A publicist. Her name's Tatiana Gripp. She might be able to . . . help us out." Well, Rubicon thought as she dialed, red-eyed and with a ragged, aching heart, *Celebrity Big Brother*, here I come.

Sirens wailed up Sheen Road as tabloid celebrity rushed to greet these two old friends.

A NOTE FROM THE AUTHOR

If you enjoyed this book, I would be very grateful if you could write a review and publish it at your point of purchase. Your review, even a brief one, will help other readers to decide whether they'll enjoy my work.

Please sign up on my website, danaburnell.com, for news about my upcoming work.

AUTHOR BIOGRAPHY

Dana Burnell has written for the *London Times Sunday Magazine*, *The Guardian Weekend Magazine*, *Time Out New York*, *Show Business Weekly* and others. A former contributing associate for *Harvard Review*, co-founder of Firewater Films in NYC and arts editor for *Inside New York*, Dana was awarded a Mellon Foundation Grant for Fiction from Columbia University. Dana lives in New York City, and *The Tame Man* is her first novel.